For Jessica.
I love you to the moon and back.

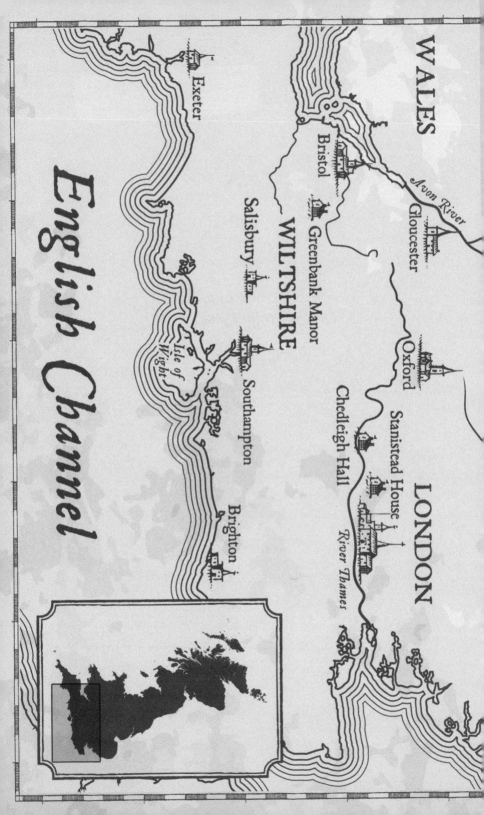

THE
ILL-KEPT
OATH

Jim
Enjoy!
CCAune

C.C. AUNE

ISBN 13: 978-1-945769-02-3
eISBN 13: 978-1-945769-01-6

Library of Congress Catalog Number: 2016937263
Printed in the United States of America
First Printing: 2016
20   19   18   17   16   5   4   3   2   1

Cover and interior design by Steven Meyer-Rassow

Wise Ink Creative Publishing
837 Glenwood Ave.
Minneapolis, MN 55405
www.wiseinkpub.com

To order, visit www.SeattleBookCompany.com or call
(734) 426-6248. Wholesaler and reseller discounts available.

CHAPTER ONE

Edingham-Greene, Wiltshire
20 April 1819

Clarence Weston's nerves came to life in a shower of prickles, and an upwelling of dread surpassed the anxieties that usually consumed him. Though nothing specific had sparked this sensation, apprehension soon gave way to gut-clenching terror. An insistent pounding began down the hall, startling him to his feet in a cloud of silk banyan. He glanced at the mantel clock—a quarter past midnight.

"Who would call at *this* hour?" Heart squeezing wildly, he scanned his study for a means of defense. In all four directions towered floor-to-ceiling shelves crammed with hundreds of books, useful for research but ineffectual as weapons. He rifled through the rubble that littered his desk, sending pamphlets and inkwells and scrolls to the floor.

The pounding now alternated with muffled shouts.

"My lord! Lord Middlemere! You must let me in!"

The earl backed toward the hearth, his shaking hand sliding round the shaft of a poker. "Dear heavens!" he croaked. "*Carson! Help!*" After what seemed like an interminable pause, he heard his butler unbolting the front door. Someone spilled into the hall and spoke animatedly. The earl huddled against a bookshelf, wincing and shuddering at each amplified word.

The study door opened, and Carson stuck in his head. "Will you receive Mr. Johnson, sir? He asserts that a giant ate his horse as he passed through the Heywood an hour ago."

Mr. Johnson had a reputation for enjoying his drink. Middlemere, however, thought at once of his ledger. Two and a half pages full of tenants' complaints . . .

He shook the poker at Carson. "I will not see him. He's shattered my poor nerves enough as it is. Put Mr. Johnson in a cart and have Sam drive him home."

The butler bowed. Sensing hesitation in his mien, the earl drew nearer. "Well, what do you think? Can we believe Johnson's ravings? Shall I add his report to my ledger?"

Carson glanced down the hall. He shut the door softly and said in a grave voice, "My lord, Mr. Johnson is covered head-to-toe in offal. Short of his falling into a butchering tub, I cannot see how else he could have effected such an appearance."

Middlemere took in a long, trembling breath. "Oh, God!" He leant against the desk. "This could be nothing more than a lone rogue with illusions of grandeur. Or . . ." Here he met Carson's eye. "Or else someone more powerful has issued a challenge."

"Let us hope it is only the former, my lord."

"I'll alert Bancroft. He will know what to do."

London
20 April 1819

Prudence Fairfeather awakened with a start and sat up in bed. With effort, she checked her breathing and lay slowly back down. The bed hangings loomed over her, heavy and shadowed in the early morning gloom. Throwing an arm across her sweat-speckled brow, she squeezed shut her eyes.

Today I am eighteen years old, she thought. *I could be married before the year is out.*

This was no sudden revelation; her whole purpose lately involved finding a husband. All penniless girls—especially orphans—faced the same task, which boiled down to sparing their relatives the burden of always caring for them. Prudence's kin would by no means leave her to languish as a governess or indigent spinster, but she was determined not to spend her life beholden to them. To that end, she must marry and marry quite well. For weeks, she'd practiced accepting that her future depended on the partiality of a yet unknown man. Resignation, she found, helped to settle frayed feelings—resignation and stuffing down her heart's disappointments. This time, however, a stray burst of homesickness slipped to the surface; she doubted her guardian had grand plans for this day. Miss Amelia Staveley showed her affection as ants show interest in picnics—with much fervor and little selectivity.

Gulping back incipient tears, Prudence slipped from bed to begin her toilette. Shortly, the chambermaid entered to help dress her hair. Prudence enjoyed these quiet hours best, whether alone or in the company of affable Nell; the rest of the morning would be filled with tutors and lessons. After luncheon, she and Aunt Amelia would set out on their calls. Paying calls in London was wholly unlike the same activity at home—pure strategy and lacking any semblance of neighborly warmth and wit. In a word, dreadful.

At breakfast with her aunt, a letter from Lady Josephine Weston momentarily dispelled Prudence's longings for Wiltshire.

"Arthur Grant asked after you the other day," wrote her cousin and foster sister. "He loves you in his own way. He's hoping you'll have bad luck and settle for him."

Prudence smiled. Had she been there in person, she would have scolded Josephine for disparaging their neighbor. Yet Josephine was correct: dull, reliable Arthur, with his boorish sensibilities, would make an intolerable husband. A lifetime on the shelf held greater appeal.

Please, God, give me someone who's at least cheerful and clever.

Aunt Amelia claimed her attention by placing on the table an oval brooch set with garnets. "On the occasion of your birthday, I'd like you to have this, which I wore at your age."

Prudence exclaimed, "Why, thank you, ma'am. It's beautiful!" She fixed it to her scarf and turned to the aunt, whose gaze had meanwhile gone strangely vacant. "Is something wrong?"

Amelia blinked into focus and produced a stout smile. "Old memories, that's all. Now, if you've finished your meal, I would have a word with you in my chamber."

Curious as to what had inspired this mood, Prudence tucked Josephine's letter into a pocket and followed her upstairs. Amelia went straight to an armoire, threw open its doors, and gestured toward a box squatting alone at the bottom.

"That was your mother's," she said gruffly. "Go on, take it."

Prudence's heart stopped. Slowly, she collected the box and stood hugging it in her arms. It did not seem to have the heft that it ought. Constructed of maple, dome-lidded, and devoid of all ornament, the battered chest lacked a functioning clasp and was held shut by a strap. "My mother's?" she said. "Dear me, I never expected to receive a bequest. What a lovely surprise!"

"*Bequest?*" snorted the aunt. "'Tis meaningless rubbish."

She went on in a low and portentous mutter, "And were I not compelled to, I would never have given it."

"Pshaw," Prudence said, moving to unfasten the strap. "Rubbish doesn't merit nearly two decades' worth of custodianship."

"Stop!" shrilled Amelia. Prudence stepped backward, her knuckles tightening against the box as she braced to protect it at all costs. She had no time to puzzle at this, for the lady went on, "I'll thank you to view it in your own chamber, dear."

"If this box so distresses you, I am entitled to know why."

"*Curse* these impulses!" Amelia collapsed into a chair. "Yet answer I must. The tokens in that chest have been handed down through countless generations. Some of your ancestors possessed . . . ah, never mind!" She flapped her hands, as if by doing so she could sweep away their whole conversation.

Normally, Prudence would never challenge authority, but her guardian, having conjured this evocative subject, might as well have touched a spark to gunpowder. Curiosity gave way to burgeoning wonder. A throb of imperative seemed to flow from the box into Prudence's skull.

She advanced on the old woman. "My dear Aunt, you cannot expect me to accept 'never mind.' Lord Middlemere has told me next to nothing about my family. Who can blame an orphan for being curious about her parents? My ancestors possessed *what?*"

Amelia emitted a groan of duress. Tautly, she replied, "They possessed a rare set of talents called the Inheritance."

Prudence's eyes went wide. "Fascinating! What sort of talents?"

Aunt Amelia, however, had unburdened herself as far as she was willing. "It matters not. That tradition is dead; you and your brother are among the last of the line. As for those heirlooms, they're useless. Think of them as a remembrance, for they serve no other purpose."

"But—"

"Take that thing from my sight! It has haunted me for too long with its unpleasant memories. Ask me no more, and never, *ever* speak of it to anyone else."

Vexed but preempted, Prudence shut her mouth with a snap. She went to her room and set the chest on the bed. *So this is Amelia's birthday scheme. 'Tis awful peculiar.* Her hand caressed its battered wood grain. *Mother!*

For years she had schooled herself to suppress yearnings for her parents. They were gone—it was impractical to suppose how her life might have been different. She had last cried for them at age seven or eight. Indeed, Josephine's periodic lamentations for her own deceased parent had firmed Prudence's resolve to stuff it all down. Not once in ten years had she wondered about the people who had given her life; now this ugly old box had appeared without warning, awakening thoughts she preferred not to have. Apprehension slid down her spine like a trickle of sweat. Taking a deep breath, she undid the buckle and flicked open the lid.

The relics appeared to have been crushed hastily inside, and considering their volume, they shouldn't have fit. One by one, she lifted them out: a purple velvet overgown, Elizabethan in style; a pair of elbow-length gauntlets, missing a couple of fingers; and a wool cloak, so flecked with stains that it took her a while to summon the courage to even touch it. Underneath the cloak lay two other objects.

Her eyes went at once to a shining gold ring, a filigreed band cast in intertwining knots. Beautiful though it was, the stone had gone missing. Now she frowned at a sword with a dented cross-guard, its blade broken off to a few jagged inches. *It really is rubbish!*

Disappointed, she threw herself facedown on the bed. Something small and hard rattled in the box. Prudence peered inside and found an oval-cut ruby, half its surface blasted with black, oily soot. It struck her as an ominous gem, bloodred and ebony, and a likely partner for the filigreed band. Staring in horror, she fought back the sensation of a faint aura of death. *I can't—I won't—I mustn't think about that.* She scooped everything up, crammed it back into the box, and stuffed the whole lot under her bed.

The bell rang downstairs, signaling the arrival of a tutor. Prudence rose, smoothed her dress, and exited the room.

Whatever her ancestors' mysterious talents might have been, now was not the time to think about such things. She dismissed the box entirely, and as such did not have to pretend its contents had not shaken her. Lessons led to luncheon led to afternoon calls. As the day progressed in tedium, with no visit lasting more than a quarter of an hour and all remarks confined to noncontroversial topics, Prudence's thoughts drifted to her cousin. Poor Lady Josephine! Her turn to debut would come in two years. Sensitive and impatient, she was bound to fare badly under Aunt Amelia's tutelage. Prudence had tried to craft her letters as veiled warnings of this, but Josephine had simply assumed she was fadging:

> *Thanks for your good-hearted attempt to portray London as dull, but don't think me so bird-witted as to fall for such a plumper! It cannot possibly be tiresome paying calls on fine houses, especially when one has dozens of new frocks to show off.*

You have no idea, Prudence thought as she and Aunt Amelia exited the last house of the day. She fought off the idea of her life stretching on in a similar manner, month after month, year after year.

"For shame!" fretted the aunt once they were back in the carriage. "You nodded off against my shoulder. What if Mrs. Grisham had been someone truly important?"

"What if her son possessed half a brain?" hissed Prudence. "I don't give one whit about connections or money. I want a husband with whom I can have a rational conversation."

Amelia looked heavenward. "As you gaze into each other's fever-glazed eyes in a draughty garret, I suppose? Don't be dramatic, Prudence. A husband with a fortune is merely your *entrée.* Plenty of wives don't love their husbands. Do your duty, of course, and then find fulfillment elsewhere. You can spend his money and your hours however you choose."

"Oh? Is that what paramours are for?"

Aunt Amelia recoiled. "What? Such impertinence!"

Repentant, Prudence laid a hand on her arm. "Please forgive me. I suppose anxiety has brought out all my sharp edges."

"Ah, how could I not?" Aunt Amelia said, her voice warm with affection. "Besides, I am certain Society will soon see what I now behold: a great beauty, a 'diamond of the first water,' as modern folk like to say. You, my dear, shall have your choice of gentlemen."

The heat of modesty rose in Prudence's face. "I have no such pretensions. Besides, a fair countenance won't make up for my deficiency in fortune and name."

They pulled up at Amelia's aging Georgian manse. As a footman hurried to hand down the two women, Stanistead

House's ivy-covered brick edifice loomed overhead, itself the personification of loneliness and advanced years. They parted ways to dress for supper. It had already grown dark, and rain thrummed steadily against Prudence's windows. She pondered her reflection in the warped glass panes: her honey-brown hair plaited to precision, her figure willowy yet mature in persimmon-red silk.

Who is this creature? She is like a stranger to me.

She'd spent six weeks in London undergoing this transformation. Gone was the country girl who climbed trees and rode bareback; gone forever her girlhood spent in the idyllic hills of the west. Until now, she had directed no thought toward her future. Love might have found her in Wiltshire without the fuss and fumble of a London Season.

If only. If only.

Not for the first time today, Prudence's chin trembled. While external bravery in the face of these trials might reassure her loved ones, it did not always temper her inner unrest. Clenching fists, she muttered, "There now, what would Josephine say? You mustn't dispel her shining illusion of you."

Just the other day, her cousin had written, "I admire you, Prudence. You do what you have to, and usually without complaint."

Josephine probably meant this as more of a gesture of goodwill than genuine feeling, for compliance in her lexicon ranked just above blind submission. Yes, Prudence had been blessed with a stout heart, but she'd wept bitterly in private the night she learned she must go to London. Josephine had mourned loudly enough for them both.

Such recollections caused a fresh onslaught of homesickness. Prudence ran to a window and pushed open the sash. After a moment's hesitation, she thrust her head into the downpour, where flowing tears mingled with a cold springtime rain.

CHAPTER TWO

Edingham-Greene, Wiltshire
29 April 1819

Lady Josephine Weston slumped in a chair, regarding the dried mud caking her boots.

I have no one to talk to, nothing to do, and I'm staring at mud.

Exhaling with pointed unladylike verve, she addressed her companion. "Really, Maria. Life these days is so unspeakably dull. Until Prudence was gone, I never realized how much I depended on her to promote good discussions."

"Not a-mention good behavior," added the blunt yet well-meaning matron who served as her nursemaid.

Maria's household status rankled more than her words. Although Papa had retitled her as "lady's companion," she had been, and ever would be, Lady Josephine's nurse. The girl jerked to her feet and stood with clenched fists.

"Will you start a quarrel, then, over something I did ages ago?"

Maria lifted her chin against this hyperbolic barrage. "What quarrel? Have I not license a-reference, even in passing, the uproar 'ee caused over thy cousin's departure for London?"

Josephine's frown deepened. She was in retrospect greatly ashamed of that time, but these days she had little forbearance for anyone, especially Maria. "I raised a breeze, and I'm sorry. Must we belabor the point?"

"Gently, my lady. Thy attitude continues to smack of resentment."

Josephine flopped into her chair and threw a leg over one arm. "I own it!" she snapped. "I see no reason why we couldn't have all gone to Town. As much as I love Greenbank, this house feels like a prison. It's not fair that Papa set free only Prudence—she who had no desire to go!"

Maria frowned at her charge's inelegant posture. "Now, now. 'Ee have the liberty of the village and thy entire estate. Anyway, surely 'ee realize such parting was due. 'Ee girls must marry and lead separate lives."

"Oh, I doubt Papa has any such plans for me. Why do you suppose he brings a musket on our rides if not to drive away young men who might dare to show interest?" In truth, Josephine could not for the life of her figure out why her father went about armed.

"A musket? I know nothing. What reason dost he give?"

"He claims it's for the buck that's been eating the roses, but I know he hasn't the heart to kill an innocent creature. Don't you see? Papa is my warder. None shall pass through Greenbank's gates, nor shall I leave here for the rest of my miserable, lonely, pitiful life!"

As these words fell in half-jest from her tongue, Josephine was gripped by a wave of despair. *Oh my lord, it's the truth. I shall never have a Season, never meet gentlemen outside my closed sphere. I shall spend the rest of my life keeping house for a fearful and hermitlike parent!* An unchecked tear trailed down one cheek.

"I—er . . ." Maria covered her mouth to stave off a laugh. "Honestly, my lady, how 'ee do love to embellish."

However innocently the nurse had meant this, the barb struck too deep.

"You know very well I am justified in that particular concern!" Rising again, Josephine marched from the drawing room and ascended to the landing of Greenbank's grand staircase. There, in her window seat overlooking the rear gardens, she sprawled behind the curtains and worked up the passion to have a good cry. After only a moment, she thought better of it. Instead, she drew close her knees and put her arms around them.

Everyone expects me to act immaturely. Somehow or other I must win their esteem, yet how shall I accomplish it without my cousin's assistance?

No immediate answer materialized, so she picked up a novel lying nearby. For an hour or two, *Northanger Abbey* kept her in thrall until she roused to the unmistakable sound of many marching feet. After taking a moment to establish that she had not imagined the din, Josephine hurried upstairs to the sitting room, which afforded the best view of Greenbank's front drive. A platoon of soldiers filed up the lane, led by an officer on horseback.

"Good Lord!" she breathed, pressing her nose to the glass. She had never seen anything more beautiful than that field of bright crimson on fifty broad chests. The whites of their breeches and ebony of their accoutrements were bested only by the glint of sunlight off half-a-hundred muskets. Boots crunched across gravel. Arms swung in perfect unison. Shortly, the soldiers reached the base of the porch. Someone called an order and the column ground to a halt.

"What's this about, then?" Josephine fumbled to push open a narrow side-window. At the squeak of its hinge, the mounted

officer glanced up. She flung herself out of sight. After waiting
for what seemed like a significant pause, she peered out again
and was treated to a sly wink. She fell back with a yelp.

A jangle and a thump told her the officer had dismounted.
Josephine scurried back to her landing and hid behind the
drapes, a place that afforded earshot with little chance of
detection. The bell rang, and Carson materialized. Josephine
heard only bits of their ensuing conversation: Lieutenant Such-
and-Such, who'd been sent from Headquarters to "get to the
bottom of the recent disturbances," desired an audience with
the earl.

Her ears pricked up. *Recent disturbances?*

Carson asked the officer to please hold his explanations
until he found himself in the earl's presence. Josephine stifled
a growl as Carson showed the lieutenant to Lord Middlemere's
study and pulled the door shut. She yanked off her boots
and padded silently downstairs. Moving catlike through the
shadows of the back hall, she approached her father's door.

"—could you describe, sir, the nature of the mischief you
have thus far observed?"

"I do not vouch for it personally. I am a scholar and not
inclined to engage in the details of rural pursuits. For that I have
my nephew, who, when he is not off at Oxford, tends lovingly
to Greenbank. It pleases me that Mr. Edward Fairfeather, who
is also my foster son, has taken such an interest in the estate of
his maternal forebears—"

Oh, Papa, get on with it! thought Josephine, expecting at any
moment to be nabbed at the keyhole.

"—yet of *this* matter he is wholly ignorant, and I should
like it, if possible, to remain that way. In short, Lieutenant,
these complaints are gleaned from my tenants and neighbors. I

daresay they're reliable, for in close to twenty years I have not known them to repeat anything wilder than an old ghost story, and that much laughed-at."

Out in the corridor, Lady Josephine rolled her eyes.

The officer said patiently, "Well, then. And may I know the particulars of their recent concerns?"

"Indeed, I have made notes in this ledger." The rustling of pages indicated a consultation of said book. "My entries began about three months ago. I did not at first keep an accounting, but after a fortnight of trouble I went back and recorded each previous incident. You will note the rash of fences smashed, granaries broken into, *et cetera, et cetera*. Here is the tally of wounded and missing livestock. It always happens at night, with surprising stealth, I might add. Not one sober soul has yet to encounter the culprit. Speculation as to its identity runs to vandals or wild dogs."

"Forgive me, Your Lordship, but I wonder why you did not direct your people to organize a party and attempt to track down the troublemaker yourselves?"

Josephine's father seemed unsettled by this question, for he hemmed and hawed awhile. "Well," he answered finally, "beyond my foster-son there is no other capable young man available in these parts, and as it is out of the question to involve Mr. Fairfeather in such doings, I felt I should enlist outside help before somebody got hurt or . . . or *worse*."

"So you are not convinced this is only vandals or wild dogs."

"You will no doubt find it unsatisfying, Lieutenant, when I say my fear is based on personal experience that I am not at liberty to discuss. It cannot be silenced by polite reassurances. You received your commission from someone who understands this, and as such it is your job merely to investigate my claim."

"Which I shall begin at once," the lieutenant replied. Floorboards creaked as the officer stood. "Are you certain you won't mind if we camp on your lawn? I agree the arrangement is conducive to daily communication, but we soldiers can be a troublesome lot—"

"Oh, no! It is most agreeable to me, and I can't think why it should put anyone else out of sorts. You and your junior officers shall, of course, board with us."

"That is gracious of Your Lordship, but I must respectfully decline. A camp cot and tent will serve perfectly well."

His footsteps were Josephine's signal to hasten back to her nook. A moment later, the lieutenant rejoined his men. Orders were shouted, and a camp began to sprout up.

Josephine huddled in her window seat, maddened by curiosity, not to mention other impulses altogether new to her mind. Of these "recent disturbances," she had previously heard nothing, save for the late-night ravings of an inebriated villager. That her father desired to keep Edward in the dark amazed her a good deal; that he considered their neighbor Arthur Grant incapable intrigued her still more. The supreme element in all this, though, was the arrival of the army. Josephine had grown up in the company of several young men, every one of them like a brother to her. These men were decidedly not her brothers. The sudden flutterings in her breast signaled a watershed change.

She spent the rest of the afternoon peering out windows as the soldiers scratched and sweated and swore their camp into being. At suppertime, she wasted little time in quizzing her father.

"It's an exercise," he replied. "They'll be gone before you know it."

Now Maria shrilled, "My lord, forgive me for speaking my mind, but how can 'ee permit threescore men a-bivouac on our front lawn? Lady Josephine will be exposed to all sorts o' offensive behavior. I'll have a-confine her to the house, and I know not how that be humanly possible!"

"Pish, Maria, you'll manage," said the earl with a shrug.

That night, Josephine crouched in the upper sitting room watching the lights of the camp until Maria caught her and shooed her to bed.

"And I thought I'd have nothing to write Prudence about," she murmured, snuggling under the covers with a grin on her face.

Bright and early the next morning, the platoon marched off on some errand. Josephine could barely concentrate on her lessons; her mind would think only of what the soldiers were doing.

Their faces would take on uniformly doughty expressions as they shouldered their muskets and marched through the countryside, driving malefactors before them. Afterward, the officers would return and regale her with stories . . .

"Shall I tell thy father 'ee hain't writ a single line in an hour?" inquired Maria, looming over her shoulder. Grimacing, Josephine dipped her quill in fresh ink.

The platoon returned in the midafternoon, at which time she stationed herself at the first-floor sitting room window.

"What've we got?" asked the lieutenant, standing with his two ensigns in the shade of a tree near the house.

The officers, having divided their efforts into quadrants

centered on the village, launched into a discussion of the lay of the land. Josephine, who knew it too well, soon found her attention drifting back to the book in her lap. She listened vaguely as each ensign accounted for the inhabitants of his quadrant and enumerated the incidents that had taken place there.

While such events were highly unusual, the answer seemed obvious: a person or persons had grown desperate by circumstance and were inflicting revenge on the inhabitants of the district. The militia would round them up soon enough, and then it would leave.

The meeting rambled on.

"—although I cannot dispel the notion that this could be the work of trolls."

Trolls? Josephine lowered her book and edged closer to the window.

"Let us not jump to conclusions," the lieutenant said mildly. "We are all eager, of course, to put our training to use, but we'll look foolish if it turns out we are wrong. Did you want to add something, Mr. Upton?"

"Sir, I saw with my own eyes thirty foot of hedgerow ripped out like it was daisies."

"And don't forget the drunkard!" the second ensign cried.

Upton nodded. "Aye, Mr. Johnson, whose horse was allegedly eaten by a giant—"

Josephine gasped. The lieutenant glanced up. Their eyes locked through a wavy prism of glass. This time, Josephine held her pose with all the dignity she could muster. His frown indicated displeasure, but she thought she detected a twinkle in his eyes.

"Let us shift away from the house." The lieutenant gestured to his men, and they moved out of earshot.

Josephine careened to the sofa, plunked herself down, and punched at a cushion. "Stupid, stupid girl! How do you expect to learn anything if you can't keep your mouth shut?"

Next time she would use more circumspection.

CHAPTER THREE

Edingham-Greene, Wiltshire
1 May 1819

"God help me, Joanna, this horde of strangers is almost more than I can bear!"

Lord Middlemere stood by the study window, watching soldiers tramp across his rear lawn, his pulse pattering like a springtime downpour. He turned to a large portrait hanging over the mantel. The woman smiled, dark-haired, forever young, and regal as a goddess in her Grecian-style gown. "Ah, my dear wife, would that you were here to help comfort my nerves!"

He imagined her saying, *You never had bad nerves when I lived, Clarence.*

"You gave them to me, Joanna, right at the end, as a recalcitrant child gives his parents grey hairs. I could not protect you from the forces within, let alone those without."

He gave a small shudder and picked his way across the room, sidestepping stacks of books and folios overflowing the shelves. Here the gentleman-scholar conducted his life's work, hidden away from perils supposedly no longer extant. Perils like a sudden resurgence of trolls.

He sank into a chair and ran his fingers through salt-and-pepper, shoulder-length locks. "Yet I must tolerate the soldiers' intrusion, for I *shall* know exactly what, and presently whom, we are facing. I only wish I could tell whether Bancroft regards the problem seriously enough."

He thumbed through the ledger of tenant complaints. "Mad Middlemere" his colleagues had once called him—fearmonger, paranoid, *voice of doom*—but this time, to establish a sufficient degree of credibility, he had taken care not succumb to hysteria. That business with Mr. Johnson, though . . . that had been the last straw. Modestly, delicately, he'd written General Bancroft, who had promptly agreed to send out a small force of men.

Which was worrisome, really. In one breath, Bancroft had assured him his suspicions were unlikely and then validated those suspicions with an offer of aid. If a semi-retired general could so swiftly raise troops from a department long ago disbanded, then something was brewing. Still, the earl knew better than to ask, for Bancroft would simply lie to his face.

"The work of brigands," Bancroft termed Edingham-Greene's troubles. "But, to keep your people calm, tell them the soldiers have come for a training exercise."

The pretense satisfied Middlemere, so long as the problem could be solved before June. Once Edward came home, he would surely involve himself in these matters, and that could be disastrous.

Middlemere gazed up at Joanna. "You loved that life, didn't you—the danger, the excitement, the sort of authority not normally granted to women—and yet you agreed to bring about its end. I only wish it hadn't taken your sacrifice—and the others', of course. In accordance with the Oath, all three children live in ignorance of their blood legacy. The past remains buried, and if Bancroft's men act swiftly, then so shall it stay."

With those words, a memory struck like a hammer.

A rumble of wheels in the drive. Doors banging and children crying. A middle-aged woman rushing blindly into the house.

"Oh, my dear sir, our worst fears are realized!"

He charged up the hallway, nearly colliding with the woman, who carried a small child. A sullen-faced boy about four years of age clung to her skirt.

Kneeling before the boy, he said kindly, "Hullo, little man. Remember me, your Uncle Clare?" The boy kicked his shin and flew out the front door. "Poor fellow!" muttered the earl.

The woman turned, panicking. "But—"

"Let him go," said the earl, staggering upright.

Lady Joanna rushed down the stairs and halted at his elbow, taking in the tableau. The tot's plaintive cries echoed across the foyer.

"They're gone!" moaned the woman, swaying.

The earl rushed to support her. Lady Joanna took the squalling girl and walked about, murmuring the kinds of sounds at which young mothers are expert. Soon the child calmed to an occasional shudder.

"What will happen to these poor orphans?" lamented the woman.

Lady Joanna lifted her head. "Hush, dear. Edward and Prudence will be safe here at Greenbank."

"Safe!" gasped Middlemere, fighting his way back to the present. "All these years I've feared London, yet now I have trolls prowling through my backyard!" Once again, he found himself struggling to tame a skittish heartbeat.

Ironic that he had first opposed Aunt Staveley about Prudence's coming out. He'd done so partly because he had understood his ward's indifference, and partly because he had his doubts as to the efficacy of the Fairfeathers' anonymity. God knew what might happen if their true parentage were revealed; Josephine's, alas, could never be hidden. Still, he'd had to accede when the aunt insisted that rural Wiltshire could not afford Prudence a satisfactory choice of mates. At least Prudence and Edward weren't presently exposed to the fresh danger—just his precious only daughter, who was too curious by half.

"As you were, Joanna," he said with a sigh.

A knock sounded at his door and a tall, towheaded man of about twenty thrust in his head. "Greetings, Papa!"

The earl forced himself to cover his shock with a smile. "Edward! To what do we owe this unexpected honor?"

"We owe the provost of Oxford University. And because of him, you shall have this honor for most of the foreseeable future."

Damn! thought Middlemere, his heart dropping like a stone. *Not now, Edward. Not* now.

Josephine bustled into the drawing room and pulled herself up short. There, in the best armchair, sat Cousin Edward swirling a tumbler of gin.

"Getting an early start on your holiday?" she asked, glancing at the clock. It was barely half past one, and he had poured a generous portion.

Edward dashed back half his drink with a well-practiced flair. "In a manner of speaking."

She approached and bent for the obligatory kiss. "That is

not an answer," she said, challenging him with lifted brow and crossed arms.

Edward shrugged. "Very well. I was suspended three months ago and have been lodging in London. I'm home for good now, I reckon."

Josephine gave him a shove, spilling the rest of his drink down his chest. "What? You've been shamming it all this time?"

"Your words, not mine," he said, scowling at the mess. He reached for her skirt to mop up his soaked waistcoat. Josephine slapped away his hand and backed out of reach.

"Coward!" she spat. "And what has Papa got to say?"

Edward mimicked Middlemere's tolerant tones, "'There's nothing wrong with taking more time to discover one's true calling!' To think I spent months fearing I might be disowned."

"You came home because you ran out of money!" guessed Josephine. The expression on his face confirmed her suspicions. "Why?"

He cut away his eyes. "I am no scholar, Josephine."

"Oh, Edward! You're not stupid. That's an excuse for not trying harder. Your sister will be so disappointed."

He slammed down his glass, still not looking at her. "I am not comfortable with the erudites. I prefer it here at Greenbank."

"I'm sorry you lack any ambition!" she snapped. "And it's a greater pity Papa hasn't the courage to call you out on your folly. Oh, what *I* wouldn't give to attend University! I would not squander such an opportunity."

Edward burst into laughter. "And what would you study? Embroidery and hat-making? Religious symbolism in the penny romance?"

Rage arced through Josephine's breast, and she caught herself half a second before uttering a foul yet well-deserved epithet. Instead, she considered how Prudence might receive such ill treatment, and with tremendous and unprecedented reserve, she turned her back on Edward and stalked from the room.

14 May 1819

Josephine hurried down the hall with a letter in hand and drew to a halt at the last doorway on the right. There she stood in a half-daze with one hand on the doorknob. Slowly, without fully approving her own actions, she turned the knob and crossed the threshold. Despite its being nearly midday, the chamber lay in darkness. White sheets draped the furniture and a musty smell hung in the air. She snapped to attention.

"Mother's room again? That's the third time this week. You're losing your mind, Josephine Weston!" She backed away from the chamber, a place she associated with disconsolation, and hurried for the stairs to post her letter to Prudence. The past fortnight had been fraught with so much upheaval—was it any wonder she kept wandering into the wrong rooms?

Edward was responsible for it all. First, he'd taken Middlemere to task for permitting the militia to bivouac on their front lawn. Within twenty-four hours, the platoon had packed up and removed itself to the village green. Josephine had been devastated. The mystery of the troll-creatures might never be revealed! Next, with the earl's apparent blessing, Edward had established an office in a spare parlor, where he met with Greenbank's tenants and the foreman of the farm. As his credibility built, so too did his sense of self-importance, which only deepened his inclination to either scorn or ignore her.

Josephine saw right through him. "Edward has succeeded in deflecting attention away from his personal faults," she wrote Prudence. "Instead, he prefers to focus on mine, beginning with an effort to rob me of my friends."

Those friends were in fact Edward's lifelong mates, nineteen-year-old Charles Lowell and the two sixteen-year-olds, Peter Bradford and Roland Tolliver, all sons of gentry from the vicinity of Greenbank. Prudence and Josephine had grown up playing with these boys; Josephine couldn't see why they no longer welcomed her in their circle.

"They're too wild for you," Edward claims, as if they were natives of Borneo. "You need proper female friends, the sort who reflect the lady of character you aspire to become." Is he not amusing in his obtuseness? In all my life, there has not, besides you, been a girl of my age and rank within ten miles.

Having dropped this letter in the mail pouch, she loitered near the drawing room door. Peter and Roland sat there with Edward, discussing the platoon.

"They're smart-looking chaps," Roland said. "I could see myself in uniform someday."

"They're idiots!" snorted Edward. "Have you seen how they comb the countryside like they're searching for buried treasure? It's a fool's errand, I tell you. They'll never manage to outwit the clever bastard who's got them running."

"I hear it's monsters," stated Peter with an air of authority.

"Ridiculous!" howled the others, hurling cushions at his head. "How *can* you believe such a Banbury story?"

"Many of the farmers believe it," retorted Peter, deflecting the missiles. "Did you hear what happened to Old Man Johnson?"

There was a sudden pointed lull and a growl deep in someone's throat. Edward said, "Go away, Josephine! I can see your shadow stretching across the hall."

Josephine stamped into view. "What exactly is your complaint? I like company, too."

"You can enjoy our company at luncheon, my dear." Smugness oozed from his half-lidded eyes.

Josephine inhaled slowly. *Help me, Prudence, for I very much want to draw your brother's cork!* She turned heel and headed to the kitchen, thinking maybe she could sneak a tablespoon of salt into Edward's soup. Next thing she knew, she was standing in the attic.

She looked around in perturbation. "Fiddlesticks! I am really off my rocker!"

Sunlight filtered softly through the cracks in the eaves, casting bands of bright and dark across an assortment of old trunks. Dust motes whirled like snowflakes; the air felt stuffy and warm, emphasizing the already strong odor of rotting leather and body oils and mold. Like a needle to the lodestone, Josephine's eyes were drawn to the trunks. She approached the largest one and lifted its lid. Inside, wrapped in tissue, lay an assortment of books, watercolors, and bundles of letters, many signed with the various titles used by her mother.

A ripple of dizziness caused her to sway. "All these years . . ." she breathed. What little she had gleaned about her mother came from the painting in Middlemere's study and family anecdotes that bathed the late countess in an implausible light. Joanna's personal items would certainly provide a more complete picture. "Yet my family withheld them. More evidence that they have too little regard for my feelings!" Indignation blazed a fiery trail up her spine.

Still, no one has forbidden me from touching these things.

Laughing aloud, greedy for knowledge, she threw open the next trunk and the next, finding clothing and hats and all manner of female accoutrements. Her fingers explored the surface of these treasures, but she dared not remove anything, for they held an aura of sacred sadness. The fourth trunk stopped her cold. Beneath the folds of a faded Union Jack nestled a brace of silver-handled pistols, regimental banners, and masculine clothing tailored for a woman's curved figure.

"What have we here?" Josephine's eyes slid this way and that, as if at any moment someone might catch her red-handed. She mustered the nerve to lift out the military jacket, which she meant only to hold up to her body. In seconds, she'd thrust her arms into the sleeves.

Lady Joanna, if that was indeed who had once worn the uniform, had been somewhat larger in size. This did not surprise Josephine, who was petite for her age. She sniffed the warm, navy-blue wool, smiling at the imagined scent of her mother. Reaching into the trunk, she fished out a shako, which she tried to fit on, but it interfered with her coiffure.

"Josephine?" called Maria far off in the house.

Josephine took off the jacket, put it back in the trunk, and closed the lids before beating a hasty retreat. She headed to her room to compose a letter to her cousin. But how to address this problem, when thus far Prudence had pooh-poohed her concerns about the soldiers, the trolls, and even Edward's assault on her character? These wanderings, she realized, were not at all random, and they had nothing to do with strained nerves. They had brought her to these trunks, seemingly on purpose, and considering she'd had no awareness in transit, one might call them trances.

"You say everything has an explanation?" Josephine muttered, thinking of the last letter she'd gotten from Prudence. "Well, explain *this*, Cos."

She dashed out a detailed description of trances and trunks and concluded it with this challenge:

> *So, my rational Prudence, what say you now? Here is a mystery you cannot dismiss.*

Then she sat back, thoughtfully chewing the feathered tip of her quill. *A uniform, eh?* For the first time, Josephine wondered whether her mother really had been killed in a carriage accident in London. She had always respected Middlemere's reticence on that subject, but now she felt she must know the truth. Ideally, without ruffling her father's notorious nerves.

"Come now, Prudence," she whispered. "Surely you can understand my yearning, you who are motherless, too!"

CHAPTER FOUR

London
9 May 1819

"Dear, oh dear, oh dear!" tutted Prudence, gazing in dismay at the letter in her hands. She'd heard nothing from Josephine in nearly a fortnight, and now the girl had written a veritable novel, chock full of soldiers, wild beasts, and irritating older brothers. She went to her desk and began a reply.

> *All mysteries, no matter how curious, have Rational explanations. If Papa says the Militia has come to exercise, then you can be sure it is so. Be sensible, Jo!*

Prudence understood the ways of her cousin's fertile mind. Several unusual events, combined with Edward's disgrace, could build a crisis from nothing. No doubt her brother's increased officiousness could be attributed to his underlying shame.

"Edward's discontent," she wrote, "will temper with time. Meanwhile, I'm proud of you for so coolly deflecting his slings and arrows."

Satisfied she'd put to rest Josephine's concerns, Prudence

posted the letter and fell back into her routine of lessons and calls. Her cousin was not the most dedicated correspondent, so it didn't surprise her when nine days passed before she received a reply:

> *I did not mishear the lieutenant, nor can I discount his daily meetings with Papa! Let us not disregard their first conversation and the facts I overheard on the following afternoon—*

"—which can be explained by rational means!" cried Prudence aloud.

Josephine had added, "Worst of all, Edward has convinced Papa that our rides must end, musket or no!"

This gave Prudence pause. Since his early teens, Edward had taken on much of the governance of the estate, but never had he dared to discipline the girls. She wondered whether one of Josephine's moods had finally pushed him to the brink. The rest of the page was filled with an unnatural quantity of crabbed handwriting. She forced herself to read on. What followed had nothing to do with her brother, but rather a certain trunk that sat in Greenbank's attic.

"Oh bother," Prudence murmured. The contents of that trunk sounded as mysterious as those in the chest under her bed. Clearly they held her cousin in thrall, but *she* had no Aunt Amelia to hint at their history. Perhaps a few words could help Josephine appreciate their value; then again, Prudence *had* promised Amelia never to speak about the keepsakes. Did the prohibition extend to family members who shared the same history?

"I wonder what sort of special talents our ancestors had,"

she mused. "For women of their station to keep military paraphernalia would be highly unusual."

After two days of inner personal debate, she decided to unburden herself, for there remained no doubt in her mind that the girls' collections were of the same ilk. As she wrote about the chest and its peculiar contents, she considered what little she and Josephine knew about their family. Three of their parents had perished within months of each other: Lady Middlemere in a carriage accident and the Fairfeathers in a Channel shipwreck. She and Josephine had never questioned the coincidence of this, and Prudence's childhood inquiries had been met by Middlemere with glossings and shrugs, as if she and Edward had sprung out of nowhere.

Prudence glanced toward the shadow under her bed. Three people had vanished for ill-explained reasons. These hidden artifacts, which consisted largely of weapons and half-destroyed, wrong-gendered accoutrements, suggested their parents had had extraordinary associations. The fear that for nearly a month had kept her curiosity at bay receded under the force of her sudden desire to know more. *Talents, secrecy, violence, and death.*

"The Inheritance *must* have had something to do with their fates," she guessed.

She recalled Aunt Amelia's admonition not to speak about it. The truth must be more dreadful than she could imagine. Why, then, did this possibility make her want to know more? With a crash of realization, the floodgates of emotional restraint flew wide open. Her dead mother and father were nothing but never-spoken-of cyphers. This had to change. If Amelia and Middlemere refused to enlighten her, she would simply seek knowledge elsewhere.

She finished the letter and laid down her pen. To get at the truth, she would have to face those strange artifacts, no matter how strongly they hinted of violent death. She considered each keepsake and settled on the ring as an item both portable and sporting the least objectionable scars. A thrum of doubt rippled down her spine, but she thrust it away.

It's only a ring, and it's mine, so why shouldn't I do with it as I please?

Prudence knelt beside the bed. Soon, the gold band and scarred stone were enclosed in an envelope with instructions for repair. Heart beating fast, she rang for Nell. When the girl arrived, she pushed the package and some coins into her hands and sent her off to the jeweler.

Despite Prudence's usual ability to set anxieties aside, the matter ate at her conscience for the rest of that day. Did she not have the right to know more about her own family? By bedtime, she could no longer bear the strain. She went to Amelia's room and asked for an audience.

She found the old lady sitting up in bed, sipping sherry. The moment Aunt Amelia's eyes fell on Prudence's serious countenance, she set aside her glass and narrowed her gaze.

"I have been thinking about my parents," began Prudence, as humbly as possible.

"Oh, Prudence," groaned Aunt Amelia, rolling her eyes. "Now I shall have to ring for hot milk."

Prudence made a gesture of supplication. "Could you please tell me something, *anything* about them? Surely there is one aspect of their lives which would engender no pain."

"Trust me, it is better this way. Keep that door firmly closed. Dredging up even the least information could release a flood of unpleasantness."

Prudence came closer and clasped Amelia's hand. "I suppose you are only afraid to upset me with the gruesome details, yet I already suspect that their deaths were no accident!"

"Hush, girl," whispered Aunt Amelia, jerking away her hand.

"Please!" Prudence cried. "Did you think I would never ask?"

The aunt looked away. "No, though I did pray for your indifference."

"My indifference? I am not like Edward, who is content with pretending to be the son Lord Middlemere never had. I have spent a lifetime suppressing dreams about my parents, of whom no one will speak. How can you expect me *not* to be intrigued by that box and its disquieting contents?" Prudence stared at Amelia with wide, pleading eyes.

"Good *night*, Prudence!" said the aunt, turning away.

Prudence's heart sank. She had pressed matters too far; there would be no more forbearance, not even for the most casual inquiries. Taking her leave, she returned to her room and stood still for a long moment. Then, in a rare outburst, she snatched up a bonnet and threw it hard against the wall.

26 May 1819

The following week, she received a letter from Josephine, who sounded relieved to learn they shared this mystery.

> *If only you could appreciate with what trepidation I raised*
> *the subject in the first place! I was so certain you'd scold me*

for drawing unnatural conclusions. The keepsakes are unusual then, and on that we agree. I wonder, too, whether you have any thoughts on the trances that so forcefully led me to that trunk?

Prudence wrinkled her nose. That was the trouble with Josephine—one moment they were having a nice philosophical discussion, the next she was injecting flights of fantasy. Rather than criticize, Prudence wrote, "I wasn't there, so I'd prefer not to pass judgment."

Her ring was delivered that afternoon as she was dressing for supper. Once the maid had gone out, she tore open the package and beheld the restored jewel for the first time. Cleaned of the soot that had sullied its surface, the ring winked in the candlelight, no longer imposing but pretty and inviting. Prickles of excitement tingled her arms as she slid it onto the forefinger of her right hand. She expected it to stick at her second knuckle, for the ring seemed rather small, but it skimmed on as if custom made and settled comfortably at the base of her finger. A wash of warm pleasure suppressed her anxieties as she stroked the band's knotted surface. *Was this Mother's engagement ring?* She suspected it was much, much older, and that its origin had been lost deep in the mists of time.

"But for Aunt Amelia's sake," she said aloud, "I shall have to keep you hidden away." So she dropped the little jewel into a pocket at her waist and vowed to admire it only in private.

The next day, she was emerging from her room when Nell approached her with a card that had just been left by messenger. She opened the envelope and read aloud for the maid's benefit: "'The pleasure of your company is requested at a recital and supper at the estate of Baroness Elisabetha Revelle.' Huzza! My first invitation!"

Mistress and servant giggled in unison. Grinning like a schoolgirl, Prudence went to knock on Aunt Amelia's door. The old woman gave the card a quick perusal then tossed it aside. "You will, of course, refuse."

Prudence's spirits crashed, and she rushed to gather up the invitation. "But why?"

"Because this woman is the last hostess with whom we should associate."

"Madam, please! I beg you to elaborate."

Aunt Amelia waved a dismissive hand. "Reese will deliver your regrets."

Prudence drifted in a daze back to her own room.

"I ain't surprised," mumbled Nell, who was making up the bed.

"I beg your pardon?" At Nell's guilty look, Prudence shut the bedroom door. "Go on," she commanded, crossing her arms.

Nell's shoulders sagged. "I 'eard it from 'er footman, 'oo was a beau of mine last year. Lady Revelle loves to en'ertain, and plenty o' young people flock to 'er salon. Always the quality sort, mind."

"I fail to see why that is remotely scandalous." Prudence narrowed eyes and stared at the maid. Nell blinked, as if measuring the propriety of speaking more frankly.

She said in a stage whisper, "She uses 'er salon to handpick 'er lovers. I 'ear Lord Fortescue 'as ended their affair—'e's to marry a young heiress. If 'er ladyship's on the hunt, Miss Staveley will not want ye to witness such behavior."

Prudence shivered. "Lord, how sordid!"

"Forgive me, Miss, but ye did insist."

"I know, Nell. Thank you. You've been a great help." Prudence circled the room, thinking. If the objective of parties was to see and be seen, then she should attend and get on with the business that had torn her from her family. Let her finally meet the legions of gentlemen in whose hands lay her fate! It mattered little to her—nor obviously to scores of well-connected parents—that the hostess had ulterior designs.

She thrust her hand into her pocket, seeking the invitation, and unexpectedly encountered the ring. Her fingers closed over it. *I do wish I might go* . . . On a burst of impulse, she returned to Aunt Amelia's chamber. "Madam, hear me out. I want to attend this soiree."

The old woman's face darkened. "Do you question my judgment? Leave off with this, Prudence. There will be other opportunities."

Deep in the pocket, Prudence's hand squeezed the ring. Strength surged through her veins. "Shall we rely on social calls to open the right doors? My heart may not be so sanguine with the purposes of a Season, but I have accepted it as a necessary rite of my passage. I've been in London already one quarter of a year but not one event have I attended. With so little to offer I may never attract a good man. I can't afford to be selective, not when Society approves of this lady's salon. Dearest Aunt, I beg you. Please let me go!"

Aunt Amelia stared, eyes wide and mouth gaping. Finally, she said, "I can't argue with your reasoning. Very well, Prudence. You may."

Smothering astonishment, Prudence curtseyed and withdrew to the hall. Inside her pocket, the ring had somehow slipped onto her forefinger. She took out her hand and regarded the bright band. A spark-like sensation raced down her spine. Closing her fist, she gave a small squeal and skipped toward her room.

CHAPTER FIVE

Edingham-Greene, Wiltshire
24 May 1819

Josephine's interest in the soldiers and their mysterious mission waned in proportion to her ever-growing interest in Lady Joanna's trunks. She waited all week for Prudence's response. Meanwhile, she returned to the attic again and again, most of the time purposefully, although sometimes she would turn up there just waking from a trance. She found comfort in fingering the countess's treasures, occasionally even daring to try on the uniform.

"What are you trying to tell me, Mother? What do you want me to know about you?"

But no explanation came to her by simple proximity. Trying not to dwell on the supernatural aspects of her recent compulsions, she hoped Prudence could offer some rational advice.

When her cousin's letter finally came on the following Monday, Josephine ran to her nook and absorbed the stunning reply: Prudence had a collection of equally interesting items, and she agreed their parents had been involved in some kind of enigmatic activity—though she could not guess what.

But I think, my dear Cos, that it must have gotten them
Killed. This explains the Secrecy and the frightful appearance
of my Keepsakes. It also explains why Aunt Amelia grows so
unhappy at the mere mention of the Subject.

"Whatever this Inheritance is of which Aunt Amelia spoke, that is the key to everything," mused Josephine, wondering why Prudence had glossed over the trances. She had offered no advice about what Josephine should do to curtail them, nor acknowledgement of their peculiarity. "Bother! She must not believe me!" Crumpling her cousin's letter, she resolved to press the matter more firmly when she penned a reply.

That afternoon, she set off to sneak a biscuit from the pantry, when suddenly someone was shaking her shoulder. Josephine blinked until the world came into focus.

"Edward?" she asked, for he was glaring at her.

"What's this?" he bellowed. "Aren't you a bit old to be playing highwayman?"

Josephine took in her surroundings: The stile in the back meadow, the lane beyond, and a bitter smell in the air. What had become of the servant's passage with its squeaky oak floor? How could the light from a wall sconce so dazzle her eyes?

"I was daydreaming, not playing! Why must you belittle me?" She looked down and discovered that, instead of biscuits, there were pistols in her hands. "How did *these* get here? Good Lord, are they loaded?"

Edward's eyes bulged. "Don't you *know?* Are you daft, girl? One was in good working order but a few moments ago. I was riding up the lane, and—see that walnut with the fresh scar, see the bark chips on my coat?—that's how close you came to putting a hole in my head!"

"I don't understand. I *couldn't* have fired a pistol. I don't even know how!" Josephine waved her arms in distress.

"Christ, watch it!" howled Edward, ducking out of the way.

"Take them, I beg you!"

Edward snatched the guns, uncocked them, and thrust them into his pockets. "Where'd you get these and what's that damned getup you're wearing?"

"I don't know," she replied meekly, frowning at her mother's military uniform.

"Shameful, a girl your age! What if someone else had seen you in those ridiculous clothes? What if you'd actually shot me? Of all the stupid things—have you no care for your position in the community?"

Josephine's head whirled. "I don't know how this—"

"Get on inside. No more of these escapades, or I'll tell your Papa!"

She ripped off her shako and ran back to the house. Upstairs, she threw the uniform into the deepest corner of her wardrobe and fell onto the bed, sobbing. She was doomed to be perceived as an immature child, and the keepsakes seemed to make matters worse. Edward's point about her reputation had been perfectly valid, however cruelly stated, but the dangers were worse than he could possibly imagine. These wanderings, over which she had no control, might land her anywhere at any time of day. In the blink of an eye, the pleasure of touching her mother's belongings morphed into fear.

She thought about her father—his nerves, his fear of crowds, his preference for isolation. Was his eccentricity the result of a similar youthful experience? She dared not ask him, but Josephine shuddered to think she might live such a life.

Meanwhile, in the study, Lord Middlemere absorbed Amelia Staveley's latest report.

It has been a slow road thus far, and I know Prudence is anxious to be done with the whole thing, but outwardly she is patient and witty and lovely. Soon enough, she will soften the hearts of the more entrenched sponsors, and assembly halls such as Almack's will then bid her welcome.

"Brava, Prudence!" exclaimed the earl, but his delight vanished as he read further.

You should know that the box is now in her possession. O, how I'd hoped and prayed the compulsion would have abated. But you expected this, didn't you?

All those years ago he had tried to say it, but the Keepers disbelieved him. And now . . .

Wincing, he pressed on. If the bequest itself wasn't bad enough, the girl's ensuing questions had triggered yet another compulsion, forcing Aunt Staveley to reveal fragments of truth. At first Prudence had seemed unimpressed by what she'd found in the box, but later she had posed more questions about her parents. She'd even guessed they had died in a violent way.

"Oh, my dear sir," wrote Aunt Staveley, "I thought I would faint. If she only knew how I spent hours scouring that field—"

"Damnation! Why couldn't that rubbish have been lost or

destroyed?" Middlemere dropped the letter and covered his eyes as nausea welled in his throat. "Look, Joanna, how haunted I am!" He forced himself to peer at the letter's last lines:

> *Thankfully, without the application of ritual, the Talismans shall remain inactive and harmless. I rebuked Prudence soundly, and the matter is now closed.*

Middlemere squeezed the bridge of his nose. Two decades ago, he had postulated that Talismans could, even without ritual, awaken a Keeper's instincts. It was a radical theory and ignored by the authorities—justly so, it would appear. Though he'd spent sixteen years painstakingly tracking each surviving Keeper family, he had found no evidence of any heir employing the gift without training.

"Perhaps I was wrong," he said, addressing his late wife. "Considering what's at stake, I'd be happy to concede." Joanna smiled down at him, frozen in time, her elegance and femininity belying her true nature.

Picking up his pen, he wrote,

> *Prudence is an inquisitive creature; she was bound to ask questions. However, her curiosity is not proof that she actually carries the Trait, and anyway, as you say, the Talismans are useless without proper training. If we're lucky, she'll lose interest and burn the whole lot. Find a nice baron for her to fall in love with and she'll forget those old things.*

"A girl in love has no time for such silliness. Right, Joanna?" He smiled at his wife's portrait. For once, however, he did not feel so reassured.

4 June 1819

Josephine entered the house after a midmorning walk and came upon her father speaking with the lieutenant of the special militia. The officer had dropped by Greenbank frequently over the course of the past month, but until now she had seen him only in passing. With the militia removed to the village, she had no way of knowing how things stood in the neighborhood, chiefly because Carson seemed somehow to have divined her desire to eavesdrop, and so he often prowled the back hall.

"Ah, Josephine!" cried Middlemere. "Come here, dear, and let me introduce you to our most excellent officer, Lieutenant Quimby."

Josephine approached them and bobbed; the lieutenant likewise bowed. In the shadows of the hallway, she could discern little of his features except his trim build, dark-head, and age, perhaps mid-twenties. His carriage, she noted, had straightened when she'd entered, from which she deduced a certain friendliness developing between him and her father.

As she moved to take her leave, Quimby suddenly spoke. "I'm sorry we disappointed you, my lady, by moving up to the village."

Josephine froze. She glanced sidelong at Middlemere. The last thing she needed was her father suspecting she had an interest in affairs that didn't concern her. Lightly but through clenched teeth, she replied, "What makes you think I gave it any consideration at all?"

In the awkward silence that followed, Quimby coughed into his hand. "Oh, I beg your pardon. It must have been a maid I saw peering down at us that day."

Josephine flashed him a dangerous look.

Middlemere chuckled. "The whole household was in an uproar during your encampment at Greenbank. I caught two maids polishing silver with their foreheads pressed flat against the dining room window!"

"Ah, yes! Nosy girls!" said Quimby, nodding. "Some enjoy the spectacle of uniformed men, whilst others think they've discovered intrigues that in fact don't concern them."

Josephine found his manner impertinent, but there was such a smile in his voice that she could not muster too much resentment. She *had*, after all, been eavesdropping on him.

"There is another possibility," she rejoined. "Sometimes girls who read books by open windows are presumed incorrectly to hold an interest in something as pedestrian as sweating yeomen in uniform. Indeed, they can hardly be blamed for taking note of all the commotion." She curtseyed again and passed into the drawing room, pointedly ignoring the mischievous sparkle in Quimby's eyes.

CHAPTER SIX

London
28 May 1819

Josephine wrote in her usual breathless manner to complain of an incident that had once again put her at odds with her foster-brother. From what Prudence could tell, she had sneaked out of the house with the uniform and pistols and was caught in the act by a startled and aggrieved Edward.

> *I've been trying and trying to behave more like a lady—you know I have, Prudence, and you have complimented my efforts—but your brother never misses an opportunity to call me out for a child.*

"Really, Edward!" sighed Prudence.

"I beg your pardon?" said Aunt Amelia.

Choosing her words carefully, Prudence explained, "My brother has become a tyrant. Josephine is constantly at his mercy, but Papa seems not to notice."

"That boy ought to be at school. Truant puppy! Middlemere indulges him as much as he did your fath—" Amelia broke off.

Prudence took in a soft breath. She couldn't recall anyone alluding to her father's character. Gently, so as not to ruin the rare moment, she asked, "Is Edward that similar?"

Aunt Amelia's eyes closed, her face softened, and a smile crept across her lips. "No, he is not half as fiendish. Your father, rest his soul, tried *everyone's* patience. Clarence Weston was practically the only person who could stand him." She stiffened. "For shame, you conniving chit!"

"Ma'am?"

The old lady lurched to her feet. "I need a cold compress," she muttered and shot from the room.

Blast it, she's gone. Then, aloud, "My father was an insufferable fiend?" This information had come to Prudence so out of context that she felt no disappointment, only surprise. She had never formed an idea of what her parents were like. Filing away the interesting detail, she bent to absorb the remainder of Josephine's missive.

> *Anyway, the pistols are gone; Edward has locked them away. Isn't it ironic? I'd predicted tedium for myself and excitement for you, yet everything has gone quite the reverse.*

Prudence gave a short laugh. "At least *he's* got the pistols." She knew Josephine too well. A keen imagination coupled with trunkloads of old clothes could make for endless entertainment. She wondered what had *really* happened in that pasture; likely a prank gone awry.

Josephine then went on about her supposed unconscious wanderings. Prudence tsked and went to Amelia's desk to pen a reply. She couldn't in good conscience indulge such fantasies. Besides, she had her own interesting news, namely the restored ring and her invitation to attend a baroness's salon.

"Prudence!" called Aunt Amelia from the vicinity of the foyer.

"Coming!" She had one final thought, something that might inspire Josephine to give up her childish ways:

My brother's severity comes from his desire for Order and Safety, though it does go too far. You are the Lady of Greenbank, and I shall advise him so forthwith.

"Let us see what she makes of that." Grinning, Prudence folded the page and dribbled wax on its seam.

4 June 1819

As dusk fell, Prudence and Aunt Amelia took the carriage to Chedleigh Hall, an estate situated on the River Thames a few miles west of London.

Prudence's nerves thrummed as she struggled to shut out Aunt Amelia's unending chatter. She reached up to pat her hair, a high confection of curls and plaits studded with pearls. Her pale-yellow silk gown had blue flowers embroidered across the skirt and a satin ribbon at the hem. Long gloves, pendant earrings, and an azure ribbon at her throat completed the ensemble. At the door of Chedleigh Hall, she opened her reticule and unconsciously slipped on the ruby ring.

She gazed up at the house, a great shadow in the dusk. Each window emitted beams of sparkling light, like a multifaceted prism. Inside, the women divested themselves of their wraps and gave their names to the footman. Then, arm in arm, they entered the salon.

The room blazed with candlelight, floor-length windows

thrown open to admit the summer air. Such richness of color! Such a pleasant clamor of voices! Gentlemen and ladies stood in clusters, here speaking, there whispering, now breaking into sudden peals of laughter. Chaperones sat along the walls, their attitudes friendly but their eyes all business. Servants glided about bearing trays full of drinks. A quartet played in the corner, their efforts largely unnoticed.

A voice in Prudence's ear purred, "Welcome, Miss Fairfeather. Everyone is anxious to meet you."

Prudence turned and looked into a pair of blue-grey eyes, white-lashed and piercing. The woman's face, flawless and pale, was so perfectly formed it might have been sculpted from Travertine marble. Her brows arched, thin and platinum, across a high, regal forehead. Her white-blonde hair had been twisted into a turban adorned with white feathers. She was clad all in ivory, and she was stunning.

Masking her confusion at the effusive greeting, Prudence made a low curtsey. "Thank you, my lady."

The baroness turned to greet Aunt Amelia and immediately stiffened. "Aha! Miss *Staveley*, is it? What an unexpected pleasure."

"My lady," the aunt replied, her voice stilted and odd. "It has been a long time."

They glowered at each other for several crackling seconds. Lady Revelle broke the spell with a sudden, careless laugh. "You must excuse me. I have other guests to attend." Turning heel, she vanished into the crowd.

"Oh, I *knew* this was a mistake!" harrumphed Aunt Amelia.

"Are you acquainted with her?" Prudence's eyes scanned the room for a glimpse of white feathers.

"No, of *course* not! Or, rather, I did not know *she* was the Baroness Revelle. Years ago, she went by a different name."

"She seemed equally surprised to see you."

"As well she should," muttered Aunt Amelia, a dark expression on her face. She shook herself and added, "I think we should go."

"Aunt!"

"Don't argue with me, girl. I have your best interests at heart."

Prudence groaned inwardly. Here was Society, so tantalizingly within reach. Something told her if she ever wanted to do more than pay calls every day, she must continue to exert pressure on Aunt Amelia's will. Careful not to sound desperate, she said, "Please let us stay. Besides, if we go now, it might cause a stir."

The aunt followed her gaze. A half-dozen people had taken notice of them and were talking amongst themselves. The baroness joined this group and seemed to be exhorting them to make the newcomers feel welcome.

"Crafty vixen!" growled Aunt Amelia. "Very well. A couple of hours will suffice." A footman appeared at her elbow, bearing a tray filled with drinks.

"Refreshments, ma'am?"

"Indeed," agreed Aunt Amelia, snatching one directly. "But you should refrain." She stayed Prudence's hand. "You must keep a cool head."

They waded into the room. Aunt Amelia recognized several chaperones and stopped often to chat. Prudence did her best to seem engaged, but the longer she stood there, the more she desired to meet other people. She cast furtive glances round the salon, taking in the splendor of more gentlemen than she'd seen in her life. The place abounded with broad shoulders, tobacco-scented jackets, and booming male laughter. Without realizing it, she edged her way out of the circle of matrons and girls and angled her body to better observe other guests.

"Need help?" Startled, Prudence turned. Lady Revelle greeted her with a complicit smile. "Come, Miss Fairfeather. I'll introduce you around. You'll never find a mate while roosting amongst the biddies." She gestured at Aunt Amelia and mumbled something in an undertone.

"I beg your pardon?" said Prudence.

"Never mind me. I talk myself through parties to make sure I haven't forgotten anything." Lady Revelle tucked the girl's arm around hers and drew her away from the chattering aunt.

Thus ensued a dizzying round of introductions. Prudence met girls of great wealth and refinement, some with aristocratic lineage, as well as eligible bachelors of varying pedigrees. After a while, names and faces started to blur, and she felt a little faint. She wondered why Aunt Amelia had not noticed her absence.

Lady Revelle joggled her arm. "Pay attention, my dear, for here is one fellow you must not forget. Miss Fairfeather, permit me to introduce Phinneas Allerton, Viscount Underwood."

Prudence curtseyed. A tall, fair-haired gentleman surveyed her with neutral grey eyes and palpable detachment.

"Dearest Phinney!" cooed the baroness, hanging on his arm. "I've a special favor to ask. Miss Fairfeather is fresh from Wiltshire; she hardly knows anyone. Promise you'll call on her?"

Underwood drawled, "Indeed, ma'am. The pleasure will be all mine."

"Perfect!" The lady turned her gaze from Underwood to Prudence, as if assessing their compatibility.

Prudence felt a blush coming on. Behind her back, she twisted the ring, wishing she could fade away. She had not known the Marriage Mart functioned on so obvious a level. Whether she found a love match or not, she preferred not to be subjected to the machinations of a third party. Still, Lord Underwood was handsome, possibly wealthy, and definitely titled. She could do far, far worse.

Where on earth is Aunt Amelia? Prudence craned her head, scouting various groupings of chairs ringing the room.

Lady Revelle released Lord Underwood to his friends. Crooking a finger, she led Prudence aside and lifted her left hand. "Mm-hmm. I thought so. I know this ring well. Your mother was a friend of mine, Miss Fairfeather."

"She was?" Prudence breathed. "Dear me! I-I—"

Lady Revelle silenced her with a gesture. "This is no time for reunions. I'm curious, though, what Miss Staveley has told you about that and other . . . *related* subjects." A sly note stole into her voice, and her eyes narrowed to slits as she scanned the salon.

"She has said next to nothing, actually," replied Prudence.

Lady Revelle's eyes returned to hers. "No mention of Talisman Keepers?"

Prudence shook her head.

"In that case, we must meet some other time, and I'll tell you all about this pretty jewel."

"I would like that, but—" Prudence stared down at the ruby, which contrasted so sharply with the creaminess of her glove. It seemed to glare more crimson than ever. Suddenly self-conscious, she tried to pull away her hand. The lady held fast.

"Leave it on, darling. It suits you." She reached out and ran a finger along Prudence's cheek, slowly, deliberately, ending at her chin. "Yes, I can imagine how the right gentleman might be quite taken with you, and you in turn would make him a fine *companach*." Stressing the final word, she tapped Prudence's chin and flashed an enigmatic smile. Prudence stared, shivering, unable to move. The lady said nothing more, but released her and glided away.

Prudence exhaled a slow breath. Aunt Amelia had never advised what to do if someone else raised the subject of keepsakes. She couldn't deny she'd felt a sense of uneasiness in Lady Revelle's presence—of course the baroness was an energetic woman, and that kind of élan might make anyone nervous. It meant nothing. And yet . . .

She stowed the ring in her reticule and stepped from the alcove, her eyes darting about. Aunt Amelia was still nowhere in sight. Just as apprehension had begun to take root, a gentleman approached with two glasses of wine.

Smiling, he said, "Don't take it personally. Lady Revelle has abandoned us all at one time or another. Will you console yourself with this drink and a moment of my company?"

Prudence tensed. The lady had introduced them, though his name escaped her. "No, thank you, sir," she said, looking out across the salon. She had no experience with speaking to gentlemen alone and would have preferred to practice the art in an amiable group setting.

"I don't bite," teased the gentleman, ducking into her line of sight. "Will you accept this, or must I drink alone and two-fisted?"

Prudence submitted to the gentleman's gaze, which sparkled with good humor, his grin crooked yet confident. He was tall and well built, with sandy hair and long, curling side-whiskers. He had an air of confidence untouched by conceit, and neither shyness nor boredom curtained his eyes. As the moment extended, Prudence's brain seemed to fold in on itself. Never had she met a man whose appearance so pleased her. Never had any man rendered her speechless. Was this what it felt like to fall in love at first sight?

Ridiculous! she thought. *I don't know the first thing about him.*

"Forgive me," he murmured. "I am causing you discomfort. I bid you good evening." Disappointment darkened his features as he inclined his head.

"Oh, sir, d-do stay!" stammered Prudence. "I-I shouldn't want you to drink alone and, if truth be told, I haven't anyone else to speak to."

He turned an ironic eye. "So you'll settle for me?"

She reddened. "I didn't mean it like that."

"I think you did! Perhaps somewhere in this crowd you've heard terrible things about old Will MacNeal. Do they say he's moody? Unpredictable? A cad?"

"No, sir. Nothing like that." She warmed to the game. Lowering her voice, she added, "They say he speaks of himself in the third person!"

The gentleman roared with laughter. "He does *not!*"

"Oh yes, indeed. I have heard it myself."

"And this is a greater crime than the aforementioned allegations?"

"Absolutely, because either he is vain or he has something to hide."

His brows arced. "So you've more patience for a cad than a somewhat flawed gentleman?"

"Well," Prudence said with a shrug, "the cad may be silver-tongued, but at least he takes ownership of his unsavory reputation."

"Right. Then what if I told you I was moody, unpredictable, and a cad?"

Prudence smiled. "I'd find you refreshingly forthright!"

"Truce!" declared Mr. MacNeal, and they laughed together as easily as old friends. "Here," he said. "Take a glass before I spill wine on your slippers."

Prudence sipped at the wine, astonished at her burst of boldness. Buoyed by the thrill of conversational success, she strained to think of something more to say.

"Are you a veteran of such events?"

Mr. MacNeal snorted. "A grizzled veteran, you might say. Battle-worn and jaded. I came only for the music . . . but have been pleasantly diverted by a new acquaintance." He lifted his glass in a silent toast.

Flustered, Prudence shifted her gaze to the floor. "Such disdain you have for Society," she said. "Is it really that odious?"

Mr. MacNeal shrugged. "I suppose not. Please disregard my cynicism. You're a newcomer, and I have no right to influence your sensibilities. Better I should guide you through the possible hazards you might meet." There was a quizzical softness in his last statement that drew Prudence's attention back to his face.

He watched her with his intensely green eyes, a half-smile lifting one corner of his mouth, and her heart thudded like a timpani drum. As in a dream, the rest of the room fell away; sounds faded, lights blurred, and the other occupants vanished. She was aware of only Mr. MacNeal, the first man whom she thought she might like to know better. Was it her turn to speak? What should she say, now that she sensed his longing to take her hand and kiss it . . . ?

Overwhelmed by a confusing array of emotions, she again looked away. A group of young ladies stood nearby, staring at the couple with unmistakable coldness. What had they seen that offended them so?

"Miss Fairfeather, I—" Mr. MacNeal followed Prudence's gaze. "Ah, the omnipresent gossips!" he said softly. "I recommend you keep a safe distance from them."

Prudence set aside her wineglass with trembling fingers. "Perhaps we should . . ."

"Yes, if you prefer," he interposed, as if divining her thoughts.

"It is no slight to your company, only . . ."

"No offense taken. I quite understand. Society dictates the rules. We must mingle at parties, whether we care to or not."

"But how else are we to ensure that we'll meet the most fascinating people?"

Mr. MacNeal's eyes glittered. "Who says we haven't?"

Prudence drew in a breath.

He cleared his throat. "May I call on you sometime?"

"Yes, I'd like that. Stanistead House."

"You may count on it, Miss Fairfeather. I hope to have the pleasure of seeing you again."

They bowed to each other, then the crowd swallowed him up. The gossips grew bored and turned away. Prudence crossed to the phalanx of chaperones, where she found Aunt Amelia holding court. Had she been there all along? A chime sounded, indicating the recital would begin soon. The guests moved to take seats.

Aunt Amelia beckoned. "Well, my dear, are you having a good time?"

"Passably good. Where have you been? I lost sight of you in the crowd."

"Why, here, of course. I've been keeping my eye on you, and I must say you carry yourself well. Did our hostess do the courtesy of introducing you round?"

"Yes, ma'am."

"Ah, excellent!"

Strange, thought Prudence. Considering their earlier hostility, why was Aunt Amelia not alarmed by such attention?

"And did you meet any interesting gentlemen?"

There was no hint of insinuation in Amelia's tone. Prudence found this stranger still. Had she not spent several minutes speaking to a man in view of the whole room?

"I met several, actually, and I do not think I embarrassed myself too badly."

"Saucy girl!" Aunt Amelia whacked Prudence's shoulder with her fan. "Now, let us take our places, for the recital is about to begin."

"I thought you had not meant to stay long."

"What? Oh, why spoil a pleasant evening? I love music, don't you?"

Prudence puzzled over the aunt's abrupt change of tune, but she was too distrait to pursue the matter in depth. They moved with the crowd and found seats at the rear of the room. Prudence expected to be far too agitated to sit still, but she quickly lost herself in the first tender, burring notes of a cello. After several bars, a pianoforte joined in, building and melding with its resolute partner. The instruments spoke to each other like intimate friends, first echoing then leading, each in its turn. As the sonata's melody swelled, so did a thrum of passion swell in her heart. Prudence gasped, and her emotion-dampened eyes roved the audience for another glimpse of Mr. MacNeal. She did not see him again for the rest of that evening, but his words, like the cello's song, still burned in her mind:

I should guide you . . . I should guide you . . .

CHAPTER SEVEN

Edingham-Greene, Wiltshire
8 June 1819

All weekend long, Josephine thought of Prudence and her London debut. At last, on Tuesday morning, a letter arrived. Josephine retreated to the privacy of her nook, where she savored every line about Lady Revelle's salon.

"Huzza, Prudence!" she shouted, waving the page over her head.

A soft chuckle came from the shadows of the lower entry hall. Glancing down, Josephine spied a man's silhouette and two glinting eyes. It was Quimby, who said nothing, though she sensed merriment in his mien. He greeted her with a nod and walked out the door.

Josephine shrugged. Her attention returned to Prudence's letter and its talk of Talisman Keepers. She agreed it would be interesting to plumb Lady Revelle's knowledge, yet something about this proposal troubled her. As shamelessly as she employed underhanded tactics of her own, flouting Aunt Amelia's heartfelt warning was another matter. Eavesdropping was only a question of politesse, but a plea for circumspection suggested something more vital was at stake.

"Careful, Prudence!" she said. "Oh, I hope she's not too eager to invite a stranger into her confidence."

Josephine went to bed that night certain her bout with trances had passed—it had been days since her last wandering—and awakened to find herself standing in the dark at the edge of the Heywood. Mildly vertiginous, she threw her arms wide and discovered a pistol in each hand. How this was possible she couldn't guess; she had not seen them since Edward confiscated them a fortnight ago.

She cast a glance downward and found herself clad in the oversized jacket, boots, and breeches from her mother's trunk. The shako perched cock-eyed atop her loose tumble of hair.

"Blast it, not *again!*"

Voices rang in the distance. A twig snapped nearby, followed by animal-like snufflings. Stifling a whimper, Josephine wondered what she should do. Run? Back away slowly?

Her eyes flicked to the pistols. Small comfort, since they weren't loaded.

Anyway, I haven't the foggiest idea how to shoot the dratted things.

She raised her useless weapons and trained them on the woods. Another twig snapped—louder. Closer. She inched backward, heart racing, preparing to bolt for the house.

In an explosion of claws and unholy shrieks, a muscular beast plunged from the thicket. It skidded and wheeled on her, spitting and snarling. Josephine stood transfixed, staring in horror at the hellish figure. A blast of musk assaulted her senses, rousing her as swiftly as a sharp dose of salts. With a throaty cry, she squeezed the trigger of one pistol. The weapon discharged, belching fire and smoke. The beast stumbled, screaming, then regained its footing. Somehow she had shot it square in its left eye. The beast cast about with its remaining orb, seeking revenge.

"Oh, help," she whispered.

The beast's roving eye fixed on the source of its pain. Through a fog of pure terror, Josephine perceived an intake of breath and gathering of muscles. It took a step toward her, nostrils twitching as it drew in her scent. Puttylike lips lifted, revealing its teeth, which were yellow and countless and lethally sharp. A long rope of saliva dangled from its mouth. Josephine watched, fascinated, as the mucus stretched downward, reached the point of release, and dropped to the ground with an audible plop.

She was so mesmerized by the repulsive details of the creature that she failed to notice it had crept nearer. Now she blinked and swallowed and found herself staring up at its chest. The thing sniffed her over, as if to assess her edibility. Its blown eye socket gaped dark and grisly; rivulets of ocular fluid had already begun to harden on its pelt. The odor it gave off—rotting flesh and old, rancid lard—staggered the senses.

Josephine comprehended that she was an instant from death.

The instinct to survive took over. Quick as lightning, she palmed the other pistol. Pressing the muzzle point-blank to the beast's chest, she fired again.

Her weapon's report rang out across the field, followed by a pause and a moan and a reassuring thump. Dogs barked, shouts grew nearer, footsteps pounded through the woods. Josephine bent over the corpse, trying to make sense of its alien features. In the faint starlight, she could see very little, but it was enough.

This creature was unlike any animal in her knowledge. If she had not previously heard the soldiers' musings about trolls, she would never have been able to identify the truth: this was a being of supernatural origins.

Someone's hands closed over hers, and a voice said, low and firm, "I don't think you want to be found here, my lady, especially like this." It was Quimby. "May I have these?" he asked. Josephine nodded and gave the pistols up gladly. He tucked them in a pack, then undid his cloak and threw it over her shoulders.

Josephine was vaguely aware of the lieutenant fastening his cloak at her throat and afterward bending to examine her face. "Are you hurt?" he murmured. She shook her head.

I killed something. I nearly died. Oh God, I nearly died! It took every ounce of her willpower not to stagger against him and shed relieved tears.

"I'm taking you home," he said, nudging her away from the corpse. He hailed an approaching soldier. "I've dispatched the creature. Have the men burn it and scatter the remains. Oh— and will a crown help you forget who else was here?"

"Aye, sir!" The soldier caught the shining coin as it sailed through the air. His eyes flicked to Josephine before looking away.

Lieutenant Quimby resumed his pressure against the small of her back, propelling her toward Greenbank's old mill and over the race. As they circled the pond, he said, "Well, then. Tell me how it is you came to kill my quarry in the middle of the night."

Frightened and shocked as she was, Josephine thought he had some nerve. She snipped, "I'd rather not say. Besides, gentlemen don't take credit for others' achievements."

Quimby chuckled. "Ladies don't gad about in breeches firing guns. You ought to thank me, you know. You might make it back to bed before anyone realizes you're gone."

Josephine hadn't time to be furious at his cheek. He had marched her up the lawn, and they were close to the house. Quimby pointed toward a dark side-entry. "Here you are, madam. Good night."

All of a sudden, the door burst open and Edward staggered out, shrugging a coat over his rumpled nightshirt and cradling a musket in one elbow. He spied them and goggled like one who has lost his mind. "Bloody hell!" he cried, lurching forward.

Quimby threw up an arm. "It's not what you think! The men and I were conducting an exercise and inadvertently flushed our quarry into the path of Lady Weston."

"I heard shots—"

"The beast was killed. No harm has been done."

"No harm!" Edward turned on Josephine, his eyes ablaze with fury and concern. "Why in God's name are *you* abroad late at night?"

Normally she would have stood up for herself, but in this instance Josephine had no ready retort. Shaking her head, she stepped backward into the officer's sheltering stance.

Lieutenant Quimby interposed. "That very point, sir, I have already impressed. I'm sure Lady Weston is duly contrite."

How could she be, for her actions had not entirely been willful? Regardless, Josephine murmured, "Thank you, Lieutenant. It shan't happen again." She brushed past the two men and darted inside. Upstairs, she changed clothes, hid Quimby's cloak, and lay down on the bed. Visions of the slavering, one-eyed beast kept jolting her awake. There was no use trying to sleep, so she lit a candle and staggered to her desk.

"Oh help!" she scrawled.

Maybe now Prudence would finally believe her.

9 June 1819

The next morning, Josephine awoke to find Maria standing by her bed. "And what, young lady, might 'ee be doin' with *thic?*" She held up the countess's uniform.

Josephine kicked herself inwardly for not hiding it. "I found it in the attic. Why on earth would my mother have owned such a thing?"

"'Twas for a costume ball, no doubt. In those days, thy parents attended many a grand party."

Doubtful, but after the events of last night, Josephine no longer cared. "Put it away, would you, please? It's too morbid to bear." Maria flashed an expression of relief. "While you're about it," Josephine added, "have someone put proper locks on those trunks. Someday I will go through Mother's effects, but not yet, I think."

"Certainly, my lady." Maria turned to leave.

"Oh, and one other thing. Lately, I've been having such terrible nightmares. Might you indulge me for a few days by sleeping on a cot by my door?"

"Why, o' course, 'ee poor child! I'd do anything for my girl." Maria hugged the offending articles to her chest and hurried away.

Josephine lay back with a shudder. "I cannot believe I almost perished last night! This Inheritance seems a dangerous business— no *wonder* Aunt Amelia doesn't want us meddling about."

And those trolls, which Lieutenant Quimby was so obviously hunting? That meant another set of secrets, both of which had converged so explosively in one night. What did Edward know about these beasts? Had his return to Greenbank been by coincidence or design? Then Josephine remembered him calling Quimby's exercise a fool's errand, and that he had ridiculed Peter for invoking the notion of monsters.

"Edward has no idea what Quimby supposedly killed last night," she whispered. This gave her a brief dose of satisfaction, but just as quickly the shudders came back. She was not, perhaps, as adventuresome as she had always believed.

In the days that followed, Lady Middlemere's trunks were padlocked, and Josephine kept close to Maria. The nurse established herself on a cot in the girl's room, by the door as requested. The strategy worked; Josephine had no more recurrences of somnambulism.

Which is not to say that her troubles had vanished.

On the morning after she killed the troll, Edward ordered the women confined to the house. Fear forced Josephine to accede to his wishes, but it was the height of summer and the out-of-doors called to her with its siren song of freedom. She missed her rides, her solitary rambles, and paying calls on the neighbors. These losses she forbore willingly until one evening when, as family and friends rose from supper and advanced to the drawing room, Edward stopped her in the hall.

"Would you ladies please spend the evening upstairs? In fact, make yourselves scarce every night and the rest of us would be grateful."

Josephine guffawed. "You must be out of your mind, Edward Fairfeather, if you think you can banish me from my own downstairs parlor!"

"Ah, my lady, let the boys be boys!" advised Maria. "Give 'em a few nights o' their secret society; they'll soon beg for our return."

Edward's upper lip twitched.

"Give them the drawing room and they'll soon have half the house!" Josephine retorted. "On no account will I give in. Speak of manly things all you like, sir. You shan't alarm my sensibilities."

Edward changed tack. "If you must know, Grant's taken up smoking and doesn't want to offend you."

This was a lie and Josephine knew it. "Indeed, I *love* the smell of tobacco. Oh, Arthur!" she called. "Will you let me help you light your cigar?"

Arthur, who stood in the drawing room, turned and frowned. Edward jerked shut the parlor doors and loomed over her. "You're being difficult to spite me, aren't you?"

Josephine drew herself up to her full height. "Not at all. It's a matter of principle. You gentlemen may confabulate anytime and anywhere you like so long as it doesn't affect my rights in this house. I've had enough of your dictatorship! In fact, my grievances are many, and henceforth I shall not hesitate to enumerate them with Papa."

"You wouldn't dare upset milord with your petty complaints!"

"No, but I could always stage a frightful tantrum. Isn't that the sort of tactic you'd expect from Josephine Weston? I know: what if I refused to eat until Prudence came home? *She* would shake apart your autocracy!"

"Oh, ha! You haven't the stones!" However blusteringly he said this, Edward looked most uneasy.

"Care to wager on that?"

As they stared each other down like two duelists poised to shoot, Josephine felt a thrum of unaccustomed power surge through her veins.

Finally, he muttered, "I ain't that stupid."

"Then stand aside, and we'll forget the whole thing."

Edward's nostrils flared. He grasped both handles and flung open the doors. "Your parlor, madam," he announced tightly.

Josephine entered first, holding open her arms. She couldn't help noticing the smiles on the three younger boys' faces—in her view Arthur Grant's opinion counted for nothing—and she basked in their pleasure. *Brilliant! I got my way without yelling or stamping my feet.*

"Play us a tune, Peter. Come here, Charlie. I feel the sudden urge to dance!"

Soon, the French doors stood open, letting in the lush smells of summer. Music and laughter trickled out across the lawn. For the moment, Greenbank was as it should be. And like her father had done for many a year, Josephine drank deeply from the River Lethe.

14 June 1819

Lieutenant Quimby's cloak had now lain folded in her bureau for nearly a week. Josephine had no particular reason for keeping it; a servant could have returned it to the camp in the village, but something told her it might come in handy. One day, she awakened with the kernel of an idea.

At breakfast she announced, "Today I shall visit Mrs. March." Before Edward could protest, she added, "Maria and

I will take the carriage, and if it so pleases Edward, he can arm
Harry and Sam. At the very least we might bring home a rabbit
for supper."

Edward glared, but Middlemere laughed.

"That's a capital idea!" agreed the earl. "Please be sure to
take her some wine as a token of my affection."

Josephine glanced sidelong at Maria, who shook her head.
Later, in the carriage, the nurse said, "All these years, Mrs.
March has waited so patiently for thy father, hanging on each
gift. I wonder if the poor lady will ever get her reward."

"'Tis one of my fondest hopes," Josephine concurred with
a sigh. She was forever attempting to foster romance between
her father and the sweet-faced widow who resided in a cottage
at the edge of Edingham-Greene. The earl, as always, remained
detached and oblivious. She patted the basket wherein lay
the bottle selected by Lord Middlemere himself, cushioned by
Lieutenant Quimby's cloak.

The ladies rode the scant mile into Edingham-Greene.
The village green looked strange with its occupying army. As
there had not been enough households to billet all the men,
more than a dozen were obliged to camp out in the open.
Their tents stood in smart rows, interspersed here and there
with smoldering cookfires. Off to one side loomed a pavilion,
its flaps tied back. The troop's colors and a Union Jack were
posted nearby. Several soldiers, among them Quimby himself,
huddled round a traveling desk propped on a crate.

"Will you pull up right here, Sam?" said Josephine. "I have
an errand to make."

Maria gave her a narrow look. They came to a halt beyond
the pavilion. It would not do to hail a soldier in public, so she
waited for someone to notice. Presently, an ensign nudged

Lieutenant Quimby, who approached the carriage and bowed.

"Good day, ladies," he said pleasantly. "May I help you?"

This was the closest Josephine had seen him in broad daylight. He was quite young—probably in his early twenties— and had chestnut hair, bright blue eyes, and a healthy, tanned complexion. There was a respectful quietness about him that contrasted with every other youth she knew. True, he had teased her before, but she wondered if it came from a spirit of interest rather than one of meanness. She would test that by seeing how he treated her now.

"No, sir, we are only passing by, but I have something you inadvertently left at Greenbank." Josephine reached into the basket and drew out his cloak. Maria turned on her, mouth open, eyebrows arched in horror. Josephine trod hard on her foot.

"How kind of you," replied Quimby, visibly pretending not to notice. "Lady Weston, would you care to take a cup of tea with me?"

Josephine hadn't expected this turn of events. "I'd be delighted, Lieutenant." His eyes met hers, twinkling mischievously. "Wait here, Maria. I'll be but a few minutes."

As Maria gaped like a fish, Quimby helped Josephine down and led her to the pavilion. The junior officers moved off. Josephine and her host sat on folding chairs in the shade. The sergeant bustled by to inform them that tea would be along shortly. In the interim, she handed Lieutenant Quimby his cloak.

He said, "Thanks, but you needn't have troubled. I visit your father regularly; you could have left that with the butler."

"Indeed, I didn't think of it once till I chanced upon it today. Maria and I are visiting a friend in the village, so I brought it along in case I should happen to see you."

Quimby's lips curved in amusement. "I see," he replied.

The sergeant returned with the tea and moved out of earshot. Josephine wondered how to get round to her actual objective. "I did not mean to take up so much of your time. I can see that you're busy."

"Oh, but I welcome the interruption! It's not every day a soldier may entertain a young lady. Nor is it every day that young ladies come to trade me cloaks for pistols."

Josephine set down her teacup with an indelicate clatter. Lieutenant Quimby leant his chin on one palm, blinking expectantly. He was surely the most cheerful teaser she had ever encountered. A peculiar niggle tickled her belly.

Do not banter with this man! It's a waste of your time. He is only a soldier.

But he's clever and witty. What harm can it do?

Conscious of his eyes boring into hers, she said, "Well, now that you mention it . . ."

"I supposed I *had* to. How else were we going to get to the real reason you're here?"

"You discredit me. I am perfectly content with tea and conversation."

"For which I'm grateful," he replied gently. "But we ought to conclude our business first, don't you think?" He gestured to his sergeant and whispered in the fellow's ear. The sergeant fetched a bundle wrapped in white linen. "Here you are," said the lieutenant. "I took the liberty of cleaning them for you."

Josephine accepted the bundle, and they drank their tea in companionable silence. She could feel Maria's eyes from all the way across the green.

"You showed remarkable composure that night," said

Quimby. "More than some of my best men. I'm sorry you couldn't receive proper credit for dispatching that beast. Did you think I stole it to save my own vanity?"

She lifted one brow. "In a word, yes."

"I promise you, that wasn't the case. Only a fool would begrudge help in a matter this serious. No, I had a suspicion Mr. Fairfeather wouldn't take kindly to being upstaged by a female."

Josephine's eyes widened. How could he have known?

Quimby went on. "Mr. Fairfeather's desire to protect his property is well known. Bad enough that he must compete with trained soldiers. Word of your achievement would have shattered his tightly-wound sensibility."

"You have no idea," agreed Josephine.

"Did you have any trouble after he discovered us together?"

"N-n-no! Your explanation sufficed. My cousin is far too distracted to linger overmuch on imagined midnight trys—" She inhaled sharply and reddened.

Lieutenant Quimby said quickly, "No matter. What's important is that you and I are understood."

Josephine nodded, unused to consideration in any young man. Indeed, his easy manner made her reluctant to end their conversation, yet with cups empty and accounts settled, that moment approached. "Will you be leaving us now that the creature has been destroyed?"

He shook his head. "Not yet. We believe there are several more; perhaps as many as half a dozen." Then he frowned, as if wishing he hadn't volunteered so much.

"So many! But what on earth *are* they?"

"I can't tell you, Lady Weston, and it would be best if you didn't concern yourself. Just trust that my men will soon secure your district."

"And how do you expect to accomplish that without my expertise?" she said impishly.

He threw her a crooked smile, then admonished, "You *must* stay close to home, as your family desires, but if you mean to arm yourself with fancy old pistols, then someone ought to instruct you. As it turns out, the creature wasn't entirely dead and you might've been mauled."

If this news was disconcerting, his veiled offer was doubly so. Josephine dropped her gaze. "I doubt that would be possible . . . much as I should like it." She heard his soft intake of surprise as she lurched to her feet and collected the bundle. "Thank you, Lieutenant."

Quimby escorted her to the edge of the pavilion. She did not meet his eyes as they bowed to each other. "Be careful with those things," he said in a low voice. "Promise you won't touch them unless you're properly trained."

"I promise."

Back in the carriage, Maria huffed with impatience. "How shocking! Where'd 'ee get that infernal cape, and what's this he's given 'ee?"

"We spoke but a few minutes and in full view of the village. Drinking tea is surely the most harmless act in the world! *Really*, Maria!"

Did her bluster sound cool enough to mask the irregular thread of her pulse? Holding her chin high, Josephine tucked the bundle by her side, and they proceeded to March Cottage. Later, when confronted with the necessity of turning the pistols over to place in the locked trunk, she let her hands linger on the bundle.

"He is an awfully nice man," she whispered to herself, and on impulse she hid it in the bottom drawer of her bureau.

CHAPTER EIGHT

London
11 June 1819

Prudence floated on air during the days that followed Lady Revelle's salon, but she kept her excitement stuffed deep down inside. It would be unwise, she decided, to build up her hopes about Mr. MacNeal. Wittiness and good looks were not the only qualities that made a fine match. If and when he chose to make an appearance at Stanistead House, Aunt Amelia could then root out the more practical details, such as pedigree and wealth.

Speaking of which, how long did men typically wait before paying a call? Prudence had no idea, nor dared she ask. Her dignity prevented her from exposing such idle thoughts to her aunt.

Meanwhile, Josephine continued to claim that she suffered from trances, which she attributed somehow to the countess's uniform and pistols. That she would blame her actions on inanimate objects baffled Prudence to no end. Was the girl only doing this to seek some attention? Hoping to deflect her, Prudence penned an abridged report about her debut. Josephine wrote back, calling her bluff:

How dare you gloss over the best aspect of the affair? Two
men in one evening! You hardly said a word about the viscount.
What does he look like? Has he come to call? And the attentive
Mr. MacNeal, though untitled, deserves more consideration.
What is his background? I see prospects, my dear!

Prudence frowned. She'd given the barest outline of her
encounter with MacNeal, merely to prove she had not spent
three hours standing against a wall. Never once did she
intimate there'd been any spark between them—she'd kept *that*
to herself. She hurried off to meet her tutor, thinking, *I'll set the*
record straight later.

But the following day brought another missive, one that
banished her thoughts of possible suitors. Josephine had killed
something—a troll? Good heavens! Or perhaps only something
large and rabid—who really could say? No point in arguing the
details. By all indications, actual violence had occurred. Prudence
felt faint. Her dearest friend had come close to being killed!

As she sat contemplating this nightmare, Prudence noticed
another envelope, with directions given in the hand of her
brother. Odd . . . Edward never wrote letters.

Josephine is up to no good, and I know you're aware of it,
for God knows the two of you share every second of your lives.
Do you realize her antics are putting her in GRAVE DANGER?
Be a peach, won't you, Sis, and tell me what she is up to?
  Yr. loving brother,
  Edwd. F.

"Is something wrong at home?" inquired Aunt Amelia,
bustling in.

"No, no!" Prudence assured her. "Just the usual familial unrest: Edward and Josephine continue to butt heads. May I have the morning free so I can post both letters by noon?"

Amelia nodded. "Of course, dear. How sensible! One must not put off a family crisis, for it will lead to distraction. A lady's finishing requires complete concentration."

Prudence excused herself and went at once to her room, where she paced for a long time. She had, to an extent, believed her cousin's wild claim that she'd slain something down by the woods. Edward's confirmation of real danger only added to the shock. He might want information, but she had no idea what had actually happened. Besides, she refused to sacrifice Josephine on the altar of his scorn.

"I shall redirect him," she decided.

Meanwhile, she must hope Josephine's brush with danger would be enough to temper her curiosity about the keepsakes. They weren't playthings, and her cousin had no business pretending otherwise. As for those purported creatures—surely they were bears or some other ordinary thing!—let the lieutenant do his job, and they would soon be gone from the region. With calculated slyness, she wrote:

> *My dear brother,*
>
> *I'm sorry you're having so much trouble managing Greenbank. Would it help if I came home for a few weeks? Aunt Amelia would dislike it, but I'm only too glad to help.*
>
> *Yr. loving sister,*
>
> *Prudence*

16 June 1819

If Prudence's words swayed her brother in the least, his actions gave no sign. In the aftermath of the incident that had nearly gotten Josephine killed, Edward continued to tighten his reign over Greenbank. Josephine had begun to champ at the bit:

> *The battle chief of Greenbank goes everywhere armed. He walks the grounds twice each day. He's hunting bears or wolves—he's not certain which. One often sees a mate or two swaggering along. Only yesterday, it seems, they were playing with pop guns.*
>
> *Late each evening, fortified with wine and weapons, the menfolk march off to war. It's a wonder no one has gotten shot! Papa appears concerned but bites his tongue. If only he would take his rightful place as head of the house!*

Prudence shook her head, tsking. At least Josephine had asked Maria to lock up the trunks; that should put a stop to the girl's escapades. As for the creatures Josephine referred to as trolls, Prudence offered the following information:

> *Here in London, the newspapers have begun to speak of "an inexplicable Rash of Violence toward the livestock of southern England." According to one naturalist, "it is most likely a startling Resurgence of the species* Ursus arctos, *the European brown bear, which had been considered Extinct in the British Isles for three hundred years."*

Prudence nodded smugly. Providing Josephine with an explanation fulfilled her a great deal; knowing the buccaneer games had ended satisfied her sense of unease. She signed the letter and let her gaze drift in the direction of her bed. Thoughts of Josephine's pistols reminded her of her own keepsakes, as yet unexplored. These days she could think of nothing except the very charming Mr. MacNeal. He could be forgiven for not coming directly after the soiree—likely he'd had prior commitments—but sooner or later they would come face-to-face, and *that* was the only kind of exploration which now occupied her mind.

Happily, today was Wednesday, that day of the week when she and Aunt Amelia received callers. Before Lady Revelle's soiree, Prudence had only marginally preferred Wednesdays over the others. Since then, she quite looked forward to them, for one never knew when Mr. MacNeal might turn up.

Their afternoon was, unfortunately, dominated by bored debutantes. Just before teatime, the bell rang once more. When Reese brought the visitor's card to Aunt Amelia, there was no mistaking the flash of glee in the old lady's eyes.

Prudence's heart pounded. Unconsciously, she sought her pocket and the gold band within. There was no time to rub color into her cheeks.

Reese opened the door. "Lord Underwood, ma'am."

The ladies rose and curtseyed. Underwood showed a fine leg, then stood in the doorway like a statue at the Roman Forum. Aunt Amelia said, "Do come in, Your Lordship, and be seated. We're delighted you chose to spend your time with us today."

Without a word, Underwood established himself in a chair and fixed his gaze far to the left of his hostesses. Astonished, Prudence stared, taking in his features. He had longish hair the color of wheat, and a tan complexion that suggested a love of the outdoors. His aquiline nose and cleft chin lent an aristocratic air to an otherwise ordinary face. She reckoned he must be about thirty.

Underwood sniffed, recrossing his legs. Prudence would not speak first. She shot a look at Aunt Amelia, who seemed flummoxed.

"Well, sir!" exclaimed the old lady. "How did you enjoy the music at Chedleigh?"

Over the next quarter of an hour, Amelia labored to extract little more than monosyllables from Underwood. Prudence put in a word or two, but she soon lost interest in trying to draw him out. Clearly, he was here only to fulfill an obligation to Lady Revelle. He'd be gone soon enough, never to return.

Aunt Amelia thought otherwise. No sooner had he departed when she set to howling about Prudence's good fortune. "Oh, such an honor! Do you realize how exceedingly wealthy he is? You have charmed him for sure!"

"How could you tell?" Prudence asked. "He barely said five words."

"Oh, hush! Such sauciness is not to be tolerated!"

"He came as a favor to Lady Revelle; I witnessed her issuing the command. He doesn't like me one whit—in fact, I doubt he likes anyone better than himself."

Aunt Amelia scowled. "Mark my words. We shall see him again."

Prudence hoped the aunt was wrong. She would much prefer to see Mr. MacNeal. Eleven days had gone by . . . not that she was counting. Why had *he* not come?

Writing to Josephine had become a great challenge, one which Prudence faced again that same evening. She described Underwood's call with ambivalence, though she did not dismiss him. Of Mr. MacNeal's continued absence she hesitated to write, for fear that her partiality would be too evident.

You're a fool, you know. It's been nearly a fortnight.

"Oh, goodness, he's busy," Prudence said aloud.

Marrying a man like Lord Underwood would make you an important lady.

Prudence balled her fists. "I'd find contentment with Mr. MacNeal were he poor as a churchmouse!" Then she blushed at her audacity.

He's not coming, can't you see that? You're the one who is poor.

"I know," she sighed, reaching automatically for the ring.

If you can convince Josephine that he matters nothing to you, then perhaps you *may begin to accept it as fact.*

So Prudence forced herself to pen several indifferent remarks. It felt false repudiating MacNeal without reason . . . any reason, that is, beyond his absence.

It'll get easier, the voice in her head added.

17 June 1819

Thursday dawned brilliant blue, the finest day yet that summer. Such weather was almost indecent for a day destined for calls. Aunt Amelia, however, made a surprising proposal.

"What do you say to a stroll in Hyde Park? My joints are feeling well, and I desire some fresh air."

They took the carriage, disembarked with parasols, and walked along the perimeter of the Serpentine. A dozen or so children, watched carefully by nannies, dipped their toes or pushed toy boats in the glittering water. Prudence looked on wistfully, envying their freedom.

Looking up, she spied Mr. MacNeal with two other gentlemen strolling toward them. She fought to control a jagged intake of breath. Desperate though she was for his acknowledgement, she wondered in what manner she ought to respond. She'd presumed his absence could be explained by a journey out of town, but his presence in the park seemed to indicate otherwise. Perhaps a touch of nonchalance was what he deserved.

Threading her arm through the aunt's for support, she fished for a casual topic of conversation. "Such a pretty place for children to play," she said brightly. "Where did you grow up, ma'am?"

Aunt Amelia launched into a detailed reply, but Prudence barely heard a word. She had attention only for the approaching trio of men. They gesticulated wildly, so engrossed in their banter they failed to realize they'd entered the earshot of women. Mr. MacNeal uttered something, and all three roared with laughter. Walking sticks flew against shins. Curses ensued.

Aunt Amelia puffed up like a fighting cock. "Attention, louts!" she exclaimed. "There are ladies present!"

Prudence covered her mouth. A strained silence fell over both parties.

"How now?" demanded the old lady. "Are you half-wits? Speak up, someone! Apologize to my niece, who has been traumatized by your brutishness."

Prudence, hoping they would not believe this allegation, allowed a smile to creep into one corner of her mouth. Mr. MacNeal uttered a gasp of recognition. "Is it not . . . why, surely you are Miss Fairfeather, whom I recently had the pleasure of meeting?"

Blushing, Prudence nodded. Aunt Amelia jabbed her

sharply. "Yes, sir," Prudence yelped, remembering to curtsey. "Allow me to present my aunt, Miss Staveley." That was all she could manage, for her determination to stay aloof had vanished along with his name.

Fortunately, he seemed to perceive her dilemma. "Delighted, madam," he said with a bow. "I am William MacNeal, and these are my associates, Thomas Perkins and Stephen Tate. Miss Fairfeather, I must apologize for the company I keep. I believed my superior charms would improve them, but, as you can see they are quite beyond help."

Prudence replied gaily, "It is vanity, sir, which induces you to set too high a price on the quality of your influence." This produced another jab from the aunt.

The men laughed uproariously. Prudence sensed they understood the reference rather too well. Her courage died, and with it her smile.

"Of all the childish nonsense!" scolded Aunt Amelia. "I am of course appalled by my niece's impertinence, but see how you've embarrassed her! Take yourselves off at once, you scoundrels! Shoo!"

Mr. MacNeal said hastily, "Forgive us, madam! Your niece and I were sharing a bit of a joke from our previous conversation. It was not impertinence, and I'm sorry these addlepates made a jest of her remark." He looked directly at Prudence. "I wouldn't dream of insulting you, Miss Fairfeather."

Aunt Amelia glowered. "Is what he says true?"

"More or less," replied Prudence, holding Mr. MacNeal's gaze.

"In that case," said the aunt, "we should welcome you at Stanistead House, but do not presume to bring along your wicked compatriots."

Perkins and Tate looked ready to burst. Mr. MacNeal stayed them with a gesture. "I thank you, madam, and I shall not forget the terms of your kind offer. Good day to you both." The gentlemen passed on by. Prudence's eyes followed Mr. MacNeal until she could no longer see him without turning her head completely. At the last moment, he glanced back with a grin. She gulped and cast her eyes forward, heart thumping. A tiny inner voice intoned, *Charming as before, sir, but where have you been this past fortnight?*

CHAPTER NINE

Edingham-Greene, Wiltshire
19 June 1819

Josephine leant her chin on one hand, fanning herself idly with Prudence's last missive. The air in the drawing room was stuffy and hot. Maria snored in her chair. The mantel clock ticked out its persistent taunt: *no walks, no rides* . . . Oh, this dreadful confinement! Josephine was so bored she wanted to scream.

Hoofbeats clopped up the drive. She heard the greeting of the grooms, then Lieutenant Quimby's reply. She wriggled upright. Maybe he would stop in and visit awhile; certainly, he was the most interesting person around. She folded her hands and turned an expectant smile toward the doorway.

Carson materialized from nowhere. Josephine sat up straighter, ready to beckon the visitor. The door opened, and the lieutenant had just stepped into the foyer when footsteps sounded on the landing, followed by a curt, "Oh, it's you, Quimby."

"Good day, Mr. Fairfeather."

"New excuses today?"

The lieutenant coughed. "Sir, we're doing what we can. As I was about to tell His Lordship, we've got a particularly good lead."

"By all means, hurry along. Wouldn't want to miss the free coffee." Edward walked out the door sans parting courtesy.

Lieutenant Quimby bowed his head. Josephine, assuming he would not like to know she had witnessed this exchange, sat back out of view. Quimby straightened his spine and spun, heading for the study.

"Oh, Edward," she whispered. She thought of his sister's words, clutched there in her hand.

Without his Studies, of course, Edward has nothing better to do than play Lord of the Manor. He has always been attached to Greenbank, though he has no Chance of inheriting it.

Josephine nodded dismally. How tragic indeed that he should not stand to succeed to an estate that had been held by his maternal relations for hundreds of years! For Greenbank had come to Middlemere through his union with its sole heiress, Lady Joanna Greene, and someday, barring the discovery of some Weston male heir, it would pass to his only daughter's children.

Yet if it weren't for Edward's stewardship, the estate would surely fall to pieces. He *had* to know, thought Josephine, that he was doing it in vain. Was this then the source of his increasing disaffection? Perhaps, but what had a man like Quimby, who had nothing to do with the fate of Greenbank, done to earn Edward's especial scorn?

If she could appreciate the source of his grievance, maybe she could learn how to diffuse his wrath. She got up and walked about, lost in thought. Of course! It boiled down to jealousy: Edward was jealous of Josephine's right to Greenbank, and he resented not being included in Quimby's briefings regarding the same. What then could she—

"You're locked up like a bird in a gilded cage."

Startled, Josephine turned. "Lieutenant Quimby, is that you?" He stood a step beyond the doorway, obscured by long shadows.

"I feel responsible," he went on. "Every day I fail to complete my assignment, you sit in this house, bored and bereft of society."

"And for every such day, you endure the undeserved contempt of my cousin."

Lieutenant Quimby moved into the parlor. "I understand Mr. Fairfeather much better than you might think. We're both trying to make the best of the hand life has dealt us."

"So you dislike your career?" she wondered, confused.

"On the contrary, my career suits me fine. One has choices in that regard, but none when it comes to one's place in a family."

Uncanny! thought Josephine. She stared hard at the lieutenant. It was the sort of statement that hung there, demanding further inquiry, yet she dared not inquire because it was none of her business.

"I-I beg your pardon," he stammered. "It was impertinent of me to suggest I had any understanding of your family's affairs."

"But you—"

"No, no! I don't know what came over me." He glanced down the hall. "Well, I must be going. Good day, Lady Weston." He made a quick bow and strode out of sight.

"What on earth did *he* want?" grumbled Maria, rousing from her slumber. "Don't Quimby have anything better a-do than disrupt our peace and quiet?"

Josephine, still staring at the place where he'd just stood, gave a hollow laugh. "He's here to *restore* the peace, silly! He was leaving Papa's study and stopped to greet me, as any gentleman would."

"Gentleman! We know nothing about him. Look what thy trickery has wrought, young lady! 'Ee gave him tacit pre-mission a-be overly familiar. He's a nobody from nowhere who thinks he can flirt with the earl's daughter."

"Good Lord! If that was flirting, then he's the most unromantic nobody I ever met!" Josephine seized Prudence's letter and stalked out. From the window of the upstairs parlor, she watched Quimby disappear on horseback. She blamed her breathlessness on stairs and the spat with Maria.

"Flirting!" she scoffed. "'Don't fire those pistols!' 'I understand your cousin!' Maria is right. No gentleman would behave so presumptuously. Good riddance to you!" she cried through the open window, and with a great exhalation she crossed her arms and sat down.

"But he wasn't at all rude," she murmured. "Rather kind, actually. Does that constitute flirting?" She threw up her arms in a gesture of defeat. "Oh, what would I know? I'm accustomed to nothing but teasing and abuse from that sex!"

Her thoughts returned to Prudence's letter, which had puzzled her for its notable lack of alarm concerning the troll. There were the usual platitudes—the 'oh dears!' and 'good heavenses!' and 'are you sure you are wells?'—but Prudence didn't seem shocked by the central matter at hand: that Josephine had killed an erstwhile fairy-tale creature. Indeed, she'd said little about the shooting itself and had pointedly enclosed a newspaper clipping about European brown bears.

She still *doesn't believe me,* Josephine thought. She trudged to her room and began a letter:

Dearest cousin, the creature I encountered had great yellow eyes and a huge nose that sprang from a heavily ridged brow. Its mouth was broad and entirely separate from the snout. I swear to you, no bear ever looked like this.

She looked over Prudence's missive and carefully replied to each of her points. The last page contained at least one positive tidbit: Lord Underwood had paid a call at Stanistead House. Of that other gentleman, the one whom Prudence pretended not to favor, there was but one small reference:

Fine looks, fine Speech, and likely an empty pocketbook. I mustn't allow myself to be charmed by that kind of Man.

20 June 1819

Josephine arose the next morning feeling unusually inspired. She would not let her forced internment spoil the rest of her summer. Edward might play His Lordship out of doors all he liked, but *she* would rule the house.

Maria bustled in and paused, frowning. "Wot's this gleam in thy eye?"

"I am making plans to topple the Fairfeather Empire."

Maria looked alarmed. "My lady, I wish 'ee would not quarrel with Mr. Edward—"

"—as soon as he stops picking quarrels with me. Edward's imperiousness may please him at University, but it shall no longer be acceptable in my home."

Maria gaped. "*Thy* home?"

"Aye, *mine*. Am I not by rights the mistress of Greenbank?

I shall now assert that right, with all the responsibility and respect it entails."

"I see," said Maria dubiously. "Well, 'ee'll be right busy, that's sure enow."

Josephine was making out a task list when the maid brought in a letter. "Two days in a row! Good tidings, I hope." Alas, Prudence's missive began with a lecture:

> *Lieutenant Quimby obviously likes you. Why else would such a busy man offer to teach a female how to fire Pistols? Tread carefully, Josephine. You must avoid any further encounters that smack of Impropriety!*

"Well, then!" exclaimed Josephine, blushing a little. Quimby liked her? It couldn't be true—nay, she would not allow it. Shaking her head, she muttered, "You've misread him, Prudence. He's a busybody, cut from the same cloth as your horrid brother." She put down the half-read letter and took out a fresh page. Soon her pen flew in heated refutation:

> *For shame! I am the earl's daughter; Quimby feels obliged to show his respect. Anyway, he couldn't possibly aspire to snare my affection. Consider our difference in stations. Edward and Maria would drive him off in a heartbeat.*

Nodding in satisfaction at this reply, Josephine added privately, "Yes, he'd be a fool to pursue me, and Quimby's no fool. Prudence has invented this nonsense to tease me." She resumed reading and discovered the real reason her cousin had written so soon: there had been another sighting of Mr. MacNeal.

"Oh, I *knew* he fancied her!" Josephine said with a grin.

Who cared that he had not called right away? Who cared that he consorted with ill-mannered friends? Their encounters were so *deliciously* romantic!

Then Josephine sagged. "Unless he fancies her fine but discovered she hasn't a penny to her name. Oh, fiddlesticks! Is that why our hero has yet to call?"

If Mr. MacNeal needed an heiress more than he wanted love, it wasn't the worst crime in the world—plenty had gone there before him. Prudence herself would do so if need be. It didn't make him an awful man, no more than did his apparent decision to let Prudence go. For she suspected *that* was why MacNeal had never called. Too bad for Prudence—indeed for them both—that their attraction had increased during this second meeting. If she could have seen past his charm, she might have guessed he never meant to come.

The result of this reflection was that MacNeal actually grew in Josephine's estimation. He had sacrificed his happiness to protect Prudence's future. Such was the epitome of tragic romance. But what about Prudence? She would have to reach that conclusion alone.

"For if I told her," said Josephine, "then she would only love him more, and their heartbreak would be greater." Thus she answered with cautious enthusiasm, tempered with inquiries about Lord Underwood, after which she sallied forth to take command of Greenbank.

Tucking a copy of Maria Jacson's *The Florist's Manual* under one arm, she found Gardener Perry and informed him they would replant the beds adjacent the rear terrace. Perry, a nut-brown man with wiry arms, pushed back his hat. "Huh!" he rejoined, scratching absently at his shoulder.

"These days, all the best gardens are being converted to a wilder look. You'll adore it, I promise."

Perry thrust his spade into the earth. "'Ark a'ee, m'lady. I h'a'en no time for thic—I got branches a-clean up." The gardener stomped away, leaving Josephine agape.

"Of all the cheek!"

"He's had free rein for two decades," observed Maria from her seat on the terrace.

Josephine's nostrils flared. "Well, then! I shall do it myself and earn his respect." She kicked off her shoes and waded into the planting bed.

"'Ee must be joking!" exclaimed Maria, sitting bolt upright.

"No, indeed!" Josephine seized Perry's spade and thrust it at the roots of an offending perennial.

"But 'ee will dirty thyself!" Josephine flapped a dismissive hand. The nurse lumbered off to fetch her charge some old shoes and an apron.

Three days later, the terrace beds had been transformed into a dizzying mass of wildflowers. Josephine was putting the final touches on her new garden when a horse approached, bearing a familiar crimson-coated figure.

"Good day!" called Lieutenant Quimby. "Such enterprise on so warm a morning."

Josephine blotted her forehead. She had long since discarded the straw hat, exposing her sprung coiffure. Maria's apron had failed to protect her day dress, which sported damp rings under the arms. She looked a perfect mess, but what difference did it make? The last time she had seen the lieutenant she had shouted 'good riddance.'

Quimby drew his horse to a halt.

"Good day, sir," she replied. "The gardener does not

subscribe to my horticultural theories, so I have been obliged to take matters into my own hands."

"Aha." He pointed his riding crop at one of the perennials. "I remember that from my childhood. Wallflower, isn't it?"

"Yes, that's right. *Cheiranthus cheiri.* It has a pleasing fragrance."

"Hmm, pleasing indeed." Lieutenant Quimby stared down at the flower as if it were the most inspiring thing he'd ever seen. Josephine waited for him to continue, but it soon became apparent he had lost his train of thought.

"Don't let me keep you, sir. You obviously have important things on your mind."

Lieutenant Quimby looked up. There was no playfulness in his eyes, no smile, no hint of flirtation. "Is it that noticeable?"

"You *are* very grave these days. I'm sure it goes hard for you, not to have secured the district in a more timely fashion."

Quimby cleared his throat. "I would prefer it, my lady, if you remembered this is only a military exercise."

"Come now, sir," Josephine said with a laugh. "We are not speaking in public. I saw what I killed, and if that thing was a bear, then I'll eat my hat!"

His fingers tensed on the reins. "For the purpose of this conversation, it was absolutely a bear. Your neighborhood, Lady Weston, has a prodigious number of bears. Now, my shako could make for a bit of tough chewing, but since you lack a bonnet . . ."

"*Prodigious?* How many?" she asked, diverted from his jest.

Quimby reddened. "I say, you're awfully persistent."

"I prefer to think of it as curious," she rejoined. "Do your superiors know how poorly you keep secrets? You have a way of blurting out just enough information to pique a person's interest,

when I suspect your mission is to do exactly the opposite."
Lieutenant Quimby jerked on the reins, causing his mount
to rear. When he had stilled the horse's nerves, he wheeled
it back round. "I never had any trouble doing my job until I
encountered a certain inquisitive young noblewoman!"

His voice had a strange edge to it, and his eyes flashed,
bright and blue. Josephine immediately regretted her words.
"I beg your pardon. What I said was unconscionably rude, and
you did not deserve it."

Quimby's horse snorted. "Hush, Ivan," he murmured,
patting its ivory neck. When he spoke again, the tension was
gone from his voice. "I'm not offended. In fact, I am indebted
to you for having identified a shortcoming of which I was
unaware."

Josephine peered up at him through her lashes. Surely he
must dislike her now, though he was too much of a gentleman to
show it. Yes, whatever Maria might think, he was a gentleman
at heart.

"Well, then," said Quimby. "I must attend your father. Good
day, Lady Weston." With that, he kicked his steed and cantered
off toward the stables.

"Oh, drat!" whispered Josephine. "Drat! Drat! *Drat!*" She
stumbled around the terrace wall and sank to the ground.
There, she leant back against the stone ledge and fought back
hot tears. "Why must I always inject myself into other people's
business?"

The crunch of footsteps approached. Peeking around the
ledge, she saw Perry stop and scowl at the new beds. She
pressed herself back out of sight.

"Gurt stubbrun gell," Perry spat and stalked off.

That was the final blow. Josephine put her face in her hands and wept for a while, then strode inside and called for a bath.

Later, she lay on her bed in a dressing gown, arms flung wide, staring at the ceiling. The windows stood open, admitting a stale summer breeze.

I don't know that I shall ever learn how to be a real lady.

Truly, though, she couldn't recall the last time she had publicly resorted to hyperbole, let alone thrown a tantrum. That *had* to mark an improvement.

The window sash rattled, and a distant rumble warned of a storm on the approach. A burst of air caressed her face. It would be raining in London by nightfall. She pictured her cousin, waiting by a streaming window for a man who would never come. In today's letter Prudence had written:

> *Once again we received Underwood, whose ironic name most fittingly describes his stilted manner. I swear he possesses not one ounce of wit! There has been no sign of Mr. MacNeal, who still elects to snub me.*

"Poor besotted darling." Guilt gnawed at Josephine's conscience. She should have addressed the matter three days ago and perhaps nipped it in the bud. The longer it took Prudence to comprehend the obvious, the more likely she would obstruct her chances with Underwood, or anyone else, for that matter.

A sudden flash of lightning streaked across the sky, leaving a sharp tang in the air. That's what Prudence needed—a jolt of reality. "I don't know that I have the strength to give it," Josephine said with a sigh.

The wind rose. Raindrops blew through the open window. The storm burst over Greenbank with exceptional ferocity. Josephine rose to slam shut the window. Padding into her parlor, she sat down and wrote,

> *Forget that persistent bore of a viscount! Disregard the other neglectful brute! I submit that neither merits further consideration. A Season should be a whirlwind of flirtations. By now you ought to have had men dueling for your favor!*

She stared down at this cheerful, sidestepping confection. Yes, she had taken the cowardly way out, but it seemed far kinder to propose a cleansing of the slate than to tell her cousin that the man she admired needed money more than her. She signed her name with a flourish and watched the rain beat down on her garden.

CHAPTER TEN

London
20 June 1819

Prudence stared unseeing out the carriage window. Somewhere above the grey edifices of London, past the dust and grit and noise, the sky sparkled clear blue. Days like this intensified her yearning for home. Home, where friends, family, and the sublime beauty of the English countryside formed the cornerstone of her earthly happiness.

God, I hate this city!

The London Season had become a blur of sitting rooms and carriage rides. Day after day, she and Amelia paid their calls, leaving cards in the entry halls of fashionable townhouses. Occasionally they were asked in, but no real acquaintance could be formed in a mere quarter of an hour. Besides Lady Revelle's soiree more than a fortnight ago, Prudence had been invited to no other event. If she failed to attract the interest of Society hostesses and did not gain that all-important voucher for entrance to Almack's assembly rooms, her marital prospects were limited to those gentlemen who frequented less exclusive entertainments— in short, the same gentlemen who of necessity sought heiresses.

Prudence, however, couldn't stop thinking about William MacNeal. Since their Hyde Park encounter three days ago, she no longer doubted he reciprocated her interest; it was only a matter of time before he called to prove it.

"—aren't you?" came an inquiry, penetrating her fog.

"Hmmm?"

"Come, dear. We've received permission to enter. This is the home of Mrs. Wymstone, an intimate of Lady Sefton."

This needed no further explanation. Prudence knew by heart the names of the seven lady patronesses of Almack's, of whom Lady Sefton was one. Without a patroness's sponsorship, the upper echelons of London's *beau monde* would remain forever out of reach. As she descended the carriage, her hand went absently to her hip. Through the layers of morning dress, she stroked her mother's ring for good luck.

The drawing room contained five ladies of varying ages. Mrs. Wymstone, a plump matron, came forward to greet them. She and Aunt Amelia seemed to be on friendly terms. If Mrs. Wymstone indeed had the ear of the famed Lady Sefton, this interview could easily change Prudence's fortunes.

Miss Wymstone, her daughter, was a stunningly unattractive creature, pale and red-haired with sad eyes and an overbite. Prudence felt an instant sense of affinity for this afflicted young lady—she imagined the lifetime of humiliation Miss Wymstone had already endured. It was bad enough to lack money and name, but in London, to lack beauty was perhaps the greatest social crime of all. Miss Wymstone might frequent Almack's, but she would find it nearly impossible to marry for love. Prudence smiled at the girl, looking her directly in the eyes, which, she intuited, others rarely did. Miss Wymstone's surprised intake of breath confirmed her suspicion.

The other party consisted of a pinched-looking chaperone and her two charges, Lady DeLacey and Miss Kimball, who greeted the newcomers with identical sneers.

"Miss Kimball and I really must be going," Lady DeLacey announced.

Mrs. Wymstone would hear none of it. "Please stay," she insisted. "I should be indebted to you both, for I promised Miss Staveley I'd help her niece make acquaintances. She's from the country and doesn't know a soul."

"Such a dreadful shame," said Lady DeLacey in a flat voice.

"Yes, it *is*," agreed Mrs. Wymstone, "but that can easily be rectified. I am certain you, my lady, are the perfect candidate to assist Miss Fairfeather, for you and Miss Kimball are real veterans of the Marriage Mart."

However sweetly spoken, the words were both insult and threat.

Through thin, angry lips, Lady DeLacey asked, "Pray, what service can I offer?"

"Kindness. Suggest Miss Fairfeather's name for every event. Sing her praises whenever she is spoken of. Include her in your inner circle."

Lady DeLacey's left eyelid twitched. "As you wish."

"Oh, thank you, Lady DeLacey!" gushed Aunt Amelia. "Mrs. Wymstone, we are indebted to you!"

Their hostess's gaze never left Lady DeLacey's face as she replied, "Pshaw, Miss Staveley! *You* owe me no obligation." An ugly silence followed.

Miss Wymstone stammered, "S-s-so, Miss Fairfeather, what is it you miss most about the countryside?"

"Riding. My cousin and I like to go out early, when dawn is touching the sky and scrolls of fog still linger in the vales."

Lady DeLacey rolled her eyes. Miss Wymstone sighed. "It sounds lovely! Perhaps here in London you'll snare a ride in a gentleman's phaeton."

"Speaking of which," interjected Miss Kimball, addressing her companion, "when will Mr. DeLacey take me out behind his beautiful matched bays?"

"Pish! Frederick hasn't the time of day for you!" sniffed Lady DeLacey.

Miss Kimball paused. "There's only one other pair in London that could rival your brother's, though I suppose I shouldn't dream of securing *his* favor."

Lady DeLacey turned on her. "How *dare* you say such a thing?"

"I-I was only making conversation!" exclaimed Miss Kimball. "Surely everyone knows your brother bought those horses because he so admired Mr. —"

Lady DeLacey let out a shriek and fell back against the sofa in a full-blown fit of vapors. The chaperone, who'd been dozing, jerked awake with a yelp.

"Dear Lord!" groaned Mrs. Wymstone. "Quick, Alice, fetch my salts!"

Prudence looked on in wide-eyed amazement as Miss Kimball seized Lady DeLacey's fan and beat the air by her face. "Look, she revives! Someone bring water!"

Miss Wymstone's glass of water and smelling salts were brusquely refused. Under Miss Kimball's ministrations, however, Lady DeLacey soon ceased her gasping. "Enough, Grace!" she snarled. "You'll give me windburn!"

Miss Kimball stopped, stared curiously at the offending instrument, and chirped, "Well, what do you know, Emmeline? I thought you had burnt everything he ever gave you."

"*Be quiet!*" raged Lady DeLacey, knocking the fan to the floor.

"Sorry!" howled Miss Kimball.

Mrs. Wymstone brought the visit to an immediate close. Loudly and contentiously, Lady DeLacey's party departed. Aunt Amelia followed Mrs. Wymstone into the hall. Miss Wymstone stopped Prudence with a touch on the arm.

She bent to retrieve something from under the sofa. It was the discarded fan that had caused Lady DeLacey such grief. "Here," she said, pressing it into Prudence's hands. "Keep it as a reminder of the kind of person you must never become." They smiled at one another.

In the carriage, Aunt Amelia was aquiver. "Well done, my dear! Mrs. Wymstone says she will speak favorably of you. Mark my words, you'll be dancing at Almack's within the fortnight."

"Do you think Lady DeLacey will?" Prudence asked cheekily.

"Good heavens, don't remind me of that wretched experience. I'm positively depleted! Let us find some refreshment, shall we?"

They stopped at a confectioner's shop and secured a small table. The waiter brought them a pot of chocolate and cakes. Prudence, who'd never before dined at any sort of restaurant, gazed in delight at the fashionable folk all around. For a moment, she forgot her distaste for the city.

"Much better!" sighed Aunt Amelia. "Was that not the most vulgar scene?"

"Astonishing, indeed. I hardly expected her to be overcome at such harmless conversation."

"Lady DeLacey gave you the cut, of course!" Aunt Amelia's stentorian voice rose above the din. "But Mrs. Wymstone put that chit right back in her place. She doesn't abide snobbery; she was a country girl, herself, once. She will be a powerful ally."

Hereupon, someone exclaimed, "Dear me, it's Miss Staveley!"

Aunt Amelia looked up and crowed with delight. A matron and her husband seated themselves nearby and, after a quick round of introductions, they fell to talking about old times. Prudence remained lost in her own thoughts.

"Did she swoon?" whispered a voice at her elbow.

"I beg your pardon?" asked Prudence, startled.

"Lady Emmeline DeLacey. She was once engaged to be married, but the offer was undone. I hear she swoons whenever anyone invokes his memory."

Prudence, who couldn't turn from a conversation she should at least purport to attend, swiveled her head slightly to view the person who'd addressed her. A girl, accompanied by an elderly gentleman, sat at the table immediately behind her. She was tall and thin, clad handsomely in pinstriped muslin and a cocoa-brown pelisse. A tall-crowned bonnet obscured her face, exposing but a slice of pointed nose and sharp cheekbone.

"I prefer not to confirm rumors overheard in a shop."

Prudence's neighbor inhaled. "Indeed. Forgive me. You must think very ill of me, but your companion's voice . . ."

"Of course," Prudence interjected. "But I cannot give credence to your uninvited deduction. Please excuse me."

"Are you still ensconced at that draughty villa of yours . . . Stanistead House, isn't it?" the acquaintance was inquiring.

"Oh, yes," replied Aunt Amelia. "I'm quite fond of the place, draughts and all."

"The parlor is warm," observed Prudence.

"Not warm enough," remarked the aunt, giving her acquaintance a significant look. "Not warm enough."

24 June 1819

Mr. MacNeal did not come to lend his warmth to Stanistead's parlor: not that day, nor the next, nor even the next. The certainty with which Prudence had believed he favored her faded again.

The increasing frequency of Lord Underwood's calls added to her distress. His visits, though they pleased Aunt Amelia, remained unremarkable. He would go through the motions of politesse, then fix his eye on some point high up on the wall. Minutes would pass in total silence, filled only by the ticking of the clock and the old woman's desperate small talk. Afterward, Aunt Amelia would prattle on about Underwood's noble silence, his obvious devotion to Prudence, and the exquisite perfection of his pedigree and fortune. Such talk perplexed Prudence. It seemed perfectly apparent that he performed these calls as if duty bound. If this was love, where were the endearments, the heated glances, the stolen touches? Where was the electricity she had felt in the presence of Mr. MacNeal?

As the aunt chattered away, Prudence succumbed to the force of sweetly inflated memories. MacNeal's last backward glance at Hyde Park now included his lips forming the words, "I love you." She smiled absently, her thoughts drifting down secret pathways.

One day, Lord Underwood had just departed when Aunt Amelia clutched Prudence's arm. "I think it's only a matter of time before he realizes his bachelor days are at an end!"

Prudence covered her eyes. "Ma'am, to be honest, I am not fond of Lord Underwood."

"I beg your pardon?"

"I don't especially like him. I'd prefer to consider other prospects, and perhaps find a husband for whom I might care a little."

Aunt Amelia held a hand up to one ear. "Bless me, but I fail to hear the stampeding footsteps of this romantic herd of prospects!"

But there is one other . . . don't you remember?

Prudence tried to say it, tried to speak his name aloud, but for some reason she couldn't. She should not have to debase herself by singling out any man, especially one who might then prove unworthy. She blinked back tears and remained silent.

Aunt Amelia glowered. "Men do not like to be trifled with, Prudence. Once they're ready for marriage, they see no reason to wait on a lady's whim. Someone like Lady Emmeline DeLacey, with beauty *and* titles, can easily replace you. You could lose everything in your naïve quest for love."

"There's always Almack's!"

Aunt Amelia shook her head. "We haven't got that voucher yet, have we? Such matters are delicate and cannot be rushed. Mrs. Wymstone will propose you to Lady Sefton at the first opportune moment, and then the Lady Patronesses will consider you at their next meeting. The process is entirely out of our hands."

"Then let Underwood come, but I shall not encourage him."

Aunt Amelia's mouth tightened. "I think you're making a grievous mistake."

"I need more time." Prudence pressed a hand to her hip and felt the outline of the gold band in her pocket.

She dared not write a word of her agony to Josephine, for fear her longing would expose her as a love-sodden fool. Instead, she teased Josephine about the handsome lieutenant. Her cousin's life held so much promise when hers seemingly held none.

And so this gloomy prospect continued to bear itself out. On the following Tuesday afternoon, Prudence sat alone in her room, staring at the empty hearth. Twelve days—*twelve days!*—had passed since she had last seen Mr. MacNeal. If he was, as he'd professed, so eager to see her, then why had he not come?

Lord Underwood dropped by frequently; he'd grown comfortable in their presence and now spoke of his interests, mostly sporting related. The voucher for Almack's still had not materialized. Aunt Amelia put less stock in it than Prudence, who dreamt at night about meeting MacNeal at the Assembly. Sometimes, he was pleased to see her; other times he didn't know her. Those mornings, she woke with dark circles under her eyes.

You must end this obsession.

Idly, she snapped open Lady Emmeline's fan. It was a gorgeous example of Italianate artisanship, with mother-of-pearl sticks, hand-painted flowers, and fat putti hovering about in gold-leafed medallions. She ran her hand along one edge.

A reminder of the person you must never become.

That kind of person was obsessed and embittered, possibly even unmarriageable. Prudence closed her eyes, wondering how anyone could be driven to such extremes. Poor Emmeline . . . she must have loved her beau so dearly . . .

A startling image rose up in her head. A man and a woman stood in a large, dimly lit space. There were crates stacked everywhere; among them lay urns and statues and huge, gilt-framed paintings. Shadows fell across the couple's faces. Then, as if Prudence had entered a theatre in the middle of a play, the scene began to unfold:

"Lord, how gorgeous!" the woman said, fishing the fan from a stack. "I must have it."

The man's body froze. "Not that one," he answered, eyeing the fan. "I have at least two dozen others from which you may choose."

Like a hawk on the wing, she dove toward the prey. "If it's that priceless, then I want it all the more." She unfurled the fan and fluttered it coquettishly, closing on him, batting it near his face.

He crossed his arms. "That fan is already spoken for."

"By whom?" she demanded, a pout curving her lips.

He glanced away. "I-I am unable to say . . ."

The fan snapped shut. "I don't care. I shall have it."

"My lady, I beg you to listen—" He stepped forward, tensed to wrest the fan from her grasp. She held it aside and arched her back, defying him to take it. He continued to close on her. "That fan is the one thing I ask you to forsake."

"No!"

He took another step. They stood face to face, his head bent over hers. She closed her eyes and tilted her chin, ready to receive a kiss.

Seeing her poised thus in artful submission, he curled his lip in disgust. His hand closed over her wrist. "Unhand it!" he cried.

She thrust the fan into her bodice. "Take it, then! I dare you!"

For a moment, he appeared to consider the challenge, but then he recoiled and looked away. "I'll have the groom drive you home."

She sniffed, "You'll send me off alone, will you?"

"I think it's for the best."

"People will talk. They'll know we quarreled. They will misconstrue the situation."

He bent over his invoices. "Let them," he said dispassionately.

"You can't be serious!" She took in a shuddering breath. "Do you mean to end it like this?"

His head shot upright. "End what?"

She realized, too late, that she had exposed her presumption. "Today's ride," she replied heavily.

"That, my dear, is certainly done." And he strode for the doorway to beckon the groom.

Prudence dragged herself awake and looked wildly about.

"Prudence!" called the aunt, far away in the house. A knock sounded at her door.

"Ma'am, Miss Staveley desires you downstairs. Lord Underwood is come."

"I'll be right there." Prudence went to the looking glass to powder her sweat-dampened nose. "There you are, Phinneas: no freckles for His Lordship." She sighed dejectedly. "Must I become Lady Underwood? Really, how terrible would that be?"

Downstairs, she found Underwood standing by the fireplace. He spun at her footstep. "Aha, th-there you are, Miss Fairfeather, and don't you look well today!"

Prudence bobbed a curtsey, barely registering his compliment. As she moved to take her usual seat, he beckoned her to him. She glanced at Aunt Amelia, who opened a book. Prudence moved slowly to the fireplace.

"I have something for you," Underwood said in a low voice. He produced a long, lacquered box and pressed it into her hands. Prudence gave a start. She grasped one end of the box and extracted a fan made of ivory paper, painted with delicate gold scrolls.

"It's . . . lovely," she forced out. "Thank you."

"I'm so glad you're pleased. I know nothing about such things."

"You've done well," she assured him. She ought to have added that she'd treasure the fan always, but it was all she could do not to burst into laughter at the viscount's ironic choice of gift. She couldn't see herself ever swooning at the sight of it or longing for the company of its dull-witted giver.

Underwood glanced at the clock. "Well, look at the time. I really must be going." With a bow, he fled. When the front door had closed behind him, Prudence fell into a chair, giggling.

"What on earth is so funny?" snapped Aunt Amelia, clearly displeased with the brevity of the proceedings.

"It's a fan!" chortled Prudence, waving it about.

"I see that."

Prudence fanned herself with vigor, cackling away. "As a friend once suggested, 'keep it as a reminder.' Heavens, I certainly shall not forget *this!*"

CHAPTER ELEVEN

Edingham-Greene, Wiltshire
26 June 1819

After breakfast, Josephine climbed to the roof of Greenbank's turret and stationed herself on the wide stone ledge. Behind her, at the front of the house, the lawn lay lush with morning dew. Before her stretched the rear gardens, which blended into barley and meadow and the woodlands beyond. The sun crept higher, touching the landscape with its warm, orange glow.

Despite the poor results she'd achieved with Perry the gardener, she had continued to forge ahead with her campaign to conquer the house. Her next sortie had involved an invasion of the kitchen, where, kindly and delicately, she'd won over the cook. It turned out Cook had for many years desired to improve the household receipts, so Josephine agreed to lend her support. The rewards were immediate. A long-hated terrine presented at lunch yesterday was deemed "rather edible" by Edward and "marvelous" by Mrs. March, who requested Cook's presence for personal praise.

"Oh, don't thank me, madam," Cook had said, twisting her apron. "'Twas milady who suggested I add pork an' herbs."

Smiling now at the memory of her triumph, Josephine

broke the seal on a new letter from her cousin. After scanning it in vain for the names Underwood or MacNeal, she began from the salutation. Prudence, for whatever reason, had no news of her own but had written to discuss the recent doings at Greenbank. She was especially interested in how things stood between Josephine and Edward. She wrote:

I'm glad to know you have both stood down from your conflict, it proves that my brother is not really such a tyrant. "

Josephine rolled her eyes. "It proves nothing! His despotism and rudeness persist, although for your sake I no longer dwell on it in writing. Your brother could use a good setting down, Prudence. If I cannot deliver it, then I pray it comes by some other means!"

The letter continued to disappoint. Prudence not only said nothing of her two suitors, she even managed to turn the tables on Josephine:

Edward and Maria aside—what do you think about the lieutenant? I'm certain he's taken with you, for he engages you in Conversations every chance he gets. Think on it, and see whether I am not Right.

"Vexatious creature!" cried Josephine.

Well, what about Quimby? He was kind, dutiful, and well mannered. Their last encounter notwithstanding, he displayed an evenness of temper far surpassing that of any other man in her sphere. He was handsome, too, though perhaps the uniform lent him that extra dash of quality. She knew little else about him, not even his given name. Of course she liked him—very well, in fact—but she had a duty as a gentlewoman not to let herself yield to such feelings, and as a common officer he was wholly beneath her consideration. Prudence could sound her out all she liked, but Josephine couldn't and *wouldn't* let herself fall in love with that man.

"And so I shall tell her." Josephine slid off the parapet. A flash of red and white glinted far off through the trees. Her heart immediately sped half a beat, doubtless from the exertion of having stood up too quickly.

That night, Josephine jerked awake to a loud crash, her eyes straining in the dark to see what had caused such a racket. It seemed to have come from outside. The bedroom windows stood ajar. Crickets chirped in the woods. Maria lay snoring on her cot, oblivious to the din.

Someone hallooed. A fierce shushing followed. Horses' hooves clicked against cobblestones. Buckles and spurs clinked. Josephine eased out of bed and pulled on her dressing gown. She squinted at the mantel clock as she moved toward the window. Half past three. Below, a pair of sleepy grooms collected the reins of four horses.

"I'll fetch Carson," said Edward with a hint of elation. "Meet you in the drawing room. Think you can make it there on your own feet, old boy?"

Someone grunted his assent. A quartet of shadows moved into the house.

Josephine darted across the room, skirted Maria's cot, and slipped out the door. She tiptoed downstairs, pausing in her alcove until Carson and Edward entered the drawing room.

Cautiously, she advanced and pressed an ear to the door.

"I hope you don't mind that we started without you," said Charlie Lowell, his voice strangely high-pitched.

"No, indeed," returned Edward. "And from the looks of that thigh—oh, I *say!*—you'll be requiring much more than a nip of the sauce."

"Keep still, sir," advised Carson.

There was a loud intake of breath, then—"Blast you, that hurt!"

"I'm only trying to help, Mr. Lowell. The pain, I daresay, comes with the territory. If you prefer, I'll leave the tray of plasters and Mr. Fairfeather can attempt to dress it."

In the darkness, Josephine grinned at Carson's cheek.

"Gawd, just do it, curse 'ee to hell!"

"Take it like a man, Lowell," admonished Peter. "It's not every day one has an actual brush with death!"

"Curst thing—didn't see it in the dark! Ow!"

Edward laughed. "Then you must be deaf and without sense of smell. It was devouring a whole deer when you stumbled upon it. Such crunchings!"

"Such a reek!" added Peter. "Our dear Heywood will never be the same."

"'Twasn't Heywood but *my* land," Arthur corrected. "We followed those spoor pretty far tonight. We cornered it in Grant Park."

"Ho! That's a bit too close for comfort, what?"

"Not as close as the one here last month," Edward said grimly.

Out in the hall, Josephine felt her heart squeeze, but Edward made no further reference to that earlier incident.

Carson spoke. "May I ask, sirs, how Mr. Lowell received this wound, and what happened to the, er, *animal* of which you speak?"

"I shot it 'tween the eyes!" boasted Peter.

"You scalped it, dimwit," Edward contradicted. "I shot it in the chest."

There was a flurry of scuffling and muffled laughter.

"Fiend seize it, you spilt my drink!" complained Charlie. "Bist 'ee done yet, old man?"

"Yes, nearly. Will you gentlemen be needing anything more?" Carson's tone was taut yet patient. Josephine could tell he'd seen and heard enough.

Edward said, "Not if there's another bottle of brandy in the cabinet . . . Yes, go on back to bed, Carson. You have our hearty thanks."

"I shall send for the doctor, Mr. Edward, if you are amenable."

"Yes, yes, though I think Lowell's more weakened by the sight of blood than the loss of it."

"Yes, sir. And I expect you'll want to inform Lieutenant Quimby, as well?"

"What for? It's *our* trophy, and we mean to fetch it come morning."

"Yes, sir."

Josephine dropped deeper into the shadows. The butler emerged from the drawing room, shaking his head and tutting under his breath. She waited a while longer, thinking she might learn still more, but the boys had grown silent. She pictured them nursing drinks and lolling about, growing drowsy in the half-darkness. On chilled feet, she stole upstairs and climbed back into bed.

The following morning, she arrived early in the breakfast room and settled back for the show.

"Where's Edward, I wonder?" inquired Middlemere presently.

"Sleeping, I expect." How had her father missed the mayhem in the night?

A thump sounded across the hall. Mild curses followed, then groans. A door creaked open, and four figures emerged. Josephine watched as each boy shook off his stupor before entering the dining room. She stifled a smirk.

Edward strode in first, swaggering and beaming. "Good morning. Don't you look pretty today, Cousin?" Josephine raised a dubious eyebrow.

Charlie limped in on Arthur's arm. They looked haggard and unshaven but hid it well in their triumph. Last came Peter, chest puffed out and face flushed.

"Good morning, my lord," he cried. "Isn't it a fine day, Lady Weston?"

"What's the occasion, lads?"

"Last night we killed some kind of strange animal!" exclaimed Peter, who then blanched when he realized he'd stolen Edward's thunder. Edward inhaled sharply but remained sanguine. Middlemere, Maria, and Josephine gasped in unison.

"Edward, please tell me you're joking," the earl said in a quiet voice. "I thought your hunting parties were only for appearance's sake. We have soldiers in the neighborhood who can handle such things."

Edward adopted a heroic pose. "Indeed, it's true. We shot the thing and left it lying at the edge of Grant Park. We wanted to drag its carcass behind the horses, but they refused to go near. We'll bring it round after breakfast to show you."

Middlemere looked horrified, as did Maria, who cried, "Mercy, no! Do not bring it here to frighten us! Turn it over to the authorities!"

"It's my trophy, and I intend to keep it," declared Edward, sitting down to a plate laden with sausages.

"Too late, I'm afraid." Josephine tilted her chin toward the window.

Peter and Edward leapt up, their chairs banging to the floor. Everyone's eyes fixed on the distance, where a black smudge of smoke rose above the woodlands.

"I'll kill that bastard!" shouted Edward.

"Mr. Edward!" admonished Maria.

He wheeled on the nurse. "I have every right to be angry. He's stolen what's mine. Who's with me, boys?"

Arthur and Peter joined him at the door. Charlie remained seated.

"You go ahead," he said, waving them off. "I've had enough for one day." His cohorts needed no further encouragement; they dashed from the room. No sooner had they gone when Charlie slumped sideways in his chair, pallid and sweating. "Dear me," he whispered. "I feel awfully faint."

Maria howled, "Help! What's thic? Dear Lord! What's happened to the boy?"

Middlemere put a hand to his mouth and stifled a small cry.

In an instant, Carson was kneeling by Charlie's side. "Come, Mr. Lowell. I have a carriage waiting outside. Dr. Swinton will meet you at home. I couldn't raise him any sooner, for he was out on call last night."

Josephine helped Carson get Charlie to his feet. Together, they guided him to the front stoop, where the footman loaded him inside the carriage.

"I'm coming with you," announced Josephine, moving to climb aboard.

"No, milady," Carson said firmly. "*I* shall accompany Mr. Lowell."

His voice was so forceful that Josephine was obliged to comply. As the carriage rattled down the drive, she made her way back inside. She sat down in the parlor, kneading her hands as a terrible foreboding knotted her stomach. Maria's sobs continued in the dining room.

"He'll be fine," Josephine whispered. "Charlie will be fine."

An hour later, a great tumult broke out in the front drive, wrenching the Westons from their devotionals. Stamping boots, clashing spurs, and shouting burst through the front door. Clearly, this was no report about Charlie.

"Unhand me, damn you!"

"You have no authority—"

"The earl will put a stop to this outrage!"

Josephine glanced at her father. His eyes had gone glassy, the classic first sign of impending nervous distress. "I'll manage this," she said and hurried from the drawing room. Out in the foyer, half a dozen soldiers struggled to contain Arthur, Peter, and Edward, all three in shackles. "What is going on?" she called above the din.

"My lady!" exclaimed Lieutenant Quimby, peeling himself from Edward's side. He crossed the hall to greet her. "Would you be so good as to summon your father? We've had a minor disagreement with Mr. Fairfeather and his colleagues."

"Papa is indisposed. We've had a shock, you see. One of the boys was hurt badly and has been taken home in a swoon. My father—" Josephine glanced in consternation at the ongoing mêlée. "Will you put them outside? I can hardly think, and the racket is upsetting my father. Then I'd like a word with you in private."

Lieutenant Quimby spun to issue the order, and the battle shifted out to the front porch. Josephine beckoned him into the dining room. Here, the morning sunlight afforded her a better view of the officer's disheveled appearance. He was sweating and soot-streaked, filth coated his neckcloth, and an epaulet had been torn clean from one shoulder.

"What happened?" she asked.

"Well, your father—" he began.

"—is still indisposed," she reminded him. "Perhaps you have noticed, sir, that he is a bit of a recluse?"

"I should not have brought them into the house, but I thought a dose of His Lordship's displeasure might quell their exuberance."

"I do not know what effect it might have on those miscreants, but it is unlikely to help Papa's constitution. Now, if you could at least summarize what's happened and let me pass along the necessary information, then maybe Lord Middlemere can help you sort out your grievances."

Lieutenant Quimby flapped his gloves against the palm of one hand. "Very well. I gather you understand the gist of what transpired overnight. Your butler apprised me of the situation, after which my men and I marched to Grant Park to dispose of the carcass."

"Why?"

"It is our *policy*," he replied tautly. "We had the remains nearly cleared away when in charged the aforementioned miscreants—er, gentlemen—who picked a fight with my men. Mr. Fairfeather attacked me with his fists, claiming we'd stolen what was rightfully his. I had the party clapped in irons, but I'll release them if they promise their patrolling days are over."

Josephine turned away, deeply embarrassed for her cousin. "Oh, Edward," she murmured. She looked back at Quimby. "You haven't the authority to keep Mr. Fairfeather from guarding our property."

"No, but two months ago I appealed to him as a gentleman, and he swore on his honor, that should he and his cohorts encounter a beast, they were to send for me at once. Not kill it, not claim it, nor speak about it to anyone."

Josephine covered her eyes.

The lieutenant went on. "He put his friends in terrible jeopardy, and worse, he broke his word. I understand Mr. Fairfeather's innate desire to protect home and hearth, but he has no idea what he's dealing with. He must leave this matter to the experts; otherwise I may be forced to place him under arrest."

"He means well!"

"He's a reckless fool!" Quimby countered savagely, then colored at his own outburst. "Forgive me, my lady. I'm tired and cross."

Her throat swelled with an unaccountable compassion for him. Sighing, she said, "Edward is an honorable young man. H-he's just . . . aimless."

"I know. Like I've said before, he's very much like me. The difference is, he wants what he can't have, and I have what I don't want."

This puzzled her, but Lieutenant Quimby did not seem inclined to elaborate. He stared out the front window, beyond which stood the soldiers and their trio of aggrieved prisoners. Edward had ceased arguing and stood to one side, his chest thrust out in silent indignation. Lieutenant Quimby stroked his chin, then shook himself back into the moment.

"Let us help Fairfeather glean some lesson from his poor judgment. If Lord Middlemere can in any way lend authority to my sermon, I'd be obliged."

Josephine nodded. "Give me a few minutes to brief Papa, and then you may escort Edward back to the study. You can serve the lecture and Papa will nod supportively. I'll make myself scarce, so as not to cause my cousin any further embarrassment."

"Thank you, Lady Weston."

"No, thank *you*, sir," she returned, and in so saying, a thread of emotion escaped. "I suppose it's the strain," she said, touching her throat.

"Most understandable."

She flashed him a wan smile. "Let us finish this business and release you to your duties, which I daresay are daunting enough without that lot's interference. Needless to say," she added, "we'd be better off, sir, if your men finished this task soon." She lowered her eyes and ducked from the room.

The ensuing meeting went more or less as planned, although Edward rankled under the force of the lieutenant's address. Arthur and Peter rated lesser scoldings and were sent home. Edward tramped upstairs without a word of apology. Not long after, Carson returned home, and Middlemere and the women gathered to hear his report on Charlie Lowell's condition.

"Mr. Lowell's wound has ulcerated and he's dropped into a coma. Dr. Swinton says it's blood poisoning. He doesn't give the family much hope."

"What?" cried Josephine, clutching the back of Middlemere's chair. Maria moaned and covered her face.

Carson looked distressed. "I did everything I could. I cleaned the wound and rode ten miles to fetch the doctor, but he was off attending a difficult birth and couldn't be spared." His Adam's apple bobbed up and down. "That Mr. Charlie, he was—he *is*—the least troublesome pup of the whole lot. I cannot believe—" His voice broke, leaving him unable to finish.

"We understand, sir," Lord Middlemere said in a distracted whisper. "Now, go get some sleep. The rest of us will stand vigil and pray for a miracle."

"We're very grateful for your help, Carson," added Josephine, touching the butler's arm.

Carson bowed and took his leave. The family sat quietly for the rest of that day.

Next morning, Edward came down to breakfast and found Josephine, who had only managed a little tea. Carson had been to the Lowells' and back; the news was not good.

"Don't look so smug," Edward said, flinging a pile of toast onto a plate. He crossed the room and slumped into the chair opposite her.

Indignation and fury rose in her breast. "I swear, Mr. Fairfeather, you have the perceptiveness of a stone! The expression you observe is one of barely suppressed anguish. We have a friend who lies in a coma whilst you sleep away your worthless hours and stuff your face with cold toast!" The tears she had been holding back now started to flow.

Edward jumped to his feet, sending his chair crashing backward. "What—Charlie?" She nodded. "Why did no one tell me this?" he bellowed, slamming a fist on the table.

Josephine winced but kept her voice calm. "You made yourself unavailable, Edward. You chose not to join the family."

"By Jupiter, that's the limit! It's not about family! Am I not the factor here? Do I not at least deserve to know when an emergency has arisen?"

Josephine held her handkerchief up to her face. "This *is* about family," she croaked. "Charlie is like unto your brother. Oh, Edward, you—"

Then Josephine bit her tongue, for as much as he maddened her, she hated to see her cousin in pain. She wanted to say that a good factor would not have defied a gentleman's promise. A good factor, caught in a mistake, would not have hidden away and sulked. She wanted to point out that he had already known Charlie was hurt.

Edward wheeled around the room, bumping into furniture and flailing at the drapery. He seemed to have forgotten her.

"What'll I do?" he asked plaintively. "Oh, I am indeed punished!" He made several complete circuits of the table, then turned to her and said, "I've been such a fool, Jo. Can you ever forgive me?"

She lifted her chin and replied in austere tones, "I have not the power to grant you forgiveness. That is between you, the Lowells, and God."

Edward's visage went white. "Oh, Charlie!" he cried and ran from the room.

CHAPTER TWELVE

Edingham-Greene, Wiltshire
29 June 1819

Edward fled to the Lowells' home, where he begged their forgiveness and gained permission to sit vigil. Josephine stayed at Greenbank, anxiously awaiting Carson's reports on Charlie's condition. The young man remained in a deep coma. His body raged with fever, and the wound on his thigh continued to putrefy.

Carson came into the Weston drawing room two evenings later and reported in hushed tones that Dr. Swinton was now talking of amputation. Lord Middlemere gave a small groan and staggered off to bed. The butler inclined his head toward the ladies and turned to follow his master.

"Wait, Carson!" Josephine leapt to her feet and pursued him to the door. "I can no longer sit idly by whilst our friend wastes away. Please ready my horse—we leave at once for Lowell Ridge."

Carson shook his head. "My lady, I'm afraid I cannot help. I must attend your father."

Josephine fixed him with a determined look. "Then you must find me a suitable escort, or I shall be forced to go alone. Perhaps, under the circumstances, Lieutenant Quimby might be the right man for the job?"

Carson blinked in surprise and put a hand to his chin. Finally, he nodded. "If you insist, then I suppose I can send the stableboy to find him."

"I insist," replied Josephine. She hurried upstairs to change into some old clothes. Around nine o'clock, she met the lieutenant in Greenbank's front hall. His boots and breeches were covered in a thick layer of dust.

"Hunting tonight?" she asked. Quimby nodded grimly. "Sir," she went on. "Forgive me for pulling you away from your duties, but I require an escort to Lowell Ridge. I won't stay here another minute, not when I can be of some use to Charlie's family. You should know that if you refuse, I'll go anyway. There is no one to stop me."

Quimby's jaw worked a moment before he said, "Very well."

They walked through the gathering dusk to the stable, where he personally saddled her horse. In a few minutes, they were cantering southward. Neither said anything for most of the three-mile ride. Josephine kept her eyes forward; she was in no mood for conversation. She sensed the occasional glance from her silent companion, but she had not the temerity to return his gaze. It was full dark by the time they reached Lowell Ridge. Quimby dismounted first and handed her down.

As Josephine turned to thank him, he touched her forearm and said in a low voice, "My lady, this situation, I think, is beyond your ken. If you like, I can wait a few minutes, and should you change your mind I—"

"Thank you, sir, but I am determined to confront this ordeal. The family needs me. My *cousin* needs me, whether he realizes it or not."

Quimby's eyes glittered, reflecting the lamplight shining through the front windows. "You are intriguing. A soldier and a lady wrapped up in one package. I admire your courage."

It was, perhaps, the greatest compliment anyone had ever paid her. Josephine's lip quivered. Blinking rapidly to suppress tears, she tossed off a careless chuckle. "Pshaw! 'Tisn't courage at all, but pure, mule-like stubbornness. Now, return to your men, and I'll see what I can do to help the occupants of this house."

He bowed and backed away as she stepped through the front door. There was no one to greet her. Servants bustled to and fro, fetching seemingly every lamp and candlestick and torn sheet in the house. The dining room doors stood wide; here was the locus of everyone's activity. Josephine laid aside her spencer and gloves and drew unnoticed toward the opening.

A raging fire blazed in the hearth, and over it stood a kettle of boiling water, attended by a maid. Footmen rushed in and out, placing candles and lamps on every available surface. The dining room had taken on the look of a chapel, with its scores of small flames marking a hundred pleas to the Almighty. Mr. and Mrs. Lowell hovered over the table, on which lay the inert form of young Charlie. They moaned in unison, their grief rising with each passing moment.

"Make your peace now, Mrs. Lowell," said Dr. Swinton, who was sorting his tools on the sideboard. "We are soon about our business—there must be no more delay. Will somebody please help the parents away?"

Josephine stepped forward, but the housekeeper interceded, pulling at Charlie's parents, urging them to leave so the doctor could save their son's life. They let her guide them out, past Josephine, and thence up the stairs. Josephine followed them with her eyes; they were in no condition to accept her words of empty comfort.

She threw back her shoulders and approached the surgeon. "I'm here to help you. Tell me what to do."

"Wash your hands in that basin and put an apron over your frock," he replied without looking up. "I'm glad you're here, Lady Weston. We could use a cool-headed nurse."

Josephine stuffed down her surprise and went to do his bidding. As she tied the apron strings, Edward ducked in, looking hollow-eyed and sleepless, his hair freshly combed back, his shirtsleeves rolled up. He startled at the sight of her.

"What are you doing here?" he asked, putting his hands on her shoulders. His tone lacked any trace of hostility, as if for once he did not regard her as an unwanted intruder.

"Oh, Edward . . ."

Torment shimmered in his eyes. Josephine stepped forward and slipped her arms round him, pulling him close for a tender embrace. He shivered and pressed his cheek against the top of her head.

"Ready?" Dr. Swinton asked with an impatient glance over his shoulder.

Josephine and Edward broke apart and hurried over. Edward apparently had been apprised of his role, which involved pressing a small paddle against Charlie's femoral artery, since the wound lay too high on the leg to permit the use of a tourniquet. Josephine would hand Dr. Swinton the instruments he needed and help hold the leg still at the appropriate moment.

"It's a grisly business, my lady," the surgeon said kindly. "At least, in this case, the patient is unconscious. We could call a footman instead."

Josephine shook her head. She kissed Charlie's pale forehead and stationed herself at Dr. Swinton's right elbow. Edward stood opposite the surgeon and grasped Charlie's exposed thigh. Everyone took a deep breath, and the procedure began.

The first part went swiftly. In one deft movement, Dr. Swinton made a circular cut round the whole upper thigh. In three or four more strokes, he had severed the muscles which encased Charlie's femur. Gangrenous liquids drained from exposed tissues, pooling in gruesome, greenish-brown stains. As the stench of putrefaction curdled the air, the surgeon's assistants fought not to retch.

"Do not for an instant let up on that pressure," he reminded Edward, who stared down in white terror. Various unpleasant sounds accompanied this phase, making Josephine wish she could stop up her ears. She handed Dr. Swinton sponges and small flaps of muslin, though she dared not observe closely what he did with those things.

"The saw, if you please, madam." Josephine flinched when Dr. Swinton laid a bloodied scalpel by her left hand. "The saw?" he reiterated. Trembling, she seized the dreaded tool from its box. It was a hideous object, heavy and wide and ridged with bright teeth. Taking it from her, the surgeon assessed her composure. "I'm afraid this will be rather traumatic, yet it's the critical part. Try not to focus too much on the noise. Breathe slowly through your mouths. Do not let go his artery, Mr. Fairfeather, and if anyone feels faint, call a servant to replace you."

What followed was the most grievous experience in Josephine's life, worse even than the troll attack, which had been comparatively brief. She concentrated on not letting Edward down; if *he* must endure, then so could she. She held the leg exactly as Dr. Swinton asked, and when it fell away from the boy's body, she covered it with a towel and slid it down the table. A servant came forward and bore the ravaged limb out of sight.

The rest of the procedure passed in a blur. Dr. Swinton closed the blood vessels and sewed up the skin. Josephine gave over various plasters and dressings. Then it was done, and several footmen came in to carry Charlie to his room.

"And now we commend his fate to Providence," said Dr. Swinton as he washed his hands in the basin. He awarded his assistants an appreciative nod.

Josephine looked across at Edward, who had barely spoken since the operation began. A roaring in her ears had been building for some time. His mouth formed the words "thank you," but she heard neither syllable as the floor rushed up to meet her and the whole room went dark.

She woke moments later with her head in his lap. "Always deflecting the attention to yourself, eh?" he said dryly.

"Yes, well, I reckoned the moment called for a bit of comic relief."

Edward showed his teeth in an expression that was not precisely a grin and gave her a hand up. "Brava, Nurse Weston. You've acquitted yourself well. Now go home. I'll sit vigil with the patient."

"You may have the first watch," she agreed, "but I'm going no further than the sofa in the drawing room. Call me when you need to sleep."

Edward cocked an eyebrow and nodded. In a moment, he was gone.

CHAPTER THIRTEEN

London
25 June 1819

Prudence knelt beside her bed, peering into the dim shadows where squatted the old maple chest. For weeks, the Marriage Mart had occupied all her attention, distracting her from examining her other keepsakes. Now she craved a diversion from this ill-favored Season, which seemed daily to edge her toward a lifetime of disillusionment. Steeling her nerves, she opened the box and regarded its contents.

"Where do I begin?"

The gauntlets lay atop everything else. They were dark brown, the palms worn and cracked and stiffly shaped like a real pair of hands. Gingerly, she touched the gaps where three leather fingers had been detached, two on one hand, one on the other. Sheared clean away.

"You don't frighten me," she said.

Grimacing but determined, she pulled them straight on. They fit snugly in the palm and extended up her forearms. Fringes dangled from their cuffs; a few sported beads that clinked as she turned her hands this way and that. Her fingers jutted, white and clean, from where the leather digits were missing.

A sudden pain shot across her hands. Prudence jerked off the gauntlets and threw them back into the chest. Deep, throbbing red lines slashed across the same trio of fingers that were missing on the gloves. All at once, the marks vanished.

"I imagined that," she muttered. "'Twas a reasonable assumption about the former owner's experience." She strapped shut the chest and shoved it back under the bed. "I'll make an example of this to Josephine," she decided. "The mind plays tricks on us, particularly when we are under exceptional strain."

She hurried to her desk and a half-finished letter to Josephine, which began with the story of Underwood's clumsy gift-giving. The scene inspired by Lady Emmeline's fan had not figured in that telling; Prudence had dismissed it as an ordinary dream.

Variations of that dream haunted her, however, over the next several days. She convinced herself they were the product of a great nervous energy, of which the viscount was the chief cause. In truth, Lord Underwood provided the least source of her strain; trying to forget William MacNeal required near-constant discipline.

Alone at night, Prudence would unfurl Lady Emmeline's fan and waft the air. As expected, it performed like any other fan would. The ruby ring resided as always in a pouch in her skirt. She sometimes slipped it on, glaring at it as if daring it to effect some change. Nothing, of course, happened. Why would it?

"That I would admit the possibility of some such occurrence simply goes to show how much Josephine's silliness has distracted me," she sniffed.

As for the tattered gauntlets, they frightened her a bit. While she dared not put them on again, she examined every seam, rend, and fringe of their makeup. The beads and their tiny incisions caught her particular attention. She stared at them but still could not manage to divulge their significance. Far in the back of her mind, she wondered what Lady Elisabetha Revelle, who had immediately recognized her mother's ring, would have to say about these gloves.

Lord Underwood paid another visit on the second of July. He was in an ebullient mood, having won a racehorse in a gentleman's bet. The viscount's enthusiasm ran toward the minutiae of The Thoroughbred horse. Prudence liked horses well enough, but she had never been an ardent admirer of all things equine.

"Could you not at least try to show some interest in his pastimes?" asked Aunt Amelia once he had gone. "Imagine what people will say about a wife who is so visibly bored by her own spouse?"

"It is not my objective to marry a boring man!" declared Prudence.

"You may well have no choice!"

"Perhaps, but I will not leap into matrimony with the first man who comes calling unless I am sure he's the last who ever means to come. I am but two months out, dear Aunt. Are you counseling me to seal my fate so soon?"

"I'm counseling you not to burn your bridges."

"Precisely. The way I see it, leading Underwood along would solidify his intentions too soon, the result of which will be a bridge engulfed in flames."

Aunt Amelia's jaw trembled. "You're impossible!"

"I am only being rational."

Aunt Amelia peered at Prudence. "What's wrong with you lately? You're distant, you're peevish, you pick at your food. For a while, I had begun to think you were in love."

Prudence laughed nervously. "I do not love Lord Underwood."

"Someone else, then?"

An image of MacNeal rose in her mind. "*Who*, madam?" she asked, gesturing round the empty parlor.

Aunt Amelia's shoulders sagged. Abruptly, she sat upright. "That's it. We're going to the theatre tonight. Will you promise to be lively?"

"Yes, Aunt. I promise to be utterly and completely engaging." Prudence's tone was saucy, but her intent sincere. Though it had grown ever more improbable that her favor would be requited, she hoped nonetheless for a glimpse of a certain handsome man.

CHAPTER FOURTEEN

Edingham-Greene, Wiltshire
3 July 1819

In the days that followed Charlie's surgery, Josephine and Edward took turns nursing the ailing young man. They managed the dressings on his stump and drizzled broth down his throat, freeing his parents from the drudgery of keeping him alive. For it became ever more apparent this was all that could be done; though the site of the surgery healed as it should, Charlie did not awaken from his coma. Dr. Swinton dropped by to see his patient several times each day, but the outlook remained grim.

"Too late. Too late," he muttered under his breath. "I have never seen the likes of such a wound."

Through the open windows at Lowell Ridge, Josephine heard occasional reports of gunfire, far off in the hills east of Edingham-Greene. One morning, as she rode home with Carson to rest for a few hours, she spied a smudge of smoke rising low over the horizon. Quimby was out there somewhere, apparently making some progress at eradicating trolls. She suspected Charlie's plight had inspired these redoubled efforts.

The edifice of Greenbank was a welcome sight. Josephine couldn't wait to bathe and relax, free from the pressures of her unending duties. Engrossed as she had been with Charlie's condition, she had given little thought to how Prudence fared. A letter waited in the front hall; she tore into it eagerly, hoping for good news. She found quite the opposite: Prudence had for some reason developed a sudden interest in the old gauntlets, and the scene she described prickled the hairs on Josephine's neck.

Prudence professed that the marks on her hand had been an accident of her mind. "Is it not a fantastic display of nervous imagination?" she asked. "Clearly Lord Underwood's attentions have got me in a tizzy, and I don't even like him."

Josephine shook her head. It sounded like a supernatural event. Not a trance, which was akin to sleeping . . . no, more like a vision. Despite her exhaustion, she trudged up the stairs and sat down to reply:

> *You say it was your imagination, but acute pain cannot be conjured by the idly dreaming mind. Separate, therefore, what you* believe *is true from what you* know *to be true. Ever since we first encountered those keepsakes, things have happened to us that defy reason. Dare I suggest we are dealing with . . . with* magical *things?*

There. She had said it.

Another idea she had been withholding now rose up in her brain. What if these relics were too dangerous to be handled by uninformed girls? What if *they* were the source of all their bad fortune? The magical keepsakes and mythical trolls, both the stuff of fairy tales and fables. And after what she'd seen happen to Charlie . . .

Josephine refreshed her pen.

Prudence, this is no game, nor is it merely some old secret. If you persist in handling the contents of that box, trouble is sure to find you. You must resist them completely—if you love me at all, heed my plea and abandon your keepsakes!

9 *July 1819*

One night, on Edward's watch, Charlie Lowell passed away. He was buried two days later, on the morning of July the eighth, after which Edward adjourned to his rooms at Greenbank.

When twenty-four hours had gone by with no sign of her cousin, Josephine began to worry. Guilt was surely a harsher sentence than Lieutenant Quimby could dispense, but Edward must not let himself think that he'd personally slain his friend. With Lord Middlemere and Maria both steeped in their own grief, Josephine took it upon herself to try to draw Edward out. She filled a tea tray with his favorite jam tarts and rapped lightly on his door.

"Good*bye*, Josephine!" he roared.

She pressed her cheek to the door. "Have something to eat, Edward. Don't starve yourself, please." Silence. She tried the door; it was locked. "Charlie wasn't a child. He *chose* to be there that night."

"Good*bye*, Josephine!"

She left the tray beside his door and wandered downstairs. In the lower hall she encountered Lieutenant Quimby, just departing. He beckoned and said, "I'm glad you happened by. Would you be so kind as to accompany me outside?"

They went out to the drive, where a groom waited with his

horse. Quimby took the reins and stroked the gelding's nose; for a moment, he seemed rather loath to explain. "My platoon has received orders to decamp. We've killed five of those creatures, likely the whole lot. Meanwhile, other districts are experiencing similar difficulties."

She had always known that sooner or later the militia would leave, but the sudden force of her feeling caught her off guard. "Well!" she exclaimed with false cheer. "Bravo, sir, for a job well done! Within the year we'll be hearing about the famous *Captain* Quimby, who saved our nation from a scourge of wild beasts."

Quimby shook his head. "You'll hear nothing. Our assignment is clandestine, as you guessed. I have told you this in confidence because you have shown yourself to be a rational person who does not run off sharing her particular knowledge with others. Anyway, I don't intend to let the next campaign run on so long, and I hope never again to let the locals get a good look at our quarry."

A trill of laughter burst from her throat. "Yes, we locals can be awfully vexatious!"

"Not *all* of you," he countered.

It was his usual style, she reflected, to make comments that invited pursuit. Considering their difference in rank, this struck her as inappropriate, though certainly interesting. No matter. Their acquaintance was now at its end. She held out her hand. He bowed low, coming within a hair's breadth of touching it to his lips. At the last instant, he hesitated to take that liberty. He straightened and gave her a radiant smile.

Josephine's stomach flopped. With effort, she said, "It has been a pleasure knowing you, sir. We're grateful to you for restoring the security of Edingham-Greene."

His fingers squeezed hers ever so slightly. "The pleasure has been mutual. My only regret is that I never followed through on my promise."

"Promise? What promise?"

Quimby's sun-bleached brows arched over cornflower blue eyes. "Have you forgotten? I offered to teach you how to handle those pistols."

"Gracious!" Josephine laughed, flustered by his gaze and the insistent pressure of his hand. "I never expected you to uphold such a scheme."

"I did," he said earnestly. Unnerved, she looked away. Loosing her hand, he placed the shako on his head. "Well, goodbye, Lady Weston."

Reluctant to speak for fear of betraying her emotions, Josephine could only nod. Lieutenant Quimby mounted his horse and rode off down the lane. She watched his crimson-clad back fade until he passed through the front gate. Once he had vanished altogether, she realized she'd been holding her breath. She exhaled a great lungful and sank down onto the front steps, her eyes blurring slightly. They would probably never see each other again.

"Oh, fiddlesticks!" she muttered, then burst into tears.

For too many weeks she'd labored to repress the flowering of a true admiration for Quimby. She had lied to her dearest friend and lied to herself. She'd faced the object of her interest with a mask of cool impartiality, though perhaps, from time to time, he'd seen through her disguise. Would he carry that knowledge like a trophy, expecting at his next posting to have the same effect on another young thing? Somehow, she doubted it.

Josephine rubbed her eyes on the back of her arm and

stretched out along the bottom step, staring blankly up at the sky. She went inside an hour later sporting a very sunburnt nose.

With the troll threat eradicated, Josephine ventured forth for a long, satisfying walk. At the end of her circuit, she passed the millpond. How she longed to plunge in and splash about in the cool water! She had her boots and stockings off before she thought better of it.

"Young ladies don't swim," she muttered bitterly. *Indeed, they don't do much of anything of interest, especially not mooning over unsuitable young men.* She recalled Quimby's hand on the small of her back the last time she had walked here. Fear and pride had clouded her senses that night, and he had still been only an impertinent cipher. When had she realized how much she admired him? It had come on so slowly; perhaps their quarrel had brought it out in the open. "'Tis all a moot point," she reminded herself. Her stomach felt hard as a tightly clenched fist. Restoring her footwear, she carried on toward the house.

In the days that followed, Edward began to take nourishment from the tray by his door. Josephine did not attempt to interact with him, but she saw to it that food was delivered at intervals. Her father's mood had likewise improved, and before too long Lord Middlemere ventured from his chamber.

"This is good," she told Maria as they strolled the garden one afternoon. "I've never seen Papa recover so quickly from a shock. Is it possible to hope that soon we might have our old family back?"

"That depends on 'ee."

Josephine lifted a brow at the guarded expression on the nurse's face. "What's that supposed to mean? I daresay I have acquitted myself as calmly as any young lady might."

Maria shrugged. "'Ee've been in a pet, too, or hadn't 'ee noticed, Miss High-and-Mighty?"

"A *pet?* I'm in mourning, Maria, like everyone else."

A sly smile crossed the nurse's lips. "Ay, but *whom* bist 'ee mourning?"

"*Whom?* Why Charlie, of course!"

"Nay, I reckon 'ee feel more keenly the loss of a certain handsome officer."

Josephine's face grew warm and her stomach fluttered in sorrow. How long had Maria known? Well, there was no point in denying it. "Time heals what reason cannot," she quipped.

"Time . . . and *distance,*" added Maria with a self-satisfied nod. She linked arms with Josephine. "Take heart, my darling. There are plenty o' fish in the sea, and some are much, much better than others."

CHAPTER FIFTEEN

London
7 July 1819

The next week brought two pages' worth of warnings from Josephine. Prudence stared down at the girl's handwriting, at one word in particular:

༄ *magical* ༄

"Oh, Cousin," she sighed. "This is the limit. You plainly underestimate the power of the human mind." She sat at her desk and wrote,

> *The contents of our Mothers' boxes signify nothing. There are no fairy tale Creatures prowling about Wiltshire, and there have been no Supernatural Phenomena—only a series of interesting coincidences.*

To further prove her point, she fished the Elizabethan overgown from the chest and slipped it over her shift, then strolled about the room for a good half an hour, daring it to unleash some inexplicable result. She finished the exercise by staring hard in the mirror. The lavender velvet was a bit moth-eaten but clung flatteringly to her body, its pleats and deep gores flaring out at her hips. With her honey-gold hair falling like a curtain across her shoulders, she could almost imagine herself as a royal lady-in-waiting.

"'Tis a costume or a great-great-great-grandmother's vestment, nothing more," she murmured, removing the gown. A full description of this experiment went into her letter, which she posted before noon.

At midday, a messenger arrived with an express from Middlemere announcing the demise of Charlie Lowell. While this unhappy outcome moved Prudence to tears, she refused to believe it signified anything more than an unfortunate accident.

Josephine had other thoughts, which she shared in a letter that arrived shortly thereafter:

> *The manner of his death and the sort of creature that caused it has, in my mind, only magnified the seriousness of our family's secret. There is a relationship here between the past and present, proven by my father's first words to Lieutenant Quimby: 'My fear,' he said, 'is based on personal experience.' Would* Ursus arctos *have caused a man's lifetime of seclusion? No, I think not.*

Prudence registered but one word from this passage. Her eyes shot immediately to the blotter on Amelia's desk: *Aha! The magnifying glass! That is how I might identify the markings on those beads.*

The next morning, when Aunt Amelia left to spend an hour with a friend, Prudence quickly laid hands on the magnifying glass. Upstairs in her room, she spread out the gauntlets in a patch of bright sunshine. As she'd suspected, the marks were fine inscriptions carved into the glass and stained with black ink for legibility.

KINGSBURY 11.4.1795
KILKARNEY 17.1.1798
ORMOND 16.9.1799

She could not for the life of her deduce what these names and dates signified. "I dare not ask Aunt Amelia. Hmm. One wonders what a certain baroness knows about such events . . ." She copied down the inscriptions for Josephine to consider and asked her to have a look at Middlemere's atlas.

> *As for the supernatural Idea you raised, 'tis an interesting Hypothesis but it goes against Reason. Experimentation, not fear, is how One proves points. What Fools we will feel when we realize our Presumptions have far outstripped the actual Truth.*

She was signing her letter when Aunt Amelia burst in crying, "Oh, rapture, my darling!"

Prudence lunged from her desk and strode to the middle of the room. By the window lay the gauntlets in full view, and Amelia's magnifying glass beside them. "Ma'am?" she asked as calmly as possible.

The old lady, however, had something else on her mind. "How I adore Mrs. Wymstone! She is a pearl among women! Here in my hand is an invitation for you to join her and her daughter for a grand boating party. Are you not perfectly charmed?"

Prudence smiled at the thought of meeting Miss Wymstone again. "How interesting! When are we to enjoy this merry holiday?"

"The day after tomorrow. As I have no fondness for watercraft, you'll have to go it alone. Oh, you'll be dancing at Almack's by the middle of next week! Of course, a smile for a certain nobleman wouldn't hurt—"

"Dearest Aunt . . ." Prudence intoned.

Amelia gave her an arch look. "You know I am right."

"In all likelihood you are," the girl averred, "but Almack's will afford me the chance to bestow my smile on many others." She linked arms with the aunt and guided her to the door. "Now, please let me finish my letter before lunch. I'll see you in ten minutes?" When Aunt Amelia had gone, Prudence glanced back at the gauntlets and exhaled in relief.

10 July 1819

The boating party cast off late Saturday morning with a score of giggling girls, several matrons, one or two dogs, a fleet of small boats, and a half-dozen boys to perform the labor. The girls talked constantly, praising the oarsmen's strong arms, shuddering when the boats rocked, screaming in mock fear, and chiding the dogs.

"You're quiet today," lisped Miss Wymstone as they reclined in their boat.

Prudence smiled over her shoulder. "Our companions more than make up for it."

"My mother dines with Lady Sefton tomorrow."

Prudence twisted round. Anything she might say, from feigned disinterest to restrained pleasure, would come across as banal. "I won't pretend that I don't desire a voucher, but it is not in my nature to affect friendship for personal gain. In fact, I've been wondering why you have not called on me."

Miss Wymstone put a hand to her mouth, for such was her habit when covering a smile. "We've been in Hampshire these three weeks. My sister gave birth to a baby girl."

"How lovely!" laughed Prudence. She dangled a hand in the cool waters of the Thames. Liquid flowed around it, gurgling merrily in its wake. *See, there is an explanation for all things!* She flicked a handful of water back at Miss Wymstone, who squealed in delight.

The party lunched on a shaded riverbank. Miss Wymstone lay at Prudence's feet and asked her about Greenbank. Then she inquired, "Do you think you will marry for love or for money?"

Prudence's breath caught. "Gracious, a little of each, I suppose," she replied. "'Tis out of my hands, though. In the end, I have a duty to spare my family the burden of my upkeep."

Miss Wymstone sighed. "I'll always have a living but, alas, I do not think it will be enough to buy happiness." She gestured helplessly at her face.

Prudence said with great feeling, "I am truly sorry for you."

Presently, it was time to head back downstream. The hampers were loaded, and the ladies clambered aboard, clutching as they went at the boys' outstretched hands. Prudence was the last of the girls to enter her boat. As she stepped into the prow, a dog dashed down the riverbank and hurled himself onboard. The force of his landing tore the mooring line from their oarsman. The boat surged backward into the river.

Prudence circled her arms, fighting for balance. The dog barked wildly, leaping over girls and rocking the vessel. Prudence was undone; she plunged into the Thames and came up gasping. The river was shallow here, no more than waist deep, cool against her flushed, prickly skin. The situation was so ridiculous that she started to laugh. Miss Wymstone joined in. She flung a handful of water at Prudence, crying, "There you are—I've paid you out, though I daresay you've fared worse than I!"

"I'll get you for that!" Prudence said in mock-threatening tones. She slogged toward the boat, pretending to reach for Miss Wymstone. Then an awful thought struck her. She felt for the pocket that contained her mother's ring—it was gone.

Ignoring the oarsman urging her into the boat, Prudence dove underwater and groped all about. Her hands clutched at silt and slippery twigs. She opened her eyes but could see nothing through the swirling brown soup of the river. On resurfacing for the third time, she was jerked from the water and hefted soggily into someone's arms.

"Put me down!" she demanded. "I'm looking for something!"

"Oh, I thought you were drowning."

"Pish-posh! Not in two feet of water!"

Her hero's chest quaked. It occurred to her that his voice was far deeper than the average teenaged boy's. If only she could pull her fallen coiffure away from her eyes! But with her arms pinned in the clasp of her would-be savior, she was sightless as a mole. Water drained noisily from her favorite day-frock; her shoes had vanished.

"Drat you, now I'll never find it!"

"What, pray, are we fishing for?"

"Never mind! Put me down."

"Damned mud," muttered the hero, shifting his weight. "Oh, hell," he added.

Prudence felt herself falling. She hit the water with a great splash and was on her feet in an instant, trudging toward shore. Someone draped a blanket round her shoulders. She dropped to the ground and burst into tears. Several girls tittered.

It's gone! Gone forever!

The well-meaning Samaritan waded ashore and stood dripping nearby. "If it's any consolation, Miss Fairfeather, I too am now shoeless."

Her heart nearly stopped. She peered between her fingers. *Mr. MacNeal? Oh my God!*

He knelt beside her and said in a low voice, "I've been abroad these three weeks and returned late yesterday. I meant to call on you this morning, but my mother had already engaged me with yon company. Yet here we are! Serendipitous, wouldn't you say?"

Prudence picked silently at her ruined stockings, her stomach churning in turmoil. So *that* was his excuse? Perhaps he was too embarrassed to admit he'd falsely promised to call, but why would he come to her aid if he wanted to snub her?

As if reading her mind, he added, "After a scene like that, though, I suppose you'd prefer never to see me again."

Prudence began to weep all over again.

"Are you coming, Sir Galahad?" someone shouted.

Mr. MacNeal shifted his crouch. "One moment!" he called. "Well?" he asked softly.

Prudence, conscious of dozens of watchful eyes, found herself in the grip of agony and euphoria. He did not comprehend her dilemma: concurring with his statement would drive him away, yet refuting it was unthinkable, for she could hardly ask him to come see her. Had he instead asked permission to call, she could have said "yes." She huddled in silence, hoping he might somehow perceive his error.

"Right." Resignation thickened his voice. Mr. MacNeal got to his feet. "One moment. Weren't you looking for something?" He produced a lump of linen, which he dangled before her. Prudence took the pocket, tipped out the ring, and looked up in gratitude. Mr. MacNeal gave her a sly wink. "I was fishing around for my shoes and found that instead."

Her stomach clenched, and the ring warmed on her palm. She tried to convey through only her eyes her sincerest desire to see him again. No words could possibly correct her predicament.

"Oy, Quixote, the windmill's this way!"

Several of Prudence's party giggled, only to be shushed by their chaperones. Everyone had grown bored of the waning drama.

"I must be going. Good day, Miss Fairfeather." Bowing, Mr. MacNeal squelched over to his companions, who had pulled their boat ashore, and swung lithely aboard. They clapped him on the shoulders, calling him a hero. An elegant woman bent to kiss his cheek.

The oarsman helped Prudence into her boat. She settled herself near Miss Wymstone and stared down at her lap, feeling stunned and embarrassed. They pushed off and glided into the main current of the Thames. As the girls broke their silence and began waving to passing boaters, Prudence raised her eyes. Mr. MacNeal's party floated some fifty yards downstream. They were a convivial lot; their occasional outbursts echoed across the water. MacNeal glanced her way. Prudence felt dizzy.

"Do you know him?" murmured Miss Wymstone.

Prudence blushed. "We—we've been introduced."

"His eyes are following us. I think he's smitten with you!"

"Oh, hardly!" protested Prudence, ducking her head.

"And the feeling is mutual! Who is he, pray tell?"

"William MacNeal." Prudence peered at her hopefully. "Do you know aught of him from Almack's?"

Miss Wymstone shook her head. "No, though that signifies nothing, for I've only attended the assemblies since May. You have met just this once?"

"Twice before, actually. The second time but briefly."

Miss Wymstone smiled. "Then that's thrice now, and memorably so. You haven't seen the last of that gentleman."

"But I treated him so abominably!"

"He doesn't seem to mind."

Prudence looked back across the water. Mr. MacNeal inclined his head in a final salute before turning to his companions.

She arrived home filthy and forlorn. Aunt Amelia bustled into the foyer and instantly froze. "I think I shall scream."

"Please don't." Prudence moved toward the stairs. "Could we talk later? I desperately need a bath."

"What happened?"

"I fell into the Thames."

"I have a dreadful feeling it wasn't quite so simple."

"No. A dog knocked me in, you see, and then I dove underwater to retrieve my missing pocket, and there was also a gentleman . . ."

"A gentleman?" queried Aunt Amelia sharply. "What gentleman?"

"He thought I was drowning, but of course I wasn't, and since no one else offered to help, he leapt in and hauled me up, but I was so distracted by the loss of the pocket—"

"The *pocket?* Please tell me you didn't ruin your whole future for a rag!"

Prudence winced. "I was distraught. I thought he was one of the boys, so I ordered him to put me down."

"*What* gentleman?" pressed Aunt Amelia.

Prudence was too ashamed to admit the truth. "I don't know. My hair covered my face. Anyway, I doubt it matters."

Aunt Amelia sighed. "We'll find out soon enough, won't we? Now get along with you." She gestured up the stairs where Prudence duly fled.

12 July 1819

The repercussions of the boating mishap were not immediately felt. Prudence had caught a minor sniffle, so she and Aunt Amelia stayed home. On Monday, a welcome caller appeared.

"Miss Wymstone!" cried Prudence. She took her friend by both hands. "Here at last," she murmured, pressing the girl's cheeks.

"Here by extreme contrivance," replied Miss Wymstone. She raised her voice to add, "Will you please show me your garden, Miss Fairfeather? It's a lovely day, and I'm desirous of exercise."

Aunt Amelia waved them along. The two girls, arm-in-arm, strolled out into the sunshine.

"Something's wrong," guessed Prudence. Miss Wymstone's arm stiffened beneath hers.

"Oh, dear! Mother is fit to be tied. She would lock me up for a week if she knew I was here."

"But I don't understand!"

"Forgive her—she wants only what's best for me. Because of my appearance, she controls my environment and the quality of each person who shares my company. People have been talking, you see, and there is now a taint about you—"

"A taint?" exclaimed Prudence.

Miss Wymstone reddened to the roots of her bright orange hair. "A rumor . . . of mental instability. People are saying you tried to drown yourself in the Thames."

"What?" Mortification welled in Prudence's throat. "You were there. The dog knocked me overboard."

"Yes, but there were five other boats boarding at once, so no one else seems to have witnessed the event. Because the three girls with us were trampled and upset, their stories are prejudiced. All anyone knows is what was observed after your fall—the diving and splashing and howling at your rescuer."

Prudence blinked. "I had lost something precious."

"They say you raved nonsense and plunged your face underwater."

"And what do *you* say?"

Miss Wymstone squeezed her hands. "I support you entirely. Unfortunately, my mother has a horror of controversy. She has declared you can no longer be my friend and that she shall cease her campaign for your sponsorship at Almack's."

Prudence said weakly, "I didn't do anything wrong."

"Of course not, but I had to warn you and assure you I had nothing to do with it. Now I really must go." Miss Wymstone embraced her. "Has he called?"

Prudence shook her head, too beside herself to speak.

"Be patient. He shall." They entered the house and crossed to the front door. Here, the girl lisped, "I'm very sorry things have turned out this way. You're the only person who has ever treated me with genuine kindness."

They parted in tears, after which Prudence retired to her room. She lay on her bed and placed her mother's ring in her palm, studying the way it caught the light and wondering how such a simple thing could have caused so much trouble.

That's ridiculous! she thought in defiance. *A chance occurrence, nothing more, has brought about this misfortune.*

CHAPTER SIXTEEN

London

14 July 1819

For several days thereafter, no other callers appeared, not even Lord Underwood. A dismissive note from Mrs. Wymstone had hardly improved Aunt Amelia's mood, but she did not berate Prudence for the loss of the voucher. Perhaps she expected still more repercussions, even if she didn't know in what form they would come.

Directly after lunch on Wednesday afternoon, the bell at Stanistead began to ring and ring yet again. Aunt Amelia delighted in all the attention, but Prudence, forever thinking the next caller was MacNeal, quickly grew frazzled. Worse, their callers consisted of mostly strangers who peered at the young lady of Stanistead House as if expecting her to erupt into incoherent speech. Prudence's nerves wore thin trying to elicit the simplest remarks about weather.

At last, the aunt cried, "Turn them away, Reese. That is enough! Apparently we are the zoo and Miss Fairfeather the prized wild animal. Oh, woe is me, what am I to make of all this?"

Prudence held her head in her hands. "That half of London thinks I'm mad?"

"I'm going out," resolved Amelia. "I must establish what we're up against. Meanwhile, Prudence, do not answer that door! I'll give Reese instructions about what to say."

The old woman departed, and Prudence drifted upstairs. She attempted to read but found herself sliding into an uneasy doze. Somewhere far away she heard a bell ring. *More gawpers*, she thought and sank back into oblivion. She awoke with a jerk. *Or Mr. MacNeal!*

She dashed downstairs and burst into Reese's small parlor.

"Yes, madam?" asked the butler as she stood panting in the doorway.

"That caller moments ago. Who was it, please?"

"I don't know."

"He left a card, did he not?"

The butler drew thoughtfully on his pipe. "Aye, miss, but I didn't read it. I turned him away and burnt it, as Miss Staveley instructed."

"Burnt it?" Prudence stared in horror at the grate. "Well, what did he look like?"

"Like many gentlemen, miss. Tall, well-dressed, gloves, cane, hat. I didn't study his face, for I assumed he was another curiosity-seeker. I'm sorry I cannot be of more assistance."

Prudence groaned and stomped away.

Aunt Amelia returned at suppertime. Her expression was grim as she seated herself at the table. "Only the soup tonight, Reese. I do not think I could possibly manage anything else."

Prudence bowed her head, bracing for the lecture.

"Your alleged crimes are extensive. Some say you attacked Miss Wymstone. Several testify that you dove into the river, screaming like a lunatic. One suggested it was a brain fit. Another said you kicked the gentleman rescuer and he collapsed in pain.

It goes on like this, and I am now made perfectly ill." Aunt Amelia daubed at her eyes.

"Do you doubt me?" Prudence inquired softly.

Aunt Amelia seized her soup spoon. "No, of course not! The lesson here is that the tiniest aberration can spawn a multitude of interpretations."

"Then I shall endure the gossips and convince them I'm sane."

"Just so," agreed Aunt Amelia. "It may well pass. However, I am concerned about what important people like the viscount are thinking."

Prudence held her tongue. She would not be sorry if her escapade dissuaded Lord Underwood. Only William MacNeal's feelings mattered. Dear, kind Mr. MacNeal, of whom she knew nothing except how gallant and handsome he was. But, thanks to her fit of speechlessness, not to mention the probability he'd been turned away from her door, she had little expectation of ever seeing him again.

"There is one glimmer of hope," continued Aunt Amelia. "Are you certain you can't guess the identity of that gentleman? If he were to say the right things to the right people, it might put you in the clear. The gossips have suggested three or four candidates, one of whom is the Prince of Wales himself. Imagine that!"

Prudence inhaled her soup. Coughing, she rasped, "Who, pray, were the others?"

"Lord Diddlebury. Sir Francis Ingleside. And Mr. William MacNeal. Hmm . . . was that not the rascal we encountered in Hyde Park?"

Prudence's heart thundered. "Yes, ma'am, the same. And—"

"And did I not give him leave to call?"

"Yes, ma'am, you did, but—"

Aunt Amelia sniffed. "But he never came. Well, that was a snub if ever there was! I doubt anyone with such effrontery would leap to a maiden's aid. It can't have been MacNeal."

Prudence suffered yet another fit of coughing. "Don't be so hasty," she managed. "May I suggest you make inquiries with each of those gentlemen, excepting, of course, the Prince of Wales? If at least one rumor is true, then we may, as you have suggested, be able to salvage my reputation."

"Indeed," agreed Aunt Amelia with a satisfied lift of her chin.

Prudence resumed eating her supper, swallowing her guilt along with the soup. She should confide in her aunt, but the simplest solution seemed fraught with complication. *Please, Aunt Amelia! Discover the truth of the matter on your own, and save me the discomfort of looking like a fool!*

18 July 1819

In the days that followed, curiosity seekers continued to flock to Stanistead House. Prudence greeted everyone with a gracious smile and sparkling conversation. The first wave of visitors, which had consisted largely of cynical persons hoping to see a beautiful lunatic, was gradually replaced by those of a more authentic sort, including a quantity of male admirers. Notes arrived, expressing sympathy and good wishes. Prudence attended a luncheon without mishap, and on three occasions as she rode in the carriage gentlemen tipped their hats.

Invitations and visitors began to flow in; Aunt Amelia forgot about the lost Almack's voucher. Prudence, however, had not forgotten poor, lonely Miss Wymstone. Would her mother absolve Prudence like so many others had done? She hoped so. Above all, she prayed that news of her redemption would soon fall on William MacNeal's ears.

"Well, we've ruled out Lord Diddlebury," declared Aunt Amelia, holding up a notecard one afternoon. "He's in Bath and has been since the first of July. It doesn't surprise me, really, for I cannot imagine him ruining a suit of clothes for anything!"

Prudence laughed, but her merriment faded when the doorbell rang and Lord Underwood was shown in. This was the first they had seen of him since before the Thames debacle.

"Sir, what an honor!" Aunt Amelia enthused. "We have missed your company."

"I thought I'd give Miss Fairfeather a few days to dry out," drawled the viscount.

Prudence bit back a snort of derision. "I am quite dry now, thank you, my lord."

Aunt Amelia turned and glared.

"And how is your horse?" added Prudence with a smile. Lord Underwood spoke at length about some malady that afflicted his favorite hunter. After he departed, she turned to Aunt Amelia. "Will you continue your inquiries, then?"

The old lady shrugged. "What's the use in stirring up trouble, now that Lord Underwood has returned to the fold? Why, you're more popular than ever."

Prudence stared at the aunt. "So you'll abandon the project?"

"In a word, yes. It hardly seems worth the effort."

"But what about Miss Wymstone, whose mother requires flawlessness even if Society does not? Our friendship was uprooted before it could flourish. It would be worth soliciting those other gentlemen, if only to assuage Mrs. Wymstone's sensibilities."

"I appreciate your good intentions, but do not forget how Mrs. Wymstone turned on you. She is a dangerous ally; likely her daughter is cut from the same cloth. No, Prudence, I disagree. There is no longer anything to be gained by pursuing that matter."

Prudence's throat tightened. Her best hope for restoring herself in Mr. MacNeal's favor had been crushed. She excused herself, went upstairs, and sat down at her dressing table. When after a long while not one tear had appeared, she told her reflection, "Good day, Lady Underwood." The words were as hollow as the eyes that stared back.

The late afternoon post brought a tirade from Josephine, who'd received two letters in succession and found reason to be alarmed by nearly everything in them.

> *This is the third time in a fortnight you've mentioned those keepsakes. Admit it: your fascination is beyond your control. Think of the misfortune that ring has caused you: both your reputation and your chance for love, gone in one blow. I shan't be a party to your misguided experiments. I refuse to investigate those dates from the beads. Prudence, please hear me: put the relics away and never touch them again!*

"That's absurd!" cried Prudence. "How *has* she managed to draw such conclusions?" The ring itself couldn't be blamed for her falling into the river. Social cruelty, not supernatural powers, had caused her companions to misinterpret her attempts to find it. Josephine's rebuff stung, especially since it went against her usual inquisitiveness. "These are not magical tools of disaster," scoffed Prudence, "they're fascinating artifacts that may help us to understand our heritage. So be it. With or without her assistance, I shall carry on."

23 July 1819

Prudence frowned at the blank sheet of paper, a quill poised in her right hand. Only one other person could help her interpret the significance of the inscriptions—a person whom Aunt Amelia clearly disliked. She stared at her ring, which lay glittering in the sunlight, and weighed the gravity of her choice. "I'm entitled to know *something* about my own parents," she decided. She dipped the quill and wrote:

> *Dear Lady Revelle,*
>
> *Perhaps you may remember me from the night of your most excellent Musical Soiree? We spoke briefly about a Ring you recognized on my hand. I am Hesitant to write, for I was told not to pursue this matter, but I confess I'm Curious to know more about my Family. Meanwhile, I wonder if you might be aware of the significance of the following Places and Dates?*

Here she copied the list she had compiled from the beads, then she signed and sealed the letter. Afterward, she summoned a footman and bade him deliver it across town. She squeezed the ring against the palm of her hand, feeling energized by her unprecedented act of rebellion.

1 August 1819

At the home of Lord Driby, Prudence found herself seated for supper beside Mr. MacNeal's associate, Stephen Tate. Aunt Amelia, who sat opposite, did not seem to recognize him. A surge of hope lifted Prudence's mood. Maybe, just maybe, she could learn something interesting about Mr. MacNeal. First she must discover whether Tate remembered her from their encounter in Hyde Park. This, as it turned out, required no effort.

"I hope you don't mind dining next to an addlepate," he teased.

"Not at all," replied Prudence. "I'll speak slowly, if that helps."

Tate's face lit with amusement. "Ha-ha-ha! *Touché!*"

Servants descended with wine and the opening course. Meanwhile, politeness dictated that they address the other persons beside them. To Prudence's left sat a florid man who loved his own voice and pretty young girls. A soup course and poached fish made the rounds before his wife could reclaim his attention. Prudence chuckled inwardly at the woman's jealous scowl.

At this juncture, Tate leant close and gave her a nudge. "I hear you're an avid swimmer," he said with a grin.

Prudence felt a blush creep up her neck. Had he learned this from rumors? "I've been called many things this past month, most of them unflattering."

"I advise you to disregard such talk. It's the price of admission to this game we're all playing." He gestured with his fork to indicate the present company.

"Easier said than done, Mr. Tate. I am these days viewed as the town oddity."

"Not by *everyone*," he said with a significant look. Prudence's heart skipped a beat. Tate added in an undertone, "Have you any message for your champion? I shall see him next week when I am in Paris."

Champion? He speaks with impunity about me yet never comes to call? Prudence looked away. "That is hardly a proper question," she murmured, carving nervously at her roast beef.

"Do I take that to mean you have no further interest in his acquaintance?"

Prudence laid down her cutlery. "You puzzle me, sir. He has shown no inclination to pursue my company beyond our several chance encounters."

"He called once and was turned away. He thinks you're angry with him."

A gasp escaped Prudence's throat. Across the table, she felt the weight of Aunt Amelia's inquisitive eyes. *Look away, Aunt. Look away!*

But the old woman kept her gaze fixed, so Prudence had no choice but to continue obliquely, "I wasn't the least bit offended. We had a misunderstanding. The dismissal was the result of unfortunate timing."

Aunt Amelia's forehead crinkled. Tate's eyes flicked her way. "I see," he replied. "I am gratified to know this."

Later, in the carriage, Aunt Amelia huffed, "What on earth did that horrid man say to distress you?"

"It was nothing," said Prudence. "He made a political

statement and repented, thinking he had offended my sensibilities. I assured him he had not."

"You were too kind to him. It's a shame he turned out to be such a boor."

"On the contrary, ma'am. Mr. Tate was neither a boor nor a bore," Prudence replied. "He was positively full of fascinating information."

CHAPTER SEVENTEEN

Edingham-Greene, Wiltshire
2 August 1819

In western Wiltshire, the rest of July passed in relative peace. Now that people could again go abroad without fear, their rural enterprises resumed. The fields were bright with acres of healthy grain, the meadows bursting with summer color. The Weston family sank into its familiar rhythm.

Frustrated as she was by her cousin's state of affairs, Josephine had her own challenges to overcome, such as her propensity to search the horizon for crimson coats on horseback. Craving a distraction, she went to Middlemere and threw her arms round his neck.

"Papa, dearest, everyone in the neighborhood has been cooped up all summer. Wouldn't it be lovely if we held a dance here at Greenbank?"

Middlemere remained silent, leaving Josephine to rue her moment of impulse. Finally, he smiled. "That's a capital idea! Oh, it has been ages since we entertained; the ballroom must be in terrible disrepair."

Josephine beamed. "I'll manage! The draperies, for one thing, are quite moth-eaten; may I order new ones?"

"Yes, yes! And don't forget to have the parquet polished! Do you know what you're doing, my pet? There are the musicians to hire, refreshments, invitations, and heaven knows what else . . ."

"Never you mind. Maria will assist me."

As they talked, a youthful glow sprang up in the earl's face. The careworn lines softened around his eyes, his cheeks grew pinker, and Josephine thought fervently, *If only he might let himself fall in love with our dear Mrs. March!*

The date of the dance was settled for the nineteenth of August. Josephine wrote to ask Prudence whether she could come home for a few days. She even offered to invite Mr. MacNeal, "for it is ever so clear that he still thinks of you!"

Indeed, she had squealed so much at Prudence's recounting of the supper at Lord Driby's she'd been obliged to tell her family what pleased her so well. She made light of it, saying, "There is a gentleman whom Prudence sometimes encounters. They get along famously, but he is like a rabbit popping in and out of holes: here today, gone tomorrow."

"Sounds like a bounder to me!" remarked Edward.

"We have thought so, on occasion, but it seems he may have been unfairly judged. For the time being, though, he's in France, so Prudence must be patient."

Maria frowned. "What about the viscount? He seems so perfect for her."

"Yes," agreed Middlemere. "Aunt Staveley says Underwood is an attentive fellow, and it's only a matter of time before he proposes."

Ordinarily, Josephine would've agreed, but a burst of romance had fired her imagination. "Prudence tells it differently," she said with an air of confidence. "Lord Underwood is hopelessly uninteresting, and he has yet to show any real affection. I think she would be miserable in a marriage with him."

"Dear me!" cried Middlemere.

Josephine instantly regretted her lapse in discretion. "Oh, Papa! Prudence is keenly aware of her duty to establish herself well, but you cannot blame a girl for holding out hope."

"But how long must she wait?" demanded Maria. "She could grow into an old maid before this other fellow returns."

"She'd be a jinglebrain if she turned Underwood down," opined Edward around a mouthful of ham.

"Thank you for that bit of wisdom, sir," Josephine said dryly. "I'll be sure to repeat every word to your sister."

"Please do!" Edward replied with a grin. "And don't forget to credit me when it turns out I was right."

Josephine kept busy consulting with carpenters and drapers, planning refreshments, and meeting with the village dressmaker. So distracted was she that one day as she rummaged through her bureau for gloves, she encountered an unexpected package crammed far in the back. She stared in dismay, knowing full well it was the antique pistols.

"I was perfectly content having forgotten about you."

Whether this meant the weapons themselves or Lieutenant Quimby was not clear, even to herself. At any rate, at least a fortnight had passed since either she or Prudence had spoken about their keepsakes. Josephine had even released Maria from her nocturnal guard duties. Would the trances begin anew, now that the pistols had resurfaced? She bit her lip with unease.

"I should have Maria lock these up." As she tossed the bundle onto her bed, a slip of paper fluttered out and she spied the words, "Dear Lady Weston . . ." Intrigued, she unfolded it and read,

> *I couldn't help admiring this lovely brace of pistols, for I am somewhat of an aficionado of antique firearms. The inlay and silver filigree are in pristine condition, and the works are clean as a whistle. Based on their markings, I'd date them to the late 1720s. It's a wonder you didn't get hurt, considering the tremendous kick they must give. Again, it would be my pleasure to instruct you in their proper use and care.*
> *Your servant,*
> *Robt. Quimby*

Feeling slightly dizzy, Josephine clutched the note to her breast. "Such audacity!" she breathed as a blush crept into her cheeks.

Gentlemen—especially those of a lower social class—did not write notes, innocuous or otherwise, to ladies with whom they had the barest acquaintance. They certainly didn't use said notes to reiterate a scheme of dubious propriety. All those weeks, Quimby must have expected an acknowledgement from her. Josephine bit a knuckle. Well, how would she have responded had she found the note before he left Wiltshire? The question set her atremble. She recalled the sensation of her hand held warmly in his, and her heartbeat surged with mingled ecstasy and shame.

"No!" she gasped. "It's for the best! Oh, it would have been useless—nay, *shameless*—to encourage his attentions! My family would not permit such a match. Besides, I've likely blown the matter all out of proportion. There isn't a single romantic word in that note." She reread it to prove the point, though the mere fact of Quimby's having written it continued to enthrall her. "Very well," she said, "let's have a look at these weapons he purports to admire so much."

Josephine locked her bedroom door and laid the pistols out on the bed. Knowing an expert thought highly of them, she could better appreciate their beauty. She examined one handle and found the following inscription:

OUR GRATEFUL THANKS FOR SERVICES RENDERED

HRM KING GEORGE II

Who had earned this reward? What service had been rendered to the Crown? She considered her father's reticence on the subject, as well as Aunt Amelia's exhortation regarding the importance of secrecy, and suspected the answers did not lie in any history book. She carefully rebundled the pistols and clasped them to her breast. "His name is Robert," she murmured dreamily, tucking the note inside her desk and pushing the bundle back into the drawer.

9 August 1819

Preparations for the dance were now in full swing, and it was often evening before Josephine managed to catch up with the post. In the drawing room, she received Prudence's latest missive: just as Mr. MacNeal might finally get a chance to express his interest in her, Lord Underwood had begun to show signs of increasing devotion. As Prudence described it,

> *Aunt Amelia excused herself and stepped out of the Parlor.*
> *No sooner had she gone when he commenced Staring at me.*
> *"My lord," I exclaimed, "is there something on your mind?"*
> *To which he stammered, "I sh-should be most pleased if you would Consent to go d-driving some time."*
> *I paused a long Moment, then Told him I'd be honored. What else could I say? He looked so genuinely Pleased that I couldn't help thinking, You old Goose, he isn't half bad-looking. But what terrible Timing! What if Mr. MacNeal should come along and see us?*

Poor Prudence! Josephine tried to put herself in the same shoes. Could she be sanguine under such circumstances?

"Maria," she asked, "would you have been a dutiful wife if Providence had placed you well, but with a man you couldn't love?"

The nurse furrowed her brow. "I married my duty, 'ee might say, through lack o' choice, which is practically the same thing. I've found satisfaction in the service I've given. It never occurred to me a-gainsay my fortune."

Josephine rolled her eyes. *Must she always find the parable in things?* She turned to Edward and his three friends, ensconced at the card table. "What about you? If the roles were reversed and you married for money, would you be miserable or content?"

"That depends. Is she ugly?" Edward grinned sidelong at his mates. Their subsequent chortling died under Josephine's glare. "Very well," he relented. "Let us posit the notion that my wife is wealthy, tolerably handsome, but distant of feeling. Your question is whether I could lead a life of relative fulfillment?"

"Precisely."

Edward held her gaze for a long moment, then turned to wink at the others. "I'd thank my lucky stars! Marriage, Jo, is a social contract in which both parties seek a compromise. Since there can never be perfection in any relationship, why suffer also from poverty?"

"That's the most depressing thing I've heard all week."

"But it's the truth," he rejoined. He looked at her again, and his expression was inscrutable.

CHAPTER EIGHTEEN

London

12 August 1819

Three weeks had passed since she made her appeal to Lady Revelle, but Prudence had yet to receive a reply. Perhaps the lady considered it a terrible impertinence; perhaps she'd changed her mind. Prudence endeavored not to dwell on useless speculation. The knowledge that Mr. MacNeal still regarded her fondly was enough to sustain her. Then came the inevitable moment she had tried to forget: Lord Underwood pulled up in his curricle sporting a pair of grey Thoroughbreds and invoked her promise to go driving with him.

Courage, Prudence thought as she endured the fussings and admonitions of her excitable aunt. Underwood helped her into the two-seated carriage, then popped up beside her with the ease of a cat. Aunt Amelia waved madly as they set off down the street.

An afternoon ride in London was a popular affair—the object, of course, was to see and be seen. Regent's Street thronged with pedestrians, riders, and horse-drawn vehicles of all kinds. From the clothing and fine hats to the teams and conveyances themselves, everything and everyone was on display. Only the hardest of hearts would have hated this spectacle, and so gradually Prudence began to enjoy herself. To her surprise, Underwood as a driver was a man transformed. His usual diffidence vanished and his hooded eyes opened wide. He sat proudly erect, nodding at acquaintances passing by.

With a sinking feeling in her stomach, Prudence comprehended that Underwood was showing her off. To offset the impression that she relished the role, she pressed herself far away from him and adopted an expression of regal aloofness. She could do nothing, however, to prevent him from steering his team into the quiet lanes of Regent's Park.

No, no, no! she thought, panicking. *He wouldn't do this. Not now . . . he has barely spoken five words to me in our entire acquaintance—*

They came to a halt beneath a spreading oak tree. Underwood took her right hand and brought it to his lips. "My dear Miss Fairfeather, I've grown rather attached to you. Will you permit me the honor of paying you court?"

Prudence's heart pounded. *'Tis not an offer, at least, but bless me if I know what I should do about this.* She forced herself to focus on the essentials of the matter. If she gave her consent, that would preclude entertaining other suits. If she didn't, there was a good chance she'd have no suitors at all. "Dear me!" she croaked. "This is so sudden."

A frown line appeared between Underwood's wheat-colored brows. "I've called many times. You cannot be surprised at the depths of my interest."

She *was* surprised, actually, but that point was moot. *What to say now?*

"Sir, you are always welcome at Stanistead, but if you were to interpret this as some kind of promise—"

Underwood seemed to lose heart. "Dash it all, I *knew* it! You dislike me, don't you?"

"No—I . . . !" Prudence struggled to think. She felt through her skirt for the outline of the ring. *For heaven's sake, you dolt, don't frighten him off!*

Taking a deep breath, she slipped her hand round his and gave it a squeeze. "My lord, I've been so caught up in the Season I hadn't realized your attentions were an indication of deeper feelings. Please understand, you truly have caught me unawares."

Lord Underwood stared down at their clasped hands. She sensed a wave of emotion, tinged with awe. He had never touched a woman for this long.

"I am your slave, madam," he said huskily. "What would you have me do?"

Her voice remained calm, and her confidence grew. "Be patient with me. I'd like to finish the summer unencumbered by promises."

He brought her hand to his chest. "My dear Miss Fairfeather, I'll do whatever it takes to win your heart! What say you to this: I leave on the morrow for my country estate. You are free to associate with whomever you please. One month from today, we shall see how things stand."

"That is . . . more than generous of you," replied Prudence, trembling in relief. Misunderstanding her emotion, Underwood attempted to give her a kiss. She turned her face so his lips glanced off her cheek, but he did not seem to mind. Grinning like a madman, he grabbed the traces and clucked to his horses.

Back at Stanistead House, Aunt Amelia hovered in the front hall. Prudence deliberately removed her bonnet and gloves, then unbuttoned her spencer and handed it to Reese. Finally, the old lady could stand it no longer.

"Cruel girl! You have the nerves of a duelist. How fares Lord

Underwood?"

Prudence sidled into the parlor. "His Lordship desires to be my only suitor. I requested some time to think it over."

Aunt Amelia went scarlet. "You little fool! He is the finest bachelor you'll ever attract! This isn't a game, Prudence."

"I didn't turn him down. I only asked for a postponement. Underwood himself proposed the terms of our deal."

"Deal? *Deal?* Impossible girl!" cried Aunt Amelia, storming from the room.

"No, no," whispered Prudence, smiling to herself. "Not impossible. If anything, quite the opposite. Perhaps now my hopes are not utterly dashed."

13 August 1819

At breakfast the next morning, an envelope labeled only with her name lay by Prudence's plate. She slid it discreetly into her lap, saving it for a more opportune time. Once her lessons had ended, she went to her room and opened the note. It was written in tall, angled strokes:

> *Slow down, darling, you're getting ahead of yourself! I have a question for you: Whom shall you trust? The guardians who have lied to you all your life? I shall tell you this much— your name is not Fairfeather. No such family exists.*

The note ended here without signature. Prudence stared in disbelief. "No such family? What does that mean? Amelia and Papa have hidden things, but why would they lie?"

She reached into her pocket, gave the ring a quick rub, and made her way to Aunt Amelia's sitting room. She settled herself on a stool at the old woman's feet.

"Yes?" queried Amelia, counting the stitches on a slipper she was embroidering.

"What is my real name?"

"I beg your pardon?"

"My real surname. I have been wondering whether Fairfeather might be an alias."

"What, pray tell, would lead you to *that* conclusion?" asked Amelia, setting aside her sewing and glaring at Prudence.

"Intuition. Guesswork. It explains why you never want to speak of my parents."

Aunt Amelia heaved a great sigh. "You are the most maddening, overcurious creature! Very well. If you must know, when your parents died, you and your brother were given an alias and a contrived distant relationship with Lord Middlemere's wife. In truth, you share no blood with Lady Joanna Greene, nor even Lady Josephine."

That was far more than Prudence had expected to hear. "B-but why?" she stammered, starting to cry.

"For your safety. Oh, come now, Prudence! You desired the truth, did you not? Well, the truth can be cruel." After a moment, Aunt Amelia seemed to repent her harsh words, adding, "Thankfully, our arrangement has withstood the test of time. You have moved comfortably in Society without fear of identification. Henceforth, however, you assume certain risks. You must brace for the possibility that someone, someday, might attempt to expose your secret."

"*My* secret?" exclaimed Prudence. "This arrangement was none of my doing. What if I am found out? A nobleman's family—Lord Underwood's, for instance—might not take kindly to fraud."

Aunt Amelia made a calming motion with her hands. "The chance is slight. Lord Middlemere has created a mountain of paperwork to protect you."

"Protect me? I—"

"Prudence, you may as well accept it, for there is no undoing the scheme."

"Yes, but why were Edward and I in jeopardy, and why the cloak of darkness surrounding the identities of our parents?"

"I can tell you no more. That would make you vulnerable to those with a wicked agenda. I cannot impress on you strongly enough the importance of turning away anyone who would woo you with more knowledge." The old lady's voice trembled. "They would have taken a solemn Oath—we *all* took that Oath—never to speak of it again."

The image of Lady Revelle's face flashed through Prudence's mind, and a feeling of shame rose in her stomach. She had allowed a perfect stranger to plant the seed of doubt in her head, yet here was her guardian answering questions, albeit reluctantly. Lady Revelle had not only attempted to place a wedge between them, she had broken a serious vow.

What kind of trouble have I set in motion?

"Forgive me," she rasped. "I see that my inquisitiveness pains you, but could you at least tell me one real thing about my parents?"

Aunt Amelia reached out to touch a strand of Prudence's honey-gold hair. "She was tall and elegant, like you, though her hair was much fairer. You have *his* eyes. In appearance alone, you resemble your father. Edward favors your mother."

Prudence laid her head on Amelia's lap. "Oh, why did you

give me that box?" Aunt Amelia sighed. "I was compelled to. Believe me, if I could have, I'd have gladly destroyed it. Limit your contact with those accursed Talismans. Better yet, make your peace with them and burn the whole lot."

Prudence shuddered.

"No?" queried the aunt. "Then at the least you must always leave them at home."

So Amelia guessed what Prudence almost lost in the Thames! She kissed the old lady's hand. "Are *you* my relative anyway?"

The aunt shook her head. "You and your brother have no living family. I truly am Lady Josephine's great aunt, but even *I* am a fraud . . . I was not born Amelia Staveley. My identity was changed around the same time as yours. See? You and Edward are not alone in your plight—countless others were also bereft of their past."

"So the Inheritance also runs in Josephine's blood?"

Aunt Amelia's nostrils flared, but she answered nonetheless. "Like the color of one's eyes, Inheritance is the expression of certain traits from both parents. Not everyone would receive this gift in their blood—even you, Prudence, might not have it. Whether you do or do not makes no difference now. I ask you to accept that and go on with your life."

Prudence spent many hours absorbing the blow. After debating whether or not to inform Josephine, she decided her friend was entitled to know everything she did about this baffling Inheritance, especially since Middlemere would likely never give her even a basic understanding.

It struck Prudence as ironic that the keepsakes—or Talismans—had proved the weakest link in her guardians' scheme. Some overwhelming force had bound the aunt to bequeath them, and in Prudence's hands they had prompted a new chain of events. The Talismans had piqued her curiosity, leading her to ask questions; compulsion had made her send the ring for repairs; the ring broadcast her identity when she wore it in public; and now, thanks to that foolish inquiry, Lady Revelle showed an unsettling interest in her.

"I will never again make that kind of mistake," she said after sealing this difficult letter. "As much as I desire to know more about the history of my Talismans, I refuse to let curiosity supersede what is right."

She made this last vow to herself, for she'd withheld the action which had set this unhappy revelation in motion. Josephine would never know she had contacted Lady Revelle, would never know she had not merely deduced that Fairfeather was an alias.

Prudence squeezed the bridge of her nose, ashamed but resigned that secrecy and subterfuge were the unfortunate cost of maintaining her pride.

CHAPTER NINETEEN

Edingham-Greene, Wiltshire
12 August 1819

If it wasn't bad enough that Lord Underwood might any day state his intentions to Prudence, the twelfth instant brought Josephine still more unhappy tidings: Prudence would not be coming home for the dance. Aunt Amelia, anticipating a favorable turn of events, had no desire to leave London, and Prudence would not budge from the one place where Mr. MacNeal could find her.

Four days later, as she bustled into the dining room, Josephine caught the words "never figured her for a fool!" tumbling from Edward's lips.

"What've I done now?"

"Not you—my pigheaded sister has refused Underwood's suit!" Edward gestured in disgust at the letter in Middlemere's hand.

Josephine's breath caught in her throat. She eyed a second letter which lay by her plate. "I'm sure she has her reasons."

Maria huffed, "It's that rabbit 'ee mentioned, what loves France better than her!"

"Now, all of you!" cried Middlemere. "She did not refuse Underwood altogether. She merely put him off for a while."

"Right. Let's see what she has to say for herself." Josephine snatched the other letter and retired to her nook. Prudence's explanation astonished her. Josephine admired her cousin's determination, but what if this bold and reckless decision had all been for naught?

If it weren't for that conversation with Mr. Tate, she'd be engaged now, realized Josephine. "Oh, Prudence," she murmured, "I don't suppose either of us was meant to have the men who charmed us so."

She went upstairs to compose a reply:

> *I commend you for arranging things so well. Now Underwood has no claim if a better offer comes along. But, truly, will it ever? You have one month to decide. Will you (barring any new developments) accept a loveless, albeit sound, match?*

Afterward, she chewed thoughtfully on the end of her quill, a smile lifting one corner of her mouth. "However," she added aloud, "this is the single most willful and irrational thing you've ever done, Prudence Fairfeather, and I congratulate you for it!"

After posting that letter, Josephine grew so busy she could scarcely find time to eat, let alone reflect on the state of affairs in London. On Wednesday morning, she was surprised to receive yet another missive from her cousin. She carried it out to the orchard and under the shade of an apple tree broke open the seal.

> *My dear Josephine, I hope you're sitting down, for I have staggering news . . .*

19 August 1819

The day of the dance finally arrived. Josephine had closeted herself all afternoon, and now she waited, beaming and trembling, inside her front door.

Beside her stood Lord Middlemere in a coat of bright blue, with buff breeches and silk stockings, and a cravat artfully tied. His long hair was queued; his clothes were not at all rumpled. Josephine, in fact, had never seen him look so well. A sidelong glance at the enraptured Mrs. March revealed she held similar thoughts.

Equally splendid in a dark green coat and mustard waistcoat, Edward attracted attention of his own, though he seemed determined not to notice. He bowed to the guests with stiff-spined aloofness, speaking largely in monosyllables.

Josephine, feeling the burden of a double challenge, whispered, "Be patient!" to Mrs. March. Next, she elbowed Edward, hissing, "Smile!" He obliged her by revealing his teeth.

The party moved into the ballroom, which had been utterly transformed. The restored parquet and brass sconces shone; the upholstery and draperies were crisp and bright. An army of liveried footmen trooped about with trays of refreshments. An orchestra played a grand march as the gathering entered. Everyone gasped. Most folks hadn't set foot inside Greenbank in years.

The orchestra sounded a fanfare. Josephine stepped to the center of the room. "Dearest friends and neighbors, welcome to our home. May this day begin a new era for Greenbank!"

All the guests cheered. Josephine looked over at Edward, whom she expected to join her in the first dance. Instead, Middlemere stepped forward with his gloved hand outstretched. The orchestra struck up a minuet, and, for the first time in her life, she danced with her father. He followed the figures stiffly but with obvious expertise. When the minuet was done, she steered directly for Mrs. March and pressed that lady's hand into his. Embarrassed and awkward, they nevertheless obliged her by dancing two or three tunes. For the rest of the evening, Lord Middlemere could be found at Mrs. March's side.

Meanwhile, Josephine took a turn with nearly every male in the room. During one interval, she found herself standing by Edward, who'd thus far avoided what he called "that infernal activity." He had finally relaxed, striking a gallant pose and chuckling at the drunken antics of his friends.

Josephine elbowed him. "Mr. Fairfeather, is this not marvelous to see?"

"If you say so, milady."

Roland and Peter staggered by, spilling punch as they went. Roland squinted at Edward. "How can you, you dog? She's languishing!"

"I beg your pardon?" inquired Edward coolly.

"Lady Josephine, sir, whom you are supposed to be squiring, has no partner, and you haven't even the decency to give her your arm. You ought to be ashamed!"

"We'd happily offer our services," added Peter, "but really, old boy, she's wearing us out! Could you not take her off our hands for a while?"

Josephine laughed. "Poor Edward can't abide the humiliation he'd endure if I had to guide him through the figures."

"That does it," declared Edward, handing Peter his glass. He faced Josephine and bowed low. "My lady, wilt thou do me the honor of tolerating my two left feet?"

Josephine could not contain her astonishment. She

curtseyed in return. "Indeed, sir, I'd be delighted." She gave him her hand and they entered a swift reel. Edward was in fact an accomplished dancer. His expression soon softened, and Josephine thought he might even be enjoying himself.

"Your tutoring has paid off," he remarked as they came together and parted.

"I'm a natural," said Josephine the next time they passed.

"The tutor was for your sister."

Edward guffawed and then added, "That's a pretty frock."

"Mine?" puzzled Josephine, for he had yet to look directly at her.

"Of course!" he laughed, suddenly meeting her eyes. "Whom else's should I mean? It's a becoming color for you."

Her gown had tiny, embroidered flowers scattered across a field of pale peach silk. Her hair was done up in a twist on the crown, set with ivory combs that had once belonged to her mother. Long chestnut tendrils cascaded down her neck. She had taken great care to look her best, but she had not expected Edward of all people to remark upon it.

"Edward Fairfeather, I believe that's the nicest thing you've ever said to me."

"You deserve it and more. You're the finest lady in this room."

He said this so sincerely that Josephine's lip trembled with surprise. "Heavens, Eddie!"

The reel ended and the orchestra struck up a another tune, one of those newfangled dances which foreigners called the "waltz." The crowd murmured. Josephine suspected they all secretly wanted to know it, but they'd heard it was improper and banned by the best assembly rooms. She glanced about, wondering who had ordered this piece. Now Edward would bow out, and just when he had finally been coaxed to stir a leg.

Instead, he slid an arm across her back and took her right hand in his left. "Let's see what a natural you *truly* are, m'dear! I'll talk you through it. We start with a short march. Put your arm around me, and we'll show these bumpkins a thing or two!"

Edward's voice and firm touch led her along like a beacon. The dance began with an intimate, face-to-face pirouette. As it gradually increased in complexity and tempo, Josephine struggled with the challenging footwork. For the final section, Edward took her waist and guided her, swooping and whirling, round the floor. The other guests stood back, watching in astonishment as they demonstrated. Presently, several of the braver ones joined in, until half a dozen couples completed the dance and came to a halt in a swirl of applause. Edward and Josephine staggered off arm in arm, laughing and breathless.

"You're a fraud!" she accused. "Where on earth did you learn how to waltz?"

Edward smiled slyly. "When I was exiled in London, I was known to frequent the assemblies. I made a point of learning to waltz, as all rebellious souls do. How the matrons swooned when I endangered their daughters' precious reputations!"

"Naughty boy! You jolly well kidnapped me!"

"You enjoyed it, didn't you?"

A guilty blush crept up Josephine's cheeks. "Anyway, don't ever let me hear you disparage dancing again!"

"But I detest it!" he said without conviction. They grinned at each other in a rare moment of harmony. For some reason the blood was rushing in Josephine's ears and she felt herself tumbling into the ocean of Edward's eyes. He reached down and lifted her hand. "Ah, Josephine—" he began.

Peter Bradford jostled by. "I say, Fairfeather!" he slurred. "How smashing your cousin looks tonight! If you don't kiss her, then I shall!"

Edward's hand grabbed for Peter's cravat. "Shove off, you drunken fool!"

"See here—!" protested Peter.

"Oh, Edward, leave him be!" chided Josephine.

Edward released his captive, who quickly retreated. "Forgive me, Jo. Perhaps I should take some air. Will you . . . will you join me outside?"

Josephine nodded. As they wended their way through the crowd, Edward seized and downed a glass of champagne. They exited the ballroom and took refuge on the terrace. It was a beautiful, cloudless night. Crickets chirped in the shrubbery, and the sound of the orchestra was muted but sweet. Josephine swayed to the music, circling Edward as she continued to practice the waltz. He stood in one spot, watching her with hooded eyes.

She nudged his shoulder with an elbow. "I should punish you for causing a scandal during my first outing as hostess. Why do I think you personally ordered that dance?"

"Not like that," he replied. "You've added a fourth step. The waltz is in three-quarters time. Let me show you again." He stepped forward and placed his right hand on her waist, then lifted her left hand and held it lightly by the thumb and forefinger. As they pirouetted slowly on the balls of their feet, he said, "The first part is simple. Mirror what I do."

"That's the trick, isn't it? I've never danced so closely before." She had nowhere to look except straight into his eyes. *Lord have mercy, no wonder the matrons dislike it!*

They moved together in the darkness, Edward counting out

the beats. "Now for the Sauteuse. Turn and hop, then *bourrée*, mind my toes *s'il vous plait.*"

The last part, the Jeté, was by far Josephine's favorite. She would have liked to leap about forever, dipping this way and that, supported by a partner's strong arm. After a second complete circuit of the terrace, Edward stopped and gave her a quick twirl. When she came to a halt, they stood so closely their knees nearly touched. They remained in that pose, panting, hands held aloft, for a very long moment until he twined their fingers and lowered them together.

"You look exceptional tonight," he said. "Have I told you already?"

Josephine felt again that strange rush in her ears. "Yes, you said something rather complimentary, I think."

"The truth is, dear Jo, you are always lovely to me."

She was so astounded by this statement and the husky manner in which it was said that she stood motionless as Edward stooped nearer and nearer. He reached up and caressed one side of her face. Slowly, purposefully, he tilted her chin. Her breath faltered in puzzlement as the tip of his nose feathered her cheek.

"Edward?" she squeaked.

Now his mouth fell against hers and he drew her close to his chest. Josephine had kissed boys before, in her younger, more impulsive days, but never had *she* been anyone's target. The act of kissing improved, she reflected dimly, when one's partner kissed back. Without thinking, she let an arm curl round his neck; this only encouraged him to redouble his passion. It wasn't remotely a sweet sort of kiss, but a desperate one, as if he'd thrown caution to the wind.

For a moment, she reveled in his unfettered longing; the

warmth and closeness of his body and mouth answered some primal need locked deep inside her. Then reality crashed.

Wait! This is Edward! What on earth am I doing?

Prudence's letter had made everything so complicated. Josephine pulled back with a gasp. "We shouldn't be doing this!"

"Why not?" he asked, nuzzling the curve of her jaw. "I think you rather enjoy it."

She *did*, that was the trouble. Now her legs turned to jelly as he discovered a sensuous place on her throat. Josephine yelped and dug her fingernails into his shoulder. "Stop! It isn't proper! I shouldn't even be out here, alone with you."

Edward gave a sharp laugh. "Now, I *must* be foxed, because I can't imagine what could be improper about cousins sharing a breath of air on the terrace."

"Sharing a breath of air?" she rejoined, extracting herself from his arms. "Is that what you call this? Oh, Edward! We are *not* cousins, and that's the least of my reasons."

He took her by the elbows and peered into her eyes. "The wiser part of me says if it's true, all the better. Let us kiss again and afterward consider your other objections. The fool compels me to ask *what in God's name are you talking about?*" His voice rose in volume, bespeaking a dangerous shattering of nerves.

"I'm sorry, but it's true. I found out yesterday. Prudence revealed everything—we are not cousins, nor blood relations of any sort. I am also in shock." Without explaining why the subject had been raised, she summarized the facts of the Fairfeathers' alias. Eyes brimming with tears, she added, "But it matters nothing to me. You and Prudence will always be my cousins."

Edward chuckled bitterly. "I should be happy we are not! So why ain't I, Jo?"

"You're making no sense. Come now, Edward. It doesn't change a thing."

He shuddered as if his soul was turning to ice. "On the contrary, it changes *everything!* I'm not even your poor relation. Now I am merely poor."

"No, no! You shall have a healthy portion. Papa will see to it."

Edward's nostrils flared. "Did the last few minutes mean nothing to you? Josephine Weston, it's not the portion I desire!"

It was Josephine's turn to be stunned. "That's not fair!" she lashed out. "You cannot ask me to find meaning in an event that was so wholly unexpected, and I'm sorry if my reaction led you to believe I had been hoping for it!"

Edward turned heel and strode toward the ballroom.

"Edward, come back!" Josephine gathered her skirt and hurried in his wake. By the time she reached the doorway, she could see his head bobbing distantly over the crowd. It passed through the main entrance and thence out of sight.

Josephine sighed. She had no time to dwell on Edward's flight. The hour was late and guests were beginning to take their leave. Peter and Roland sidled up, fully in their cups. Peter leant forward and kissed her clumsily on the cheek.

"There. I told you *someone* must do it, and God knows dour old Eddie hasn't the nerve!"

"Get back, odious whelp!" hissed Josephine. It took her moment to realize his accusation was innocent. She exhaled to calm herself. "Speaking of Edward, where's he gone off to, anyway?"

Roland gestured toward the door while stifling a belch. "Did you and he have another of your famous tiffs?"

"Go home," she said tightly. "I'll cuff anyone I find here in the morning!" The young men fled. "One of our famous tiffs," she muttered. "Indeed!"

Josephine spent the next hour seeing off each of her guests. As the servants doused the sconces, she made her way to Edward's room and peered inside. He lay sprawled in an armchair, still booted but in shirtsleeves and perfectly unconscious. Josephine pulled a half-empty bottle of gin from the crook of his arm, then fetched a pillow and the coverlet from his bed and arranged his sagging head in a more comfortable way.

"Poor Edward!" She ran a hand along his brow, smoothing back the forelock of bright-yellow hair. On impulse, she bent and bussed his cheek.

Edward shifted and murmured but did not awaken. Josephine smiled tenderly at the young man she had known all her life. It was a rotten trick to find out he was half in love with her, though it explained almost everything he'd done over the last several months.

"This will complicate things," she murmured, blowing out the lights.

As for the sensation she had felt when he kissed her on the terrace, well, it signified nothing. While she'd indulged Edward's curiosity—and admittedly her own—she had imagined herself in the arms of another man altogether.

21 August 1819

She slept late the next day and didn't write Prudence until Saturday morning. The interlude with Edward she pointedly left out. After breakfast, she took a book out onto the terrace. The sound of footsteps broke her concentration.

"Hullo, Jo," Edward said meekly. This was the first she had seen of him since the dance.

"Hullo, Eddie."

He slouched against the balustrade, hands in his pockets. Josephine patted the end of her chaise. He settled at her feet, eyeing her like a dog who expects a beating.

"Listen," she said. "I don't care about the wretched alias. I don't care where you came from. Do you think, though, that you could keep this revelation from Papa?"

Edward shrugged. "What's another obligation after a lifetime of them?"

"Please, stop that."

"Very well, if you insist."

Josephine's eyes flashed. "Stop it, Edward. I don't like to see you submissive, but I won't quarrel with you either."

"No quarreling. No, indeed." His eyes drifted around the terrace, where everything had changed between them two nights before. "It felt good, getting along with you. Quite splendid." As he smiled at this memory, the angles of his face softened. He turned and put his hand over hers. "I'm sorry I ran out on you. That was very bad form."

Josephine had been dreading this part of the conversation. "So what do we do now?"

He regarded her hopefully. "If you're amenable, we could explore the possibility of a romance between us. I know you're still young. I had not expected to alert you to my feelings so soon. It just happened, I suppose."

Josephine shut her eyes. "Edward, the notion that we have no blood connection is disorienting enough . . ."

"Don't you see? As long as everyone thinks we're cousins, we have the advantage of constant intimacy. We could keep our affair clandestine for as long as it suits us."

Josephine's breath caught. "Your plan violates every accepted mode of behavior!"

"Right then. I retract the suggestion, though you can't blame me for thinking it." Edward lifted her hand and brought it to his lips. Josephine gently but firmly withdrew it. Her expression must have conveyed the strength of her hidden convictions, for he scowled and leapt to his feet.

"Well, if that's how it shall be, then I'm returning to Oxford."

"But—"

"I'm not some shiftless sod!" he declared, backing away. "Perhaps, with hard work, I can *earn* your respect. Now, if you'll excuse me—"

He turned and strode off, leaving Josephine agape. The next morning, as promised, Edward departed Greenbank.

CHAPTER TWENTY

London
24 August 1819

O ver the past fortnight, London had emptied itself of most of the *beau monde*. Prudence now saw how pointless her postponement of Underwood had been; there would be no major events for many weeks to come. Nonetheless, she and Aunt Amelia had been invited to attend an early season foxhunt at the Hertfordshire estate of Sir Waltham de Pelvain. Prudence had no idea how they'd managed to secure the nod— likely Underwood had something to do with it. However it had been done, she needed a more fashionable riding kit.

In the meantime, a letter came from Josephine concerning the dance. It began with an agonized lament about their false consanguinity, which she had for some reason, relayed to Edward. Prudence winced, wondering what impact this had had on her brother. As Josephine did not elaborate, she contented herself with the recounting of the dance, much of which she read aloud for the amusement of Aunt Amelia. The old woman was especially attentive during the passages about Edward.

"Do you think your brother is fond of Lady Josephine?" she asked.

"It seems so, does it not? That would explain his odd behavior all summer."

"Hmmph. It would not be a poor match," mused Aunt Amelia, tapping her chin.

Prudence guffawed. "On the contrary, it would be the worst match imaginable! They'd break all the dishes inside of a week!"

Aunt Amelia glowered sidelong at her. "She's still a child. Her temperament will improve. Anyway, he is not yet worthy of her hand. Your brother, Prudence, needs to sort out his head. Give them a couple of years. We shall see where things go."

Prudence was still laughing when Reese announced the dressmaker, who'd come for a fitting. Aunt Amelia, unfortunately, had grown inspired by these idle thoughts of matchmaking. As the dressmaker made her adjustments, the old lady fired off inquiries about the latest fashion in wedding gowns.

"Madam!" screeched Prudence, popping several pins from her waistline.

The dressmaker howled. Prudence tried to convince her that a riding costume required some latitude for movement. When her argument failed, she inhaled rebelliously to expand the upper measurements. After that mishap at the boating party, she must not have any cause to dread a scene at the hunt; fainting from an overly tight bodice posed exactly that sort of threat. Then she glared at Aunt Amelia, who had resumed the topic of wedding finery.

Soon she'll be planning the nursery! thought Prudence miserably.

Another week went by, and the deadline with Underwood was three-quarters expired. He had been as good as his word, making no contact whatsoever since the day he left London—of course, neither had Prudence heard aught from Mr. MacNeal. Now, to her consternation, Josephine began to give counsel about Underwood's return:

> *You might learn to love him. Besides, you can easily find fulfillment in a world of such privilege. Honestly, a fate at Underwood's side does not sound that terrible!*

"I suppose not," Prudence muttered. Her spirits were lifted, however, by a diverting story from home.

Edward had evidently made some kind of arrangement with his friends to look in on Josephine after his departure. Every day, one or more of them would drop by for a visit. Roland and Peter had taken up a new hobby: they had purchased an old fencing manual and a pair of rusty foils and planned to teach themselves to fence. Greenbank's front drive made the perfect staging area. Josephine liked to watch them from a comfortable chair placed out on the lawn.

Arthur Grant happened by one day and found the youngsters hard at it. He tore off his jacket, crying, "Tolly, give me your sword!" then grabbed a foil and advanced toward Peter. His blade flashed repeatedly, landing touches all over Peter's chest until the boy collapsed onto the gravel, gasping for mercy.

"For heaven's sake, Arthur!" complained Josephine. "Leave them be."

Arthur drew a sleeve across his sweat-dampened forehead. "Without proper instruction, they will never be anything more than hacks."

"It's unconscionable of you to mock them. Their fathers aren't rich enough to hire a fencing master. Why don't *you* teach them, if you think you're so expert?"

Arthur glanced from Roland to Peter. "Very well, I shall. You fellows will obey me, hear? Any cheek, and I'll take Lady Weston riding instead."

The boys shrugged, and Arthur started in directly, beginning with static poses. Roland and Peter champed at the bit—they had no desire to master their patience; they wanted to get on with the exciting business of sword fighting. Arthur, however, had them at his mercy. Josephine could only pray that he had not spoiled their fun.

By the end of the letter, Prudence was laughing so hard she attracted Aunt Amelia's attention and was compelled to read it aloud all over again.

"One thing is certain," remarked Aunt Amelia. "That Lady Josephine has the neighborhood wrapped around her little finger."

Prudence agreed. "And she's blind to how deeply her sycophants worship her."

Bolton Manor, Hertfordshire
4 September 1819

The weekend of the cub hunt began without any hint of trouble.

Prudence stood before the looking glass, admiring her attire. The bright blue wool jacket had ruching across the shoulders and frills at the cuffs. Its matching skirt ended in a long train that flowed to the left, designed to drape elegantly as she rode in the sidesaddle. A crisp white neck ruff completed the ensemble. She'd performed enough contortions during the fittings to ensure reasonable flexibility. Smiling, Prudence slipped on the matching blue bonnet, pulled loose a couple of pin curls, and fluffed the white ostrich feather.

"Too bad the gentlemen will be more preoccupied with their hounds than a beauty like you," said the aunt, chucking her under the chin.

They descended to the rear courtyard and assembled with the others. The air was chilly for early September. Weak fingers of daylight probed through broken clouds. Fog crept over the house and clung to every corner.

Prudence took her place in the mounting block queue. One by one the grooms led forward the mounts and helped the ladies situate themselves. The mare that Aunt Amelia had brought for her was an indolent creature, but Prudence didn't mind. She had only eight days left of freedom and she meant to have a good time.

The party filed from the courtyard, led first by a phalanx of important men, then a throng of eager younger gentlemen, followed by the young ladies and three carriages full of elders. On the lawn, they met the hounds held in check by their handlers. Many were young, barely out of puppyhood, here to sample their first taste of a kill and to cull the neighborhood's fox population of its younger, weaker members.

The field moved sedately, backing the hounds as they were driven by the huntsmen toward a distant covert where foxes likely hid. The ladies and gentlemen trailed the pack for more than half an hour when there sounded a blast followed by the baying of hounds. The first part of the field surged forward. Two or three ladies galloped after. Prudence, who had no desire to find herself unhorsed, hung back with the majority. It soon began to mist. The ladies reined up to discuss whether to return to the house. Everyone seemed of an accord: their interest in the hunt had waned with the weather.

One woman turned to Prudence. "Well, Miss Fairfeather, what say *you*? Shall we press on so you may get a glimpse of the dashing William MacNeal?"

A ripple of interest flowed through the group. Prudence, who was startled by this assertion, said, "You're mistaken, Miss Postlethwaite. He is not a member of this party."

The others concurred: Mr. MacNeal was definitely not at Bolton Manor.

Miss Postlethwaite disagreed. "But I saw him below my window, standing apart from the others, with unshaven face and gimlet eyes. He looked positively *wild!*"

Several ladies oohed, others tittered. Prudence was puzzled. Surely Miss Postlethwaite was trying to bait her, but why would anyone connect her with Mr. MacNeal when she hadn't seen him in two months? She waved a dismissive hand. "Shall we head for the house?"

"How coolly she parries!" taunted Miss Postlethwaite. "What would Lord Underwood think if he knew her other lover was here?"

"*Edwina!*" screeched another rider, prompting a fresh ripple of titters.

Just then, a fox burst from the tree line and scampered between the legs of their horses. Mounts reared, ladies screamed, and everyone leant forward, fighting for control. Now a pack of barking dogs burst into their midst. Prudence's mare had had enough—she bolted for the woods.

Though brush, over logs, and zigzagging between trees, the mare ran full tilt as Prudence fought to keep her seat. Nearly a mile away, at the edge of a deep defile, she finally reined in her mount. She let the mare pick her way down to the stream for a drink.

"Dear me!" muttered Prudence, thrusting her gloves into a pouch slung across her chest. "Why do I always find myself in such horrid predicaments?" She plucked at the briars stuck all over her train, thinking uncharitable thoughts about Edwina Postlethwaite. Her hands grew cold and drifted back to the pouch. She reached for her gloves and pulled them on, scanning the forest for other members of her party. Her fingers were stiff, making her elegant gloves of kid leather feel coarse, as if hardened by years of weather and use. The gloves slid on without hesitation, beaded fringe jangling as they went. Prudence kept her gaze fixed on the ridgeline above.

She sat up straight, head cocked. Somewhere nearby, water gushed in great torrents. Prudence looked down at the stream bubbling gently at the mare's feet. Now she became aware of a dozen other sounds, like the flapping of geese high overhead and a pair of deer stepping through the underbrush two hundred yards away. She perceived a hidden squirrel gnawing on a nut and the hum of bees in a hollow log. Then she heard the sound of a rider on horseback.

Though she could see no one, Prudence sensed he was there, above on the ridge.

She opened her mouth to hail him when a gunshot rang out and something whizzed past her ear. Startled, she spun her mount, urging the mare up the embankment. Another shot sounded, followed by a sharp tug as a ball tore through her left sleeve. For a long, frozen moment, she stared in fascination at the twin holes that had punctured the pleat before detachment gave way to a spasm of alarm. Remaining horsed at this point seemed suicidal—it made her a much clearer target. Prudence unhooked her leg from the saddle and threw herself to the ground. She landed, sprawling, on a carpet of wet leaves. The mare clambered out of the defile and sped away without her.

Prudence lay motionless, trying to collect her wits. Her nose wrinkled against the onslaught of leaf particles and mold. Earthy dampness seeped through her dress.

"What'll I *do?*"

In her mind's eye, she distinguished a pair of hands loading a pistol. Powder whisked down the length of a barrel. She heard the plunk of a metal ball rammed home with a rod. The cold deliberateness of it chilled her. This ordeal was no accident, and it would not end until her life was snuffed out. Over the scraping of her own ragged breaths, she thought she could make out another set of hoofbeats; whether rescuer or accomplice, she could not tell. Rather than risk hailing the new rider, she scrambled through the slippery loam and dived behind a clump of exposed roots. The instant she reached shelter, a third shot was fired.

"Stop!" she shrieked. Peering between the gnarled roots, she spied a man sitting on horseback about fifty feet away, a smoking pistol in hand. A wool scarf obscured the lower part of his face, but his brow furrowed in an unmistakable scowl. He seemed to be scanning the opposite ridge. His gaze shifted downward, halting when it came to rest on her crude hiding place. He nudged his horse in her direction.

"Dear God," breathed Prudence. "I'm going to die!"

Just then, the roots shifted under her and the embankment collapsed.

The drizzle had grown so heavy that the three open carriages had already turned back. Everyone was eager to get close to a fire. They were passing along a road edging a wooded ravine when a figure on foot lurched out from the underbrush. The ladies screamed. When they saw the figure carried an unconscious woman, they screamed yet again. All three drivers brought their vehicles to a halt.

"Who is this, sir?" called Lady de Pelvain. "What has happened to her?"

The man staggered forward. No one recognized him, for he was covered with mud and had a scarf round his mouth. "It's Miss Fairfeather!" he panted in a muffled voice. "There's been an accident. Is there room in your carriage?"

"Prudence!" shrieked Amelia Staveley. In a mad scramble, footmen helped elders in and out of the equipages until they had made room for the victim. The anonymous Samaritan lifted her onto one of the seats, then crouched beside her, brazenly clutching her limp hand to his breast. The coaches lurched into motion.

"What happened?" demanded Miss Staveley. "We heard shooting in the woods."

The stranger did not take his eyes from the girl. "She fell off her horse, and then the streambank collapsed."

Miss Staveley's eyes narrowed. "What do you mean? Where are the others? Was she alone in that ravine . . . with *you?*" Conscious of an audience, she clapped a hand to her mouth.

"No, ma'am. Her horse had apparently run off from the ladies' entourage. I happened by as the accident occurred." As the carriages neared the stables, he added, "I'll go for the doctor. Madam, what is his direction?"

Lady de Pelvain described the way. The stranger sprang from the carriage and ran toward the stables. They pulled into the courtyard in a tumult. A servant carried Miss Fairfeather upstairs, trailed by her aunt, the hostess, and several chambermaids.

Meanwhile, the elders gathered in the parlor, speaking in horrified whispers, insensible to their mist-dampened clothes. The younger ladies began to arrive, breathless and ignorant of this latest development. Now the murmurings began, and they continued for another hour until the menfolk returned.

Prudence fought her way back to consciousness. She parted her swollen eyelids and Aunt Amelia wheeled into view, but the throbbing pain in her skull forced her to close them again. On a later attempt, she observed a serving girl and some gentleman who must be the doctor.

"Hallo," she murmured through thickened lips. "Am I going to live?"

"You're a very lucky girl," the physician affirmed. "Bruised ribs and a mild concussion are all that you suffer." He turned to Aunt Amelia. "Bed rest and no traveling for one week."

"Thank God! Oh, Prudence!" Aunt Amelia clutched at her hand. "My dear child, how did this happen?"

"Let her be," the doctor said sternly. "The explanations can come later." He ushered Aunt Amelia out, leaving Prudence in the care of a chambermaid.

"Water, please," Prudence croaked. "And pen and paper. Are you able to write?"

"Lud miss, no, and I don't think the doctor would like you to, either."

"Well, I simply must. Only a few lines, I promise. Will you help me?"

A search of the room turned up the essential supplies. Wincing, Prudence rolled onto her side and scratched out a brief note. She ended with:

> *Josephine, I despair, for someone with evil intent must have discovered my true identity! Why else would anyone want to kill me?*

She sealed it and bade the maid post it as soon as she could. Then Prudence lay back, exhausted, and fell into a fitful sleep.

Muffled cries. Oh, God, she was suffocating! A gasp as fresh air flooded her lungs. Strong arms cradled her shoulders. Her eyes would not open. All her senses were overwhelmed by strangely amplified sound.

"It's so loud!" she moaned. "Make him stop shooting at me!"

"I made him stop. He's gone now. I won't let him hurt you."

Scraping noises, then the sensation of her body being freed from a great weight.

"Dear God, are you shot?" She didn't know. She was numb all over. Now came the sound of rending fabric. "No, praise be! 'Tis but a very near miss." He was gone for a moment, then returned and cupped a hand to her lips, saying, "Here's a little water. Drink if you can."

As she sipped the cool liquid, she opened one eye and took in the pulled-down hat and the scarf wound round his face. The shooter!

She flailed wildly at him, but it hurt so much to move. In the end, she could only scream and faint dead away.

She woke with a start. The maid rushed to her side and applied a sponge to her face. "Lud, mum, you sure had a fright!"

Prudence clutched the bedclothes, breathing rapidly. The same man who'd tried to kill her had then saved her life. How could that be?

5 September 1819

She woke reluctantly, for her head hurt something awful. The chambermaid brought her a tray with tea and porridge, then handed over a note, saying, "Yesterday a gen'leman gave it to Nob the Groom, who gave it to Hayes, who then gave it to me."

"A gentleman?"

"Ay, th' one what saved ye, the one as was wearin' the scarf."

Prudence stared at the maid, her heart seizing with fear. *What could he possibly have to say?* With shaking hands, she unfolded it and read,

> *I didn't shoot at you, I swear it! Do you have some enemy you're aware of? I long to explain, but I must fly. The groom stands ready—*
>
> *One favor I beg: pass no judgments, nor make any decisions till I can see you again.*
>
> *– W.M.*
>
> *P.S. I placed those strange gloves in your gear.*

Prudence crumpled the page. A cascade of pain shot through the back of her skull. *W.M.* . . . William MacNeal? Certainly—who else? Relief and confusion worked at odds with each other. She longed to see him and ask what had happened in that ravine.

So, by his own admission, he *had* been at Bolton and he *was* the man she had seen holding a gun. Half-formed questions swirled in her mind. Had he come to Bolton to see her? Or to kill her? No, the shooter couldn't have been MacNeal. If he'd wanted her dead, he'd have left her to smother under the landslide. But *someone* had fired at her . . .

There was a knock at the door, and Aunt Amelia poked her head in. Prudence shoved the note under the bedcovers and beckoned her forth.

"The others are leaving," said the aunt. "They've been asking after you."

It was too early in the morning for a general departure. "I didn't hear much music last night. Did they cancel the ball on my account?"

"No, but the mood was subdued and most retired before long. Lady de Pelvain is disgruntled, but that's neither here nor there." Aunt Amelia leant in close and added in an undertone, "Tell me, my little troublemaker, have you got any of those artifacts here?"

Prudence furrowed her brow. "Not at all! I swear it! Why do you ask?"

"Never mind." The aunt gave Prudence a probing look. "Do you recall hearing gunshots?"

Prudence froze. If she divulged everything, Mr. MacNeal might be accused of trespass, or poaching, or assault. She had to protect him until he got the chance to explain. He had brought her to safety; she owed him that much.

She shook her head. "It all happened at once. I remember a roaring noise, which I suppose was the landslide." Her hand stole under the covers and brushed MacNeal's note. The sound of drumming hoofbeats rang sharply in her ears, causing her to wince.

Aunt Amelia leapt from her chair. "Heavens, child, I've fatigued you with my questions! My quarters are adjacent. Ring this bell and I'll run straight to your side."

When the aunt had gone, Prudence drew out MacNeal's note. She imagined him scribbling it against one propped-up knee, his forehead creased with worry. He handed the paper to the groom with a shilling on top. His expression was grim as he mounted a horse. By all indications, he had come to Bolton to see her . . .

So where was he now?

Three more days went by as Prudence lay helplessly in bed, and the deadline with Lord Underwood now fast approached. Aunt Amelia anticipated returning to London on the twelfth of September, the selfsame day His Lordship expected an answer. Meanwhile, there was still no sign of William MacNeal.

Odious men! thought Prudence. Sometimes, when she was alone, she shed tears of frustration. An express came from Josephine, full of querulous confusion:

> *We were shocked yet reassured by Aunt Amelia's note, but then your own statement followed. Tell me your head injury gave you those wild thoughts. You* must *have been mistaken about the gunfire!*

"I most assuredly was not," muttered Prudence. She had the evidence to prove it. Yesterday, when the chambermaid laid her riding habit across the foot of the bed, she saw her pause and stare hard at the left sleeve. The rent flaps of cloth, when placed back together, formed the unmistakable silhouette of a ball entering and exiting. Shrugging, the girl had folded the garment and laid it in Prudence's trunk.

On a wrinkled sheet of paper that the maid had nicked from Sir Waltham's study, Prudence told Josephine,

> *On the contrary, someone* did *nearly shoot me, either by Accident or Design. Nobody has yet guessed the identity of the anonymous man. Edwina Postlethwaite, I think, will not hesitate to state her Theory, which is too close for comfort and will only cause a Scandal.*
>
> *Meanwhile, what shall I do? I was nearly prepared to accept Underwood; now my resolve falters. Do I wait for MacNeal's explanation, or give over to Underwood . . . that is, if he will still have me?*

CHAPTER TWENTY-ONE

London
13 September 1819

Prudence sat in her room at Stanistead House, looking over a stack of letters dating back a fortnight. The journey home had been physically trying, though otherwise uneventful. Now she could recuperate in familiar surroundings.

The dreaded deadline had come and gone with no sign of Lord Underwood.

"Do you think he is somehow repelled by the accident?" she had wondered aloud over supper the previous night.

"It's possible, of course." Aunt Amelia flapped a careless hand. "But I'm certain that is not the case. He's a gentleman. He knows you've had a difficult journey. He'll call tomorrow."

But Underwood hadn't.

Not that Prudence minded. She shook herself and bent back over her letters. Presently, she began a missive to Josephine reviewing the aftermath of the Bolton Park incident. Mr. MacNeal said he had not been her attacker, and she wanted to believe him, but why had he trespassed when he might've called on her in London? Why had he not returned? Above all, why had he been armed?

I'll tell you what I think. MacNeal went to Bolton because somehow he knew Lord Underwood planned to offer for me. I do not mean to Flatter myself, but in word and deed, he shows every sign of being a Jealous Lover.

Well, what did she feel about a man capable of committing violence in the name of love . . . and then disappearing yet again? Prudence rubbed her forehead. A vital piece of information was still missing. For instance, at whom had MacNeal been shooting, and why had that person been shooting at her? She could not sort out her feelings until she had those answers.

And what about the last line of his note, which had made absolutely no sense?

I placed those strange gloves in your gear.

Prudence went to her bureau and retrieved the riding pouch. She reached inside, expecting to pull out a pair of ordinary kid gloves; instead, she laid hands on the hoary old gauntlets. The fashionable gloves she had worn at the start of the hunt had sunk to the bottom. She must have switched them somehow when she stopped to remove the burrs, but how had the gauntlets made their way into that pouch in the first place?

She had no recollection of handling the Talismans since sometime around the middle of July, and then with great caution. Once her attentions had shifted to her two prospective suitors, she had lost interest. Prudence stared at the gauntlets, remembering the dream and the painful red slashes across the tips of her fingers. The slashes that had led Josephine to propose that the Talismans were dangerous—and magical.

"As I stated before, the idea is ludicrous and illogical in the extreme. Still, those sounds I heard in the forest . . ."

Biting her lip, Prudence slipped on the gauntlets.

Somewhere down the street a stray kitten mewed. The scullery maids chopped vegetables and gossiped, three floors away in another wing of the house. Aunt Amelia, at her desk downstairs, pushed back her chair and walked down the hall.

Prudence's right hand drifted unbidden toward Mr. MacNeal's note. As glove and page came into contact, entirely new sounds burst to life in her head. Men's shouts, a clang of metal, and the thundering of hoofs. Gasping, she tore the gauntlets from her hands and threw them under the bed. Then she sat perfectly still, her heart pounding.

22 September 1819

Prudence pretended to be engrossed in a novel, but it had lain open to the same spot for a quarter of an hour whilst her thoughts roamed elsewhere.

Four times this week she'd experimented with the gauntlets. At first, she had been overwhelmed by a cacophony of ambient noise. Then she had hit on the idea of conducting her tests late at night, when the household and neighborhood had grown more subdued. This enabled her to sort through the breathing and snoring of her dozen or so housemates and focus on identifying a few nocturnal sounds: the clicking of mouse feet, a tree tapping against the house, and the unmistakable creaking of floorboards in the pantry.

Matt the groom, she had deduced with a smile.

She catalogued everything, adding to the notes she had collected from the beads. Though she longed to share her observations with Josephine, she guessed what her friend would say: "I told you to burn those dratted Talismans!"

But then how will you ever find out what happened to your parents?

Prudence dearly wished she could deny the mounting evidence of the Talismans' magical character. She made a point of turning to the next page in her book, but her ruminations were broken by Reese's sudden arrival in the parlor.

"Major General Morris and Miss Helen Morris beg your permission to call."

"Well, who on earth are *they?*" complained Aunt Amelia.

"I couldn't say, ma'am."

"Are they young? Old? Fashionable? Goodness, man, one must have some forewarning about surprise visitors, else one must send them away to avoid possible shocks!"

"No, please don't!" exclaimed Prudence. "I long for a diversion. Let them in, whoever they are."

Aunt Amelia gestured reluctantly. In came a spry-looking elderly gentleman and a very tall girl, somewhat younger than Prudence.

"You will, I hope, forgive our intrusion," began the gentleman when he had taken his seat. "My granddaughter recently returned from a month at Bath, and when she heard Miss Fairfeather was recovering from some mishap, she insisted we pay a call. Of course, I don't believe we've been introduced . . ."

"—the confectioner's shop, three months ago," interjected Miss Morris with a conspiratorial smile. "I was eavesdropping shamefully."

Prudence blinked. The memory of a bonneted silhouette

rose up in her mind. "Oh, yes," she said, immediately on guard.

Miss Morris looked downcast. "I see I made a poor first impression."

The gentleman said, "I admonished Helen afterward, didn't I, dear? She wanted to call on you right then, but I said Miss Fairfeather was sure to turn her out."

Miss Morris sat forward to engage Prudence's eye. "We have at least one thing in common: a dislike for the gall of Society's finest diamonds. Oh, please forgive me! I've come to make amends."

Prudence glanced at Aunt Amelia, who looked perplexed by Miss Morris's speech. This was the single most interesting call she had ever experienced, unconventional in its lack of polite nothingness. She couldn't bear it to end now. "Very well," she consented, ignoring the huff from Amelia.

"Brilliant!" exclaimed the girl, clapping her hands. "I see we have overstayed our welcome, but you must come to High Street tomorrow and spend the entire day with us. Mustn't she, Grandfather? Say you will let her, Miss Staveley!"

Major General Morris shrugged good-naturedly and agreed that if Miss Morris desired it, then it must be so. Aunt Amelia stammered, but she could think of no reason to prevaricate. After the Morrises took their leave, she lectured Prudence on the hazards of becoming intimate with persons who were not of the highest quality.

"I have found little pleasure thus far in my dealings with the so-called Quality," replied Prudence. "Besides, those persons are scarce to be found in town at the moment. No one will know, and anyway I rather like this Miss Morris."

"I dislike her," sneered Aunt Amelia. "She lacks grace and tact, she doesn't know when to mind her own business, and she hasn't enough respect for her betters."

Prudence's mouth curved into a smile. "Perhaps I can help her improve on those faults."

When Prudence arrived at High Street the next morning, she was greeted at the door by Miss Morris herself. "We shall have the best time, you and I," declared the girl, linking arms with her. They went into the parlor and settled down at a small table. "Grandfather won't join us until lunch. We have the house to ourselves."

"Have you no governess or lady's companion?"

"Heavens, no!" Miss Morris shuffled a deck of playing cards. "How is a person to think if someone is forever stifling one's ideas? Grandfather serves as both teacher and chaperone; he and I get along famously."

Prudence couldn't help feeling somewhat envious of this arrangement. Picking up the cards Miss Morris had dealt her, she studied her companion. Miss Morris had an almost exotic appearance, with her pointy face, high cheekbones, and exceptionally dark eyes. Her black, violently curly hair was pulled into a topknot that threatened to burst at any moment. She towered over Prudence, herself taller than most girls. Everything about Miss Morris seemed thin and angular in an arresting way, but she did not, according to *beau monde* standards, have a pretty countenance.

"Have you debuted yet?" asked Prudence.

"Not officially, although I've stood along the wall at a couple of events. I am not yet seventeen. I shall come out next Season, or perhaps the one after that. I'm in no particular hurry. I may never marry. I warn you, Miss Fairfeather: I'm a bit liberal in my view of Society."

"I haven't that luxury," Prudence said with a smile. "My whole future depends on the Marriage Mart . . . little good though it has done me so far."

"Come now! Things can't be as gloomy as all that. I heard you were publicly embraced on the Thames by one of London's most eligible bachelors."

"Which bachelor was that?" sniffed Prudence. "No one seems able to agree."

"I have it on good authority he was Mr. William MacNeal, third son of Sir James. Don't tell me you didn't recognize him—I attended the soiree at Chedleigh Hall. You and he were thick as thieves that night. Several people remarked on it."

Prudence slapped down her cards. "Goodness, you *do* love your gossip!"

"Forgive me," soothed Miss Morris, touching her arm. "I didn't mean to sound flippant. I only wondered whether you knew you were the object of some talk."

Her concern was so evident that Prudence's fury vanished.

"Only recently did I surmise it, which puzzles me, for he didn't call all summer. That mishap in the river was the last time I saw him." To Prudence's mind, swooning in his arms in Hertfordshire didn't qualify.

"Well, it was enough for the wags. I heard about the sodden dress, his embrace, and the intimate conversation held in undertone. Such details also made their way to one rather unforgiving Lady Emmeline DeLacey, formerly affianced to the selfsame gentleman."

Prudence's head reeled. Here at last was the true nature of that man! MacNeal *was* a cad, one with a history of casting off women! She dared not allow herself to feel or react, not in the presence of a virtual stranger.

Miss Morris said gently, "I can see by your expression you had no idea. Well, perhaps now you can understand why you've had such a hard time. I'm very sorry for you." She took Prudence's hand. "Oh, goodness, it's even worse than I thought! I see tears—oh, my dear!—this news has wounded your heart!"

Prudence looked away, eyes stinging. "A little," she admitted. "But it doesn't matter. I am not surprised. Might we talk about something else?"

"Of course!" Miss Morris squeezed her hand. "Let us have some fun."

Prudence enjoyed the rest of her visit. She adored Miss Morris's grandfather, who was indulgent and encouraged them to speak their minds. The girls chatted and played cards until late afternoon. Alone in Aunt Amelia's chariot, Prudence's smile faded.

Pass no judgments, he had said.

How liberal must she be in her belief in his good character? Until now, she had given Mr. MacNeal the benefit of the doubt— after all, he intended to explain why he had fired those shots. But Helen's words called into question the very constancy of his soul. His words and deeds implied a deep attachment for her, but perhaps he once had said the same to Emmeline DeLacey.

In a spasm of grief, her arm shot sideways, seizing by chance a curtain hanging at the window. Crushing it between her fingers, Prudence let out a loud sob. The curtain tore from its rod, and she pressed it to her face. She had held in her tears all day long, but now she released the full depths of her anguish.

CHAPTER TWENTY-TWO

Edingham-Greene, Wiltshire
16 September 1819

All about Greenbank there hung a delicious scent of mown hay. Throughout the valley, fields rippled with ripening grain and kitchen gardens brimmed with their bounty. Josephine walked through the orchard, plucking apples straight from the trees. The chore of canning was soon to begin; this year, for some reason, she looked forward to it.

Prudence had returned safely to Stanistead House. Although her friend's ordeal had been terrifying, Josephine doubted the incident had sprung from evil intent. No one but Lady Revelle knew Prudence's real identity; and in that case, Aunt Amelia would have whisked Prudence from her salon if the woman had posed a true threat. No matter how bizarre the events at Bolton Park, there must be an explanation that made perfect sense.

"Everything can be resolved except for those wretched gauntlets!" complained Josephine, grimacing at a worm poking from her half-eaten apple. How had they ended up in Prudence's bag? Prudence couldn't explain it any more than Josephine could explain how she had laid hands on the pistols the night she killed the troll.

"Burn them!" she'd written Prudence again this morning.

"Need we any more proof of their terrible power?" She had experienced enough violence this summer to last her a lifetime. Now the trolls were all gone, along with her trances and an uncontrollable fascination with her dead mother's keepsakes. So what if it had meant a return to her old, boring life? A boring life meant a safe life. A safe, predictable, innocuous life, free of soldiers in red coats riding ivory stallions . . .

Josephine shook her head to clear it.

A commotion on the front lawn heralded the arrival of her cavaliers. Flinging away her bad apple, she ran down the slope and rounded the house. Arthur Grant, who took seriously his self-appointed fencing master role, stood in the driveway limbering up while Peter and Roland ran laps around the lawn. Rain or shine, Arthur drilled the young squires every day.

"I think they're responding to your regimen," said Josephine.

"It would seem so," agreed Arthur, tossing aside his jacket. "They hate repetition, but it's the only way to teach them balance and grace. I must engrain it in their very souls."

Josephine sat down to study the menfolk. Even in the awkward efforts of a novice, there was an elegance and dignity to fencing that transcended the brutality of ordinary combat. As they went through their paces, she moved her arms and legs slightly, mimicking their poses. Later, she wrote Prudence:

> *How unfair it is, sitting still whilst the boys tear about, having such fun! I think I could do as well as they, perhaps even better. After all, there appears little difference between dancing and fencing.*

Arthur, for some reason, did not show up one day, whereupon Peter and Roland dropped all pretense of discipline and commenced slashing at each other until Peter sustained an injury on his upper left arm. Carson, pursing his lips, patched up the invalid with his usual expertise. Afterward, the two rascals threw themselves at Josephine's feet and taunted each other until they came close to starting a brawl.

"Children!" she cried, smacking them with her parasol. "If you had a student to teach, you could reinforce your skills instead of bickering. Someone give me his sword. Let's see what I can do."

Roland and Peter laughed raucously, but Josephine persisted in demanding a blade until they placed one in her hand. Moving out onto the driveway, she threw back her shoulders and demonstrated the skills she had learned by observation. She finished with a satisfied exhalation.

"There! That's easy enough. I'd like to go through the lunges, but I can't move properly in this frock. If I found something more suitable to wear, would you be my teachers?"

Roland and Peter exchanged glances.

"I don't think we'd better," said Peter. "We mustn't risk hurting you, and if Grant should find out, we'd catch hell from him and Fairfeather both."

Josephine put her hands on her hips. "They won't know the first thing about it! We can meet in the east pasture each morning at seven o'clock—that's when everyone thinks I'm out riding—and we'll review everything you've learnt on the previous day."

Roland guffawed. "Why should we crawl out of bed so curst early to waste our time teaching a girl how to swordfight? Begging your pardon, m'lady, but you *know* there's no sense in it!"

"By helping me, you'll improve yourselves. Don't you want to get better?"

"Not especially. It's Grant who's taking the whole thing so dashed seriously."

Josephine took a deep breath. How maddening that men should have all the opportunities when women might make better use of them! "If you refuse to assist, I may be forced to tell Edward you're the ones who ruined his favorite top hat last summer."

"What proof have you got?" bellowed Roland.

Josephine regarded them coolly. "I saw you down at the millpond, lining it with dead fish. What was it Roland said? 'If Fairfeather came along now, he'd squeeze the pulp out of us!'"

There was a momentary silence.

"That's b-blackmail!" stammered Roland.

"He'd kill us!" groaned Peter.

Josephine nodded.

"Done. Done!" they exclaimed, throwing up their hands. "When do we start?"

After settling upon Saturday morning, Josephine dismissed them and went directly to Edward's room. She rummaged through his bureau for clothes he'd outgrown and in no time had the makings of a fencing ensemble. That night, she set to work with needle and thread.

20 September 1819

"My lady, we're on pins and needles," said Maria at breakfast on Friday. "It has been more than a week since Lord Underwood was supposed a-have returned. Bless me, how can 'ee read that letter with so impassive a face?"

"Because Lord Underwood has yet to call," explained Josephine. "Listen—" and she read aloud an excerpt from Prudence's account:

Underwood's absence has stretched on, and Aunt Amelia fears rumors about the hunting Accident have finally reached London. She sent Reese round with an Invitation to dine, and thus we learned that his lordship was in fact Nowhere to be found. The butler was frantic, for his master had left Essex over a fortnight ago.

The dining room fell silent.

"What sort of rumors?" puzzled Middlemere.

Josephine waved a dismissive hand. "An assignation in the woods—complete nonsense, of course."

"Why would anyone say such odious things?" cried Maria.

"Oh, Prudence has endured all that and more since her arrival in London!"

The earl leaned forward, eyes wide with surprise and concern. "What? Then whatever can this mean?"

"It means Prudence's best chance at getting married has been dashed!" howled Maria, reaching for a napkin to cover her tears.

Josephine groaned. "Hush, Maria. It's not nearly as bad as you think." She excused herself and went upstairs to finish reading Prudence's letter. The rest was less than encouraging.

Thanks to the loquacious staff at Bolton Park, the servants of Stanistead House soon knew there was a Bullet hole in my sleeve. Thus, I had to concoct a Lie.

"Twas an accident," I told Nell. "I was mistaken for Quarry by a jumpy huntsman. He has already apologized. Please speak to the others, so that Miss Staveley is not upset by False rumors."

Josephine's shoulders sagged as doubt pierced the heady optimism of a few days ago. Mr. MacNeal still had not returned to account for his actions. She went to her desk, muttering, "I question the honor of any gentleman who would let a lady dissemble on his behalf." To Prudence, she wrote,

I am uneasy, my dear friend. I think you must prepare yourself for an unfortunate outcome. Don't be a fool. You know not whether MacNeal is even worthy of your protection.

"Prove yourself, you scoundrel!" she grumbled aloud.

Early the next morning, she rode out in her hand-crafted ensemble, which consisted of trousers with two flaps of wool skirting tacked to the waist. Roland and Peter stumbled late into the clearing, half-asleep and ill-attired, as if they hadn't believed she would really dare to come. Her outfit elicited frowns but no direct comments. She didn't care; it worked perfectly, affording her the flexibility she needed while maintaining the guise of feminine modesty.

As Josephine had predicted, the boys began to take pride in demonstrating what they had already learned. Though she had spent hours in her chamber practicing proper form and footwork, she pretended not to understand the subtlety of certain parries so that they must show her again and again. Before long, she could see the effect this repetition had on their confidence, and indeed it produced a great change in her, too.

She moved more nimbly and ceased to tromp up and down the staircase. Her eye became more attuned to the movements of others. She imagined herself growing powerful enough to vanquish any fiend with the nerve to cross her—whether it be Prudence's assailant or a whole swarm of trolls. Most importantly, fencing gave her focus, a goal she could strive toward in the secret depths of her heart.

CHAPTER TWENTY-THREE

London
24 September 1819

Prudence squinted in dismay at Josephine's latest letter, which contained a detailed account of her morning practice sessions. "Lord, if anyone were to find out about those silly fencing lessons . . ." Hurriedly, she scrawled,

> *For shame, Josephine! You'll be seventeen in a few months. You've worked so hard all Summer to earn everyone's respect, yet here you are playing Buccaneer and threatening teenage boys with Blackmail!*

When she had finished her scold, she changed the subject to that of Miss Morris and the awful information she had learned about William MacNeal.

Josephine's reply came on the thirtieth instant. She commented cheerfully, albeit cautiously, on Prudence's friendship with Miss Morris, but she withheld nothing in her censorship of Mr. MacNeal:

> *That barbarous snake! Men come and go at will, and it's always the ladies who suffer. He's made it look like Lady*

Emmeline's fault, and he'll do the same to you. Shun him, Prudence! It is the only way. Oh, I pray Underwood reappears soon and pleads for your hand. Security is what you need, though you dream of true love.

Prudence groaned. She'd shed countless tears over MacNeal's failings, yet she still clung to the possibility that his actions had been warranted. For the first time, however, a tiny part of her agreed. As a potential helpmeet and friend, and as a keeper of solemn vows, William MacNeal was wholly and fatally unreliable.

8 October 1819

One morning, Miss Morris arrived on horseback in Stanistead's forecourt, hallooing for Prudence. Prudence leant out her window.

"What in heaven's name are you doing?"

"Such fine weather we have today! You and I must take a long ride. Hurry up, then, lazybones! Tell your aunt I've got a groom and a hamper with lunch."

Prudence ran to secure Aunt Amelia's permission, then hastily changed into her mended riding clothes. Soon they were trotting west out of London.

"Where are we going?" asked Prudence, glancing round at the dwindling number of passing coaches and riders. Her palms grew damp, and she tightened her hold on the reins.

"Be patient," soothed Miss Morris.

They rode for an hour before turning into a narrow lane

that wended its way south until it ended at a cart path on the Thames's north bank. From here, the little party proceeded upstream. Grand estates fronted the river, their vast landscapes sprawling down from neatly tended terraces. Prudence began to relax and admire the changing leaves and marble statuary gleaming against verdant expanses of lawn.

Abruptly, Miss Morris turned her gelding's head and spurred him to a gallop. Prudence shrugged and sped after. They raced up someone's lawn and skidded to a halt on a neat gravel drive. Two liveried grooms materialized. As the girls dismounted, someone beckoned them from a pair of open French doors.

Thus, once again, Prudence came face to face with Lady Elisabetha Revelle.

"Close your mouth, dear!" chided the lady. "Sheldon! Lunch!"

Trapped by the dictates of polite society, Prudence took her place at a table set for three.

"I have wanted to see you, Miss Fairfeather," Lady Revelle said, "especially since I received your letter a few weeks ago, but arranging this meeting has proved excessively challenging. I'd have sent an invitation, but I did not think your aunt would consent." Her laugh was silvery, like miniature bells.

Prudence glanced at Miss Morris.

"Lady Elisabetha was a friend of my late mother's," explained the girl. "She is my mentor. Oh, Miss Fairfeather, please forgive this little deception! She has been after me to get you here somehow."

"And so here I am." Prudence turned to her hostess, resolved not to play into her hands. Lady Revelle returned her gaze with an ingenuous smile.

Over lunch, they conversed about innocuous things. Then,

as if by some prearranged plan, Miss Morris and the servants withdrew. When the door closed behind them, Lady Revelle said, "I asked Helen to leave us because she is not yet old enough to be introduced to the Inheritance."

Steel yourself, thought Prudence, returning a blank stare.

"Come now, my dear. Don't play ignorant. You contacted *me*, or have you forgotten?"

"I have since re-examined where my priorities lie."

"I think your aunt has instructed you to suppress your fascination."

"She is a very wise woman," Prudence replied, lifting her chin.

"A woman who lies to you and requires you to bear a burden of secrecy that eats into your soul. That cannot be satisfying."

Prudence returned a cool stare. "There are many things in life which duty asks us to endure."

"Like marriages of convenience?" asked Lady Revelle dryly. She looked hard at Prudence, and her eyes glinted like blue fire.

"Like abiding the strictures of one's guardians," rejoined Prudence.

Lady Revelle leant back and swept her arm in a grand arc. "Picture a world, Miss Fairfeather, where a handful of people possess skills that set them apart from the rest of society. With the assistance of their Talismans, they wield power beyond your wildest dreams. It is by necessity a secret society; the common folk cling to their superstitions, and one wouldn't want to be burned at the stake. But the ambitious ones who share their confidence with only a select few can build brilliant careers of unlimited potential. Intuitive advisors. Uncontestable persuaders. Untraceable spies. Imagine the value of such persons to a king."

Her mellifluous voice wove its provocative song, and all the while she spoke, Lady Revelle stared unblinkingly at Prudence. Now she paused and tilted her head, as if measuring the girl's interest in the tale she'd begun.

"I sense you would like me to continue, my dear."

Prudence swallowed. This was precisely the situation against which Aunt Amelia had cautioned. She stood and walked to the window. "On the contrary, I beg you to stop."

But Lady Revelle did not stop. Like a blossom unfolding, she rose from her seat and spread wide her arms. The fall of her sleeves shimmered, pearlescent blue in the sunshine. Closing on Prudence, she went on, "These people called themselves Keepers, and they came to enjoy privilege and fortune and regard. That world was *ours*, Miss Fairfeather, until snatched away by functionaries who thought they knew better. They stole our gifts by forcing us to sign an Oath disavowing the Inheritance. They offered us bribes for compliance and promised assassination for those who dared to dissent."

The lady stood behind Prudence, cupping her shoulders, and her voice dropped to a whisper. "Do you think it was just, that more than two thousand years of history and service should be wiped out like that? Are you not a little curious to know what it would feel like to be a fully trained Talisman Keeper?"

Prudence shook her head. "I trust the story isn't quite as simple as that. My guardian has advised me not to pursue this matter."

The lady came around to face her head-on. "Amelia Staveley and I happen to view the matter differently, but that doesn't make me wrong." She reached out and lifted Prudence's hands. "You're not wearing your ring."

"I never do."

"Not true. You were wearing it when we met, and I can't imagine it would allow you to leave it behind. It found its way back to you following your dip in the Thames, did it not?"

Outrage arced through Prudence's body. She snatched away her hands and took a step back. "I must go. This interview was not at all what I had in mind when Miss Morris proposed a long ride."

"Don't blame her!" laughed Lady Revelle. "She knows nothing about the Talismans. No, I have my ways of discovering the truth." She held up her right hand, displaying a ring similar to Prudence's, but with a large diamond setting.

Prudence stared at the jewel, and her hand drifted unthinkingly to the pocket at her hip. She shot an angry look at her hostess. "You know nothing about me!"

Lady Revelle's eyes glittered. "I know more than you think." She raised her two forefingers and touched them to Prudence's lips, saying, "*Ithidh an cat do theanga.*" Prudence looked at her in puzzlement, but the baroness merely smiled. "Come back when you're ready. I'll show you things, my dear girl, that you never imagined possible." She clapped her hands and called, "Helen! Miss Fairfeather tires and you both have a long ride."

Out on the driveway, Prudence could hardly contain her fury. Miss Morris had not only brought her here by duplicitous means, she'd befriended Prudence at the request of Lady Revelle. She wheeled the mare this way and that, weighing the wisdom of riding off alone. Could she find her own way home? What would she tell Aunt Amelia?

"Do not look so grave!" cried Miss Morris. "Your aunt will never know you strayed so far."

Prudence whipped the mare into a gallop, letting the horse slow once they turned north onto the back lane. Meanwhile,

Miss Morris and the groom had kept silently apace.

"Isn't Lady Elisabetha a goddess?" queried Miss Morris. "She knows all the best families. Perhaps she can find you a handsome duke."

Prudence did not immediately answer, for she was bent on trying to understand what role the girl was playing. She turned and asked tartly, "A handsome duke, you say? It's tempting, if a girl wants only security and prestige. Will the lady also do this for you?"

"Ha-ha, I'm *never* getting married! I shall live alone and have torrid affairs!"

Prudence saw by her smile that Miss Morris was jesting and likely unaware of her idol's scheming nature. Forgiveness did not come so easily. "I would rather be friendless and not marry a duke than trust in anyone who thought fit to deceive me so boldly," she rejoined. For the rest of their journey, she remained silent. Miss Morris stared straight ahead, visibly struggling to maintain her poise.

Prudence returned home exhausted and disheartened. Fearing Aunt Amelia would perceive her distress, she left a message with Reese begging off supper and hurried upstairs. She sat down to pen a confessional letter to Josephine and afterward sat wondering what Aunt Amelia would do if she knew at least one person in London could blow the gaff on her pedigree. Prudence felt the band in her pocket, that tangible connection to her dead mother. The prospect of relinquishing her Talismans was unbearable.

How, then, might you justify keeping your silence?

She *had*, as instructed, rejected the lady's overtures; never would she succumb to the wiles of that woman. Then there was Miss Morris, who, despite her complicity, had no knowledge of the Inheritance, let alone the importance of keeping its secrets. Without Prudence, she was destined to fall completely under the thrall of her mentor.

Even Amelia would agree it's your duty to shield her!

"If I don't need help resisting Lady Revelle, then there is no reason to speak up," Prudence reckoned aloud. "And, for Miss Morris's sake, there is every reason *not* to."

Soon, the decision had made itself.

Prudence had no plans to go to High Street the next day; given Miss Morris's unwitting deception she thought it best to spend some time apart. Thus, when the doorbell rang, she was surprised to hear the voice of the Morrises' footman. A moment later, Reese came into the drawing room.

"Miss Prudence, your young friend is outside. She begs you step into her carriage for a brief conversation."

Prudence pulled a shawl round her shoulders and went out to the courtyard. In the chariot, she found Miss Morris crying.

"I'm sorry I displeased you, though I'm sure I don't know why! I had *so* hoped you would deal well with Lady Elisabetha, for I am devoted to her."

Prudence sighed. "I don't mean to disillusion you, my dear, but surely you realize not everyone finds Elisabetha Revelle the *crème de la crème*?"

Miss Morris froze, then nodded, her eyes round, dark saucers.

"You, of all people, should appreciate the power of a rumor. While Society may indeed love the lady's salon, few people desire any real intimacy with her." Prudence patted Miss

Morris's knee. "I appreciate your good intentions, but I'd rather not associate with her. I can't afford any more controversy."

"Yes, I suppose—"

"One other thing: I like you, Miss Morris, I honestly do, but if your friendship springs solely from the whim of Lady Revelle, then I think we must end it."

"Oh!" exclaimed Miss Morris, pressing both hands to her mouth. "Oh, Miss Fairfeather, my affection for you is genuine! If you could find it in your heart to forgive me, I swear I shall never deceive you again!"

Prudence gazed thoughtfully at Miss Morris. The girl seemed utterly guileless, as earnest as a puppy fetching a thrown stick. Prudence embraced her. "Go home. I'll visit you tomorrow."

Miss Morris's eyes shone. "Thank you! You won't regret this, I promise."

CHAPTER TWENTY-FOUR

Edingham-Greene, Wiltshire
27 September 1819

Josephine wrinkled her nose at Prudence's torrent of harsh words.

"Pooh! I care not one whit what anyone thinks about my fencing. Besides," she added, settling into a deep *en garde* position, "I happen to think I'm rather good." Pausing, she wrote,

> *By this time next year, I'll have to put aside such whims and be grown up forever, but for now I see no harm in enjoying a bit of fun. Wasn't that your reason for asking Underwood to wait?*

The conclusion of Prudence's letter had not improved her mood. Bad enough some odd chit named Miss Morris had burrowed her way into her friend's life, but that revelation about MacNeal and Lady DeLacey was the absolute limit. Josephine seized her riding crop and leapt around the room, pretending to slice off Mr. MacNeal's head.

"Oooo, MacNeal, you barbarous snake!"

She hurried over to her desk to add precisely that sentiment and ended up spitting out a lengthy harangue. What worried her most was Prudence's intention to, if warranted, bestow forgiveness on MacNeal. To Josephine's mind, he did not deserve it.

> *How* dare *that man ask for another moment of your patience? If he had any morals, if he cared about your feelings, he'd have returned to your side before you left Bolton Park. There is no explanation that can justify his habitual absences.*

"He had better watch himself," she growled, flexing her hands, "or I shall pierce his heart with my blade as surely as he has pierced the heart of my friend."

The first of October brought worse tidings from London. Underwood had been missing for nearly a month, and Prudence relayed rumors of nefarious doings. Relatives and staff scoured the country without finding any trace of the viscount. His disappearance made no sense; he was by all accounts a dull sort of fellow, and not the least bit inclined to fits of spontaneity. The deeper grew this mystery, the more Aunt Amelia panicked. It was widely known that Underwood had paid many attentions to Prudence. Would her name once again be dragged into scandal?

The remainder of this letter sang the praises of Miss Morris. Josephine fought the urge to crumple and burn it. The white-hot violence of her jealousy surprised her; she had never felt this way during Prudence's brief friendship with Miss Wymstone. On reflection, however, the difference was obvious:

She's a gossip and an enigma, so I caution you not to put so much trust in Miss Morris. You have a duty to preserve your family secrets—do not squander sixteen years of security in one careless conversation!

"Oh, I hope this girl has some flaw that will drive them apart!" Josephine's eyes flashed fire as she pressed her signet ring into the wax.

5 October 1819

"I've had another letter from Quimby," Lord Middlemere said. "He says the crisis has passed. Next spring all Special Forces will be absorbed into regular companies."

Josephine smiled. If the Army had truly eradicated the trolls, then perhaps Prudence's obsession with her magical keepsakes would likewise decline. She had long suspected a connection between the two phenomena. "Excellent! Maybe now we can put behind us that unhappy time." A sudden thought struck her. "Dear me, will they now send him overseas?"

Maria threw her a narrow look.

Middlemere shrugged. "I couldn't say, though it seems likely. Many soldiers are off to India these days. I hope the Army serves Quimby well. He hasn't much family and spent his youth away at school."

"How sad!" remarked Josephine. Maria rolled her eyes.

"I've been thinking," continued the earl. "After so many months in the field, he would doubtless appreciate a holiday. I shall extend an invitation to Greenbank on the occasion of his next leave." Maria made an unhappy sound, which Middlemere ignored. "Josephine, is the bedchamber across from Edward's in acceptable shape?"

"Yes, Papa. I've had the housekeepers in there recently, in case our aunt and Prudence came for a visit." Josephine tried not to look smug, but she couldn't help herself—it was a rare moment indeed when Maria was put in her place. She and the nurse exchanged rude faces.

"Excellent," said Middlemere. "In that case, I'll tell Quimby to come at his soonest convenience."

"We'll be ready, Papa." Josephine's heart pounded. Under the table, she squeezed her napkin into a tight ball.

Within days, Lieutenant Quimby wrote to accept the earl's invitation. He awaited orders from headquarters but had put in for a furlough to be taken before traveling to his winter post. The Westons should expect him sometime in the next fortnight.

Josephine spent the interim enduring numerous peaks and valleys of emotion. It was pointless to continue harboring a *tendre* for a man whose pedigree precluded a possible union, and yet she enjoyed fantasizing about him. Alone in her nook, she lay with her eyes closed, trying to remember the best of his features. Then, like a spooked cat, she would tear outside for long, cleansing walks.

"Good heavens, 'ee'll kill thyself, child!" Maria yelped in alarm as the girl burst through the front door on a soggy afternoon.

"Pshaw, 'tis fine, bracing weather," Josephine replied. Perfect for cooling her fired-up blood. Assuming an attitude of false dignity, she flung back a clump of sodden hair, stalked upstairs, and called for a bath. Afterward, she sat in her wrapper, drinking strong tea and reading Prudence's latest letter.

"What?" she cried, slamming aside the cup and spilling tea all over. "Dash it all, Prudence!" She held the letter at arm's length, her blood boiling now for an altogether new reason: Prudence had confessed to the Chedleigh Hall affair. Josephine grimaced. "Brava, my friend! You withstood the lady's attempt at seducing you into breaking the Oath, but did I not tell you to watch out for Miss Morris?"

Yet Prudence had absolved her!

In reply, Josephine raged:

Are you mad? That chit will be the ruination of you! Discard her. Tell Amelia everything. This intolerable secret has gone on long enough! There are no coincidences here, Prudence. The baroness means to own you and your magical Talismans, and I do not believe she will give up so readily.

Think of the innocents whose lives have already been affected by trolls. Think of Quimby, who must fight them, and of Charlie, who paid the ultimate price. Can you not see the connection between the baroness's scheme and the raids in the country? She has outlined the plan; you mustn't remain passive. We have to find someone who will listen to us!

By "we," she meant Prudence, for no one in Wiltshire could help them with this. Perhaps, when he came, she could find a way to tell Quimby, but merely thinking about him made her feel dizzy. On second thought, perhaps not. The last thing she wanted was to misjudge his role and cause him to scorn her.

Oh, what do I do?

"We shall see," she murmured, biting a knuckle.

17 October 1819

Early one crisp morning, Josephine met the boys as usual at the edge of the east pasture. Under a kaleidoscope of red and gold leaves, she and Peter stood *en garde*, poised for a bout. Roland stalked back and forth, making observations. As always, Josephine made sure to stand a bit incorrectly. They rarely criticized her form; perhaps they figured there wasn't any use. It surprised her, therefore, when Peter said, "Not quite, my lady. You'll leave your forearm open to attack if you let your blade droop."

"What if I attacked first?" she asked, lunging. Peter parried and backed away. She closed on him, advancing and thrusting without mercy. At each stroke, Peter gave more ground until, four or five retreats later, she had him wedged against a tree with the point of her sword at his throat.

"Beg for mercy," she growled.

"Now that's an unusual sight!" said a voice somewhere behind them.

Peter's eyes bulged. Releasing him, Josephine pivoted sharply. Lieutenant Quimby watched them from horseback, an amused expression on his face.

"We're in the suds now!" whimpered Roland.

Josephine's pulse thundered. "He won't say anything," she assured him. Handing Roland his sword, she walked over to the lieutenant and dipped a neat curtsey, spreading the panels of her makeshift fencing skirt. Could he see her hands tremble?

Quimby bowed and touched his shako. "Good morning, Lady Weston. Who is teaching whom?"

"They are teaching me. I got carried away."

"Indeed!" he said, eyes sparkling. "You were one flick of the wrist from slaying your opponent."

"Hardly. These swords are worse than dull." She glanced at Peter, well aware that his dignity was at stake.

Quimby caught her hint and shifted the topic. "My word, you have an unusual sense of fashion." He nodded to indicate her thinly disguised trousers.

Mortified but determined not to let on that she was, Josephine shrugged and turned to Peter and Roland. "Thank you, gentlemen. That'll be all for this week."

Peter shot his sword into its scabbard. Roland gave Josephine a leg up onto her horse and bade them both a good day. Once the boys had faded from view, Lieutenant Quimby and Josephine turned their mounts' heads for Greenbank.

"We weren't sure which day you'd come," she said as casually as possible, "but we certainly didn't expect you to arrive at sunup."

"Nor did I expect to find you threatening young squires in the meadow. The truth is, Ivan threw a shoe yesterday as I was nearing the village. I left him with the blacksmith, and in consideration of the late hour, I elected to board with a certain Mrs. March. She sends your father her fondest greetings, by the way."

Josephine laughed. "She has spent more than fifteen years hoping Papa will propose marriage. He inadvertently fans the flame by sending her gifts. We wish he would take her seriously, for he deserves the diversion of a pretty companion."

"Don't we all?" Lieutenant Quimby asked, flashing a grin. For one heart-stopping moment, his sparkling cerulean eyes held hers. Then, all too soon, they darted away. Without warning, he bent and seized her horse's reins, bringing them both to a halt. "Shh!" he hissed, jerking out his pistol and training it on the woods.

Josephine's gaze followed his to an outcropping of exposed granite, sprawled like a felled giant some thirty yards to their left. She squinted, unable to spot the source of his apprehension. Then she heard it: ragged breathing in an inhumanly low register, marked now and then with the keen of a wounded animal.

"Stay here," Quimby said brusquely, steering his horse off the trail. Once he had closed half the distance to the boulders, she nudged her own mount along in his wake. She had gone only a few feet before the lieutenant's pistol went off, followed by an oddly familiar roar.

"Damn!" exclaimed Quimby, tearing at his saddle-pack. He produced a musket and fumbled for a cartridge. Several yards beyond him, a silhouette rose from the shadow of the boulders and staggered forward with an earsplitting bellow. Quimby bent to his task with supreme concentration; his horse, trained to withstand the chaos of battle, nonetheless rolled its eyes in bald terror.

A flare of protectiveness rose in Josephine's breast. She spoke to her mount, which balked and sweated and nickered uneasily. Knuckles white on the reins, she turned it to face the danger head-on, yet the horse refused to move. From the corner of her eye, she saw Quimby still loading as the monstrosity drew closer.

"Giddup, then!" she raged, smacking the gelding's rump. It screeched and surged forward. As they drew abreast of the lieutenant, Josephine leant out from her saddle and wrenched his sabre from its scabbard. Momentum carried her on at the same crazy angle, like an itinerant trick rider she had once seen in the village. The troll now shifted its furious attention to her, but Josephine had no time to register misgivings. She raised

Quimby's sword, yelling like a banshee. The blade scribed a deadly and glittering arc, then descended without mercy.

It struck with a thunk, burying itself firmly in the sinews of the troll's neck. The force of the impact threw Josephine from her saddle, and she fell with a shriek into a deep drift of leaves. She righted herself in time to see the troll lunging straight for her, Quimby's sword still wobbling from its throat. She took in the full scope of its matted hirsuteness, the threads of saliva stretched across its maw. Its powerful torso, black and leathery like an ape's, tapered to an emaciated abdomen. Desperation blazed in the beast's sunken eyes.

"Stay down!" ordered Quimby, and he fired his musket. The troll pitched to the ground inches from where Josephine lay, so close she felt a puff of air as it exhaled its last breath.

The lieutenant leaped from his saddle and ran to kneel by her side. "Good God!" he exclaimed, hesitating a fraction before folding her into his arms. Pressing Josephine's head to his chest, he stroked her disheveled hair. "Are you hurt?" he asked hoarsely.

"Not at all," she rasped, giddy from the scent of soap and gunpowder infusing his coat.

Far too soon for her preference, he held her at arm's length and regarded her with dilated eyes. His expression wavered between concern and irritation. Had she been a man, he would no doubt have lost his temper. Instead, he said through his teeth, "May I ask, Lady Weston, what on earth you thought you were doing?"

Josephine weighed the idea of pretending to swoon, but whatever creature comfort she might gain from his embrace would likely be offset by his lowered opinion of her courage. She settled for directness. "Saving your life. The troll closed in as you were loading the musket."

Quimby sighed. "It was already dying." He helped her to her feet, and together they stood over the stinking corpse. "See this?" he asked, pointing to an old wound in its left leg, so angry and inflamed that patches of greasy pelt had gone missing and the flesh had swollen out of proportion to the matching lower limb.

Josephine cupped a hand to her nose. Seeing a troll in broad daylight for the first time, she could see why a harried victim might call it a bear. In truth, it bore no resemblance to that species. Its body was designed to shuffle mostly upright. It had elongated feet and opposable digits. This beast could not possibly be classed with *Ursus*.

Quimby crouched beside it, careful not to touch the area of open putrefaction. "I suspect it took a bullet from one of my men and has lain here ever since, living off whatever game wandered within reach. Have there been any reports of trouble?"

"No. The neighborhood has been quiet."

Quimby stood, his mouth a tight white line. "Based on the quantity of scat and bones in this hollow, the creature has sheltered here for months without causing a stir." He looked away and swallowed hard. "This oversight could wreck my career."

Josephine lifted her chin. "Then don't file a report."

"I must. My honor supersedes my pride."

"Sir, no harm has been done. What would your peers do if faced with this quandary? They would not, I suspect, offer to fall on the sword." She touched his sleeve. "As for your pride, I daresay your only witness has her own dignity at stake. I'll keep your secret if you agree to keep mine." She flapped a hand to indicate her fencing attire.

Quimby gave a hollow laugh. "An Amazon and a rebel," he murmured, taking a step toward her. His hand closed over her right wrist, which was covered in a spray of odiferous dark blood. "Your jacket is torn," he said gently. "Are you certain you're not hurt?"

Hereupon, an appalling, earthy sound emanated from the troll's corpse. Quimby tsked and pivoted. "We must burn that thing. Will you help me gather some brush?"

Together, they built a pyre and cleared the area around the troll's body. Quimby struck a flame from his tinderbox, and they stood back to watch the blaze, shifting whenever the god-awful stench blew in their faces. The fire consumed its fuel unnaturally fast. When the deed was done and the ashes fully doused, Josephine mustered the courage to say, "Tell me, sir, truly. Do you think it's over, this infestation, I mean?" She held his gaze steady with hers. "I respect your mandate for secrecy, I do, but you *know* you can trust me. If this were part of something much, much larger than it appears, would you share that information with me?"

She held her breath, eager and expectant. This was her chance, and completely unrehearsed—she depended on him to have faith in her. Quimby did not answer.

"Lieutenant," she pressed, pointing at the smoking pile. "*That* is not normal. That creature and its brethren appeared on these shores without any precedent I know of, and the Army assigned you to eradicate them. Clearly, your superiors want to hide the truth from the populace. I shan't ask you why. I want only your assurance: does or does not this creature signify an approaching upheaval?"

Quimby exhaled. He did not break her gaze. "My lady, I

would indeed share such confidence with you, but the truth is, I don't know. I am only a lieutenant, and my orders are never to ask deeper questions. I don't know what that thing is, or where it came from. I don't know what its presence in Wiltshire signifies. We had a job, and we killed them all, save, of course, this one. My orders will keep me in the West Midlands this winter; beyond that, I cannot say what the Army expects."

Josephine sagged. She might have guessed Quimby had no further knowledge. Someone in the Army, however, directed his actions. Someone out there understood the connection between trolls and the Inheritance. Alas, Quimby could not help her. His unquestioning approach to his mission only amplified her reluctance to raise the issue of magic.

Softly, she said, "Should things change, will you tell me?"

He nodded. "I will. I swear it. Your family means the world—" His voice cracked, and he turned brusquely away. "I say," he added in a cheerier tone. "Speaking of the Westons, I expect they shall miss you soon, don't you think?"

"I expect so," she said. Quimby cupped his hands and boosted her into the saddle. They rode soberly back to Greenbank, where he helped her down.

"Well, then. Let us hope that reception has no bearing on the rest of my stay."

Josephine shuddered. "When I think how many times I have passed that outcropping of rocks . . ." She added stoically, "I must wash and change clothes before anyone else sees me. Will you ring at the door and let Carson admit you in proper fashion?"

Quimby bowed. "As you wish. And, Lady Weston—?"

"Yes?"

"If you'd still like those lessons in marksmanship, why not

keep on with your morning routine? Since you've released your other tutors . . ." His voice died, leaving the obvious unsaid.

Josephine stared at the ground. "Sir, I've known those boys my whole life, but I hardly think it's proper—"

"No, of course. I presumed far too much."

"I really must go." Josephine strode away, fighting the urge to turn around and run back to his arms. In the privacy of her chamber, she screamed into her pillow. Oh, God! She could hardly wrap her head around the events of the morning, the violence and the fear and the thrill of saving and then being saved. Handsome men rescuing maidens—these sorts of things happened only in books. Quimby had acted with honor, ever the perfect gentleman. Was it possible he could've grown that much more handsome in only three months? Lord help her, she wanted to pursue his offer more than anything in the world, but she knew what Prudence would say: *Meeting in secret with a man is wrong, no matter what the reason!*

Well, she had done the right thing. Now Josephine stumbled to her closet, muttering, "Oh, fiddlesticks—I must face him at breakfast. What'll I wear?"

CHAPTER TWENTY-FIVE

London
16 October 1819

Another week went by, during which Prudence grew resigned to the likelihood that neither of her *beaux* intended to return. Josephine, meanwhile, had harsh words to say about the unexpected meeting with Lady Revelle. She blasted Miss Morris and urged Prudence to report everything before matters got out of hand. Using phrases meant to induce guilt and alarm, she claimed Prudence had a duty to stave off rebellion.

Prudence begged to differ. Her only duty, she reckoned, was to keep herself and Miss Morris safe from the machinations of unscrupulous rebels. She outlined her reasons for not involving Aunt Amelia, then went so far as to put away the ring.

"Enough of this business," she said with a frown.

She sat reading that afternoon when Nell came in with a parcel wrapped in brown paper. "'Ere's your order from the book merchant, miss. The delivery boy asks if you will pay in cash or put it on credit."

Prudence blinked to mask her surprise. Inside the package was a bound copy of Lord Byron's poem "The Corsair." *What on earth . . . ?* she puzzled, running her hands along its marbled cover. As she flipped through the pages, pondering the book's significance, a folded paper bearing her name slid from the frontispiece. The handwriting looked familiar.

She glanced up at Nell. "Give the delivery boy a cup of tea and tell him I shall need a few minutes to decide." The maid curtseyed and left. With shaking hands, Prudence bent to read the enclosed note:

Dear Miss Fairfeather,

Please forgive this unorthodox mode of communication, which I shall attempt to defend. First, I pray you are recovered from your trauma. As I've already said, I'd have sooner slain myself than cause the slightest harm to your most excellent person.

You probably despise me by now, yet I long to explain my absences and also to impart tidings of a sort you and I should discuss before sharing them with your aunt. I realize such a conversation, like this communiqué, violates the dictates of propriety. Let me therefore risk it all by begging leave to meet with you in some public place. Name the time and location, bring a trusted confidante, and return your reply through my messenger. (No coin is necessary. The delivery is a ruse, and the book is mine, or rather, now it is yours.)

Yours truly,

W. MacNeal

"Oh, mercy!" exclaimed Prudence, pressing the book to her breast.

Why didn't he call like any other gentleman would? What tidings must be discussed without her guardian? And why, oh why must he force her into making a decision that ran against the very fabric of accepted behavior?

"What'll I do? What'll I *do?*" she breathed, pacing the room.

She should spurn him, of course, but after so much waiting and hand-wringing and idle speculation she couldn't imagine expunging him so easily from her heart. Gathering her courage, she composed a reply.

> *Mr. MacNeal,*
>
> *There are many reasons why I ought to tear up your note, yet Curiosity demands that I agree to this Rendezvous. In so doing, I shall reveal myself as an Incautious Female, which is precisely the sort of lady a True Gentleman would scorn. However, being an avowed Cad, surely you will not hold it against me.*
>
> *If it is not raining early tomorrow morning, I intend to go riding in Hyde Park. –P.F.*

17 October 1819

"You're both mad!" exclaimed Aunt Amelia, who stood shivering on the doorstep in dressing gown and curl papers. It was a clear, bracing autumn day, the kind of day where leaves swirled noisily in corners, trees groaned overhead, and the wind slapped a person's cheeks pink.

"In Wiltshire, I ride all the time in crisp weather," Prudence assured her. "Please, ma'am. We haven't too many days left before we're trapped indoors."

"Well, don't catch a chill." Aunt Amelia glowered and hastened inside.

A shiver ran down Prudence's spine, but her blood was on fire at the prospect of seeing William MacNeal and finally learning the truth. She threw her friend a nervous smile.

"Is this really what you want?" asked Miss Morris, clearly disapproving.

"I know it is wrong, but I simply must go."

At Hyde Park, the girls found themselves alone on the popular riding path known as Rotten Row. They moved slowly and without speaking, for the wind bit like knives. Presently, Mr. MacNeal emerged from a distant line of trees.

"Just in case," murmured Miss Morris, pulling aside her jacket to reveal a small pistol tucked into the waistband of her skirt.

"In case of *what?*"

Miss Morris shrugged and nudged her horse until she was barely out of earshot. Prudence turned to Mr. MacNeal, her heart beating wildly. He halted beside her, their mounts head-to-flank. Her eyes met his, and all those weeks of trying to forget him came undone in an instant.

"How well you look!" he said warmly. "And I see your companion cares deeply for your welfare!" He nodded toward Miss Morris; Prudence glanced back. The pistol was now draped casually over the girl's forearm.

Prudence exhaled through pursed lips. "Perhaps you should begin."

Mr. MacNeal's cheeks flushed. "I must first apologize for my ill-timed absences. You see, my father is a collector of the Arts and Antiquities, and I am his agent. I neglected to warn you that I would be departing Lady Revelle's salon early to meet a shipment of artifacts at Southampton. It took me a fortnight to supervise their unpacking and disbursal. All the while, you stood foremost in my thoughts, as if an unseen force were tugging me back to your side.

"I returned to London with mere hours to spare before I must sail for France. As I crossed Hyde Park to pay you a call, I happened to encounter Perkins and Tate. Suddenly, *there you were!* Encouraged by our conversation, I went to Paris floating on a cloud—"

"—leaving me unattended, vexed, and confused!"

Mr. MacNeal grimaced. "Yes, once again, I failed to say the right words. In Paris, I could think of nothing but you. I would've called my first morning back had it not been for my mother, who had promised Lady Trilby I'd go boating with her."

"Oh, why should I care?" sniffed Prudence, though deep within, her long-hurt feelings had begun to soften.

"Why?" Mr. MacNeal reached out and took her left hand. "Because you should know that circumstances alone have kept us apart. Except . . ." Here he looked piercingly at her. "Except for that time on the riverbank, when I asked permission to call but you would not answer."

"It wasn't like that! You reckoned I didn't want to see you again. My choice was either to agree or refute, but begging, sir, is beneath my dignity."

Mr. MacNeal went pale. "By Jove, I *am* a fool! I did try to call on you at Stanistead House, but the butler sent me packing. I now know your aunt was turning away visitors that day, but at the time . . ."

Prudence squeezed his hand. "Never mind. What then? How did you come to be at Bolton Park?"

"I overheard three gentlemen joking about a certain nobleman's passion for Miss Prudence Fairfeather. They were taking bets as to whether he'd yet screwed up the courage to offer for her."

"I asked him to put it off until the middle of September." Prudence closed her eyes, remembering the ache of waiting for him.

MacNeal continued, "Curious, I made inquiries. My rival had titles, land holdings, and an impeccable reputation—assets I could never hope to equal. I couldn't blame you for moving on; I understood your situation. I did wonder whether you loved him."

Prudence shook her head. He let out a sigh.

"Desperation emboldened me—I had to meet with this Lord Underwood and take my measure of him. I went to his home in Essex and asked for an audience. The butler said he was away, whereabouts unknown. A crown encouraged speculation: perhaps the master had gone to Hertfordshire to watch over his lady-love.

"I rode for Bolton all night and arrived shortly before dawn. I mingled amongst the hunters, but none answered to the description of Underwood. My spirits soared when I caught a glimpse of your face. I decided that must be enough. I was about to ride away and never look back when again I felt a sudden need to find you. I knew something dreadful was imminent."

"A premonition?" Prudence asked tremulously.

He nodded. "I broke away from the field and rode hard through the woods until instinct told me to rein in. I spotted you in the ravine and opened my mouth to halloo when I spied a rider on the opposite ridge. To my horror, he proceeded to shoot at you, twice. I tore out my own weapon and fired a volley, and of course you know the rest." A strange look came into his eyes. "He eluded me all over Europe, but rest easy, Miss Fairfeather, because your assailant is dead."

"He's *dead?*" exclaimed Prudence, jerking away her hand. Miss Morris snapped to attention.

"Hush!" hissed Mr. MacNeal, nudging his horse closer and grasping her elbow. "Gentle, now, my dear, this is no place for such talk."

"You killed a man on my behalf?" she shrieked. "Tell me who he was!"

"I beg you to please lower your voice."

Their horses stood so close that Mr. MacNeal's knee pressed against hers. Their exhalations misted and mingled together. Prudence fought to stay clearheaded. Her first thought sent a chill coursing through her body. Whomever MacNeal had killed, that person must have discovered her secret. "Who was he?" she repeated. Suddenly, she knew. And with that same certainty, she realized her identity had nothing to do with the shooting. Her free hand flew to her mouth as she felt the color drain from her face.

"It was Lord Underwood, wasn't it? You came to Bolton to dispose of a rival, but your shots went wild and you nearly killed *me*. You concocted this tale to cover your blunder!"

"Not true!" he exclaimed. "I thought to protect you. I shot only once, and I wish I hadn't had any cause to!"

Prudence narrowed her eyes. "Did you think I would praise you for murdering your rival? You'd have *had* no rival had you called sooner. Well, thank God you didn't—I am glad to know the true nature of your character!" She tried to break from his hold, but Mr. MacNeal's fingers dug into her sleeve.

"I didn't *murder* him, I swear it, and I have proof he meant to kill you. I know it sounds mad—"

"Let me go!" Prudence slashed at him with her crop. MacNeal loosed his grip. She wheeled the mare and bolted toward Miss Morris. In no time, the two girls were flying from Hyde Park.

"Whatever did he say?"

"Never mind!" Prudence shook so hard she could barely clutch the reins. It mortified her to think she had entrusted herself to—had even lost her heart to—a murderer. "Emmeline DeLacey doesn't know it," she panted, "but she should bless the day she gained her release from that monster!"

They returned to Stanistead House and handed their lathered horses to the groom. Prudence fled into the garden. When Miss Morris caught up, she was sobbing her heart out on a bench.

Miss Morris sat, took Prudence's shoulders, and said softly, "Do you trust me enough to tell me what happened?"

Prudence sagged. Josephine could not help her now. Aunt Amelia would be apoplectic if she found out about the tryst. She had no one else on earth in whom to confide. So she disclosed to Miss Morris Lord Underwood's unwanted attentions and how they had clashed with her hopes for a romance with MacNeal.

"I heard what you exclaimed in the park. Did he really kill someone?"

Prudence shuddered. "Remember that to-do in Hertfordshire? He shot at Lord Underwood whilst I stood between them. And that's not the worst of it—" She seized Miss Morris by the forearms. "Afterward, he hunted Underwood down!"

Miss Morris's eyes went wide.

"What'll I do?" demanded Prudence.

"You'll do nothing."

"What? Is it not my duty to see that justice is done? Surely we must call for the Bow Street Runners."

"But no one will believe you. Just because MacNeal said so, you have no reason to assume Underwood is actually dead. Where's the body? Besides, MacNeal is a well-regarded man with no reputation for violence. You'll be compared to Lady DeLacey: bitter and hysterical."

Prudence threw up her hands. "He'll get away with murder!"

"If you had adored Underwood, I could understand your need for vengeance, but you were indifferent to him and so you should remain. You must think of yourself. There is a good chance you can escape this without any taint. Seize upon that. Feigning ignorance is the best choice you have."

"I don't think I am strong enough!" Prudence buried her face in her hands.

"You have me to support you. Now, listen carefully, dear. This kind of knowledge gives you the power to destroy Mr. MacNeal. You must convince him you have nothing to gain by his ruin; otherwise you could be in very grave danger."

"Oh, God!" exclaimed Prudence.

"Shh," soothed Miss Morris, pulling out the pistol. Prudence recoiled. "Not to worry. I'm quite proficient." Miss Morris slipped the weapon back into her pocket. "Now, the first thing you must do is to start calling me Helen. The second thing is to invite me to stay at Stanistead House."

"Very well, Helen, although I must admit I am baffled. What do you have in mind?"

"I'm going to take care of you," Helen said with a smile. "And if that scoundrel tries to harm you, I will know what to do."

19 October 1819

Helen Morris moved into Stanistead House that day, filling the stodgy old place with giggles and gossip. Aunt Amelia's staff was unused to such liveliness, but they seemed to relish the change. Nobody noticed the girls spent an inordinate amount of time peering out the front windows.

"Anyone out there?" Prudence queried. Helen shook her head. They repeated this routine a dozen times each day. Prudence expected relief, but for some reason she always felt disappointment.

"It's eleven o'clock. Race you to the music room!" challenged Helen, her dark eyes sparkling. They bolted into the corridor and tramped down the stairs like a herd of wild cattle.

Aunt Amelia stood at the bottom, a glare of perturbation on her face. She thought poorly of Helen, but she had permitted her to stay on the condition she partook of Prudence's lessons. The girl was boisterous and untutored, the aunt had complained in private, and lacked the necessary refinements to be a proper lady's companion.

"There is a fine line between high-spiritedness and wildness," she scolded. "I expect you to set a good example, Prudence. We shall not run, especially when there are persons here who travel between households."

"Yes, ma'am." Prudence had lived so sober a life these past seven months that Helen's mere presence, coupled with weeks' worth of emotional drama, had reignited her enthusiasm. She took Helen's arm. Quietly, reservedly, they sailed into the music room.

"Why is it you have no governess?" asked Prudence later that day.

"I discharged my last one a year and a half ago," boasted Helen. "She was horrid and nosy. Mind you, since then I have kept up with my studies. Grandfather is the dearest parent. He has taught me all sorts of wonderful things, things a girl never gets to learn, like hunting, gambling, how to light a cigar, and the proper appreciation of single malt whisky."

"You drink whisky?"

"Not as a rule, but some occasions rather call for it, so Grandfather says." Helen went to the bedstead and lifted the mattress. "Ah, good! It's still there."

"What's that?" Prudence wondered aloud as she broke the seal on an envelope.

"Grandfather's pistol. I keep it under the mattress in case of emergency. I wanted to ensure the chambermaid hadn't found it."

Prudence shot her a pained look. "Helen Morris, you give me the shivers!" She glanced down at Josephine's letter. "Though you're not the only uncommon female I know—it seems my cousin nearly skewered a neighbor boy." She read aloud Josephine's account of a recent duel with Peter Bradford.

Helen grinned appreciatively. "Well done!"

Prudence skimmed the rest of the letter, learning among other things that Middlemere had invited Lieutenant Quimby for a short repairing lease. She let out a long breath. "Oh, I do hope this fellow isn't taking advantage of Papa's friendship to seduce his young heiress."

"Your concern is justified," said Helen. "By way of example, we need look no further than our murderous friend's ill-starred union with Lady DeLacey."

Prudence shuddered. "Do you mean to say he only craved the financial benefits of a marriage with her?"

"I'm speculating, of course, but, as the third son, William MacNeal likely needed a marriage of convenience. Lady Emmeline is beautiful, so perhaps he did love her, at least for a while."

"How did he break it off?"

Helen stretched along the length of the sofa. "That part is legendary. He told her he was destined to love another woman. Tact, I think, is not his strong suit."

With a jolt, Prudence remembered a long-ago dream.

That fan is already spoken for.

She pressed a hand to her mouth, stifling a cry. She'd never connected real people to that particular vision. Now she understood Lady Emmeline's purpose and the price she had paid for her arrogance. This also she knew: William MacNeal would never, no matter how deep his misery, have broken with Emmeline if they had truly been attached.

"What is going on in your head?" Helen asked.

Prudence parried with a new thought. "Perhaps he was referring to his ideal, a Woman of Destiny."

Helen leant forward, her eyes bright with inspiration. "What if he believed *you* were that woman, and when he thought he couldn't win you, he was driven to the edge?" She inhaled sharply. "Oh, Prudence, he and Underwood must have dueled! Perhaps that's what he meant when he said it wasn't murder."

Something shifted in Prudence's head. There were two sides to every story—the fan had taught her that much. Mr. MacNeal claimed to have proof that Underwood was a villain, and he'd looked so shocked when she accused him of murder . . .

Meanwhile, Helen plunged ahead. "Of course, if they had words and dueled, that would be one thing, but there is another, far more sinister, alternative. MacNeal may have meant to kill Underwood on the spot. When he realized you were his witness—and nearly his victim—he concocted that ridiculous plot . . ."

Helen continued to speculate, but Prudence wasn't listening.

Perhaps, to protect her, MacNeal had left out key information. But what did that signify? She said, "It matters not; he admitted Underwood is dead by his hand, and I hesitate to associate with that sort of man. Now, we have an hour before supper, and I should like to spend that time writing."

Alone in her room, she went straight to work. Never mind *her* heart—she had Josephine's to think about. Highly impressionable and incurably romantic, if Josephine wasn't already fond of Lieutenant Quimby, she soon would be. Maria would put a stop to things, but she hadn't any tact, so Prudence set out to remind Josephine, in the kindest terms possible, that Quimby was unworthy of her favor.

> *By all means, enjoy his Company, but do not get your feelings hurt if he has come to Greenbank only to avail himself of the free Bed and Board. That's the sort of thing One expects from young officers.*

She praised Josephine for declining the lieutenant's marksmanship lesson, then embarked on the difficult task of confessing to the odious Hyde Park affair. She concluded:

> *Rendezvousing is never a good idea, but I think I was able to impress on MacNeal my extreme Disgust for his person. He has, thankfully, made no further Contact.*

Her eye went to the slim Byron volume that lay at her elbow. She had read it, of course, on the night before the assignation. Had MacNeal seized it at random or chosen it specifically? She recalled the poem and thought perhaps it held the answer:

Yes—it was Love—if
thoughts of tenderness,
Tried in temptation,
strengthened by distress,
Unmoved by absence,
firm in every clime,
And yet—Oh more than
all!—untired by Time;
Which nor defeated
hope, nor baffled wile,
Could render sullen
were She near to smile

Prudence shuddered. These words, which three days ago had seemed so thrillingly romantic, had with certain knowledge taken on a more portentous meaning. Conrad, the noble villain—was that Mr. MacNeal? Was his soul as dark as Helen believed?

She laid a hand palm-down on the book. To be honest, she was absolutely *not* grateful that he had made no further contact. Lying was difficult, but the pretense had been necessary. No one, not even Josephine, must know how she longed for her villain's return.

With a shaking finger, Prudence traced the blue and russet marbled whorls that fanned out across the book's binding.

"'My Love! Thou mock'st my weakness,'" she whispered hoarsely.

CHAPTER TWENTY-SIX

Edingham-Greene, Wiltshire
17 October 1819

"I beg thy pardon?" asked Maria, dropping her fork and knife with a clatter.

Lieutenant Quimby colored. "Aye, 'tis true, madam, though I do not like to advertise it. I trust your family will do me the honor of keeping close such information?"

Josephine took a bite of pheasant and forced herself to chew. If not for the pounding of her heart, she could've heard the gears turning inside Maria's fertile mind.

Halfway through supper, an innocent inquiry had induced Quimby, in the humblest of tones, to reveal that he hailed from Exeter and was an earl in his own right. His father was Sir Robert III, K.G., Marquess of Farrow, former Chancellor of the Exchequer, and renowned for his diplomatic role during the American Rebellion. The old man had grown enfeebled in recent years and was estranged from the lieutenant, his only son.

One could therefore easily deduce that Lieutenant Robert Quimby, otherwise styled as the Earl of Rutherford, had not come to Greenbank for the free bed and board.

"I a'n't a gossip!" declared Maria. "Thy secret is safe with us, Thy Lordship."

"Maria!" cried Josephine. "That is precisely the sort of speech which betrays his confidence. He wishes you to refer to him as 'Lieutenant.'"

"Just so!" agreed Quimby, smiling gratefully at her.

She ducked her head, determined not to betray her feelings. She concentrated on the boiled potatoes, though she had no appetite to speak of.

Quimby turned his attention to Lord Middlemere, who beamed at the two women as if he were already in on the joke. "I must say, sir," said the young man. "You seem awfully pleased with yourself, like the cat that ate the canary."

"It's because I've known for a while—put two and two together, you might say. I'm flattered you have chosen to confide this in us, although I would have invited you here on any account."

Lieutenant Quimby gave a startled laugh. "I hadn't thought of it that way. No, it simply came tumbling out. Although I *have* felt the pressure of maintaining the ruse, for it's not healthy, I think, to keep secrets from one's friends."

Was it Josephine's imagination, or had he made a point of not looking at her when he made that remark? She watched Quimby from under her lashes. *Don't be silly, it's Papa with whom he means to be open. After all, I am forever challenging him and getting in his way.*

Middlemere nodded. "And knowing that's your philosophy makes us doubly honored to have you, whatever your title!"

Maria pressed on. "But, sir, I cannot help wondering why 'ee own such a lowly rank when 'ee might've purchased a captaincy?"

Lieutenant Quimby leant back in his chair, resigned to the nurse's interrogation. His eyes, burning with the fire of conviction, glinted in the candlelight. "I joined the Army because my privileged years were close upon me. Before I succeeded, I wanted the chance to serve our nation. The rank, by its necessary limitations, has forced me to live humbly and learn what it's like to take orders from my betters."

Sighing, Maria pressed her hands together in an attitude of worship.

Privately, Josephine worshipped him, too, though she was astonished at the speed with which the nurse had reversed her opinion. In fact, it spoiled things a little to have Maria's endorsement. *I admired him long before anyone learned he was wealthy.* Then again, she hardly dared to think he'd come to Greenbank for her, especially since his regard for the earl showed no bounds. When the family moved into the drawing room, Quimby stationed himself by the pianoforte, manned by Lord Middlemere.

"Do you sing, my good sir?" the earl asked hopefully.

Quimby hesitated, his jaw working in thought. "I do not care to compete with yourself or my lady. I would fain hear you both first." He glanced sidelong at Josephine.

A blush crept up her neck. "My voice is quite plain, so I'm uncomfortable performing for anyone outside the family."

"Forgive me. I didn't mean to put you on the spot." He turned back to the earl. "On further reflection, my lord, I have nothing in my repertoire which is not a bawdy-house tune, but I am an excellent page-turner!"

So Middlemere churned away at the keyboard whilst the officer turned pages with an exaggerated flourish, and together they entertained the women for nearly an hour. Quimby was charming; like an impresario he used an affected voice to announce every piece. Minute by minute Josephine fell further under his spell. She particularly loved the jolly humor that he brought out in her father, but she resolved not to show her hand unless she perceived a clear sign of mutual interest. Josephine meant only to be herself—neither giddy nor detached—and let the chips fall where they may. Thus she managed the hour, cool of cheek and calm of blood, with her dignity intact. The evening ended when Quimby claimed exhaustion.

"Good night, sir," he said, pumping Middlemere's arm. "I've had an eventful day, and I can't wait to enjoy the comforts of a good bed. Ladies!" After showing a leg in the direction of the women, he strode out.

He had barely cleared the doorway when Maria clawed at Josephine's arm. "Oh, my lady, now do I regret scorning thy partiality for him—"

"Good night, Maria!" hissed Josephine, and she too hurried away.

Josephine sat at her window, watching the countryside awaken, sorry she had nowhere to go. If Lieutenant Quimby hadn't happened upon her fencing with the boys, she would have kept their regular appointment. A movement below caught her eye. There it was again—a flash of bright red. Leaning forward, she spied a distinct silhouette on horseback, riding across the lawn toward the lower pasture.

"That rascal!" she exclaimed softly. Did he think she had secretly rescheduled her lessons? If so, what did he mean by trying to catch her in the act?

She waited a full hour until Quimby returned up the lawn. She was satisfied she'd foiled his plan until she saw him pause and tuck a pistol into his belt. Smoothing his jacket over it, he pressed his mount toward the stable.

Josephine fell back with a gasp. *The marksmanship lesson! He has not given up!* She scurried to the washstand and splashed her face with cool water. "Steel yourself, Jo. You must fight this temptation!"

She saw little of the menfolk until evening, when her father hosted a small dinner party in the lieutenant's honor. They toasted Quimby's health and thanked him for his service, after which he rose and spoke a few words. He glanced at her once down the length of the table, but she could not discern his expression at so great a distance.

"A pity he's only a lieutenant," remarked Mrs. March as she bid Josephine good night. "And a greater pity I'm not nineteen anymore." She patted her hair and looked askance at Quimby, who was speaking to a neighbor out on the driveway.

"Pshaw, Mrs. March, you don't look a day over twenty-one!" teased Josephine.

Mrs. March, who was plump and adorable and in truth not yet forty, returned a playful nudge. "Pshaw, yourself! He fancies you, I think. Be careful, my dear."

Josephine sniffed. "I wouldn't know, for he's done nothing to show it."

"That's just as well. Perhaps he's shy, or perhaps he's well-mannered enough to know he's not worthy of you. Have a care, Lady Josephine, that's my advice."

It wasn't Josephine's place to assure Mrs. March he was perfectly worthy. As she readied herself for bed, she wondered what had persuaded the lady to think Quimby fancied her. She wondered, too, if he would go tomorrow to the lower pasture. She could take a walk and pretend to happen upon him. But she knew what Prudence would say about these kinds of musings. Even Josephine had to admit it was one thing to meet a man for lessons in shooting and entirely another to rendezvous with hopes of a stolen kiss.

At dawn, she sat in her window and watched Quimby cross the dew-soaked lawn. An hour later, he reappeared looking slightly downcast. It was unfair to him—and a little too tempting for her—to let him go on like this. After breakfast, when he rose to keep his appointment with Lord Middlemere, she followed him into the hallway.

Quimby turned and smiled. "Hullo there! Are you going the same way, then?"

She barely registered his question before launching into her speech. "Sir, you needn't go to such trouble each morning. In fact, I beg you not to—" Her voice failed, for it had not been her intent to sound so desperate.

Quimby blinked. "Not to survey the countryside for further signs of those beasts?"

"Oh!" she cried, turning red. "I presumed you were going to the pasture."

His brows knit in an expression she could not decipher. "I've been conducting a reconnaissance . . . although I *have* made a point of dropping by the pasture. It occurred to me that, in light of our little adventure, you might have reconsidered my offer." He peered closely at her, his head tilting slightly. "Now I'm curious—what made you think I persisted?"

Josephine looked away. "I am an early riser."

"How delightful! So am I." Quimby glanced up and down the hall before adding with a shrug, "In which case, it seems a shame to waste an opportunity—"

"Please, sir, I must insist that you cease these invitations!"

Her head whirled in a fog of confusion. Oh, why did he promote her unladylike avocations? She put her hand on the newel post and mounted the first step, bristling at his condescension, faint though it might be. She was not a curious child to be humored by an indulgent adult.

In two quick strides, Quimby stood behind her.

"Lady Weston," he began in an undertone, his voice unnervingly close to her ear.

Carson emerged from the study and moved down the corridor. Josephine remained frozen in place. She dared not turn to face Quimby, not even after Carson had gone. If he saw the calf-love swimming in her eyes or the tears that threatened to spill down her cheeks, he would think her ridiculous!

She heard his intake of breath as he prepared to continue, but she cut him off. "No doubt Papa craves your attention. I wish you a pleasant day, sir." Then, without looking back, Josephine stalked up the stairs, fighting at each step to maintain her pride.

That afternoon, a letter claimed her attention. How could Quimby have made her forget her anxiety to hear the last of Miss Morris? Josephine opened the envelope and read with eager eyes.

"Oh, Prudence!" she cried, scowling at the righteous rejection of her previous counsel. Worse, now Prudence had developed an irrational need to take Miss Morris under her wing. Josephine shook her head. "I'm terrified that girl will be your undoing."

But she could do nothing more than make the most of Lieutenant Quimby's final days at Greenbank, which allowed them little time together. On Wednesday, the young gentlemen of Edingham-Greene arrived early to carry him off pheasant hunting. On Thursday, she had just joined him in the breakfast room when Middlemere stopped by to say, "I've found a reference in this volume I want to show you. Come along when you're ready."

"Yes, sir. I will, shortly."

Was there hesitation in his reply? Josephine dared not study Quimby closely enough to know whether he went reluctantly or with enthusiasm, but she felt the hours slipping past, and each lost opportunity weighed heavily on her.

As dusk approached, Josephine, feeling listless and hollow, buttoned up her redingote and wandered to the edge of the Heywood, where she'd shot the first troll. The sun had already sunk to the edge of the horizon, casting spidery shadows across the shorn fields. Refractions of darkness bent over fences and dips in the landscape. They rose up her body, hugging her shoulders as Quimby's cloak had once done but without his warmth and patient, low voice.

She pushed her hands into her muff and breathed out great clouds, recalling last week's incident with the emaciated troll and the sensation of Quimby cradling her close to his chest. All those times she'd supposed meaning from his touch, look, or tone . . . well, she must have been wrong, for he had taken no steps to substantiate his favor. She had allowed her immature heart to run away with a torch left lit for too long. Quimby felt nothing for her beyond a gentleman's concern; the sooner she accepted this, the sooner she'd heal.

A flock of pheasants burst from the underbrush, making her jump.

"You're not dressed for hunting."

The voice came from directly behind her. Josephine turned to find Quimby watching her from the top of the stile. Prickles ran up her arms, her heart thudded faster. She wondered if he could have divined her last thoughts. *Not at all, not at all.* Once again, coincidence had brought them together. *Coincidence, only that.*

"I beg your pardon?" she said. "I have never hunted anything in my life."

"Luckily I have brought along one of your cousin's fowling pieces," he continued, as if he hadn't heard. He stood and raised the musket for proof. His cheeks were flushed from the cool air, his chestnut hair boyishly tousled. The crimson of his coat set off the bright blue of his eyes. Although she ought not to indulge faded hopes, Josephine allowed herself to marvel at his charmingly cleft chin and the elegant sweep of his lips.

"W-why?"

"To teach you how to fire it, of course."

"Apparently, Lieutenant Quimby, you can't take no for an answer. We discussed this already, or have you forgotten?"

"I have not forgotten what you did the first time I found you here, nor can I pretend to ignore that you've been teaching yourself how to fence. If you persist in putting yourself in situations where such knowledge is indispensable, then I must persist in offering it." As he spoke, he rested the musket butt on the ground and reached into his hip-pouch for powder and shot. "Watch closely, for the light is poor. First you pull out the ramrod and give the barrel a good cleaning."

Why the devil must he go on about this? Is he teasing me? Josephine crossed her arms. Glowering, she labored mightily not to show any interest. "You're incorrigible, sir."

He ignored this remark and proceeded to demonstrate how the powder was measured. "Now birdshot, of course, is different from what we fire from a pistol. See these pellets? They vary in size depending on which fowl you're hunting. Otherwise, you'll mince the game to pieces. You pour this much shot into the muzzle and tamp it down with the rod."

Josephine silently took it all in. She had questions, of course, but she dared not speak, lest her voice betray the tumult of feeling swirling in her chest.

Having finished loading and half-cocking the gun, Quimby held it out. "Here you are. I'll try to scare up some more pheasant. When you're ready, pull back the hammer, lift the musket, and sight along the barrel. It's important to aim ahead of the bird's flight."

Josephine wanted to shout, "Stop tormenting me!" Instead, she curled her fingers round the stock and the barrel. The musket felt strangely natural there. She lifted the gun and sighted along its gleaming length. Quimby stepped close behind and put his arms around her to help guide her aim. A wave of dizziness fogged Josephine's senses. Fighting through it, she snapped, "If you're holding me, then who's flushing the pheasant?"

"I've got it. Be ready." He took his pistol from his belt and fired it left-handed into the underbrush.

The instant he did so, Josephine stepped out of his reach, jerked the musket skyward, and followed the rise of a large screeching pheasant. She pulled the trigger and killed it with one shot. The long-tailed bird tumbled down from the sky. She lowered the fowling piece and turned back to Quimby. "Well?"

His look of amazement bloomed into a grin. "*There's* the old fire in the belly!"

Josephine furrowed her brow. "What's that supposed to mean?"

"As a rule, my lady, I have known you to be feisty and outspoken. Indeed, your display of courage the other day was entirely within expectations, but since then you have seemed conspicuously subdued. I'd developed a conceit that *I* might be the reason."

"*You?*"

"Yes," he said, taking a step closer. "It is possible, is it not, that my presence in your house has affected you in some way?"

Josephine spun, dropped the musket, and strode to the edge of the thicket. *I knew it! He* is *teasing me!* She reached up and clutched a branch for support.

Quimby followed her to the trees. He stood next to her, hands in his pockets. "I didn't mean to offend you. We have so little time left, and I—" His voice dropped lower. "Dash it all, I *shall* be direct: ever since you turned down my offer of that lesson, I've had the devil of a time trying to get you alone!"

"Alone?" breathed Josephine.

Quimby put a hand beside hers on the overhanging branch. Their sleeves brushed, elbow to cuff. Autumn leaves rustled overhead.

He murmured, "I waited in that pasture every morning."

"I know," whispered Josephine, her heartbeat thundering.

"Have you lost interest in pistols, then?"

"Not in the least. I was trying to avoid a situation precisely like this."

"And why on earth would you want to avoid it?"

She gulped, and a tremble wracked her whole body. "Because you confuse me. Because I've ascribed meaning where there may be none, and the uncertainty of it pains me."

Quimby took her hand from the branch and turned her to face him. Here, under his direct gaze, she no longer had the strength to mask her feelings. *Let him know, then, and let me suffer the shame of rejection!*

Softly, he said, "Such a light in those eyes—like twin comets in the sky! I'm sorry it took me five days to win such sweet recompense. You keep your favor close, my dear Lady Weston."

"Far be it for me to toss handkerchiefs about for a man who has so clearly come to see my Papa!"

He squeezed her hand, and an affectionate smile lit his face. "Silly thing! Why do you think I tried to lure you down to the pasture? I came here in part to gauge the feeling between us. I did not expect these various claims on my time; indeed, they have thwarted me from my primary objective: you, my lady. You. As much as I admire your father, I'd fain rather walk in the starlight with you." He reached out and ran his thumb down the side of her face.

"Ah, sir!" squeaked Josephine, her knees going weak.

"Careful!" He buoyed her up by both elbows, but they staggered and fell against each other. He steadied her, embraced her, and pressed his lips to her hair. She lifted her face, and they gazed at each other at very close range. It seemed he would kiss her, yet after a long pause he shook his head and set her back on her feet.

Josephine exhaled sharply. "But, I—"

Quimby's face glowed pale in the rising moonlight. "Dearest lady, I want very much to express my affection, but you must understand that your age precludes me from taking advantage of you. For now . . ." He put two fingertips to her lips, then pressed them reverently to his own.

His sense of honor both maddened her and increased her esteem. As she could neither dispute his reasoning nor throw herself at him, she nodded and said, "Anyway, suppertime approaches, and we will be missed."

Quimby collected the gun and gave her his arm, and

they made their way back through the dusk to the house. Josephine wondered what would happen next; he was leaving tomorrow, and they had established nothing more than their mutual interest. He had called her too young but said it without judgment. What age made one old enough to kiss in the moonlight? Edward had not shown the least hesitation. It was half on her tongue to ask him this question, but she looked up to find him studying her face, and quite lost her nerve.

"This revelation has placed an awkwardness between us," he said. "I hope, given time, you and I can transcend it." Josephine nodded. He gave her arm a tight squeeze. In the gathering darkness, a smile curved her lips, scribed by the bliss of reciprocal feelings.

It was late when they arrived home—there was no time to change clothes. Josephine strode into the dining room, doing her best to maintain a neutral expression. Quimby ducked in once she had taken her seat. Their eyes met across the table. Josephine turned to greet the others.

Middlemere and Maria were staring at her.

"What?" Josephine challenged. Their silence stretched on.

"My lady, there is black powder on your cheek," supplied Quimby. "She shot a pheasant," he went on for the benefit of the others. "Oh, bother, did we forget to collect your trophy?"

Their stares moved to Quimby, who returned a matter-of-fact smile. The faces of Maria and Middlemere underwent simultaneous slow shifts from frowning confusion to sly understanding. During supper, the elders did nearly all of the talking. Josephine contented herself with occasional glances in Quimby's direction.

22 October 1819

She watched him, of course, as he rode away from Greenbank. He looked up at her window, but she drew back, unwilling to seem too desperately attached. Long after the plume of Lieutenant Quimby's shako disappeared from sight, she sat motionless.

When she came downstairs for breakfast, Maria pinched her cheek. "There's our gurt winsome girl and the future marchioness!"

"Honestly, Maria, would you have been half so delighted had he been styled merely Mr. Quimby?"

"Not in the least."

"And yet he is the same man, both handsome and erudite."

"No. Now he be *somebody*, which makes all the difference."

Josephine tsked and did not speak for the rest of the meal.

Later, when she brought in the post for her father, he beckoned her closer. Smoothing back her hair and cupping her chin, he said, "I saw a beautiful woman last night. Was it your mother come alive again? No! She was my little girl, my Josie, nearly grown and falling in love for the first time."

"Mercy!" cried Josephine, reddening. "Who said anything about love?"

"Nobody had to," smiled Middlemere. "But you're still young and Quimby knows it. Once you've finished your education, we shall see how things stand."

Overwhelmed, Josephine buried her face in his shoulder.

In retrospect, she was thankful Prudence's next letter had not arrived during Quimby's sojourn. Horror-struck, she read over and over again about Prudence's tryst in Hyde Park. MacNeal's confession of murder only compounded the nightmare. And now the detestable Miss Morris was living at Stanistead!

"Oh, my poor nerves!" she scrawled.

> *Between that meeting with Lady Revelle and this assignation, I'm nearly frantic with fear. If you do not write by express and assure me you are safe, I swear I shall tell Papa, whatever the consequences!*

As much as she hated to side with Miss Morris, Josephine agreed that Prudence should continue to play ignorant. Underwood's death was not yet confirmed, and if news of this love triangle should ever come out, her reputation would be destroyed.

Josephine rubbed her aching forehead. There was no time to relate what had transpired with Quimby. She sealed her reply and sent it off by express.

CHAPTER TWENTY-SEVEN

London
24 October 1819

Dutifully, and not a little worried Josephine might act on her threat, Prudence scribbled a note assuring her friend that Talismans and unsuitable suitors alike were banished from her life. She had even locked the chest inside the bottom drawer of her wardrobe.

> *I will* not, *however, go to Aunt Amelia, no matter how much you insist. I beg of you, Josephine, do not tell anyone about this Matter! As you yourself said, the Truth would undo me. Since I cannot prove Anything, I must carry on as though I were ignorant of any Crime.*

She posted this by express, praying it would meet with Josephine's approbation.

Meanwhile, the tactic of indifference seemed to be working. A few callers asked what Prudence thought about Underwood's disappearance, to which she had coolly replied, "It is not for me to say what any gentleman should do." Because so few believed Underwood had any real interest in her, it didn't take long to convince the *ton* of her lack of concern.

Disappointed though she was at the turn of events, even Aunt Amelia could appreciate this more dignified outcome. "It is better, I suppose, that you're not hysterical," she said. "But I swear, child, you do have the worst luck!"

"She doesn't know the half of it," remarked Helen when the old lady left.

Prudence rolled her eyes. "Never mind my odious *beaux*. Let us find you a fine soldier—someone who can indulge your unnatural passion for weaponry!"

Helen guffawed. "I doubt there's a man alive who wants a gangly scarecrow who can ride better, think faster, and drink more whisky than he."

"Well, we all have our challenges, don't we?"

Helen stuck her tongue out at Prudence.

Not everyone had such odious *beaux*. Several mornings later, Prudence choked on her breakfast as she read a letter from Greenbank. "Goodness gracious!" she croaked. "Josephine's in love!"

"What's this? With whom?" demanded Aunt Amelia.

"Robert Quimby, whom we thought was a nobody, but is in fact destined to become a marquess. I guess the joke is on me."

Amelia's eyes bulged like an actress's in a stage melodrama. "Pardon me, but I still haven't the foggiest idea *who* this Robert Quimby is," she said with particular emphasis on the word "who."

"Why, he led the platoon that camped at Edingham-Greene this past summer. Have I not mentioned him before?"

"I shall be writing to Middlemere, of that you can be sure," sniffed Aunt Amelia. "We must have absolute assurance that this man is no charlatan."

"True, but something tells me he's genuine. Oh, isn't it ironic that Josephine has found her match at home whilst here I sit?"

"Oh, hush!" exclaimed Helen. "In three months the Season starts anew."

"Precisely so," agreed Aunt Amelia. "Although I'd feel better if in the meantime we had an invitation or two, and better still if Lord Underwood simply turned up."

"I wouldn't have any man who'd abandoned me for two months," Helen said with a sniff.

"Thoughtless chit! He may be ill or detained somewhere out of the country. Did you ever consider that?" With a scowl, Aunt Amelia rose and sailed from the room, muttering something under her breath about Robert Quimby.

"Dear me!" whispered Prudence. "What if she's right?"

Helen tilted back her chair. "Then you marry him, I suppose . . . and take a lover as soon as possible."

Prudence threw her napkin at the girl. "Horrid vixen!"

Helen collapsed into peals of laughter and nearly fell off her chair.

Alone in her room, Prudence examined the rest of Josephine's letter, which consisted almost entirely of a diatribe against Helen. Calling her an "insidious presence" who "rules your every step," Josephine railed on for a page.

How childish it sounds, a schoolgirl with a pistol, peering through windows with paranoid expectations! I do not ask you to make public your knowledge, only to make a clean breast of it and place your safety in Aunt Amelia's far wiser hands.

Your jealousy of this friendship is wholly misguided. Who else do I know that goes about with pistols? And, furthermore,

I do not think you appreciate the strain I am under. Have done
with your judgments!

Next, she offered her heartfelt felicitations regarding
Quimby and reiterated that all continued perfectly well at
Stanistead House. Which it did . . . so long as she fought the
urge to hope for another encounter with William MacNeal.

1 November 1819

At breakfast on the first of November, Prudence found two
envelopes by her plate, one made out in a masculine hand.
Her heart thudded. Quick as lightning, she tucked it under the
napkin in her lap. Helen lifted a brow but was quelled with a
sharp look. Taking a deep breath, Prudence opened the note
from Josephine:

For now I shall restrain my impulse to go to Papa, but my
love for you is stretched beyond reason.

Prudence sighed. If only she could prove that Mr. MacNeal
was no villain, that he and Underwood had dueled like
gentlemen. Why, the evidence might lie right there in her
napkin! As the minutes ticked by, anticipation grew in equal
and opposite proportion to her appetite. It was all she could do
to down a cup of tea. When Aunt Amelia finally took her leave,
Prudence gestured furiously to Helen.

"It's from *him!*" she hissed. "Boldly transmitted, mind
you, through the morning post!" She devoured its contents

and passed it to Helen.

> *My Dear Miss Fairfeather,*
>
> *It distresses me that we parted on such unpleasant terms. You must understand: a person whom you trusted really did try to harm you. He no longer poses a threat, but I fear there are unknown others who still might. If you would but listen to me . . . I have evidence, which I would gladly show you, to corroborate my story.*
>
> *Please give me permission to call properly at Stanistead House. If you are amenable, send your reply to the direction below.*
>
> *Yours in anxiety,*
>
> *William MacNeal*

Helen handed back the note. "He's excessively persistent."

"He sounds so certain." The note slipped from Prudence's fingers and fluttered to the floor. If Mr. MacNeal could be believed, then the truth of her identity must be a secret no more. She shivered. Aunt Amelia had been adamant that her safety depended on anonymity, and even Lady Revelle had spoken in secret. Clearly, neither of them had betrayed her, so how could Underwood have guessed? And why would he knowingly pay his suit to a fraud? No, he *couldn't* have known, and therefore had no motive for murder. Her original conclusion must be correct—MacNeal had killed his rival in cold blood. Even so, if he had owned up to his rage and given her an honorable reason, she might have forgiven him.

"Of *course* he sounds certain!" hissed Helen. "He invented the whole thing. Oh, Prudence, I feel he would pursue you to the ends of the earth!"

Aunt Amelia re-entered the dining room. "What's that? Have you an admirer, Prudence? Well, who is he? Let me see that, Miss Morris." She pointed to the paper on the floor. Helen turned stricken eyes on Prudence.

Prudence plucked up the letter and held it aloft.

"William MacNeal?" cried Aunt Amelia, glimpsing the signature. "Ah, yes, the handsome rogue from Hyde Park who did not deign to call on us. Later, ostensibly, your hero on the river. From the crest, I can see he must be one of Sir James's sons. Well, I had no idea. What's this about, then?" Her voice had gone harsh, and she jabbed a finger at the note.

Why now? thought Prudence. *Now, when I want to forget him!*

"He has been out of the country and only recently heard of my accident at Bolton Park. He asks after my health."

"Hmmph! He ought to have directed his inquiry to me." Aunt Amelia stalked around the dining room, stroking her chin. "He's handsome, I'll grant you, and well-spoken, too. You like him, do you not?"

"I *did*," croaked Prudence, throwing a panicked look at Helen. "But I—"

"If MacNeal was your rescuer on the Thames, then we owe him our gratitude. He spoiled a suit of clothes on account of you, and now the dear fellow asks after your health. Honestly, Prudence—we can't afford to burn *all* our bridges. The MacNeals are well-regarded. I shall ask him to join us for supper on Thursday."

The girls followed Aunt Amelia into the drawing room, where she sat at her desk and made out the notice. "Excellent!" she cried, rubbing her hands together. "Really, Prudence, you must learn to keep your mouth shut. You're gaping like a hungry fledgling." Then she went off in search of Reese.

"Oh, I say!" declared Helen, heading for the brandy decanter.

"Now what?" groaned Prudence. "I can have nothing more to do with that man. This is absurd—I must speak to Aunt Amelia!" She reached for the bellpull.

"No!" Helen darted over and seized her by the wrist. "Let me remind you, Prudence, that it's still mere hearsay. Nothing good will come of making an outrageous accusation." Prudence nodded unhappily. "Now, let us face this together. We must think of a way to make Mr. MacNeal never want to see you again."

4 November 1819

Before supper on Thursday afternoon, the girls ushered Nell out of Prudence's bedchamber. Helen helped Prudence into a high-necked, black crape gown they had found tucked away in a wardrobe. They did up her hair in a tight, matronly coif. To complete the image, they powdered her face and rubbed coal dust under her eyes.

Helen donned the same yellow gown Prudence had worn at Chedleigh Hall. It hung a bit short, but otherwise she looked willowy, radiant, and utterly feminine. They pinned her hair into loose curls and pinched her cheeks till they glowed.

"You look stunning!" Prudence exclaimed. "Helen, you've become a classical beauty."

"I have no bosom!" lamented Helen, patting her boyish form.

" . . . girls?" called Aunt Amelia, far off downstairs.

They exchanged nervous glances.

"He's a cad, don't forget it." Helen squeezed Prudence's hands. "You must bore him to tears whilst I try to distract him. We'll make him lose interest."

They linked arms and moved to the top of the stairs. A knock sounded at the front door. The girls tightened their hold on each other. Just then, Aunt Amelia glanced up.

"Dear God in heaven!"

But there was nothing she could do. As the girls made their way downstairs, Reese admitted the guest. Prudence dared one peek at MacNeal; he looked dashing in a green coat, grey pantaloons, and shiny Hessians. As he handed over top hat and gloves, the grace of his hands captivated her. She had to remind herself that behind his beauty lay a murderous heart.

"Good evening, sir," said Aunt Amelia. "We're so pleased you came."

Mr. MacNeal bowed. "I have long looked forward to this moment." His eyes quickly sought Prudence, then widened with surprise. He said smoothly, "Miss Fairfeather, you're looking as well as your aunt claimed."

Aunt Amelia stalked toward the drawing room, muttering, "She looks like a corpse." Helen bit off a guffaw.

A stab of remorse pierced Prudence's belly. *Murderer!* her mind hissed, after which she intoned, "Thank you, sir. I have never felt better." She slumped into a chair, rested her head on one hand, and maintained this attitude for the remainder of the hour.

Helen commenced her assault. Like a seasoned coquette, she batted her lashes and patted her hair. She attended MacNeal's every word with rapturous eyes. She squealed and clapped her hands at whatever he said. Prudence wished she might've found these antics amusing, but with each passing minute she grew ever more mournful. She could hardly bear the irony of finally having MacNeal here, adoring her askance, and having to spurn him for her own good.

Aunt Amelia did her best to bear up under an evening gone awry. She peppered Mr. MacNeal with questions and attempted without success to draw Prudence in. Puzzled though he must have been, Mr. MacNeal remained unruffled. He cast Prudence several querying glances, but when these efforts failed, he engaged Helen directly and without the least acknowledgment that she was flirting with him.

The supper bell rang. On the way to the dining room, Aunt Amelia prodded Prudence. "Run wash your face, little wretch, and see that you start smiling!"

Prudence ducked into the kitchen and patted her face with a damp tea towel. She didn't need a mirror to know her complexion was still ashen. *No matter how much you want him, he is a fiend. Do not forget that.* Back in the dining room, Mr. MacNeal stood waiting to help with her chair. He took his own seat and cast her an eye-twinkling smile. She looked down at her plate.

During the meal, one could hardly get a word in edgewise for Helen's giggling. Aunt Amelia grew angrier with each passing course. When they rose to return to the parlor, she took Helen by the elbow.

"One moment, please!" she called to the others, then, *sotto voce*, "I'd like a word with you, Miss Morris."

"But I—"

"*Now!*"

They disappeared into the butler's pantry, leaving Prudence and Mr. MacNeal alone. Panic-stricken, Prudence wheeled round to face the dining room wall.

Mr. MacNeal walked over and stood directly behind her. "Why are you doing this?"

"Because I despise you!"

"I don't believe it."

"Why not?"

He bent close to her ear and whispered, "Because I sense your longing."

Outraged by the strain he was placing on her resolve, Prudence whirled on him, hand upraised. He caught her wrist with an unyielding grip and pulled her close to his chest.

"Sorry," he murmured. "I felt compelled to say that—it was, I'll admit, a calculated risk." His eyes bored deep into hers. Silence surrounded them except for their breathing, and Prudence fought the impulse that wished him to kiss her. As if in defiance of that very battle, he dropped his face closer until his mouth hung a hair's-breadth away from her own. "One conference between us will negate your suspicions. Madam, I ask you—I *beg* you to yield to your heart."

Remember he's a liar! Edging back, Prudence dropped her gaze to her trapped wrist. "Sir, I think you are trying to intimidate me."

"To what purpose? I can't imagine what I might gain by forcing your attentions."

She lifted her chin. "You know it would take but one word from me and you'd be hanged for a murderer. Well, I give you my assurance I want no part of a scandal. I'll forget your confession if you agree to leave me in peace." She was shaking now, having brought the matter into the open, and terrified by the force of her conflicting emotions.

MacNeal furrowed his brow. "What? I—By Jove, I would volunteer myself for the gibbet before I'd do anything to harm you! Miss Fairfeather, I lo—" He shook his head and chose a different tack. "I came tonight for one purpose only: to convince you of our deep attraction for each other."

Prickles ran up her arm to her spine, and somehow Prudence knew he had always spoken the truth. Even so, she made herself say, "How *dare* you?"

Mr. MacNeal's jaw flexed. "Someday you'll realize I'm not half the cad I pretend to be," he muttered, pressing something into her palm.

Footsteps startled them apart. Helen appeared, looking bitter and resentful. Behind her loomed Aunt Amelia.

"Is there a problem?" asked Mr. MacNeal.

"None at all, my dear sir, none at all." The aunt glowered sidelong at Helen. Linking arms with her guest, she glided into the drawing room. Both girls were subdued for the remainder of Mr. MacNeal's visit. No sooner had the front door closed behind him than Aunt Amelia exploded.

"You girls are the limit!" She seized a handful of Prudence's dress and gave it a jerk. "Explain yourselves at once!"

Prudence said, "I'm sure I don't know what you mean, my dear Aunt."

"That rig you're wearing, your face, your demeanor! Miss Morris prancing about in your frock and behaving like a hussy! Do you think I'm a fool?"

"No ma'am."

"Perhaps *you* do, Miss Morris?"

Helen shrank back. "No, ma'am, not at all!"

"Off to bed, ladies. Oh, I pray you have not made things worse than they already were!"

Under a shower of imprecations, Helen and Prudence scrambled upstairs.

"He cornered you," hissed Helen when they gained the upper landing. "Did he threaten you somehow?"

"No," Prudence said, not looking at her. "He seemed puzzled."

"Let him be! Poor Miss Staveley needn't worry. He won't tell anyone what we did because he knows we have the ammunition with which to strike back. I think we've seen the last of William MacNeal."

Prudence smiled wanly. "Not if Aunt Amelia can help it. She clearly adores him."

"We'll cross that bridge when we come to it."

"Enough for tonight. I'm fatigued." Prudence kissed Helen's cheek. "You should wear yellow more often—it becomes you."

Alone in her bedchamber, she produced the square of paper MacNeal had given her. There were two sheets folded together, each in a different hand.

The first, in his handwriting, said,

I neither ambushed Lord Underwood nor murdered him. I was only trying to make him come home to serve justice. As senseless as it seems, he was involved in a plot to take your life. I found the enclosed in his pocket after he expired. Were you aware you had a mortal enemy?—W.M.

The second page, which was printed in block letters, read,

Underwood, sir,

She must be holding out hope for that young rubbish merchant. Frankly, I now think she is useless to us; in fact, she has the potential to become a great thorn in our side. Can you not think of some means to do away with her? Remember, you must earn *your place in our society. A consort can be found elsewhere. You, sir, as well, can still be replaced.*

There was no signature.

Prudence flung the pages away and fell facedown on the bed. "What in God's name am I supposed to make of that?"

Had Mr. MacNeal actually foiled an attempt on her life, or had he increased the levels of deceit to support his bizarre story? Whichever the case, Helen was too prejudiced to help her untangle the problem. If only it were so simple as hating this man, but the possibly that she harbored an unfounded fear kept her heart from completely shutting him out. So, for the first time in ten days, Prudence went to her desk and spilled her heart out to Josephine.

CHAPTER TWENTY-EIGHT

Edingham-Greene, Wiltshire
29 October 1819

As it had not occurred to the Earl of Middlemere to consult with a maiden aunt on the question of his daughter's fledgling love life, he was astonished to receive this admonition via express delivery:

> *Clarence, you had better know what you're doing! Do not trifle with your daughter's feelings. Be absolutely certain that boy is who he says he is before you allow this romance to go another step further.*

But Middlemere *was* certain, and he had been for several months. He often mistook people for shades from the past; even Josephine was accustomed to being called "Joanna." The case of Robert Quimby had been a different matter. Back in June, Middlemere and the young man were discussing the state of affairs in France when the earl blurted, "Tell me, sir—at what point did you realize the New York Project was a failure?"

Quimby had returned a puzzled look, and Middlemere realized he'd had another one of his "moments," which he quickly brushed off. During another briefing, he found himself thinking for some reason of Robert, Lord Farrow, a nobleman whom he had met once, a long time ago. After Lieutenant Quimby departed, Middlemere went to his books. A brief search yielded exactly what he sought.

In a volume entitled *Diplomacy in Revolutionary America* was an entry that described the consular efforts of a certain Robert Quimby, Lord Farrow of Devonshire, during his years in New York from 1774 to 1777. The accompanying engraving captured Middlemere's attention as never before.

"Well, I'll be dashed!" he breathed. "If he isn't the very spit and image . . ."

Lord Farrow had produced only one son the earl knew of, and that child had died in infancy around 1796. Thereafter, he had no personal knowledge of Lord Farrow's doings; of course, this didn't preclude the old fellow from having fathered more children.

"Fascinating!" murmured Middlemere. The lieutenant looked so much like his father yet was wholly unlike him in character, for Farrow himself had been an infamously arrogant ass. He'd put away the book and resolved to keep silent. If Quimby wanted to disclose this connection, he'd do so in time. If he didn't, that was his prerogative.

Thus, the earl had not been surprised when the young man had taken the opportunity to reveal his parentage. Middlemere chose not to insult his sensibilities by pretending to be startled, but neither did he pry. He had sensed a thread of shame in Quimby's voice, as if the young man regretted the truth of his pedigree and would have preferred to deny it. Over the ensuing days, they spoke a little of his upbringing and briefly about his sire, enough to satisfy Middlemere that here indeed was an offspring of Farrow. He realized in retrospect Quimby had confessed in order to lay the groundwork for love.

> *Dearest Aunt—be not alarmed! Our young suitor is not disingenuous, but rather the most gentlemanly of men. I am certain of his identity and equally certain he possesses all the great qualities his father does not. His mother, so I hear, was a saint among women and died giving life to this good soul. I can think of no finer person to entrust with my daughter's future.*

He signed the letter and dropped the pen into its stand. "And things will be better still," he murmured, "if we can seal the arrangement before Josephine ever sets foot in that detestable place called London!"

31 October 1819

Josephine lay in bed, nursing a minor cold and taking in Prudence's reaction to developments with Quimby.

> *What a Scamp you are, pretending you weren't fond of him all along! You spoke of him too often to convince me of your Disinterest. At least now you won't have to Endure the dreadful regime of a Season.*

No Season? Josephine gulped. "Oh, fiddlesticks! Am I never to have any fun?" Tears came to her eyes, and her nose began to run. Maria bustled in with tea and honey.

"My lady! What be the matter?" She set aside the tray and ran to enfold Josephine.

"If I promise myself to Quimby, then my only prospect of attending the Season will be as his wife!"

"There, there," soothed Maria. "No one has made any promises. Indeed, His Lordship has yet to speak to thy father. Glances and sweet nothings do not a proposal make. Give it time, my pet. We shall see where this goes. 'Ee'll turn seventeen this winter. I expect thy father won't give 'ee up for at least a year after that."

Josephine lifted her head. "Do not misunderstand me. I really do adore him."

"Of course 'ee do, but 'ee bist only a schoolgirl. At thy age, infatuations come and they go. At least he had the sense not a-press for commitment."

"He is awfully good, isn't he?" sniffed Josephine, wiping her nose.

"The very best." Maria fetched a brush from the dressing table and smoothed Josephine's bed-tangled hair. "And how fares our Miss Prudence?" she asked, nodding at the discarded letter.

"She's happy for me, of course, and perhaps a bit jealous of my good fortune."

"She ha'n't had an easy time of it. And I was so certain we'd have a wedding by Christmas. Speaking of jealousy, bist 'ee still in a miff over that Miss Morris?"

"I am *not* jealous, I just happen to think that girl is a bad influence." Josephine paused, realizing she dared not share any evidence that could support this charge. "And she's a gossip!" she finished weakly.

"Lar!" cried Maria in mock astonishment. "I'm amazed

Prudence would have truck with anyone like that!" She smiled pointedly at Josephine, who stuck out her tongue. "Oh, my love, don't 'ee see? Miss Prudence ha'n't replaced 'ee with somebody else. She has the right a-cultivate new friends."

But this girl in particular is the wrong sort of friend.

Josephine shrugged. "I wish her every happiness, of course, but until Prudence is married, it's my duty to advise her when I see her making a grave error."

Maria shook her head. "That's Miss Staveley's job now."

Of course, Maria didn't know Prudence had refused to be forthright with Amelia, all because she wanted to protect Miss Morris. Josephine wondered how she could show Prudence the error of her ways. Four days went by, then five days and six, when it occurred to her she'd never bothered to reply to Prudence's last letter. By the same token, neither had Prudence written to ask why.

Josephine supposed their friendship had cooled. Perhaps her repeated scolds had gotten on Prudence's nerves, but at the root of it lay the divisive Miss Morris. God knew what that girl was whispering in her ear. Josephine wished more than anything she could go to London and hash it out with her old friend. But there was no use in asking, for her father would never accede, and anyway Prudence and Aunt Amelia would be home for Christmas in only six weeks.

6 November 1819

Lieutenant Quimby wrote Middlemere from the vicinity of Cheltenham, where he and his platoon had been assigned for the winter. After an amusing account of his efforts to find a decent place to billet in town, Quimby ended with, "I wish you the best of health, and please remember me to your daughter."

The earl winked at Josephine. "I don't think he's writing just to me anymore. Shall I add your own greeting when I post my reply?"

Josephine ducked her head.

"Oh, sir, I hardly think that's proper!" objected Maria.

For once, Josephine appreciated the nurse's intervention. Now that she'd won Quimby's stated interest, she preferred not to fan the flame at every opportunity. He would have to wait at least fifteen more months, and she was in no hurry to marry.

"I think your own words will suffice," she told her father.

Maria sat back with a satisfied smile.

Monday's post brought a letter from Prudence, which did nothing to settle Josephine's growing sense of unease. Mr. MacNeal had not only insinuated himself into Stanistead House, he had once again swayed Prudence's opinion of him. Overlooking the plain silliness that had gone on at supper, Josephine cut to the chase:

> *That letter he gave you proves nothing. Why would anyone try to "do away" with an innocent girl, especially one whose real identity is—by design—known to practically no one? You're far too valuable; an Oathbreaker like Lady Revelle would want you alive.*

A burst of inspiration struck her. She composed another letter for Edward, asking him to visit his sister in London. "And tell me what you think of this companion of hers, who seems to be putting the oddest notions into Prudy's head." Josephine paused, hoping she had stated this nonchalantly enough.

> One other thing: Mr. William MacNeal is now showing a great deal of interest in Prudence. He may have been up at Oxford about eight or nine years ago. Last year he broke off an engagement with Lady Emmeline DeLacey. Could you, for the sake of your sister's innocent heart, somehow identify the essential facts?

"I'll never hear from him," said Josephine, "but it was worth the try."

To her great surprise, she soon received an answer:

> 10 November 1819
>
> Dear Josephine,
>
> You've given me no specific reason why I should bolt from school just to look this chit over. Speak to Papa or Aunt Amelia. Sorry, Jo, but I can't afford to leave, not when examinations loom so closely. As for the other matter, I might be able to help. By Jove, I'll draw that cove's cork if he's some kind of loose screw!
>
> Now, what's this I hear about Corporal Quimby sniffing around Greenbank? I can't believe you'd set your cap for such an obvious gold-digger.
>
> E'd. Fairf——
> K___ College
> Oxford

"*Corporal* Quimby? Oh, Eddie!" Josephine blushed in spite of herself. So he was jealous, eh? She had hoped his feelings would have tempered with time. Well, even if he refused to help her unseat Miss Morris, at least he'd shown some interest in rooting out the infamous William MacNeal. Now she sat back and waited for Edward to deliver the killing blow.

CHAPTER TWENTY-NINE

London
5 November 1819

Oblivious that Prudence had rekindled her affections for Mr. NacNeal, Helen celebrated their success in having driven him off. The next night she persuaded Aunt Amelia to take them to see *Look Before You Leap* at the Adelphi Theatre. Though the aunt held a dim regard for such mindless fare, she seemed to enjoy the production. Prudence took little note of what transpired onstage, instead scouring the audience in search of MacNeal.

She was wholly aware of her distraction. Indeed, it troubled her greatly. What did it say about her, to be in love with a man so hopelessly flawed? Afterward, she wrote Josephine,

> *Oh, the singular Heartache of being repelled and attracted by someone all at once. I think it's almost inevitable I shall give in, for I am floating and Soulless and Nothing without him.*

"Well, it seems you have managed to frighten off yet another suitor," complained Aunt Amelia, glancing at the clock late

Sunday afternoon. "It has been three days since we hosted Mr. MacNeal, with nary a peep from him since. I am curious, my dear Prudence, what your objection was this time?"

Ashamed and confused, Prudence looked away. Helen put an arm around her friend. "Have you not heard about his infamous jilting of Lady Emmeline DeLacey? Prudence fears she might become his next victim."

"Is that so?" asked Aunt Amelia. "Well, we shall see about that." She stalked to her desk and set to work on a half-dozen notes. When she was done, she rose and intoned, "If I find you meddlers have swallowed some unfounded bit of gossip and insulted that gentleman with your infantile antics, then so help me God I will banish you both from this house!"

Helen held her chin high, but Prudence shrank under these words. She wanted more than anything to see MacNeal's character vindicated, but then she would surely pay for her actions. She bowed her head.

Ah, don't dwell on losses you cannot control! He is not your only *passion.*

At bedtime, she paced her room with a lit taper in hand. Hounded by thoughts of MacNeal, she longed for something to still her mind. Her eyes flicked occasionally toward the locked drawer of her wardrobe where the Talismans resided. She strode toward it, then paused, biting a thumbnail. "No. Josephine's right. I shouldn't handle them. Besides, don't I already have enough controversy in my life?"

This isn't controversy; it is truth, and you've been seeking that truth all summer long. Your beaux *may be gone, Prudence, but you can still find solace in your Inheritance.*

She went to her dressing table and fetched the key from a tray. Soon the traveling chest lay open at her feet. With slow, controlled breaths, Prudence viewed the box's contents. Nestled in the folds of the weather-beaten wool cloak lay the winking red gem. She scooped it up.

"What did you use this for, Mother?"

Not so fast. You are learning, though you may not realize it yet.

Prudence slipped the chest back under her bed and climbed under the covers with the ring clutched in her palm. She opened her fingers and regarded the jewel. "Very well," she told it sternly. "Reveal your secrets slowly if you must, but please do remember that I am your mistress."

Touché. *I'm happy to know you're such a quick study.*

Prudence laughed aloud, a nervous trill. "Right. A ring is talking to me. I don't suppose anyone besides Lady Revelle would explain why . . . but what does that matter? Surely I can discover its powers without her guidance." She took a deep breath and slipped the ring onto her forefinger. It quickly molded itself to the correct size.

Without warning, Helen bubbled into the room. "Good Lord!" she cried, throwing herself across the foot of Prudence's bed. "Do you really think the old girl will toss us out on the street?"

Prudence cupped her hands to cover the ring. *Pocket, pocket, pocket,* whispered the odd voice in her head. *She's hiding it from you.*

She pointed to Helen. "What have you got there?"

"Nothing." Helen shrugged and held up two empty palms.

"In your dressing-gown pocket."

"There is nothing," insisted Helen, a trifle defensively.

"Hand it to me."

A startled look came into Helen's eyes. She drew out an envelope.

Quick! Save it from the fire!

"You planned to burn it, didn't you?" cried Prudence, reaching for the note.

Helen darted off the bed, shielding the envelope behind her back. "Prudence, it's for the best. Don't let yourself be tempted."

"What makes you think I'd be tempted? Perhaps I simply desire to know what a madman writes when he contacts his victim so brazenly through the post."

Helen guffawed. "I have been watching you, darling, and you do not have the look of a terrorized female. You're in love, though you're fighting it, and I'm here to help you overcome the impulse to give in. After all, you did ask me to protect you from William MacNeal."

As she spoke, Helen backed slowly across the room. With a gasp of dismay, Prudence realized the girl now stood on the hearth with the note dangling directly over the coals. Rage shot through her, sharp as a cracking whip. "Helen Morris," she warned, easing herself from the bed, "if you drop that note on the fire, I'll make you sorry you ever walked into this house."

Helen's dark eyes wavered and she trembled, head to toe. She stepped away from the fire, her arms falling to her sides. Prudence darted forward and snatched the note.

"Be off, now! Lord, you're such a child!"

The girl turned heel and fled, an apology tumbling in her wake. "I was only doing what you wanted . . ."

Prudence tore open the note and devoured its inscription:

That your aunt has been making inquiries about me suggests a lack of conviction on your part. I appeal to you directly, one soul to another: let me show you in person how earnestly I admire you.

She felt suddenly dizzy. Urgent voices curled through her head: Josephine insisting that MacNeal was untrustworthy. Aunt Amelia howling it was improper for ladies and gentlemen to communicate by post. Helen chanting, "He's a murderer!"

Then another, which said, *Come, Prudence. I'm waiting.*

"Hush, all of you!" cried Prudence, wrenching the ring from her hand. "*His* is the only voice I want to hear!" The murmurs ended at once, leaving her wide-eyed and panting. She flung the ring back into the box, along with Mr. MacNeal's note. When her pulse had cooled, she crossed the hall to Helen's room. The girl had obviously been crying.

"I'm sorry," Prudence said. "I'm just awfully confused."

Helen reached for her hand. "Of course you are, dear." She pulled Prudence down beside her. "The way I see it, it isn't a question of whether you love him, but whether you should *let* yourself love him."

"You have a point," said Prudence, resting her head on Helen's shoulder.

"You know, I think you relish the idea of loving a dangerous man."

Prudence laughed sharply. "Well, which would you choose: a dull man or dangerous one?"

Helen's expression spoke volumes. She *did* understand.

10 November 1819

If Aunt Amelia noticed any undercurrents of disharmony between the girls, she likely chalked it up to boredom. It was the doldrums of London's Season, when the *beau monde* flocked back indoors. Many had gone to the country, not to return until well after Christmas. Stanistead House stood silent; the young ladies whose laughter once filled its rooms had become introspective and moody. Aunt Amelia would not let them grow complacent. With the tenacity of a drill sergeant, she laid out their lessons and insisted they always be ready for callers.

During those long hours, Prudence was often tormented by strange and conflicting thoughts, as if MacNeal and the ring warred for supremacy over her heart. Every day the conflict grew more stark, and it seemed not one voice in her head actually represented her own.

She awakened early on Wednesday, and without any forethought she reached under the bed and opened the old chest. In seconds, the ruby ring was back on her hand.

Postman, postman, postman, hissed the voice in her head. *Get there before Reese does.*

Prudence bolted out of bed. Pulling on her dressing gown, she padded into the hall. The household was only beginning to stir. As she inched her way downstairs, she heard a maid setting the breakfast table and another stirring the fires. Her feet had just made contact with the cold flagstone hall floor when a knock sounded on the door.

Prudence melted into the shadows. A footman arrived to admit the postman. They swapped handfuls of mail and bid each other good morning. The footman tossed everything onto the hall table.

Reese is coming! warned the voice.

Prudence darted from her hiding place, startling the poor footman. "Good morning!" she chirped, as if she had a habit of intercepting the post at dawn every day. A quick search of the pile produced an envelope made out in Mr. MacNeal's hand.

She tucked it close to her heart and hurried back to the stairs. A terrible dizziness struck her before she reached the first landing.

Don't keep it so close!

Prudence yanked the note from her bodice and clutched it gingerly between two folds of her gown. Alone in her room, she lit a candle and crouched by the glowing hearth. Numb fingers pulled open the page.

Your silence tears at my heart, for I fancied a hint of reluctance in last week's rebuff. I wish to understand your conflict; will you grant me one last chance? If you still find me distasteful, then of course I'll desist. Which shall it be? Send me a word, just a word, written in your hand. Yes . . . or no?

Prudence curled onto the floor and tears flowed unchecked from the corners of her eyes. "Yes! Oh, yes! A thousand times so!" In closed the whispers of warning and dissent. "Please," she groaned. "Leave me in peace. If I am wrong, then at least I shall have made my own choice." Through the fog of this swirling internal debate, she spied a pair of black eyes at the doorway.

"She's prepared to yield!" murmured the observer. "He will destroy her for certain! No, I *cannot* allow it!"

Prudence lifted a hand. *What gives you the right to dictate my future?* But Helen was incapable of hearing her thoughts. Frowning, she shut Prudence's door with a click.

Now the voices rose to a din until Prudence could no longer stand it. She pried the ring loose and let it fall to the floor. "I understand now," she rasped, sweat speckling her brow. "One or the other. Which shall I choose?"

She must have fallen into a swoon then until a strange

stab of pain roused her and she slowly became conscious of the sound of raised voices. People were arguing downstairs. Staggering upright, she burst from her room.

"You have some nerve!" Helen said. "I told you she never wanted to see you again."

A man's voice floated upward. "It is beneath me, Miss Morris, to state my exact regard for your opinion. Deflect me if you wish with weapons and wiles, but I shall never be satisfied till I hear a rejection from her own lips!"

"William!" breathed Prudence, plunging for the stairs.

As she gained the first landing, Helen retorted, "She despises you, Mr. MacNeal. No decent man would force a lady to speak such words to his face."

A second pang struck Prudence full in the chest. She wheeled about, clutching at her heart. A searing sensation passed through her body, rendering her incapable of speech as she collapsed to the floor. Whatever else passed between Helen and MacNeal was lost in a haze of incomprehension and despair. By the time she hauled herself upright, the front door had closed and Helen stood alone in the hall.

Prudence lurched down the steps. "How *dare* you?" she cried.

"I beg your pardon?" Helen asked, adjusting her gloves. She wore a redingote and hat. Was she leaving or returning?

"You lied to Mr. MacNeal. You misrepresented me. I *felt*— " Prudence stopped herself, recalling that sharp stab of pain. Recalling *his* pain. Yes, it must have been his. But *how?*

"You're imagining things, Prudence. Mr. MacNeal was not here."

"He was, just now, and you sent him away!"

"No, but I do wish somebody *would*. It's heartrending

watching you pine for that troublesome man. If you'd only take our advice, you might marry so brilliantly." Helen's eyes bulged, and she clapped a hand over her mouth.

Prudence stared. "What did you say?"

The reply was muffled.

Prudence yanked Helen's hand away from her mouth. "When is the last time you saw Lady Revelle?"

Helen cut her eyes. "Last month. You were there."

A phrase from that mysterious letter snaked through Prudence's head.

She must be holding out hope for that young rubbish merchant.

"Tell me. Does the baroness have an opinion about Mr. MacNeal?"

There was a long, pointed silence.

"Helen, I thought you and I were friends."

Helen looked up, her countenance ashen. "We *are*. I love you like a sister. What Lady Elisabetha wants with you is not known to me, but she is a great lady. I aspire to someday be part of her circle. I hope you will, too."

Frankly, I now think she is useless to us; in fact, she has the potential to become a great thorn in our side.

"When is the first time she encouraged you to befriend me?"

Helen shuffled her feet. Her gaze shifted upward in thought.

Can you not think of some means to do away with her?

"Around the twentieth of September, after I returned from Bath."

Just subsequent to the failed attack at the Bolton Park hunt.

"I had wanted to call on you all summer," added Helen, "but she advised me to wait."

Prudence peered through blurred eyes at the girl's candid

expression. Yes, poor, silly Helen was a pawn. Lady Revelle, it appeared, had had great plans for Prudence, and Mr. MacNeal had inadvertently upset the whole thing.

And paid the price with a broken heart.

Prudence's hopes slipped away like a collapsing house of cards. Her lover was gone. Her friend beyond redemption. What would Josephine say, now that Helen's treachery was proved? What would Aunt Amelia do?

"Helen Morris, leave this house!"

"Oh, please! Let us talk about this!"

"Go!" thundered Prudence.

Anguish tinged Helen's voice. "But my affection for you has always been real!"

Prudence lunged toward the girl. With a yelp, Helen backed away, grasping blindly for the door. She gained purchase, and in seconds she had fled.

Aunt Amelia appeared at the top of the stairs. "What in heaven's name is this racket?"

"I have sent Helen away."

Aunt Amelia charged down the staircase with astonishing speed. *"What?"* she demanded, jerking Prudence into the drawing room. "While I can't say I object, I should like to know why." Prudence looked away. Amelia yanked her face back. "Answer directly for once! Had it anything to do with William MacNeal?"

Prudence tried to shake her head, but the aunt held it too tightly. Panic rose in her throat. At the core of it lay the imperiled family secret. If Amelia should find out that she'd discussed it twice with Lady Revelle, that the gunshots at Bolton truly were meant for her, that she'd brought Helen under their roof knowing full well the danger, what then?

The Talismans. If she lost them, she'd have lost everything. *Amelia cannot know I'm an incompetent steward of my Inheritance.* Desperate, she grasped for a plausible lie.

"Helen is in love with Mr. MacNeal, and for some absurd reason she thought I was her rival."

Aunt Amelia stared. "Absurd?" she asked, releasing Prudence's chin. "Why is that so absurd?"

"Because he's an idler and a rake and a waste of any woman's feelings. When I pointed out these things, Helen flew into a rage. I said if she didn't like my opinion, she could jolly well leave!"

It was surprisingly easy to channel her grief into this falsehood. MacNeal had given up. The choice had been made for her.

"Dissembler!" snapped Aunt Amelia. "You said you liked him."

"I've changed my mind."

Amelia exhaled. "If you mean that DeLacey matter, I've asked around and not one credible source believes they were ever engaged. William MacNeal may have a reputation for enjoying his bachelorhood, but he is definitely no rake."

Prudence shook her head. "I told you, Helen's the one who has her cap set for him."

"Where do you get such ideas? That man sat right there and had eyes only for *you*, you in your ridiculous widow's weeds besides! And I'm an old fool if I didn't see that you, Miss High-and-Mighty, are equally besotted."

Prudence gripped the edge of a table to keep herself from staggering. For months she had needed Aunt Amelia's support, and now it was too late. She closed her eyes and searched for any sign of hope.

Dark shadows. Emptiness. A silhouette turned away.

She rasped, "Then I guess you're an old fool."

Aunt Amelia stiffened and drew back a hand. Only with great visible effort was she able to stay the strike. Harrumphing loudly, she stalked from the room.

14 November 1819

At luncheon three days later, Aunt Amelia threw down her fork. "Really, Prudence. Do you intend to carry on like this forever?"

Prudence had spent much of her time lately alone in her room, mourning her lost love and studying her late mother's relics. Smudges of unhappiness encircled her eyes. Her flawless complexion had grown very pale. She barely spoke to anyone, and no amount of persuasion could induce her to leave the house.

Aunt Amelia added gently, "There is freedom in the truth."

No. Only lies can protect the one thing I have left.

The old woman changed tack. "I could convince him to come back. He's not Underwood, of course, but he seems to adore you. Oh, my dear girl, you ought to give Mr. MacNeal some serious thought."

Prudence stared down at her soup, smothering the hope that sought to take root in her heart. Tempting though it was, she had trifled so much with MacNeal's feelings she doubted he would ever trust her. And why should he? She had spurned his explanations, always assuming the worst. Besides, the voices disapproved of her devotion to him; the only way to silence them had been through further exploration of the Talismans.

Then the voices had dwindled to one, and its meaning was clear—she must give up either one or the other.

"I don't love him," she said.

"Do you mean to turn down every prospect that walks through that door?"

Prudence shook her head. She would do whatever she could to avoid another Season and the unhappy prospect of encountering MacNeal at some function. "No, ma'am. I owe you better than that. This, therefore, I swear: the next willing gentleman who walks through that door I shall marry, without reservation."

"Ha! A pretty speech, but this hardly sounds like you. What sort of game are you playing?"

"No games. I place myself, dearest lady, in your capable hands."

Aunt Amelia gaped. "Well!" she declared. "Then I shall get to work at once."

Prudence nodded, satisfied by her deflection. "Now, as there looks to be a break in the clouds, I think I'll take Matt and go for a ride."

Thirty minutes later she was cantering through Regent's Park, but she took no joy in this expedition. She paid no mind to the landscape, was oblivious to the wind that chilled the tears streaming down her face. To save her Talismans, she had repudiated the man she loved. The voices said it must be so . . . hadn't they? If only she could ask her mother whether *she* had been so counseled. If she'd had her mother to turn to, everything would be different . . .

As she dabbed at her eyes, a chariot approached. The postboy seemed to beckon to her. Prudence waited in puzzlement as he brought the vehicle to a halt. A window slid open.

"Good day, Miss Fairfeather! What, no escort for you?"

The passenger leant forward so Prudence could see her in profile. Pale skin and flash of bright hair—Lady Elisabetha Revelle.

"I have an escort," Prudence said stiffly, gesturing to Matt.

"A groom? Pshaw! A pretty girl like you ought to have dozens of gentlemen eager to attend." Behind the lady, Prudence spied a small movement, enough to suggest she was not alone in her carriage.

Guessing whom that other passenger might be, Prudence raised her voice, "I had a companion once, but she has thrown her allegiance elsewhere."

A sob issued from the chariot. Lady Revelle turned away, then reappeared. "I could help you salvage that friendship."

Prudence shrugged. "I am not remotely interested in anything you have to say."

Lady Revelle's lips drew tightly together. She put her hand through the window and pointed at Prudence, mumbling something unintelligible.

"I beg your pardon?" Prudence shook her head to clear the sudden buzzing in her ears.

"I said my companion is unwell and asks to return to my townhouse. I bid you good day."

The window slid closed. A rap sounded on the chariot roof, and the post boy urged the team into motion. Prudence released a loud breath. She glanced at Matt, who waited impassively nearby. "I'm chilled. Let us go home."

CHAPTER THIRTY

Edingham-Greene, Wiltshire
11 November 1819

A lthough Prudence had gone out of her way to reject Mr. MacNeal at that ridiculous supper, her following letters reflected the mind of a woman obsessed with desire. Day after day, Josephine cringed at her friend's uncharacteristically bold language:

> *I made a Mistake, and I must have him back. I can no longer Fight the urge to have him inside my Being, mind within mind, Body within Body.*

"Good God!" Josephine exclaimed, fanning herself with the page. In reply, she wrote:

> *I am astonished you would share such musings with anyone, never mind they involve your fascination for a self-proclaimed killer.*

Then the unthinkable happened: Aunt Amelia had threatened to throw the girls from her house, and for the first time in her life, Josephine agreed with the old woman.

This letter was followed by another stunning confession. Not only had Prudence resumed wearing the Talisman ring, but according to her, it actually spoke:

> *I know this sounds Peculiar, but the Ring told me Helen was withholding a Letter from Mr. MacNeal. It assures me I am justified in seeking the Truth, and it comforts me and tries to keep the other Voices at bay. I can no longer imagine my Life without it.*

"*Other* voices?" said Josephine, pacing her room. "And still she cannot accept that the Talismans are magical? I wish she would elaborate. What should I *do?*"

She sat down at her desk and started a series of notes, each of which she immediately tossed into the fire:

> *Dear Aunt Amelia,*
> *It is my duty to inform you that Mr. MacNeal is a fiend—*
> *. . . Prudence has knowledge of a crime that was committed—*
> *. . . I beg you to drive that frightful Miss Morris away—*

"Oh, fiddlesticks!" she cried, throwing down her pen. The truth was, she dared not take action until she'd heard something, *anything* conclusive from Edward.

In the meantime, she considered what she knew about Prudence and Mr. MacNeal's history. He had saved her life. Further, he seemed to possess a sixth sense when it came to her whereabouts. The attraction between them transcended love; it was an almost . . . *magical* attraction.

Josephine drummed her fingertips on the desktop. A crack had begun to form in her prejudice against William MacNeal.

15 November 1819

First thing Monday morning, Carson handed Josephine an envelope posted from Oxford. She bolted to her mezzanine, where she devoured Edward's letter.

> *MacNeal acquitted himself well here, as a scholar and a gentleman. His reasons for leaving without completing a degree are known only to him—he was not discharged.*
>
> *That famous "engagement" of which you speak was an absolute hum. A friend of a friend happens to know The Hon. Mr. Frederick DeLacey (brother to said jilted fiancée). Not long ago, this fellow became enamored of Lady Emmeline. Mr. DeLacey counseled the besotted cove to forget his dear sister, who has a notoriously wicked temper and had previously driven away a fellow by the name of—you guessed it—William MacNeal. According to DeLacey, MacNeal called on Lady Emmeline a few times last year but never made an offer. When it became apparent he'd lost interest, she flew into a rage and resolved to punish him by telling everyone he had broken their engagement.*
>
> *If what you sought was proof of his good character, I'd say you've got it. Your fears are wholly unfounded.*

"Good Lord!" exclaimed Josephine. "I didn't expect that!"

She squinted out the window. Mere days ago she had thought of MacNeal as a lunatic and a murderer. Now she wondered whether he was the one man who could shield her friend from disaster. After all, if everything he had said was true, then someone out there knew Prudence's secret and might make another attempt on her life . . . which meant her hypothesis about Prudence's value to the rebels had been entirely wrong.

Still, she mustn't panic or jump to conclusions. She spent the day absorbing Edward's report. By happenstance, another of Prudence's missives arrived in the afternoon post. Josephine hoped to learn more about those unsettling voices, but Prudence had nothing to say about them. Rather, she announced that she had sent Miss Morris packing—that part was brilliant—but when questioned by Aunt Amelia, she had denied her love for MacNeal.

"Are you *mad?*" cried Josephine.

Prudence seemed to think she must make a choice between love and the Inheritance, but if that were the case, then the Trait would have died out centuries ago.

"You've been listening to those voices in your head instead of the one in your heart," Josephine said grimly. She copied down every word of Edward's Oxford revelations. "Don't you see? Aunt Amelia spoke the truth: Mr. MacNeal is a good man. Repent your lies, dear Prudence, while you still have a chance."

18 November 1819

Matters in London continued to worsen. By the end of the week, Prudence's letters had ceased to mention Mr. MacNeal and instead devolved to mere ramblings:

Without my Talismans, I'd have nothing left to live for. Would you force me into such Straits? If magical they are, then it's time I Mastered them. My Mother was their governor, and so too might I be.

Josephine shook her head, unable to square such language with Prudence's reserved character. Surely Aunt Amelia would've taken notice of such a strange mood. In her next letter, Prudence's thoughts sounded even more detached:

When I sleep, which is rare, I suffer dreams of great Violence. At bedtime I sit Upright, fighting waves of drowsiness. I run my hands across the box. Lovely things lie inside. Lovely, dangerous things. The Devil take Aunt Amelia's advice! If they're all I have left, why should I not Possess them?

I stood before my mirror and held aloft the Sword. I existed in the real world, Mother existed in its Reflection. She wore a frock-coat and breeches with a Cloak over one shoulder. On her hands were the Gauntlets, fringed with tassels and beads. Behind her lay a Landscape full of strange and colorless forms. Smoke billowed from blackened Ruins. Sparks rained from the sky. Half-obscured silhouettes ran this way and that. Others lay strewn about, Broken and lifeless.

Undaunted by this Scene, Mother held one arm upraised and whispered Words under her breath. A Man darted past her and cried out and fell Dead at her feet. Mother screamed out his Name and knelt to pick up an object—it was the Sword, still whole. She lifted it skyward as an alien phrase tore from her Throat. The Sword exploded in her face. My own Hand felt as though the flesh were searing off my Bones. Then everything went Black.

Josephine shuddered. Surely this dream depicted the deaths of her friend's parents. No wonder Aunt Amelia had begged Prudence not to handle the Talismans! So why had she decided she must master those things? If Josephine hadn't already known it, here was incontrovertible evidence that Prudence had lost all control.

"I've got to do something—oh, I really should have before! What, what, *what?*" She paced her mezzanine furiously, thumping a palm to her forehead. "I could send an express to Aunt Amelia. She obviously has no knowledge of Prudence's inner turmoil . . ." She came to a sharp halt. "But if I do, then I will blow the gaff on everything—magic, Talismans, lies, and dissemblances— and that would constitute a betrayal of Prudence's confidence, a betrayal of our friendship to the highest degree. Oh, I *can't!*"

Her stomach roiled, and she bent to catch her breath. "There is one other way." Mustering every bit of authority her small frame possessed, Josephine went to her father's study and said, "Papa, Prudence is behaving strangely. I must go to her."

Middlemere looked up. "Behaving strangely? How?"

Josephine faltered. Mysterious voices and strange impulses were compelling, but did she want her father to know everything that had been going on for the past seven months? If he were to learn about the dangers she and Prudence had endured, let alone the partial unearthing of his wife's dreaded secrets, he would never allow her to leave Greenbank. His sanity might even hang in the balance.

"She's despondent. She hasn't had the greatest success with the Marriage Mart, you know."

Middlemere folded his hands on his desk. "You're a tenderhearted girl, my love, but wounded feelings do not constitute a family emergency. Prudence will be home in less than a month. You can support her then. Let us not further complicate things, shall we?"

"Yes, Papa." Josephine bowed her head. She no longer had any idea what she could do.

CHAPTER THIRTY-ONE

Edingham-Greene, Wiltshire
21 November 1819

On a rainy Sunday, as Josephine walked through the village on her way home from church, she was hailed by the postman.

"More post came late yesterday with something for 'ee. I ken how fond 'ee bist of Miss Prudence, so I brought 'ee along in case I saw 'ee. Nobody likes a-wait an extar day for news, a'en 'e right, milady?" He pulled the letter from his pocket and handed it to her.

Josephine thanked the postman and picked her way across the muddy road. Despite the grim weather, she'd insisted on walking alone to sort out her thoughts. She trudged along the lane, turning the envelope in her hands. Upon reaching Greenbank's front gate, she decided she couldn't wait, so she leant against a pillar and read Prudence's jumble of words:

I miss Helen's laughter and late Night conversations. I miss Autumn rides across the golden stubble of Cornfields and the absent-minded smiles of Papa when we invaded his Study. How I long for a certain someone's adoring Eyes and the whisper of his sweet Breath on my cheek.

*All I have is that Band in my pocket, awaiting the brush of
my fingertips. If I brought it to her, she could show me its Secrets.
Then I would have the power to win back what I've Lost.*

"What?" screamed Josephine. She crushed the letter in one
hand and charged up the long drive. *This is the last straw. Aunt
Amelia must be told.*

Puffing along on her pattens, Josephine lost her balance and
sprawled facedown in the mud. As she labored to push herself
upright, a speeding horse turned into the lane, leaping over her
body and pressing on without missing a beat. Josephine ripped
the pattens from her hopelessly ruined shoes and staggered up
the drive. At Greenbank's front steps stood a panting, foam-
flecked horse. Its rider and Carson conferred in the doorway.
The express messenger turned and gaped at her.

"Blimey, milady, I thought 'ee was a log!"

"It wasn't your fault," she grumbled, brushing at her mud-
drenched clothes.

Carson gave Josephine a queer look. He said to the
messenger, "Will you please wait in the kitchen in case the lady
and His Lordship need to send their replies?"

The messenger went on his way. Carson helped Josephine
out of her filthy outerwear and handed her an envelope. "I'll
fetch a towel and some tea, madam, for I expect you will want
to read that directly."

She padded into the parlor in damp stocking feet. Positioning
herself beneath a lit sconce, she tore open the packet. She had
read no more than a line or two before her heart fell to the
floor. The message, which concerned events that had transpired
two nights ago, had been authored by Aunt Amelia Staveley.

A furious knocking had roused the residents of Stanistead from bed. Reese and Aunt Amelia converged in the front hall, rubbing sleep from their eyes. On the stoop, in the pouring rain, stood William MacNeal with Prudence slung in his arms, clad only in her nightdress, soaked to the bone and babbling senselessly.

There was no time for questions. Amelia led the way as MacNeal carried the stricken girl to her room. He deposited her on the bed and was ushered away by Reese. Nell and Aunt Amelia put Prudence into dry clothes, covered her with blankets, and stoked up the fire. Presently, Amelia went down to the study. There she found Mr. MacNeal huddled by the fire, wearing one of Reese's shirts and sipping brandy, his eyes glazed and careworn.

"We're waiting for the physician," said Aunt Amelia, seating herself opposite MacNeal. "Thank you, sir, for bringing her home. I am eternally grateful. But how did you happen upon her?"

"I was passing along yonder street and saw a wraith running toward me. 'A sleepwalker!' I thought, and collected her in my arms. Pushing back her hair, I recognized Miss Fairfeather. I hope you will not find my efforts untoward."

"Of course not," said Aunt Amelia, laying a hand on his arm.

"I am relieved, madam. I couldn't bear to think that you might question my intentions."

Aunt Amelia leant in close. "Just what *are* your intentions, Mr. MacNeal?"

He shivered. "They are to leave her in your care and try earnestly to forget her."

"Do you love her?"

"Truly and deeply, but she made her regard for me quite clear a fortnight ago. I have struggled to accept my future without her, and as such I often find myself drawn to your gate."

Aunt Amelia reached for the bottle and poured him another drink. On second thought, she also took a glass for herself. "You may yet have your reward." She sipped at her brandy. "I'm certain she loves you, but something has frightened her. Have you any idea what that might be?" She raised an eyebrow and stared hard at MacNeal.

"Frankly, no, unless it's that baseless rumor about Lady DeLacey."

"It cannot be," she assured him. "I have informed her of its falsity, yet she remains disconcerted." When he offered no other suggestions, she went on. "Sir, I shall give you the benefit of the doubt. Whatever you might have done, I think in time you can regain her trust. Are you up to the challenge?"

"Your blessing renews my faded hopes, Miss Staveley. I would do whatever is necessary to win back her heart."

"Then remain here with us until we know how she fares."

"I'd be honored to, madam."

Since then, Prudence had lain unconscious and fevered, with Mr. MacNeal and the aunt in constant attendance.

So I appeal to you, Lady Josephine, for I know you are privy to Prudence's secret thoughts. Why does she pretend not to love Mr. MacNeal? I understand your reluctance to betray

her confidence, but please weigh that against the value of her
future happiness.

Josephine wandered blindly into the parlor and dropped onto a chair.

He had saved her! How perfect! Mr. MacNeal's love had not wavered; he would finally get the chance to explain. But, oh dear God, would Prudence die before he could?

25 November 1819

The Westons waited anxiously for tidings from London. Daily expresses informed them that Prudence existed on the brink of survival. Aunt Amelia conveyed every detail of the illness, from the night terrors and sweats to the bone-trembling chills. Between Maria's lamentations and Middlemere mumbling about the city's humors, Josephine had nowhere to turn for relief. The situation reminded her too much of Charlie Lowell's last days. She spent hours sitting in Prudence's room, huddled in her friend's favorite wool wrapper.

She was thus ensconced by Prudence's window late one afternoon, contemplating the rain, when a mounted figure rose out of the gloom and drew close to the house. As he had neither the look nor the bearing of a typical express boy, she dashed downstairs and wrenched open the front door. The rider dismounted and handed the reins to a groom. He said something and pointed to a satchel that hung on the saddle. The boy led his horse away. The man saw Josephine and squelched up the steps.

"Hallo," he said with a stiff bow. "William MacNeal at your service. Might I have a word with His Lordship?"

Josephine shrieked and grabbed him by the hand. "Come in, sir! Oh, dear God, you're soaked. You'll catch your death for certain!"

Mr. MacNeal followed without argument and stood dripping in the hallway.

"Carson!" bellowed Josephine. "Help us, if you please!"

The gentleman fumbled for something inside his greatcoat as he shivered uncontrollably. "I have letters—"

"I'll take them for later, but you must rest yourself first. I see you haven't shaved. Did you ride straight through the night?"

Mr. MacNeal nodded. Carson arrived, was apprised of the situation, and immediately invited their guest upstairs. MacNeal hesitated.

"Go on!" ordered Josephine. "Just one question: is she well?"

His haggard face brightened. "She's conscious and free of fever. The doctor says she is out of danger. I wanted to tell you in person."

"Bless you!" cried Josephine, standing on tiptoe and kissing his cheek. "Now go-go-go!" She shooed him upstairs.

The next morning, they peered at him with undisguised curiosity as he entered the breakfast room. MacNeal paused, a bemused expression on his face, and glanced down at his person. "I beg your pardon. Did I get my buttons out of order?"

Everyone laughed. Lord Middlemere greeted their guest with a handshake and a clap on the back.

MacNeal's posture eased, and he took a seat at the table. "Please forgive me for sleeping late and keeping you all from your meal. I'm not usually a lag-a-bed."

"I always rise early," declared Josephine. "Then again, I did not just ride a hundred miles with rain in my face."

His eyes twinkled. "No, but I suspect you're a person for whom the day hasn't enough hours to address all the ideas crowding your head."

She grinned into her lap.

"Is he not beautiful?" Maria whispered. "Such a smile! Such good humor!"

Josephine shushed her, although she had to agree. If MacNeal weren't already attached to Prudence, she would've found it easy to worship him. His sculpted visage and flashing teeth gave her the flutters. His eyes were the color of a young woodland fern. When she giggled in response some amusing remark, Maria kicked her and hissed, "Remember thyself, hoyden!"

Josephine choked back a yelp, causing MacNeal to glance over and give her a wink. She said hastily, "We're grateful for the attentions you've shown our dear Prudence. She must have been pleased to see you when she awoke."

A cloud crossed his face. "How I wish that were true. No, Miss Fairfeather seemed disoriented in general, and finding me in her chamber added to her distress. I therefore offered to hand-deliver the news to her family, in hopes that a few days' rest would restore her faculties."

"She'll soon be her old self," averred Middlemere. "Though, circumstances aside, we are pleased to have had the opportunity to make your acquaintance. Will you stay here a while?"

"One or two days, perhaps. I am anxious to attend your ward in full and proper fashion, and I hope you will not begrudge my desire to return directly to London."

"Not at all, my good sir! But I must warn you: as soon as Prudence can tolerate the journey, she's to come home for the holidays. I expect she'll stay here for several weeks."

Mr. MacNeal's shoulders slumped, but Josephine thought it fitting that he suffer a little, for he in his own turn had caused Prudence just as much grief.

Lord Middlemere wasted no time in inviting the visitor to his study. There, when they were seated, he folded his hands and looked expectantly at the man whom he assumed would soon become his foster son-in-law. For some reason, Mr. MacNeal had turned the color of ash, and a spray of perspiration stood out on his face.

"You wished to speak to me, sir?" asked the earl gently.

"I have an awful confession to make. Back in October, I was obliged to take another man's life. I did so in defense of Miss Fairfeather's honor; unfortunately, that man was none other than Lord Underwood."

Middlemere felt the blood drain from his face. "Good heavens! Was it a duel? Does anyone know? Might you be brought up on charges?"

MacNeal shook his head. "How much do you know about the incident at Bolton Park?"

"I know Prudence fell off a horse and was buried in a landslide. An anonymous stranger saved her from certain suffocation."

"Well, sir, I was that stranger. I went to Bolton because I wanted a glimpse of your daughter. Underwood, it seems, had the selfsame idea. We converged by accident with Miss

Fairfeather between us. Before anyone had the chance to speak, he shot at me, twice. In self-defense, I shot back. He fled, and after I secured your daughter's safety, I went after him. Underwood made for the coast and took ship to the Continent. This struck me as suspicious."

"Agreed," said Middlemere. "Why fire at you in the first place, and then why flee like a coward instead of hashing it out, man-to-man?"

"We'll never know. For several weeks I pursued him. When I finally laid hands on him, he refused to speak civilly. I declared my intention to haul him home to face charges. Underwood grew belligerent. He accused me of attempting to steal his woman; his 'rightful property' is what he called her. He spoke with rough language and ungentlemanly consideration. I lost my temper and called him out."

Middlemere gasped. "Miss Staveley had represented him as mild-mannered and unassuming, the sort of man who, if he were to perceive that his rival had bested him, would concede graciously."

"I couldn't say, for he was a stranger to me, but judge if you will based on how the duel played out. We arranged to meet the following day. I hired a local man to follow him, in case he should attempt to squirm out of the bargain. That local, who was also my second, met Underwood on the agreed-upon field of honor. I arrived shortly thereafter. No sooner did I step forth than Underwood shot the second dead. He had no second of his own; that left the two of us. I threw myself upon him and wrested away his other pistol. He then produced a knife and held it to my throat."

"My God! What then?"

"At that point I had him pinned, so I tried to reason with

him. 'Think what you're doing, man,' I said. 'Would you murder me over a woman who has every right to choose her own mate?'

"'She is destined to be mine,' was his outrageous reply. I could not fathom what madness would drive a man to assert this without proof that his object held the reciprocal faith. I felt I had particular claim on your daughter's affections. At any rate, Underwood had lost interest in further debate. The blade pressed harder into my flesh—you can see the scar here. I moved to release my hold on his person, thinking to resolve our dispute at some later date. As I arose, however, Underwood knocked me down and thrust the knife toward my ribcage. We struggled for some minutes. I might just as easily have died by his hand, but in all the confusion, Underwood is the one who fell on the blade. I could do nothing to save him. He bled to death at my feet."

MacNeal paused, chest heaving. "And that is not the only source of my shame. When I realized the scene with its two corpses would be impossible to explain, I left them and fled."

"You were justified," assured Middlemere. "With no witnesses to vouch for you, the risk was too high. They would have hanged you in—where was it?"

MacNeal shook his head. "Best I don't say."

"Most understandable. Ah! The very idea that Underwood regarded my daughter as chattel bristles my spine. For the good of everyone, let us put it behind us. Should this matter ever arise, I will do everything in my power to protect your good name."

"Thank you, sir. I appreciate that." MacNeal ruffled his hair. "One other thing: Miss Fairfeather knows I killed Underwood, but she believes I did it in a jealous rage. I don't know how to convince her otherwise."

"Has she heard the whole story?"

"I have not had the opportunity to apprise her in full."

"Well, when you do, speak from your heart, leaving out the grimmer details, of course. She cannot help but see your sincerity, sir."

They shook hands and MacNeal took his leave, leaving Middlemere to stare at his departing figure. "Now *that* is a fine kettle of fish," he muttered, and he did not mean the young man's surprising travails.

Josephine intercepted Mr. MacNeal halfway down the hall.

"You lied," she said simply.

He fell back a step, startled. He looked for a moment as if he might argue, but finally he said, "I may have, a little."

"And how can you convince me that the rest isn't also a fabrication?"

"Must we discuss this here?" wondered Mr. MacNeal, glancing around.

"Point taken. Follow me." Josephine led him upstairs to the first-floor sitting room. She closed the door, crossed her arms, and stared intently at him. "I happen to know that Lord Underwood shot at Prudence, not you, or at least that's what you told Prudence when you met her in Hyde Park. So which is the truth and what else did you invent?"

"You were eavesdropping?"

She tilted her chin. "I'm the lady of the house, and nothing regarding my cousin's welfare shall be kept hidden from me. Prudence tells me everything, so don't you dare alter the facts."

"Very well. I *did* make adjustments. Whether Underwood shot at your cousin or at me is hardly the issue—what matters is the brute is now gone for good."

"And what about the letter you recovered from the body? Do you not think my father ought to know that someone conspired to have Prudence killed, or did you manufacture that detail, too?"

Mr. MacNeal clenched his fists. "I did *not* manufacture that letter! I withheld the information to protect Lord Middlemere's sensibilities."

"What's that supposed to mean?" flared Josephine.

He said gently, "What purpose would be served by divulging such alarming knowledge? I am capable of protecting Miss Fairfeather, should she be amenable, but your father seems the sort of man who is better off insulated from unpleasantness."

Josephine regarded him a long while. He gazed back unwaveringly.

"How did you know?" she asked in a voice tinged with emotion.

"I didn't. It's just a feeling I had. Your father does not tolerate crises, and you listen at keyholes to protect him from harm . . . or lying rogues, as the case may be." He made a self-deprecating gesture.

Josephine smiled crookedly. "I think I like you, Mr. MacNeal."

"I'm flattered, Lady Weston, but don't you think I'm a bit old for you?"

"Naughty man! Don't you dare twist my words!"

He caught her hand and kissed the top of it. "That, my dear, is the entire object of repartee. Master that skill and you'll be the toast of London!"

Thereafter, Josephine and Mr. MacNeal got on famously, much to Maria's consternation. She cornered her charge in the hallway on the second afternoon of his visit.

"'Tisn't a'tall proper that 'ee go about whisperin' in corners and flirtin' with Prudence's suitor!"

"How dare you accuse me of anything untoward! Anyway, Lieutenant Quimby happens to please me far better."

"Hmph! And his fortune will also please 'ee far better, though I needn't remind 'ee of that."

"Shame on you, Maria! How perfectly vulgar!"

"I wonder what Mr. MacNeal thinks of Greenbank? He would certainly improve himself by marrying 'ee. Watch thyself, I say."

"MacNeal marry *me?*" screeched Josephine.

"What's that?" inquired Mr. MacNeal, appearing out of nowhere to thrust his head between them. "Not *again*, Lady Weston! I thought I already said no."

"Oh, sir, you scandalize me!" exclaimed Josephine, quaking with laughter at the horrified expression on Maria's face.

By the time Mr. MacNeal made ready to leave Sunday morning, everyone was sorry to see him go. Josephine called for her horse and accompanied him down the lane.

"One issue remains," she said when they pulled to a halt at the gate. "How can we be certain Prudence is not still in danger?"

"We can't, which is why I've been standing watch over her house."

"You *have*? Dear me, how long have you done so, my poor,

lovesick friend?"

Mr. MacNeal reddened. "I began intermittently when she fled from Hyde Park, but enacted a schedule the day Miss Morris claimed to speak on her behalf. That meddlesome chit—thank God she is gone!"

Josephine nodded, glad to know he shared the same suspicions of Miss Helen Morris. She would've said something then about the sinister intentions of Lady Revelle, except that subject would lead them onto extremely thin ice. Besides, MacNeal still had more on his mind.

"Lovesick?" he repeated. "Yes, my lady, I am besotted to the very depths of my soul, but it is not merely love that drives me to protect your sweet cousin. An instinct deep in here—" He struck his breast for emphasis. "—that instinct tells me her life is in danger. Even if she never reciprocates my love, I should continue to guard her. Indeed, I had begun to accept that fate on the night I found her wandering in the rain. Do you—do you find that peculiar?" A shadow crossed his face.

Josephine laid a hand on his arm. "Not at all. I find your devotion deeply moving."

He returned a sad smile. "Perhaps I'm a fool for devoting myself to a woman who does not seem to share my regard."

"She shares it. Oh, believe me, she does!" A pang thrummed in Josephine's heart. If only she could explain the impact magic had had on their thus-far problematical courtship. Without those dratted Talismans, Prudence would surely be free to love him. "She loves you, sir. I know it. As for the confusion and fear controlling her mind as of late . . . well, she knows not whom to trust. Men quarreled and fired shots in her presence, and one of them has died. On the face of it, jealousy makes more sense than a murderous plot."

"Do *you* believe me?"

"Absolutely."

He reached for her hand and gave it a squeeze. "Let us return to your original question. For now, moving Miss Fairfeather to Wiltshire should keep her safe. I'll hire men to follow the coach from a distance."

"And her brother will be home in less than a fortnight. Oh, I do so wish you could spend the holidays with us!"

MacNeal shook his head. "Miss Fairfeather needs time to sort out her feelings. Best I refrain from attempting a courtship till she comes back to London."

"And *then* how shall we ensure her safety?"

"I have a few weeks to think on it."

Josephine brightened. "I've got an idea! Mr. Tolliver and Mr. Bradford could be persuaded to travel back to London with her. Neither of their families has the wherewithal to house them in Town, but they're eager to try the bachelor life before university next year. These boys are fiercely protective of Prudence. Shall I see what I can arrange?"

"Excellent!" said MacNeal. "Carry on, then, my lady, and have a grand visit with your cousin. I'm envious, of course, but I hope to have her to myself in due time."

They parted with warm smiles, but as Josephine watched him disappear down the road, she couldn't help feeling a twinge of unease in her gut. Prudence's physical illness had passed, but what was left of her mind?

CHAPTER THIRTY-TWO

Edingham-Greene, Wiltshire
29 November 1819

"I congratulate you, sir!" wrote Lord Middlemere in tall, looping script.

> *You engineered a surgical campaign against two dozen trolls, wiped them out, and disposed of the evidence. How easily you frightened the populace into believing it was bears— an explanation as nonsensical as the actual fact. But do you consider this an isolated occurrence? Does no one besides me view the events of the past summer with a troubled eye? Mark my words, Bancroft, this was only the harbinger of something far worse.*

The earl paused to look over his words. Bancroft had a tendency to dismiss minor concerns, so he had fretted for months before raising such questions. Now he had evidence, and it was time Bancroft knew. Mad Middlemere might be a coward, but he was also an Inheritance analyst of the highest regard.

Twenty years ago he had warned the Keepers that their Decommissioning Plan might fail. In his opinion, though he had no hard proof, Keepers placed too much stock in the importance of rituals. If magic ran in one's blood, if the ancestors had embedded it in their Talismans, then it existed already, ritual or not. Short of murdering all people who might carry the Trait, one could never eradicate all magic from Britain. For this reason, the Keeper authorities had focused on destroying the trappings.

"Without rituals to awaken them," the Lord Governor had told the planning council, "without Talismans to enhance them and mentors to teach them how to manage their art, new generations will live unaware of their talents. They'll intermarry with common folk, and their magical Trait will dilute. Our sacrifice today shall save the nation from splintering into future factions."

As Middlemere could offer no better option, he had helped adopt the Lord Governor's plan. His doubts had lingered, yet in all the years since he had uncovered no evidence to support his concerns. Everything had gone smoothly, and the Inheritance was presumed dead. Until now.

Glancing at a book lying open on his desk, he wrote,

I have met a young man who surely carries the Trait. Consult your copy of the Pedigrees *and see what I mean: Mr. William MacNeal, about seven and twenty. He's as naïve as you would expect of any untrained heir, but in knowledgeable hands, well . . .*

There was a time when the idea of Prudence marrying into that family would've horrified him—he realized with a jolt that Amelia must have known—but having met MacNeal in person, he delighted in the prospect. Though Prudence herself had shown no sign of the Trait, it couldn't hurt for her to spend a lifetime under the wing of someone who did.

"He's a Protector. I'm sure of it."

Middlemere should know—not only had his closest colleague been a Protector, he had also married one. Intense, instinctive, and very fierce fighters, this branch of Keepers would die to shield their more vulnerable partners, the Mages. If Prudence had indeed inherited the blood of her parents . . .

But this line of thinking nudged territory that Middlemere preferred not to enter. He shook himself and finished his letter to Bancroft. Afterward, he thumped closed his great volume of *Pedigrees*. Phinneas Allerton, Lord Underwood of Essex had featured nowhere within.

Underwood . . . such a curiosity. Middlemere weighed and discounted a number of theories. Had the viscount discovered Prudence's heritage and resolved to partner with her? A thorough search revealed Underwood possessed no Keeper blood. Perhaps a renegade Keeper, needing a proxy, had enlisted the viscount to assassinate MacNeal? Absurd. No well-heeled nobleman would agree to commit murder.

Middlemere shrugged. "He must've been a madman. Such misfortunes happen in the real world. I mustn't assume that every villain out there is part of some grand conspiracy."

Which brought him back to thinking about trolls. They had been randomly scattered; a test, perhaps, to see what the government would do. This time the Army had succeeded with relative ease, but if someone out there could breed trolls, then that someone had other tactics in mind.

Who? Who? Who?

He pulled a battered paper from the binding of his beloved *Pedigrees* and peered at it for perhaps the fiftieth time: a list of every insurgent who had survived the Rebellion, plus the names of all its known deceased members. For sixteen years, with the help of the Lord Governor's spies, he had tracked their movements and those of their offspring. Many survivors had vanished on the day of the truce; several had long since gone missing. Middlemere's forefinger traced the most dangerous culprits.

"We must find them," he muttered. "We must break them before they regain their full power, or else heaven help this poor nation."

There would be no defense. The Keeper Brigade no longer existed, and many Oath-takers had voluntarily destroyed their Talismans. Of those who remained, the youngest among them were now middle aged; a handful of old-timers would be helpless to stop an organized opponent.

Shivering, Middlemere glowered at the names on his list of rebellious Keepers. "You're not ready yet, but I'll wager it's only a matter of time."

5 December 1819

"You've filled out!" cried Prudence, climbing slowly down from the carriage.

"And you're so . . . oh my, Prudence, we really must fatten you up!" Josephine stared in dismay at her bone-thin friend, whose complexion was as pale as the dusting of snow on the ground. Prudence smiled, and the girls fell into each other's arms for the first time in nine months.

Seeing Prudence wince at the pressure of her embrace,

Josephine struggled not to burst into tears. Her friend had never once been seriously ill. Now her beauty was blasted—cheekbones jutted, her hair had gone a dull shade of brown, and her fingers resembled skeleton claws.

How could this have happened?

After Lord Middlemere offered his greeting, she slid an arm around Prudence to lend her stability. "Your room is bright and warm. We shall spend many pleasant hours there."

Prudence let out a sigh. "I'm so happy to be home." She tilted back her head to take in the silhouette of Greenbank, blurry in the mist. Behind them, Amelia Staveley descended, all in a dither about the rutted Wiltshire roads and the deplorable condition of the inn at Wharton. Maria's eyes rolled; she never enjoyed the old lady's visits.

Josephine guided Prudence inside and spent the following week attending her needs. Before long she realized her deepest held fears. Prudence had changed in more than just body; she had lost her vitality and grown emotionally distant. Perhaps illness had brought out these symptoms, though that didn't explain why she never spoke of her rescuer, the man who had nursed her during those first critical days, the man she so desperately desired. Not once did MacNeal's name leave her lips.

One afternoon, as Josephine struggled to find a way to raise this uncomfortable topic, she crossed paths with her father as he emerged from Prudence's room.

"I mentioned how much we had enjoyed Mr. MacNeal's visit," he whispered, "and she snapped her mouth shut and turned to the wall! I had no idea how deeply she mistrusts him. Are you *certain* she loved him before Bolton Park?"

"Quite certain, Papa. Indeed, she loved him as recently as early November. Somehow we've got to convince her that he didn't murder Underwood." Middlemere threw her a surprised look. "MacNeal told me about the duel," she said quickly. "Prudence fears he has a violent streak."

"In that case, we mustn't press her. We shall just give her time."

Josephine agreed, even if the matter wasn't quite so simple. That evening, Aunt Amelia summoned her for a private interview; she went to the aunt's chamber with dread in her throat.

"You will have noticed, I suppose?" began the old woman.

Josephine's stomach flopped, but there was no use in prevaricating. "Yes, ma'am. She's not behaving like a girl who's in love. I wonder why."

Aunt Amelia glowered. "I had hoped you could tell *me*. Haven't the two of you spoken about it? Does she never say his name?"

Josephine's nerves thrummed. No doubt the Talismans were responsible for Prudence's emotional state, but to say so would betray Prudence's confidence.

If they're taken from her, then so be it, but I dare not set off that awful chain of events.

"One month ago, she was deeply in love with MacNeal. I don't know why she has suddenly withdrawn her affection. Her last letters before the illness were very confused. She seemed to fall to pieces under the pressure of a certain decision she had made, a decision she didn't share and which only she understood."

She met the old lady's gaze. *Think, Aunt Amelia! Deduce it yourself! Don't make me be the source of Prudence's unhappiness!*

"You don't know why she made herself pretend to despise him?"

"I do not. I was as baffled by her behavior as you appear to be."

"What do you know of a ring she inherited from her mother?"

Josephine's heart skipped a beat. The aunt stared so hard she had to look away. Her conscience pricked. *Remember what Prudence wants.*

"She mentioned it, of course. She used to carry it in her pocket."

Aunt Amelia's eyes burned. Josephine sensed her desire to probe further. Perhaps the old lady presumed her still ignorant, and mentioning the Inheritance would only open Pandora's box.

To the devil with those Talismans! I'd spill it all if she asked outright.

But Josephine did not offer a confession. Instead, she asked coyly, "Do you think the ring has aught to do with Prudence's state of mind?"

"It's possible. She was wearing it, in fact, on the night she fell ill. When she returned to consciousness, I recommended she let me have it for safekeeping. I put it away where she cannot find it."

"Are you certain of that?" asked Josephine, thinking of the pistols.

Amelia raised an eyebrow. "*Quite* certain."

Josephine let out a deep breath. "So you *do* associate it with her illness?"

Aunt Amelia's expression was inscrutable. The truth hung between them, neither daring to address it. At last, the aunt said, "Prudence is obsessed with her late parents. She has grown far too attached to the past, which is an unhealthy practice and distracts her from what matters. My lady, we must find a way to guide her out of that dark place. We must convince her to take comfort in the future and in William MacNeal."

Josephine nodded. Perhaps the love of a good man would restore her friend.

4 January 1820

Though the winter wind gripped its claws around Greenbank, indoors the house remained merry and warm. Lord Middlemere manned the pianoforte, playing a Haydn concerto. Mrs. March sat nearby, her worshipful eyes never leaving his profile. Feeling playful, Josephine bent to whisper a suggestion.

"Naughty girl!" hissed the widow.

"Not one of us would think less of you for trying."

Mrs. March looked away, fanning her face. Josephine dropped the subject and gazed round the room. Edward slouched in an armchair, his expression despondent, while the older ladies napped in their respective corners. Peter and Roland locked horns over an epic game of chess. Arthur Grant watched Prudence, who stood turning Middlemere's music. She had regained most of her health and natural beauty this past month. In the soft glow of candlelight, she looked like an angel, all in white with piles of honey-gold curls.

Josephine exhaled softly. *If only Mr. MacNeal were here!*

With a crescendo of chords, Middlemere ended the concerto. Everyone applauded, whether they'd been listening or not.

"Now!" urged Josephine, prodding Mrs. March.

White-faced, the woman rose and approached Middlemere.

"Your Lordship," she murmured. "*Clare*, that piece was

beautiful, as always."

"Why, thank you, Mrs. . . . er, *Lucinda*. You are much too kind."

"Lucy," she corrected.

Something about the way that she said this—or perhaps it was the intimacy of her rarely used pet name—caused him to look up. "Indeed!" the earl said, his voice squeaking a little.

Hooked like a trout! Josephine cheered in her head. *Now reel him in.*

Mrs. March forged ahead. "As you know, sir, I play, too, though not so well as yourself. One piece gives me much grief, it being rife with cadenzas. Would you favor me with a demonstration of the proper technique?"

Masterful, dear. Why did we not capitalize on your skills sooner?

Middlemere leapt from the stool. "Why, of course! Have a seat, my dear Lucy, and I'll hold your hand—or rather, I-I'll show you how to hold your hands."

A giggle escaped Josephine. Prudence covered her eyes. Middlemere glanced between them. "Well, well. It seems we are being made fools of."

Mrs. March colored. Her hands fluttered as she backed away from the instrument, and tears of shame shone in her eyes. "Forgive me, Your Lordship, for I was a party to this scheme. Thank you for supper. I shall now take my leave."

Josephine's throat swelled in dismay.

Middlemere stared at the widow, his expression inscrutable. "I see," he replied slowly. "In that case, let us have a turn in the corridor whilst we wait for the carriage." He gave Mrs. March his arm, and together they withdrew.

Prudence wheeled on Josephine. "Heavens, girl! What have you done?"

"Wasn't she marvelous?" cried Josephine. "Did you see that?

Papa comprehended her misery! Before, he would've shrugged and let her go home. He has acknowledged her, Prudence. No longer can he pretend that his suffering trumps hers."

"Meddler!" huffed Prudence. "Let us pray you have not made them more miserable than they already were!"

"I don't think that is possible," said Josephine, gazing thoughtfully at the door.

"Do you think they kissed?" she wondered the next morning.

"It's none of our business," Prudence said, tugging hard on Josephine's curl papers.

"Ow, that hurt! I'll wager they did. They've adored each other for ages."

Prudence unwound another of Josephine's curlers. "Don't interfere. How would you like it if I told Quimby that you murmur 'oh, Robert' in your sleep?"

"I wouldn't mind!" declared Josephine, her face growing warm. "Heavens, do I?"

"Josephine Weston, have you no shame?"

"I own that I'm fond of a handsome young man. Surely *you* have tender dreams about your Mr. MacNeal? Ow!" Josephine grabbed her scalp. "What did I say?"

"*My* Mr. MacNeal? *Mine?* I claim no ownership of that man!"

"Oh, for pity's sake! I could hand you a sheaf of letters in which you extolled his virtues. Do you mean to say you lied on more than two dozen occasions?" Josephine's heart beat fast, for now the subject they had all so assiduously avoided lay out in the open.

Prudence lurched away and went to warm her hands by

the fire. "He was but a passing fancy. My feelings are much clearer now. I don't love him, and that's that."

What's not to love? wondered Josephine. *He's a marvelous man.*

"Why does everyone say that?" cried Prudence, whirling on her.

"Say *what?*" said Josephine. "Did you . . . did you just—?" She stepped toward Prudence with a wondering look in her eyes, certain she had said nothing aloud. "Do it again, Prudence. Here: let me think something else."

Er . . . I shall wear the mustard-colored silk today.

Prudence frowned. "What on earth are you playing at?"

"You read my mind. You reacted to a thought I had not shared aloud."

"You spoke it, plain as day. You said Mr. MacNeal was marvelous, which he isn't. He has more flaws than a cheap diamond. Now, if you persist in nettling me, I shall be forced to turn you from my room!"

"Girls! Girls!" cried Maria, flinging open the door. "Wot's this commotion?"

The two friends stood glowering at each other in nightgowns and flown hair.

"Josephine can't keep her nose out of other people's affairs!"

"I'm only trying to help!"

"Meddling child!" shrieked Prudence.

It had been ages since anyone had accused Josephine of immaturity. Never mind that Prudence had obviously slung the first insult to hand, she had struck Josephine's weak spot. Tears smarting her eyes, Josephine flew past Maria and slammed the door hard.

Middlemere drifted down the corridor, oblivious to the shouts and bangs echoing upstairs. His mind was far away, recollecting music and candlelight and the sweet smell of a woman.

Her head bent against his arm, her eyes discretely downcast, but she was anything but demure. She loved his intellect, she said, and his tenderness, too. He had no idea why he loved her. Words, his beloved friends, escaped him in her presence. On impulse, he seized her and looked deep into her eyes. "I've waited a long time for this," he murmured and kissed her hard on the mouth.

"Oh, Clare!" she breathed happily.

"Joanna!" he exhaled—

"I didn't say *that*, did I?" he groaned, slapping his forehead. He paused, sorting out the differences between last night and that other interlude from so long ago.

They had spoken a bit; mostly, he had apologized for driving Lucinda to stoop to his daughter's design. She had seemed eager to receive his querying kiss. She wept a bit afterward, happily though. No, he must have used the correct name. Their embrace in the foyer had felt comfortable. More than comfortable. Perhaps Joanna's aura had finally loosened.

Bah! Don't analyze it, you fool.

He dodged into his study, averting his eyes from her portrait. An envelope lay on his desk. Eager for a distraction, Middlemere slipped on his spectacles. Bancroft, at last!

You liked the troll campaign, eh? I've kept a skeleton staff for such an occasion. Few at Headquarters understand why, so you can imagine the complaints when I requisitioned two hundred fifty soldiers to fight so-called wild bears! As you surmised, that infestation was no accident of nature. But who would have the desire and also the means to breed those poxy

*creatures? You've got the list of our old adversaries. It isn't
over yet, my friend. The trouble has only begun.*

"And we're not prepared for it," said Middlemere. What
followed caused him to choke on his tea:

*Your discovery of an untutored Protector is not so
surprising. They pop up from time to time—didn't you know?
Ask our Northern friends for the figures. Between you and me,
do* not *send him for Rehabilitation. He might come in handy.*

"They pop up?" wheezed Middlemere after clearing
his windpipe. "How many? Which families? What is their
geographic distribution?" He stared at his *magnum opus*. At the
date of publication, it had accounted for every living Keeper in
Britain. Since then, he'd corresponded with sources all over the
land, keeping his charts current. He had thought he owned the
only master list in existence . . . how much data was missing?

Damnation, all these years I was right and they never told me.

The Governors, whom Bancroft euphemistically called "our
Northern friends," had never fully trusted their non-Keeper
historian; this cover-up might prove to be their undoing.
Outrage pulsed through the earl's veins.

What in the name of God is this procedure you call Rehabilitation?

In ten minutes flat he had penned and sealed two
extremely terse letters, one to his former colleagues far away
in the north, and one to Bancroft, who this time would have
to stop playing coy.

CHAPTER THIRTY-THREE

London
13 January 1820

Prudence had forgotten the peculiar mustiness that clung about Stanistead House. As she stood in the foyer taking in the faded wallpaper and dated furnishings, she sensed for the first time a deep, abiding sadness. She glanced sidelong at Aunt Amelia, whose expression remained neutral, and wondered many things. How had the aunt come into possession of this house? Why had she never married? Had she also been a Keeper? She must . . . why else would she go by an assumed name? In all these months of self-examination and strife, Prudence had never once considered the aunt's part in her family's history, never paused to reflect on why she had an aversion to dredging up events of the past.

To ask her was pointless, and the more Prudence thought about it, the less that she cared. Aunt Amelia—the false relation—had failed in nine months to find her a husband. Her connections were useless, her advice dubious at best. This dithering old lady hindered more than she helped. *Yes, the sooner I marry, the sooner I can escape her insufferable fussing.*

Reese collected Prudence's redingote and handed her a small card. "This arrived yesterday morning, miss," he said with a bow.

Prudence opened the card, her brow furrowing more with each line she read:

> *I had hoped to find you back in residence, but alas it is not so! When you arrive on the morrow, I'll have set off for France. It's to be an extended stay, and I cannot predict when I shall see you again. I hope your sojourn in Wiltshire has restored you to health!*
> *Warmest regards,*
> *W. MacNeal*

She flung the note onto a tray. "Oh, what do I care?"

"Is that a message from our dear devoted friend?" asked Aunt Amelia, shrugging off her cloak and handing it to Nell. "You puzzle me, Prudence. Why the dark face?"

"You and he presume more of a friendship than I prefer to admit. He has gone abroad for a few weeks; I am wholly indifferent."

Aunt Amelia wheeled on her. "How can you? That man saved your life. I brought you back here so he could pay you suit. Mr. MacNeal adores you, he's handsome, and as it turns out, he is far from penniless. He is an ideal catch."

"I owe him gratitude, but not my affection."

"Well, isn't this a fine snag," Amelia said. "First Underwood, now MacNeal? Pray, what is your plan?"

Prudence lifted her chin. "I am not finished with the Marriage Mart, dear Aunt." Their eyes met, blue on blue, verging on sparks. Just then, Roland and Peter strode into the house.

"It's fantastic! It's brilliant! What an absolute castle!"

Aunt Amelia turned her ire onto them. "It is *my* castle, gentlemen, and I insist you respect that. We'll go over the rules of the house first thing tomorrow."

"Rules?" queried Roland, giving Peter a wide-eyed look.

"Of course," Prudence said. "You knew there must be a price. We mean to civilize you two for the company of women."

Peter groaned. "What are we, wild dogs?"

"Enough!" cried Amelia, stamping her foot. "Off to bed with you, Prudence! It's after ten o'clock, and you mustn't get overtired."

Prudence threw the boys a grin. "Come, gentlemen. I'll show you to your quarters."

She led them upstairs and bid them good night. Her own chamber was cozily turned out with a fire and lit sconces. After changing into her nightclothes, she reacquainted herself with her surroundings. She crouched by the bed, her hand brushing the bow-lidded Talisman chest. Two months had passed since she'd last seen it; she had feared it might be gone.

"Good," she said, smiling and giving it a pat.

Yes, everything was in order. Time to start life anew, take her future in her own hands.

At nearly nineteen years old, she now must find *someone* to marry. Anyone but MacNeal. Whenever she thought of that man, she experienced a visceral sensation, a deep-seated revulsion she could not explain. She couldn't imagine why she had ever considered him remotely handsome, and the memory of him simpering by her sickbed repelled her. Why, the brute had nearly ravished her right in the dining room! Such behavior was insupportable. There was no other way to say it: she hated William MacNeal with every ounce of her soul.

14 January 1820

After a morning spent instructing the boys how to behave in London, Prudence pleaded the need for solitude and retreated upstairs. She had, however, an ulterior motive.

"Where is it?" she muttered, opening and shutting drawers. She searched the Talisman box five times and checked every pocket she owned, but she could not find the ring.

Did I lose it in the rainstorm?

Closing her eyes, she tried to recall what had led to her to go wandering that night.

It called to her sweetly, more than ever before. Its song was an antidote to the cacophony of voices that rang in her ears:

"Why has she rejected me? I saw affection in her eye."

"Abandon the Talismans!"

"Come to me, Prudence. You won't regret it."

She wore the ring always in the privacy of her room; despite the voices, it gave her some measure of peace. That night, it sang a new refrain.

"The time is now. Go outside, and I'll send a carriage to meet you."

Here the words faded. She bent her memory to retrieve more, but the rest was a blur of nightgown, downpour, and a winking red jewel.

Then warm breath. Arms lifting her gently. "My darling, what are you doing?"

Anger and tears. "Put me down! Oh, why did you stop me?"

William MacNeal. Always there when she least expected him. Changing the course of events. Loving her devotedly . . .

She felt a brief spark of tenderness, but then her eyes swam and hatred blazed anew. Wherever she had been headed, *he* had hindered her, and she would never forgive him.

Just before teatime, she sat reading in the drawing room when Reese came in with a bouquet, which he set in the front window.

"This came by courier, miss," he informed her, then politely withdrew.

Taking this to mean the bouquet was for her, she rose to peer at the gorgeous explosion of two dozen pink roses. A card marked with her name said,

My dear Miss F., I believe these are the exact color of your cheeks when something secretly pleases you. —W.M.

A ripple of delight ran down her spine, quickly overcome by uncontrollable anger. Crushing the card and the pleasant sensation, Prudence stamped toward the door.

"Oh, you audacious scoundrel!"

Aunt Amelia happened to enter just then. Scowling, she took Prudence's arm, steered her back inside, and there she regarded the offending arrangement. "How *can* you be displeased? Mr. MacNeal is so thoughtful."

"He's a presumptuous peacock!"

"You love him, as sure as I'm standing here!"

Prudence clenched her fists. "On the contrary, I'd rather choose spinsterhood than spend a moment under his roof! Your life doesn't seem all that bad."

"Ungrateful minx!" exploded Amelia. "How *dare* you compare your choices to mine!"

A strange depth to her rage pierced Prudence's fury.

"Forgive me," she murmured, bowing her head.

"Save your repentance," snarled the aunt. "I shall find a man for you, Prudence, or else die trying!" And with a flounce of her skirts, she stormed from the room.

26 January 1820

The days passed slowly, for the Season had not yet begun. Prudence and the aunt maintained a careful détente. They dragged the young country squires to museums and galleries and afternoon calls. Every so often, a card or gift arrived from Mr. MacNeal. He never pressed Prudence and stated only that he was thinking of her. Prudence's heart remained untouched, and she made ready to re-enter the Marriage Mart, this time a wiser woman.

Their winter evenings were not all dull. Somehow Aunt Amelia managed to secure tickets for the London premiere of Rossini's opera *La Cenerentola*. Prudence enjoyed the spellbinding performance, and afterward the audience gathered in the King's Theatre foyer for a sumptuous reception.

Feeling herself a bit like Cinderella at the ball, Prudence moved through the crowd in a lavender silk gown. She caught sight of Miss Alice Wymstone and hurried over to take the girl's hand. "Hello, dear! You look well tonight."

Miss Wymstone smiled nervously, at once pleased and ill at ease. "I heard you've been ill. One would never know it to look at you now."

Prudence felt keenly the goodness and sorrow of the homely girl's compliment. "You're too kind." She kissed Miss Wymstone's cheek. "Has time eased that taint of madness about me? I should very much like to call on you."

"And I you, but—"

"Alice?" cried a matronly voice. "To whom are you speaking?"

Miss Wymstone blanched and whispered, "I'm so glad it was *he* who saved you that night! I wish you both the best!" Before Prudence could reply, she darted into the crowd.

Prudence swallowed the lump that had formed in her throat. Her various misfortunes had robbed her of a friend and robbed that friend of the chance for intimacy, too. Brushing away tears, she spied a phalanx of young ladies, among them Lady Emmeline's spiteful friend, Miss Kimball. The girls burst into laughter and leant close together. Prudence had a sudden perverse desire to know what kept them so entertained. She advanced on them, smiling, until someone touched her forearm. Looking round, she found Helen Morris beside her.

"Don't," Helen mouthed.

Prudence sniffed and kept on. When she had drawn within a few steps of the socialites' circle, the girls fell silent. Their ranks parted, revealing Lady Emmeline DeLacey, her bosom rising and falling with the effort of suppressing fierce loathing.

Prudence curtseyed. "Good evening, Lady DeLacey."

A ripple of inhalations spread through the pack. Someone giggled. Then, in a subtle shift, Lady Emmeline's eyes ceased to focus on Prudence's face. She turned and walked away; her retinue followed suit.

"That is what they call a Cut Direct," hissed Helen before vanishing into the crowd.

Prudence swayed and her emotions threatened to spill into tears. Just then, two gentlemen closed with a hearty, "Good evening, Miss Fairfeather!"

"You seemed in want of rescuing," said MacNeal's friend Thomas Perkins.

"Aren't I always?" she asked. Stephen Tate snatched a glass of champagne from a passing tray and handed it to her; she downed its contents in two or three gulps. "That time," she said woozily, "I went looking for trouble."

"There, there!" clucked the gentlemen. "Never mind them." They guided Prudence to a chair and plied her with more wine.

Prudence's head was soon swirling. "Mercy!" she muttered, pressing a hand to her temple. "Life in this town really tries a girl's nerves."

Perkins and Tate knelt at her feet. The former said in a low voice, "Far be it from me to discredit any woman, but Lady DeLacey is an unforgiving harpy who's jealous of any female that seeks to supplant her."

Laughter rippled up from her belly. "Supplant her? Me? Gentlemen, I am astonished! Your colleague may *have* that creature for all I care!"

Perkins and Tate stared, thunderstruck. "B-b-but we understood—certainly *Mac* understood—that he's been paying you court!"

Rage replaced mirth. "What? How *dare* he! I pined for him all last summer. I accepted his excuses. I withheld my favor when I might've given it to another. But now that I see him for the scoundrel he is, I cannot shed his unwelcome attentions. No, I must also endure a shunning from his discarded lover!"

"But you misunderstand—"

"Please! It wasn't like that—"

Prudence held up a hand. "Oh, no! Do not plead his case! I am just a country girl who came to London to find herself a husband. That is spoilt now because people think I'm mad or else I've set my cap for that dirty dish. I shall die alone and an old maid, all because of Lady Jealousy and your abominable

Mr. Mac!"

In the wake of this torrent of unladylike words, she clenched her hands in tight, angry fists. Perkins and Tate lurched to their feet.

"We're v-very sorry to have troubled you," stammered Mr. Perkins. He and Tate bowed and stumbled away.

"Good riddance," muttered Prudence. Draining her glass, she stood up too fast and glowered at the crowd swirling nearby. A rushing in her ears made it difficult to think, and she needed the ladies' necessary. Spying a queue of females snaking its way down a side passage, she fell in with them, securing another glass of champagne as she went.

As she waited her turn, she sipped wine and giggled. *Well done, Prudence!* she thought. *Henceforth MacNeal will trouble you no more.*

"Careful," murmured Helen. "Do not make a spectacle of yourself."

Prudence spun on her former friend. Archly, she said, "I don't know what you mean, and I can't imagine what right you have to tell me how to behave." A loud hiccough burst from her throat. Several ladies turned and furrowed their brows.

"Lower your voice, dear. I may indeed have no right to say aught, but I care deeply what happens to you. You're quite tipsy, you know. Where is Miss Staveley?"

"How should I know? I've been busy making a spectacle of myself!" Prudence was amazed at how well her voice projected in that narrow hallway. Giggles and tsking traveled back to her ears. "They certainly take a long time in the privy, do they not? Oh my, did I say that aloud?" Horrified, she pressed a hand to her mouth.

"That's it. Come along!" Helen took Prudence's arm and

dragged her, protesting, until they emerged into the light and noise of the foyer. After an interminable search, they located Aunt Amelia. "Madam, good evening. Here is your niece. I recommend you take her home directly."

The old woman narrowed eyes.

"It's nothing untoward," Helen assured in a whisper. "Prudence has imbibed a little too much and is in danger of embarrassing herself."

This statement struck Prudence as immensely funny, and she loosed a robust laugh, bringing the evening to an immediate end.

In the carriage, Aunt Amelia hissed, "What's gotten into you, Prudence?"

"Nothing! I feel fine. I am perfectly content." Prudence hugged herself and giggled for most of the way home.

Back at Stanistead, Aunt Amelia handed her over to Nell, and before long the house descended into silence. Then, close to dawn, Prudence was wrenched from a fitful sleep by a crash in the upper corridor. She staggered into the hall, where she found Peter entangled in the matchstick remains of a small lunette table. Roland, swaying unsteadily, picked his way through a field of porcelain shards.

Aunt Amelia appeared, imposing in a mobcap and frothy dressing gown. "What's this?" she bellowed. After much hemming and hawing, Peter and Roland confessed to losing a huge amount of money in some gaming hell. "Foolish creatures! Your stay will be foreshortened if you spend your allowances in a fortnight. Don't forget: you are here by my pleasure alone."

The boys held their heads and grunted compliance.

Prudence added in gentler tones, "This is not Wiltshire, my dears. Sharpers are on the lookout for bumpkins like you."

Neither boy was listening. No sooner did Prudence finish than Roland clapped a hand to his mouth and bolted. Peter quickly followed. Prudence, herself not yet sober, broke into laughter.

Aunt Amelia turned to unleash her unsated fury. "As for *you*, young lady, I need not say how your own performance may have affected your future! Three drunken teenagers in one night! Lord save me!"

And on that plaintive note, the old lady returned to her chamber.

CHAPTER THIRTY-FOUR

Edingham-Greene, Wiltshire
18 January 1820

With half the household gone, Greenbank dropped back into its sleepy midwinter routine. Lord Middlemere seemed exceptionally preoccupied these days, though he always put aside his work to receive Mrs. March. To Josephine's delight, the couple had grown closer in a fortnight than they had in fifteen years.

Meanwhile, her seventeenth birthday approached, and a desire for refinement began to supplant her more youthful interests. Of her own volition, she tackled various texts from her father's collection, and she asked him to give her regular instruction in piano and French.

With maturity came thoughts about her future. Josephine tingled at the prospect of marrying Quimby, though engagement would mean the end of her aspirations for a London debut. She lay in the alcove, envisioning herself as a matron at her very first ball. Gentlemen admirers would flock to her side, only to be driven off by the return of her husband. But oh, what a husband! Robert would outrank them all in birthright and character, not to mention his fine looks. What fun, to be the bane of jealous debutantes!

Perhaps, she thought, *some ambitions are meant to remain childhood dreams.*

Now and then, Quimby sent a letter and Middlemere would read excerpts aloud. His platoon remained billeted in Cheltenham with little to do except maintain readiness, so the officer passed his time reading books borrowed from the earl. Josephine paid close attention to what he said about them and frequently chose to read those same volumes upon their return.

This time, he had added,

> *I adore the little watercolor Lady Weston painted of Greenbank. I've hung it by my looking glass so I can admire it each morning. I wonder whether she might attempt a self-portrait? Now that is an image I'd love to have!*

"Coo, how romantic!" Maria said with a sigh. Josephine slumped in her seat; she had no talent for portraiture.

"I know: let us have a painter come to Greenbank," said Middlemere. "Not that you aren't capable, dear, but I'm happy for the excuse to have a formal portrait made. He could make miniatures, too; one each for the lieutenant and me. I realize it's not strictly proper, but we're the only ones who will know. Will you look into it?" He winked conspiratorially at her.

"If it so pleases you, Papa." Josephine wondered at her father's proposal. Hopefully his enthusiasm for Quimby signaled his acceptance of her future beyond Greenbank's gates.

In her next letter, Prudence applauded this plan:

> *Though you must understand such a Gift indicates a level of Attachment that I am not certain you wish to encourage so soon.*

"Indeed?" guffawed Josephine. "Then you advocate I quarrel with Quimby and burn all his missives?" She and Prudence had parted company on uneasy terms, spending their last week together without making peace. Prudence had apologized for making Josephine cry, but she'd plainly felt justified in lashing out. Her return to London and MacNeal's subsequent attentions had done nothing to shake her obsession with the now-missing ring, and her letters reflected a descent into bitterness and anxiety. Mr. MacNeal's latest journey to France was ill timed in the extreme, though most women would have been placated by gifts and tender notes. Prudence, on the other hand, sounded openly hostile.

Sooner or later, she would have to face him.

And then, thought Josephine, *she may well drive him away.*

29 January 1820

Josephine's inquiries produced the name of a reputable portraitist working not far away. She invited him to come to Greenbank as soon as he could and then spent hours debating which frock she should wear.

On Saturday, a box arrived from Prudence. It contained a gorgeous straw bonnet trimmed with grass-green ribbons and ostrich feathers, a birthday gift worthy of the fashion plates of London.

"Now that's devilish smart!" said Josephine, admiring herself in the entry hall mirror. She unsealed the accompanying letter and carried it into the parlor.

Aunt Amelia and I recently dined at the townhome of Sir

Richard Keithley, Sire to a trio of lively and Good-looking sons. Sadly, each possessed his own Impediment. Lawrence found it impossible to forget a Governess he has no hope of marrying. Julian, two years my junior, could think of nothing but attending University next year. The eldest, Richard, seemed the brightest prospect. He approached me after supper and paid me Many attentions, but it soon became Clear that his interest was only Platonic.

"You surprise me, Miss Fairfeather," he said with a smile. "Goddesses are usually Aloof sorts of creatures. You are not so in the least!"

I blinked in Surprise. "What makes you say that?"

"Why, your Reputation precedes you. I have heard your Praises sung countless times."

"Wh-who . . . ?" My stomach plunged in Dismay.

"Do not feign Ignorance. Surely you know how profoundly Will MacNeal admires you!"

"You shock me," I said Tightly, "for I do not count him among my more Intimate friends."

"Play coy if you like." Keithley nodded toward the Elders, conferring in a corner. "I can't imagine why your Aunt is going to so much Trouble. I shall enlighten my Parents the moment you're gone, as would any Upright fellow. No one I know would invade another Man's territory."

"Mr. Keithley, I am not a country to be Conquered!"

He bowed. "Begging your pardon. It was only a Manner of speaking."

"Whatever you call it, I'll thank you not to refer to me in Terms of chattel," I sniffed, flouncing away.

What staggering News! Apparently, during my sojourn in Wiltshire I acquired the status of Unavailable Lady. If this should continue, then my return to the Marriage Mart will certainly fail. Ah, that horrid, horrid man!

"Oh, Prudence!" groaned Josephine. She doubted MacNeal had truly declared Prudence his own; more likely his friends had witnessed enough to deduce how things stood. They had no idea Prudence's illness had changed everything.

That bedamned illness! Leading up to it, and certainly ever since, Prudence's personality had altered. How and why, Josephine could not fathom. This notion bore itself out in Prudence's following letter. She'd done something awful in public, something Prudence in her right mind would never have done: she had lost her temper and berated MacNeal to his friends. Worse, she felt no remorse. This brought Josephine to the brink of a momentous decision.

She slept fitfully that night and arose early the next morning. By candlelight, she began the note she had long dreaded to write.

1 February 1820

My Dear Aunt,

I am disturbed by the tone of Prudence's recent letters. Her hostility toward Mr. MacNeal has grown to the point where she has twice exchanged words with others in public. Madam, I fear for her sanity. This is not our mild-mannered Prudence, who was passionately in love with that man all last summer. Something has changed her.

Respectfully yours,

Lady Josephine Weston

P.S. She is looking feverishly for the ring.

She had betrayed Prudence, plain and simple, but she was driven to it by love. Josephine sent the letter by express and braced for Aunt Amelia's reply. Two days of silence wore her nerves to the bone. She stalked the house like a Fury, snapping at the staff and picking quarrels with Maria. She even called Arthur Grant a prig in front of Mrs. March. Arthur exited posthaste without defending his honor, which only proved how spineless he was.

"What's got your dander up these days?" wondered Mrs. March, coming to sit beside her.

"I'm restless!" cried Josephine, fighting back tears.

"You need more society," guessed Mrs. March. "Mr. Grant is a boor, and your retinue has gone. Are you missing, perhaps, a certain handsome fellow of our acquaintance?"

Josephine blushed. "Oh, no! These days you and Papa keep me quite entertained."

"Pshaw! We're just old friends. You, however, must be careful not to let yourself be seduced by good looks and charm. I'm worried about you."

Josephine embraced Mrs. March. It was tempting to welcome her into her confidence. She longed to share everything about Quimby, as well as Prudence's current nightmare. She also yearned not to be the keeper of so many secrets.

The bell rang in the front hall. Shortly, Carson entered with an envelope for Josephine. She stayed him with a hand. "Wait, please, in case I have a reply. Forgive me, Mrs. March. I beg your indulgence." Josephine went to the window and opened the letter, which was, of course, from Aunt Amelia.

I gratefully acknowledge receipt of your express, which has given me the sort of information I need to take action. Trust me, Lady Josephine. If I succeed in this endeavor, you

will know rather quickly that Prudence is better. Thank you
for your confidence. I know how hard it must've been for you
to take such a step. Pray for Prudence, won't you?

Josephine said shakily, "Thank you, Carson. There is no
return message."

The butler bowed and withdrew.

"Is something wrong?" Mrs. March asked.

"On the contrary." Josephine tucked the letter into her
pocket and mustered a smile. "Will you sup with us tonight?"

CHAPTER THIRTY-FIVE

London
1 February 1820

On Tuesday Prudence received a brief and surprisingly stiff note from Josephine, thanking her for the birthday bonnet but making no remark about her encounter with Richard Keithley or the events at the King's Theatre.

That's odd! she thought, smoothing out the page. She could picture Josephine shaking her head and muttering, "Mr. MacNeal is too much of a gentleman to presume you've agreed to his suit. Society simply recognizes the mutual partiality that you continue to deny!"

"She surely felt this, even if she did not bother to say it." Prudence did not question how she knew, or even wonder at the significance of Josephine's uncharacteristic silence. Instead, she penned a note responding to her friend's unspoken rebuke:

Do you think I have sealed my Fate with those harsh and hasty words? I do not care, for I'm relieved. No, more than relieved. I am Joyous!

The sounds of distant thumps and clashings interrupted her train of thought. After much wheedling and promises of exemplary behavior, Roland and Peter had received Aunt Amelia's permission to use the ballroom to practice their fencing. She and the old lady sometimes watched the boys spar, but never did it occur to Prudence that she would like to fence, too.

"I fail to see the appeal of it," she added to her letter. "You may have your physical exertions, Lady Weston. I'll take on life's foes with the power of my wits."

The icy weather continued unabated, trapping everyone indoors. Prudence hid upstairs, immersing herself in Ann Radcliffe's *The Romance of the Forest*, and tried not to care that Josephine had yet to write.

Late in the morning on the fifth instant, Nell tapped on Prudence's door.

"Miss Staveley wants you in her sitting room, ma'am."

Prudence came along slowly, reading her book as she went. She entered, still reading, and pushed the door shut with her backside. Tucking a place-holding finger into the binding, she looked up. A cloaked person stood at Aunt Amelia's elbow. She sensed it was a man, though his voluminous cape and deeply cowled hood kept every feature in shadow. The presence of a male in their private quarters and thusly clothed shocked Prudence speechless.

Aunt Amelia said, "Permit me to introduce to you to Miss Fairfeather."

The figure approached, took Prudence's hand, and pressed it with long, bony fingers. A tingling sensation raced up her arm. She tried to jerk away.

"Wait!" he commanded, stilling her with a surprisingly strong grasp.

She felt a palm on her forehead, heard an unintelligible

phrase. A pinpoint of pain burrowed its way into the center of her skull, then burst like a small firework and radiated outward. "Help me, Aunt!" she cried. Her arms flailed; the book in her hand dropped to the floor. Now the room started to spin, and everything in it whirled by with an ever-building howl. As she hovered uncertainly at the storm's vortex, a terrifying chasm stretched open at her feet. She tried to scream but was voiceless. The world slid out of focus, and she heard the man say, "You were right; I sense two enchantments at least. She'll swoon awhile, but—"

Prudence fell headlong into the chasm and then heard no more.

She climbed out of the darkness and gradually grew cognizant of her surroundings. Voices and footsteps and a sound like swishing fabric rushed by her ears. Prudence lay on Amelia's chaise, giving no outward indication that she'd regained consciousness. Aunt Amelia and the cloaked stranger stood close together, speaking in hushed tones.

"Oh, I pray that you have managed to undo the harm! What sort of spells were they?"

"The first one was not especially powerful—a love charm of sorts, though it seems to have encountered heavy resistance. The other was far more insidious, designed to make the recipient hate someone they love. Does this reflect the behavior you had observed?"

"Yes," Amelia said soberly. "Lord, and it has been months, now that I think about it. How could I miss the obvious signs of Inheritance when I have spent so many months with her?

I assumed her obsession with the Talismans was morbid curiosity. Someone in London must have identified her . . . but why would they want to control her like this?"

"That is a question best addressed to the Governors."

"Pish! Their heads are in the sand. We need an intellect like Clarence Weston, but I'm afraid he's still in no condition to help. I dare not inform him about these proceedings."

"No," agreed the stranger. "Do not tell him yet."

"Then what can an old lady do to protect this poor girl?"

Here Prudence parted her lashes slightly, but the stranger stood with his back to her.

"You are not alone, Leonore," he said. "Bancroft says her young man is a Protector."

Aunt Amelia looked startled. "What? How could he know?"

"Middlemere surmised it during the fellow's visit to Greenbank. He's confused, but his instinct is strong, and I'm told he has acted accordingly on at least one occasion." Amelia threw him questioning look. "Alas," he said, shrugging, "the details of such are not known to me."

Aunt Amelia kneaded her hands. "Clarence predicted this, but none of us believed him. Now two Keepers have manifested the Trait without the requisite ceremony."

"Oh, they are not the first."

"What do you mean?"

"There have been others, Leonore, enough that the Governors have been obliged to develop a policy to deal with the problem."

"And what, pray tell, does it entail?"

"The subject must destroy his own Talismans and then undergo a magical voiding of that part of his memory. They call it Rehabilitation. The procedure is crude, I'm afraid; there have been a few, er . . . unexpected results." The stranger glanced in

Prudence's direction. "First things first. If I file a report, these two will be summoned to the Refuge. Assuming all goes well, they'll be spared this sort of danger for the rest of their lives. Is that what you want?"

Aunt Amelia closed her eyes. "This procedure you speak of . . . will they know one another when all is said and done?"

The stranger exhaled. "Truthfully, I cannot guarantee it."

Amelia uttered a small cry and the stranger embraced her. "For you, I shall withhold my report, though that does not discount the immediate danger. Someone obviously wanted this couple divided. I recommend getting them married as soon as possible."

"God willing. Look. She awakens."

"I'll show myself out. Try not to tell her more than is strictly necessary. She'll experience residual fatigue for the rest of the day. Goodbye." He kissed Aunt Amelia's cheek and swept from the room. Prudence flicked open her eyes to catch a glimpse of his face, but saw only the receding edge of his billowing cloak.

"My head!" she croaked, struggling to sit up. The room swirled and threatened to go black.

"Gently!" urged Aunt Amelia, rushing to her side. "You fainted. It is probably just a minor relapse of your illness. Would you like the smelling salts?"

"No, thank you. I can manage."

Aunt Amelia fussed over Prudence, giving her brandy and a shawl and putting a pillow under her head. "Rest right here. I'll look in on you at teatime."

Prudence hadn't the strength to argue. Her eyes were heavy, her head full of cobwebs. She sank into unconsciousness as Aunt Amelia doused the sconces.

6 February 1820

She slept through teatime and on into the night. Waking early the next morning, Prudence slipped down the hall to her own chamber, where she washed, changed clothes, and straightened her hair. In the looking glass, she could see no visible signs of yesterday's trial. Whatever had happened in Aunt Amelia's sitting room was no relapse, for she felt better than she had in months.

So what *had* happened? A stranger had come to Stanistead House. He'd spoken to Aunt Amelia about deep family secrets and addressed her as Leonore. They talked as if Prudence were soon to be married.

"To whom?" she puzzled aloud. "One would think that I'd know."

The young man is a Protector . . .

"Which young man?" Her head filled with fog, and a hazy silhouette rose in her mind.

A voice said, "It's over, don't you see?"

"It can't be. I love her."

"She despises you. There was no mistaking her scorn."

The silhouette hunched, hands covering its face. "I refuse to accept that. I feel . . . oh, how can I explain?" The silhouette fell silent.

"Be at peace," Prudence whispered. "I still love you, my darling." She roused from the dream, unable to identify the person she apparently loved. Unruffled, she resolved to speak to Aunt Amelia. When she joined her housemates for breakfast, Peter and Roland appeared none the wiser about what had transpired. Aunt Amelia's eyes, however, never left her face.

"Your fencing master arrives at eleven o'clock," the aunt told the boys. "I suggest you behave, for I hear he does not suffer fools."

"Oh, I say!" they cried in unison. "Thank you, Miss Staveley! That's positively brilliant!"

"They're scalawags," she chuckled after Peter and Roland had gone, "but I'm growing strangely fond of those two. Shall we retire to the parlor?"

Prudence nodded, and they crossed the hall. Amelia closed the door, turning the key in the lock. "Now," she said, "let us have a serious talk about William MacNeal."

Prudence's hands flew to her mouth. Memories flooded back of a tall, handsome man with sandy hair and green eyes. She recalled the secret glances, the laughter, and the soggy embrace. Her face fell as she also remembered the lies and evasions.

Aunt Amelia inhaled. "There is a history between you two that I wasn't aware of."

Prudence nodded.

"Oh, Lord, it's even worse than I thought."

"NO—yes! What I mean to say is . . ."

All at once, Prudence's reserve gave way and a confession spilled out. She spoke of her obsession with the Talismans, of Mr. MacNeal's part in the boating and hunting incidents, of his love notes and their emotional meeting in Hyde Park. She ended with the duel and the anonymous letter implicating Lord Underwood in a murderous plot.

Aunt Amelia's eyes bulged. "I cannot *believe* this all happened right beneath my nose!" She glowered at Prudence. "Lady Josephine knows, doesn't she?"

"Nearly everything, but please don't be angry with her! I begged her to shield me. I was terrified you would take the Talismans away."

"A needless fear," sniffed Aunt Amelia. "I can't even touch

them unless you give them to me freely. If you'd been truthful from the start, I would have answered those questions that plagued you so sorely."

"Come now! You would have brooked no substitute for perfect Lord Underwood!"

"As far as I was aware, there *was* no other candidate. Prudence, I asked you directly if your heart belonged to another."

Prudence looked away. "I tried to say it . . ."

"Yes, but you were not in full control of your faculties," the aunt added softly. "What's done is done, and now you are restored. It raises the question, however: who wants to hurt you and why? That Underwood note—do you still have it?"

"Yes, in my room. I'll retrieve it directly."

Aunt Amelia pursed her lips as she examined the note. "When I think how I berated you for putting him off . . ." Her voice trailed into silence. "If this message is authentic, it bears disturbing implications. Underwood may be dead, but he wasn't acting alone. Poor Mr. MacNeal! He had no idea what he'd gotten himself into when he fell in love with you—"

Prudence interjected, "Aunt, if we are in danger, he and I cannot afford to be ignorant of what kind. You owe us that much."

Amelia went pale. "Danger, perhaps, or only mischief . . . it's never good to speculate."

"Madam, I have bared my soul—"

"Yes, very well!" Aunt Amelia paced the room. "I've hinted, of course, about the Inheritance, which gave many of your kin certain . . ."

"—unique talents?" supplied Prudence.

"Just so. These talents were augmented by objects called Talismans, such as the ones I entrusted to you on your birthday. Since then, you have seen what they are capable of."

"Yes, but not willfully. They insinuated themselves into my consciousness. Before that, I had no idea about such things, and would have denied it in any account."

Aunt Amelia nodded. "No one expected the Talismans to exert a force of their own. We called ourselves Talisman Keepers, but our power relied on more than mere objects. Most Keepers formed partnerships that made them still stronger. In the early days, they offered their services in exchange for titles and land and became much coveted by the nobility. But a weapon can be used against its owner, and some feared the Keepers might usurp the aristocracy. Our gifts were endowed for the purpose of bolstering Britain's strength, not breaking it down, but non-Keepers misunderstood."

"So the nobility was responsible for eradicating the Keepers?"

Amelia shook her head. "The collapse came from within. Britain grew from an island of many sovereigns to a nation of just one, and as the Commonwealth became stable, the Keepers began to lose their importance. Advancements in science and weaponry often matched our abilities. The government regarded our services as increasingly superfluous, and thus less supportable."

Prudence recalled the fervor in Lady Revelle's eyes when she lamented the passing of a glorious age. Obsolescence would, indeed, be difficult to accept.

"Keepers tried to assimilate into general society, but it wasn't easy. Most had developed a taste for adventure. Some found contentment as explorers, inventors, or the recklessly idle; a

Keeper Brigade was established to help channel such energies. In its final decades, members of that body acted as spies."

"But then it all came to an end."

The old woman sank onto a settee. "The government lost interest in maintaining our cover and, under pressure from the military, urged us to disband. It offered incentives to anyone willing to take an Oath of Disavowal, more for those who chose to destroy their Talismans. As the time for compliance approached, a small opposition launched a conflict that destroyed most of the Brigade. The survivors then dismantled it and forced a ban on the Tradition."

"No more Keepers would be trained."

"Exactly. An entire generation has grown up without mentoring and rituals; the Talismans became useless . . . or at least so we thought." Amelia gazed sadly at Prudence.

An irrational question lingered in Prudence's brain. She had fought the obvious for so long—now she must know. "Aunt Amelia, does this mean we are . . . *magical* people?"

The aunt turned away. "I have said enough. What's important here is this plot"—she shook the letter for emphasis—"*shall* be brought to light. We have specialists trained to deal with such matters. Your only concern now, Prudence, is whether or not you wish to marry William MacNeal."

"But—"

"Enough, child! Do you or do you not love that man?"

Prudence exhaled. Her compulsion to dissemble had utterly vanished. "Yes, of course I do. I always have."

A smile softened the aunt's face. "Perhaps we should send for the poor fellow."

"Perhaps, but I don't think he is anywhere within a hundred miles of here."

"That you should know this," said Amelia, stroking the girl's cheek, "signifies how gravely we all were mistaken. The Inheritance, dear child, has reawakened in our people."

CHAPTER THIRTY-SIX

London
7 February 1820

Prudence required another night's sleep before she could put pen to paper. She rose on the seventh instant and set to work, beginning with an admission she never thought she'd make:

> *Dearest Cos,*
>
> *The Truth, long suppressed, is nevertheless the Truth. At last I have opened my mind to Magic, or rather I had it opened for me by a practitioner of that Art. Now, looking back over my Past year's experience, I must acknowledge, dear Josephine, that you were right all along.*

She outlined every detail of the exorcism and subsequent history lesson; the missive took her well over two hours to complete. In conclusion, she assured Josephine that she felt completely restored, and she begged her pardon for having so sorely tested their friendship.

With her product submitted to the hands of the postman, Prudence entered the parlor to greet Aunt Amelia. Disappointment crumpled the old woman's face. She handed over a note, sent that morning from MacNeal's butler:

I regret to inform you that Mr. MacNeal is out of the country and not expected home any time soon.

"Oh dear," murmured Prudence.

"It is possible your denouncement of him has lengthened his stay in France, and when he returns, he may not wish to see you."

Prudence blinked back hot tears. "If he loves me, he'll forgive me. If not, I shall accept my fate."

As there was nothing more to be done with respect to Mr. MacNeal, the women began preparations for the Winter Ball, one of the Season's inaugural social events. They visited the dressmaker to commission a new gown of pale blue silk, dotted with pearls and with a sheer scarf of white gauze to cover Prudence's shoulders. Each time she went to the shop for a fitting, Prudence grew fonder of that gown, and she wished with all her heart that Mr. MacNeal could see her in it. Such a felicitous outcome, however, seemed increasingly unlikely as the days continued to pass without any word.

13 February 1820

Josephine wrote in raptures at about Prudence's restoration, though she could not shake the idea that she had willfully contributed to her friend's suffering.

Prudence, how can you say you were at fault? It is I who should beg your forgiveness! I see now that you really have not been yourself. I wish I'd realized it sooner, instead of taking you to task as if you had full possession of your reason.

Prudence assured her that nothing could be further from the truth. Josephine could not have known an enchantment had altered her behavior. To her consternation, though, the perspicacious Josephine had found her report wanting:

I see no mention in that discussion with Amelia of your doings with Lady Revelle. Is this an oversight, or did you somehow manage to confess all without truly confessing all? *Come now, Prudence, you and I can guess whose malevolent hand bespelled you! The quickest way to gain your safety is to give complete information.*

Prudence could not deny she had failed to fully enlighten the aunt, and in retrospect, she wasn't sure why that subject had never come up; perhaps it had not seemed relevant at the time. Which was, of course, perfectly absurd, for Lady Revelle was the unifying thread throughout her misfortunes.

"Josephine's right. I should tell Amelia the rest." She paused, chewing anxiously on a thumbnail. The mere thought made her queasy. "Oh, I don't know! I *want* to tell her, and I know I ought—but I am loath to revisit the unpleasant past."

If she were to conceal such vital information, however, she must justify it to Josephine as well as herself. Prudence drummed her fingers on the desk. "The truth is, I can think of no valid reason to keep the rest secret." Still, some compulsion drove her to seek an excuse.

Then, like an epiphany, the answer arrived: if she were to expose Lady Revelle's machinations, Aunt Amelia would have no choice but to notify Keeper authorities that Prudence possessed active Talismans.

They would descend on our Family and examine everyone for the Trait, identifying you and perhaps Edward before drawing Mr. MacNeal into the net. What would happen to Us then is uncertain, but the Exorcist's description still burns in my head: a magical Voiding of one's Memory with the potential to produce unexpected Results.

Prudence shuddered, then added, "Is that not a compelling enough reason, my dear?"

She blew on her handwriting to dry it. Sleet rattled against the windowpanes. A gust of wind bowed the ancient wood frame. She wondered what Mr. MacNeal was doing at that moment.

16 February 1820

The day of the Winter Ball dawned bright and beautiful. Prudence and Amelia arrived at the assembly rooms at precisely nine o'clock in the evening. In the ladies' salon, they shed their wrappers, checked coiffures, and exchanged boots for dainty slippers.

Before entering the Grand Ballroom, Aunt Amelia kissed Prudence's cheek. "Your first ball! You'll remember this night in years to come. Have a wonderful time, my precious girl."

Prudence gasped at the sight of the glittering crowd. More silk, more jewels, more elegance she had not seen in her life. As she stepped into the ballroom, her initial confidence wavered and sank. Would this event prove yet another forum for public humiliation?

I won't let it. Come what may, I shall hold my head high.

She felt reflexively for her ring, but the comforting band had been missing for more than two months. *Just as well,* she decided, smoothing her skirt. And so, without a Talisman to lend her support, Prudence re-entered Society. She found to her relief that Emmeline DeLacey's shunning had produced few repercussions; for each person who upheld it, two more stepped forward to inquire after her health. Not everyone had marked the extent of all her misfortunes; others regarded them as uncommon bad luck. Ladies beckoned her to join their discussions. Gentlemen bowed and asked her to dance.

Richard Keithley was among those who asked for her favor. "You're different tonight," he said as they moved through figures of a popular contredanse.

"My partner's elegance improves me by his mere proximity."

Keithley made a face. "Bah, don't waste your charm on the likes of me! I am yet immune to marriageable young ladies. Try old Tate here, instead."

Without warning, Stephen Tate stepped in to replace Mr. Keithley, who sauntered off.

"Well, then!" remarked Prudence, turning in place with her new partner.

"Do you object?"

"No, but I'm surprised you'd come near me after that tongue-lashing last month."

Mr. Tate grinned sidelong at her. "We addlepates have exceptionally tough hides." The contredanse ended, and the orchestra laid down its instruments. "Ah, an interval. Poor timing!" he said. "May I get you a drink?"

They entered an adjoining salon containing tables laden with refreshments. Tate secured two cups of punch and steered Prudence off to one side.

"It's rather loud in here, is it not?" he said, projecting his voice. Prudence sipped her punch and nodded agreement. A moment later he bellowed, "Are you done with that? Here, I'll fetch you some more."

No sooner had Tate plucked the glass from her hand than Prudence was seized by the waist and yanked backward into an alcove. Someone drew a drapery across its opening, plunging her into darkness.

"What's this about?" she demanded, expecting at any moment to be knocked on the head.

"It's about finding a bit of privacy in this mob. Every pink and widgeon in London seems to have come here tonight."

"It's you!" Prudence swayed as terror collided with shock.

Mr. MacNeal moved forward to steady her elbow. "In the flesh. You summoned me, so I came as soon as I could. Now, what was it you wanted to say? Shall I take the next boat to hell?"

There was an edge to his words; Prudence couldn't blame him for thinking the worst. She wanted to assure him, but she also craved assurance that he could forgive her. Alas, she could see next to nothing, and this man whom she'd just remembered she'd forgotten to love stood inches away with an unknowable expression on his face. She closed her eyes, letting her other senses plumb his mood. In that tiny enclosure, she couldn't fail to notice the ragged quality of his breathing. A hint of gin in the air bespoke of nerves that had required some calming. Another scent, *his* scent, swirled all around her, making it next to impossible for Prudence to focus.

Yes, what had she wanted to say?

"Bless me, did I sail all the way from France only to have you fall mute?"

The smile in MacNeal's voice shook Prudence from her stupor. Her eyes opened, and she could now see his face rather well. Those cheekbones, whiskers, and curving fine lips. That brow with its boyish, sandy brown forelock. Her pulse sped, and pleasure spread throughout her body. She loved him—she always had; the veil of madness was gone.

"Oh, no, sir!" she cried, seizing his lapels. "I shall speak till I'm hoarse if that will win your forgiveness!"

His arms slid round her and he pressed her close to his chest. "There, there, my dear. No need for that."

"But I treated you so wretchedly!"

"Yes, you did, and I mean to punish you for it."

"Punish me? H-how?"

"Hmm, let me think." He cocked his head. "I shall dress you in black crape and drive you to Hyde Park at the hour when it is most likely thronging with the *haute ton*. There I will shout: 'This is the termagant who crushed my poor heart!' After which I'll push you unceremoniously into the Thames."

After a moment of silence, Prudence asked meekly, "Do you feel better now?"

"Not one bit."

Her lower lip trembled. "I'm sorry I made you so angry."

Mr. MacNeal's chest shook. "Hush! You're too clever to let me tease you like this. Can't you see I'm being absurd?"

"At this point I haven't a clue *what* I should think."

"Well, I'd be happy to help you sort it out. The first thing I'm going to do, though, is kiss you, Miss Fairfeather."

In the half-darkness, he stooped and closed his mouth over hers. Prudence sank against his body, welcoming the radiant heat of his strength. Never in her life had she felt safer than this. Never had she experienced such stirrings of physical desire. Unseasoned though she was, she gave in to what seemed perfectly natural. Her chin tilted, her lips parted, and she accepted his inquisitive yet tender foray.

His hands, which had cradled either side of her face, traveled like whispers down her neck and across the slope of her shoulders. They lingered there awhile, circling thoughtfully, then inched beneath the gauze scarf, seeking the bare skin on her back. The swirling of his fingertips, rose-petal soft, coupled with the sensuous melding of their half-open mouths, were more than enough to satisfy Prudence, but now his hands began to skim down her arms. His thumb found the cuff of one of her gloves, which he pushed down smoothly, stripping it away and tucking it into a pocket. With a quick sidelong glance to gauge her receptiveness, he lifted her hand and began tasting in turn each of her fingers. He took his time at this task, smiling roguishly when she trembled, and worked his way up the inside of her arm. The last kiss there, high up on that tender white skin, was followed by a brazen assault on the swell of her bosom.

Prudence shuddered and lifted his head with her hands. "Slowly, sir! Think! This cannot go on. Sooner or later we *shall* be missed by the others."

"Yes, of course! Seems I am beside myself in my worship. Oh, Prudence, I love you! I always did, even when I was certain you didn't love me."

She caressed his face. "Whatever I might have said, know that I never really stopped loving you."

They kissed once again, deeper, more urgently, and this time Prudence let her arms encircle the firm expanse of his torso. By now the whole enclosure was redolent with his masculine scent. It was altogether too much, this ache of happiness, yet they had no choice but to end their encounter. Strains of music indicated the orchestra had resumed.

"Shall we dance, then? I've been crouching in this damned alcove for the better part of an hour; I would welcome an opportunity to stretch my legs." MacNeal handed her back the glove, which she hastened to draw on.

"Yes, and anyway we must save Mr. Tate before he falls asleep at his post."

Mr. MacNeal popped his head through the drapery and spoke a word to his mate. After a pause, the curtain shot aside and the lovers stepped forth with neutral expressions. They moved separately through the salon and met up in the ballroom, where they joined the other dancers in a lively quadrille.

There is an aura of intimacy about lovers which radiates outward, and it did not take long for others to note their alliance. Aunt Amelia kissed her fingers and smiled through streaming tears. Several gentlemen winked at MacNeal. More and more eyes began to fall on the couple. Nudges and whispers marked their progress round the room.

"So," said MacNeal. "Once again you and I are the object of much talk." As the dance now required them to exchange partners, Prudence had a moment to consider her reply.

"Do you find it amusing?" she asked upon his return.

"Not at all, but it's best to make the most of an unwished-for . . ." His voice tapered off, and he tilted his head as if listening. "Run!" he shouted, pulling her along by the hand.

A deafening crack rent the air, and the world seemed to shatter. Women screamed. Men pointed upward. Dust and plaster rained down on the dancers. Everyone scattered like chaff in the wind.

"What on earth . . . ?" cried MacNeal, drawing to a halt. They turned and looked back.

In the center of the ballroom, Lady Emmeline DeLacey stood alone, covered head-to-toe in debris. Directly overhead hung a brass chandelier, which somehow had caused the ceiling to give way. It hung cockeyed, dripping wax and swaying as, fiber by fiber, the beam supporting it splintered apart.

"Why doesn't she move?" wondered MacNeal.

"Because she sees *us!*" hissed Prudence. "Oh, *do* something, sir!"

Sure enough, Lady Emmeline was staring directly at them. Prudence covered her eyes. She couldn't stand to watch the silly fool die, all because Emmeline refused to accept that MacNeal would never be hers. The beam groaned; the chandelier dropped another few inches. Shrieks rent the air. Several levelheaded men tried to herd everyone out.

"Come away from there, dear!" somebody called.

The doomed lady remained frozen, seemingly unaware of what loomed above. Behind and barely visible through the vast cloud of dust, a woman dressed in white pointed straight up. She was slender and regal and perfectly poised, her expression one of absolute calm.

Lady Revelle! Prudence thought furiously. *And she's using magic!*

The lady's lips moved rapidly as her gaze remained fixed on the chandelier above. Prudence wondered if she was keeping it stable until the crowd could get clear . . . or was she waiting for an opportune moment to let the thing fall?

MacNeal held out his hand. "Come here, Emmeline."

As Lady Revelle continued to whisper, she lifted her other hand and directed it toward Emmeline. The girl's eyes rolled wildly—Prudence saw that she *wanted* to flee, but somehow could not. Now she understood: Lady Emmeline was the bait and William MacNeal the mouse.

"If she won't come, then I'll fetch her," he said. "This will take but a moment."

"It's a trap!" exclaimed Prudence, clutching his arm. "No, William! Don't go!"

He chuckled distractedly. "A trap? Darling, she couldn't have possibly planned this." Then, ducking his head, he ran full tilt toward Emmeline.

Lady Revelle's mouth, still moving, lifted into a broad smile. Prudence cast about for a way to break the woman's concentration. She quickly laid hold of an empty champagne bottle. Meanwhile, MacNeal grappled with Lady Emmeline, whom he could not seem to part from her spot on the floor. Prudence stepped deeper into the dust cloud, circling its perimeter, closing with dread purpose on Lady Revelle. She came to a halt a few feet away.

"I'm enjoying this," remarked the lady. "See the puppets dance! You were never meant to have him, you know."

Behind her back, Prudence gripped the champagne bottle. "On the contrary, your plans for me have come to naught. Mr. MacNeal and I are meant for each other, and in our shining future you play no part."

"Ah, you poor, misguided child! That man would distract you, and we have much to accomplish before you are prepared for the particular glories I have in mind. Let us wipe the slate clean. Watch carefully, my dear."

Prudence drew back the champagne bottle. "Watch *this!*" she snarled and hurled the bottle with all of her might.

Lady Revelle cried out as her left arm shot up to block the

bottle, which struck her forearm and shattered all over the floor. The instant her finger ceased pointing at Lady Emmeline, the girl broke free and Mr. MacNeal swept her into his arms. Snarling in fury, Lady Revelle gestured with her right arm and the ceiling gave way.

"No!" screamed Prudence, stretching out her hand as if she could stop it.

Time seemed to stand still. MacNeal swayed as he fought to balance Emmeline's weight. Prudence remained motionless, her arm extended, focusing her mind, willing the chandelier not to fall. MacNeal stumbled and dropped to one knee. The air had grown so thick that Prudence could see almost nothing except a bright streak of flame shooting from the tapers.

In the midst of all this, a deafening pulsation roared from the floor, scrolling up her legs and into her torso until it reverberated throughout her whole body. To fight the trembling, her muscles went taut, and she imagined she had the ability to hold back the ceiling.

"You haven't the strength," Lady Revelle said through clenched teeth. "Don't you wish you had taken me up on my offer?"

"To hell with you!" muttered Prudence. She lifted her other arm and planted her feet. A great weight seemed to press down on her from within. She set her jaw and fought to resist it. She was weak, though—the lady was right. Nothing but determination had gotten her this far. As her strength faltered, her vision blurred until it receded altogether. Everything went black as the throbbing continued to eat at her will.

Will it hold another moment?

MacNeal's voice echoed in her head, though she couldn't begin to guess how. Prudence fought to steady herself. *Not much longer,* she thought. *I'm—*

All at once, her mind felt like it would burst into flames. She dropped her arms and leapt back, gasping for air. With a terrific rending sound, the ceiling collapsed.

"William!" she screamed.

For more than a minute, nothing could be ascertained through the billowing dust. Prudence picked her way forward, sightless and choking. As her vision slowly cleared, men darted in to lift away the chandelier, whilst others ran forward to extinguish a small fire.

Mr. Tate appeared and took Prudence's arm. "Come away! It's not safe!"

"Let me go! I must see him!" Prudence wrenched her arm free and jerked to a halt.

Two bodies lay beneath the rubble, one masculine, one slender. Heart in her throat, she crouched down beside them. MacNeal's blood-streaked hand sprawled lifeless to one side.

"My darling," she whispered, tucking her hand around it. They had shared but a few minutes of unhindered love. *I have lost him! I've lost him!*

The chandelier rose free and was borne away, leaving the victims in poignant repose. MacNeal had thrown himself across the lady to shield her from the worst of the impact. His pallid face lay nestled in her corona of bright hair, one arm cradling the crown of her head. The image was more than Prudence could bear.

Must I forever remember him with another woman in his arms?

She lurched to her feet and spun blindly about. Mr. Tate caught her and pulled her close as a wave of despair smashed into her. Through shuddering sobs, she heard Amelia calling, "Prudence? *Prudence!* Oh, dear God!"

Mr. Tate answered, "She's safe. I've got her, madam."

A commotion broke out across the room. "Watch it—she's collapsing!" somebody cried, and several men rushed over to support a swooning woman. Prudence half-registered the presence of a bent platinum head, but her broken heart had no room left for disdain.

"Miss Fairfeather," murmured Mr. Tate, turning Prudence to face the victims. She shook her head. "Look!" he insisted.

Her disbelieving eyes detected some movement, followed by a groan, a cough, and a shifting of limbs. To Prudence's astonishment, Mr. MacNeal sat up, frowning and rubbing the back of his head. Noticing Lady Emmeline, he bent to listen for breathing. He took her wrist and chafed it, calling, "Can you hear me, my lady?"

"She's alive?" someone asked.

"Oh, yes. Very much so." His eyes flicked toward Prudence, and he gave her a smile.

A joyous shout went up from the guests. Prudence lunged forward, but Tate held her back. "Wait," he advised.

Roused by the noise, Lady Emmeline came to with a shudder. The first thing she focused on was William MacNeal's face. "Darling!" she sighed, cupping his cheek with her hand.

"Careful," he said, pulling away. "Don't move if you can help it." He gestured to a pair of men, who knelt to lift her onto a makeshift tablecloth stretcher.

"Come with me!" she called as they bore her away.

MacNeal shook his head, gingerly accepting someone's hand up. Tate let Prudence go. She ran to MacNeal and flung her arms around him, sobbing. He in turn buried his face in her neck. "Oh . . . ow! Gently, if you please."

"Good lord, you need a doctor!"

"I need a *drink,*" he rejoined. "But first I need you." He bent to give her a kiss. Prudence was too relieved to mind that he did so in public.

Something inspired her to open her eyes and look past his shoulder. Amid the dust and confusion, she saw two gentlemen assisting Lady Revelle to her feet. The baroness stared hard at Prudence, who self-consciously pulled away from the kiss. Resting her cheek on Mr. MacNeal's shoulder, she watched as realization dawned in her enemy's eyes. Indeed, she imagined she could almost hear the words:

So he's your bloody Protector, is he? Well, that explains plenty. Go on. Find love while you may, but this certainly isn't over between you and me.

Sniffing angrily, the baroness knocked aside her attendants and stalked from the room.

CHAPTER THIRTY-SEVEN

Edingham-Greene, Wiltshire
19 February 1820

Over breakfast on Saturday, Middlemere read aloud the latest from Quimby, who remained stationed at Cheltenham with no prospect of a leave. The lieutenant's father had weakened over the winter, obliging him to travel twice to Exeter rather than Greenbank.

Although he lies abed eating nothing but gruel, Lord Farrow's tongue remains as sharp as ever. He is a wretched old man, but I will continue to honor him, for such is my duty.

Middlemere nodded. "A lesser sort would pray for Farrow's hasty demise. God knows Quimby shall benefit enormously from his father's passing, yet he never speaks of the privilege that he is soon to enjoy. He is, indeed, a very good man."

"I think so, too, Papa," Josephine agreed shyly.

"And speaking of good fellows, are we not proud of our own dear Edward, who today has reached his majority?"

"Huzzah!" cheered Josephine and Maria, clapping.

"He has had a strong year at Oxford and anticipates completing his degree next fall. And here in my hand is a dignified letter thanking me for my stewardship and financial support these seventeen years. Allow me to quote: 'I pray, dear Papa, that I never give you reason to regret your investment in me.'" The earl looked up with a smile. "We shall have to convince Edward that he is not strictly an asset, but 'tis an admirable sentiment!"

Everyone laughed. Privately, Josephine was sorry to know Edward's sense of indebtedness continued to eat at his soul.

Late that afternoon, the post brought an additional letter each for the Westons. Josephine tore hers open right in the front hall, staggering to her knees as she read Prudence's incredible tale.

"Wot's this?" queried Maria, coming upon her charge plunked down on the floor.

"I-I don't know, Maria. I'm happy, astonished, and practically speechless . . ." Josephine gestured with the letter. "MacNeal kissed Prudence—that's brilliant, of course—but afterward the assembly ceiling collapsed, hurting five or six people, including MacNeal."

"Well, that a'en't proper!"

"Did you not hear what I said? People were hurt! Every time those two get together some disaster breaks out!" Her head ached in confusion as feelings of triumph mingled with dismay.

Lord Middlemere arrived from the direction of his study. "Why out of sorts, my pet? I presume you received the same felicitous news."

"Yes, Papa! It is wonderful . . . that is, if we discount the attendant catastrophe."

Middlemere shrugged. "'Twas a random mishap. Mr. MacNeal saved someone's life. He'll make a fine husband for Prudence."

"Goodness, Papa!" she laughed. "You have them at the altar already, and they did nothing more than reunite at a ball!"

"Oh, but their marriage, my dear child, was always a foregone conclusion," he said with a smile. "One hour with Mr. MacNeal convinced me he would not have it otherwise."

"But he has neither titles nor land," complained Maria.

"Oh, you old sourpuss!" Josephine leapt up to head for her alcove, but paused at the sound of carriage wheels on the drive. Through the side-light she caught a glimpse of a gig laden with trunks. "Hullo," she said. "I think that's the portraitist."

Round-faced and ruddy, Mr. Penney sailed into the house wearing a frock coat from the last century and spectacles perched on his head. While the footmen unloaded his gear, Josephine showed the artist to his quarters.

"When do we begin?" she inquired, throwing open his chamber door.

"Dear me!" replied Mr. Penney. "One cannot hurry art. I shall need to study you first, my lady—to get to know the spirit within you. Give me a day or two, at least."

Taken aback by his strange choice of words, Josephine wrinkled her brow. "The spirit within me? And how shall you depict that spirit in paint?"

He gazed at her with rheumy eyes. "Artist's secret," he replied, smiling coyly.

The next morning, Mr. Penney began his first charcoal studies. Bidding Josephine to assume a variety of poses, he churned out sketches. He then set up shop in the well-lit orangerie, draping a chair with yards of blue satin to provide a backdrop for his subject. Carson placed a brazier nearby, since the orangerie in winter was not warm enough for a lady dressed in thin lawn. Josephine watched, aquiver with interest.

"By week's end 'ee'll be begging him a-finish!" cackled Maria. "Thy mother could hardly sit still, her grown up and a countess besides."

On the day of her first sitting, Josephine appeared in a white frock and pearls, her hair piled high and plaited with ribbons. Mr. Penney spent an hour adjusting her pose, placing her at an angle with her left forearm resting over the curved back of the chair. Then he retreated to the canvas and began to block out her image. Now Josephine understood how difficult this undertaking promised to be. When she quizzed Penney about his work, he asked her to keep quiet. When she fidgeted, he frowned. Despite the brazier, she soon grew stiff with shivering.

"I hope you won't paint me as blue as I feel!" she ventured.

"Nonsense!" retorted Penney. "You have a fine porcelain complexion. You're as luminous as the moon. Footman, stoke that fire. Your mistress is chilled!"

Thus Josephine's portrait was begun, and to her dismay the secretive artist would not permit her to observe one iota of its evolution. The week crept past. Late Friday morning, she was endeavoring not to doze off in her chair when she looked up and spied Edward in the open doorway. He seemed dumbfounded at the sight of her, bedecked in finery in the middle of the day.

"Eddie!" Josephine leapt up, ignoring Mr. Penney's stammered objections. Dodging perilously stacked terracotta and boxes of paints, she ran to Edward, clutched his arms and held her face up for a kiss.

Edward brushed her cheek with his lips. "Heavens, Jo, you look . . ."

"Freezing?" she laughed, hugging herself.

"No. Magnificent." A trace of sadness tinged his voice.

"Is something wrong? Edward, to what do we owe this unexpected pleasure?"

He removed his jacket and draped it across her exposed shoulders. "Let us talk," he said, taking Josephine by the arm. Her ears pricked at the odd thread of gravity in his voice.

"But madam!" protested Penney.

"Give me an hour," called Josephine over her shoulder. She followed Edward to the drawing room where they sat together on the sofa.

He leant back to appraise her. "I see Prudence's hand in this. You were never keen on sausage curls and ribbons, though I must say they become you."

Josephine patted her hair. "She sent me sketches from London. This coif is the current rage. I shall exude sophistication for eternity."

"Very well, but tell Leonardo to correct your lazy eye."

"*What* lazy eye?"

"The left one," said Edward with very little conviction. "Never mind! For some reason, teasing you has lost all its appeal." He rose, advanced to the credenza, and poured himself a drink. Downing half of it swiftly, he returned to the sofa and explained that he had come to Greenbank at Middlemere's behest, as they had legalities to discuss relating to his majority. He planned to stay only one night. "But I'm glad to see you in private. I would speak of a subject we have not broached since my return to Oxford."

Josephine's stomach lurched sideways. She pulled his jacket tighter across her shoulders. "I had considered it a dead subject."

"Is it? Not in my heart." Edward fumbled for her hand. "Please hear me out. Last summer, when we thought we were cousins and you were still rather young, I was in no hurry . . . but then it turned out I was a nameless nobody. I left here for your sake, reckoning I had a year or two before you'd entertain suitors. I applied myself at school because I wanted to impress you. I left here, Jo, believing you had not dismissed the possibility of an alliance with me."

Josephine's heart beat rapidly. A long, uncomfortable silence hung between them. They locked eyes, blue and brown.

Edward pressed on. "I love you; I *have* loved you for well over a year. I felt you should know this before you grow any closer to—" Here he paused to gulp. "Good God! *Quimby*, of all people! And my pain is compounded, for he's everything I am not, complete with a title. Please tell me it wasn't his rank that impressed you!" He beat a balled fist on the arm of the sofa.

"Stop!" Josephine cried, seizing his shoulder. "How can you believe that?"

"Forgive me. You're too sensitive to treat a fellow so ill. But our kiss, darling, you cannot tell me there was no feeling in that! Come here and let me show you how much I adore you."

He attempted to pull her into an embrace, but Josephine darted under his arms and stood panting at a safe distance. "Edward Fairfeather! You are forcing me to say things I didn't want to say."

He watched her with eyes that were red from emotion, and his jaw trembled under the unaccustomed strain of exposing his feelings. "Go on," he rasped, as if waiting for a judge to announce his death sentence.

Josephine exhaled. "I *was* intrigued by our kiss and not wholly indifferent, but caught by surprise, I struggled to dispel the image of you as a brother. Now I know an alliance between us would be *wrong*, and not only because we're practically siblings. We have the beginnings of a true friendship, Edward; are you willing to sacrifice that just to obtain Greenbank?"

Edward went white. "What are you saying?"

"That it's possible you have confused your love for Greenbank with admiration for its heiress."

"You think I love you only because I want Greenbank?"

Josephine shook her head. "Of course not. I'm sure your feelings are sincere. The thing is, I am in love with Robert Quimby. It's a love far, far different from the love I feel for you, and I believe he feels the same."

Edward lurched to his feet. "Well, ain't he the lucky one?"

"Not at all. Think of the quarrels he and I shall have. I'm far too opinionated to be a good marchioness."

But Edward was too overcome to listen to platitudes. He charged out of the parlor and vanished until suppertime, at which time he spoke little and never addressed her directly. Josephine refused to feel guilty. Edward would have to find peace on his own.

She never imagined it would happen so quickly.

Early the next morning, determined not to part on bad terms, she went down to the driveway to bid Edward adieu. With no sign of bitterness, he kissed her forehead.

She asked fearfully, "You're not running away, are you?"

Edward laughed. "What's the use? We share a roof from time to time."

"Please swear you won't let the disappointment go to your head."

"I shan't go off on a bender, if that's what you mean. Last night I slept well for the first time in months." He swung up into the saddle. "Just one favor I ask: if that portrait is to hang at Greenbank for eternity, have Penney paint you with a grand smile. I never want to forget how fine you looked yesterday, when you first glanced up and were so happy to see me."

Josephine ducked her head shyly. "For you, Edward, I shall."

"Bless you, Jo," he said and kicked his horse into motion.

26 February 1820

Lord Middlemere set aside the agreement he had drawn up with Edward. Depending on how things played out, the young man would likely find himself well situated someday. The earl could not possibly have put the boy's mind at ease any sooner— there had been no way to predict how well his daughter would marry. And though he hated to think of his little Josie leaving Greenbank, the promise of a union with Robert Quimby did much to buoy his nerves.

His thoughts returned to Edward, and then the young man's dead father. "Ah, J.P.! 'Tis a pity you had to disavow everything in your name to preserve your children's safety. I'll do right by Edward, I swear it."

Carson entered to deliver the afternoon mail. Middlemere slipped on his spectacles and opened a letter from Bancroft.

> *To make up for the shock I gave you last month, I thought I'd do you the service of establishing whether MacNeal has done anything to raise the attention of those who would recruit*

or rehabilitate him. Sir, let me be blunt: were you aware he may have killed another gentleman last fall?

"Blast it," muttered Middlemere. "How could anyone have unearthed that unlucky event?"

Bancroft's investigation had been exhaustive. His man had accumulated enough circumstantial evidence to draw a connection, passing directly through Prudence, between MacNeal and the long-missing Lord Underwood.

Unfortunately, sir, the authorities will someday piece the evidence together. I doubt it was outright murder, though a duel between two rivals would be viewed the same way.

There is one other explanation: if, as you suspect, MacNeal is a Protector, he may have perceived that your daughter was in danger. He could've gone to Bolton for the sole purpose of keeping her from harm. I think you should confront the very real possibility that Miss Fairfeather is a fledgling Mage.

Middlemere shook his head. He'd known Keepers his whole adult life—had been married to one for heaven's sake—and his foster daughter did not have that notable desperate personality. MacNeal specifically said he had gone to Bolton to admire Prudence from afar. If he'd anticipated foul play, surely he would have said so. No, in this case MacNeal's Protector instincts were irrelevant. Whatever Bancroft might think, a gentleman's drive to preserve a young lady's virtue had precipitated the duel. Any man would have done the same.

And any man would have been prosecuted for it.

"Damn!" Middlemere muttered, ruffling his hair.

Bancroft had proposed a solution:

> *As for the various witnesses, I'll arrange for adjustments to be made to their memories. After all, you and I both know that sometimes a bit of rule-breaking is the best way to guarantee a just outcome.*

Fascinating! thought Middlemere. Not only did the general have soldiers and spies at his disposal, but he also had a Keeper willing to flout the Oath of Disavowal. *How frequently has he done this over the past seventeen years?* The earl grimaced. Such distasteful measures would shield MacNeal from repercussions, a small price to pay for Prudence's happiness.

The last part of Bancroft's letter made Middlemere's blood run cold. It concerned the Rehabilitation policy, instituted several years ago to manage the occasional cases of Keeper mentoring or self-training.

> *Those in question receive certain corrections at the Refuge. Not long ago I would've insisted you hand over this pair, but times have changed, old boy . . . or else I'm getting sentimental.*

"Bastard!" growled Middlemere, crushing the letter and tossing it into the fire. "You took advantage of my seclusion. You let me hope I might actually be wrong. You all have seen the Inheritance manifest itself naturally and not considered the reasons why!"

Why indeed? he wondered, hands cradling his head. Was there a connection between the resurgence of Oath-breakers and the rise in young heirs exhibiting their Traits? Never in history had Talisman Keepers advanced without the proper rituals and training.

Then again, never in history had a generation of Keepers gone completely unmentored.

Middlemere exhaled softly between pursed lips.

CHAPTER THIRTY-EIGHT

London
22 February 1820

T he aftermath of the Winter Ball kept London talking for weeks, but for once the subject was not the mad debutante from Wiltshire. Rather, William MacNeal found himself celebrated as the handsome hero who had saved Lady Emmeline DeLacey. Society wags said this proved he still loved her, but those who had seen him with Miss Fairfeather knew otherwise.

"I hope you don't mind that I sent Lady Emmeline my well-wishes," he told Prudence during his first visit to Stanistead after the Ball. "She has been asking for me. I thought it best to inform her I would not attend her but to do so as gently as possible."

"Of course I don't mind," Prudence said, gazing fondly at him.

Plasters dotted his face, and his ribs and a few fingers had needed bandaging. Still, he looked beautiful to her; she had to pinch herself to believe he sat beside her at last.

They spent several minutes reliving the ordeal at the Ball, although on this subject Prudence remained largely silent. Somehow, even without the aid of her Talismans, she had performed an astonishing feat of magic. Aunt Amelia must not have noticed, thank God, for the last thing Prudence wanted was a trip to the Refuge. Indeed, she desired no further connection to the Inheritance at all.

She shivered, wondering if she could ever convince Lady Revelle to leave her alone. Mr. MacNeal, apparently sensing her unease, touched Prudence's arm. He was her Protector, they all said. Whatever that meant to those versed in the ways of the Inheritance, he seemed willing to play the part in everyday society.

For heaven's sake, do not dwell on these things!

Prudence shook herself inwardly. Oh, dreadful Inheritance, which had destroyed her parents and threatened to destroy her, too! Aunt Amelia had been right—she had *always* been right. Far better to focus on a wedding and family and a happier future.

As the aunt had done when Lord Underwood paid his calls, she always found some pretext to leave the young lovers alone. This time, of course, Prudence didn't mind. MacNeal took advantage of this opportunity by wooing her with flowers, poetry, and kisses. They were caught once in an embrace by the blundering boys.

"Hallo!" exclaimed Roland. "Is this not a public space, Bradford, old chum?"

"Too public for *that*," agreed Peter. "Methinks it's time you two got married."

Prudence turned mortified eyes on MacNeal. A corner of his mouth quirked up as he struggled to remain solemn. "Sorry," he whispered. "I didn't know those rascals were around."

"Neither did I." Blushing, she looked away.

"With a Special License we could have done with it tomorrow."

Prudence shook her head. She wanted her whole family present, which meant the wedding must take place in Wiltshire.

MacNeal chuckled. "What are you thinking that makes you shake your pretty head?"

She turned to meet his green gaze. "That for the sake of my housemates perhaps you ought not to kiss like you intend to marry tomorrow."

"Hear, hear!" chimed Roland, flinging himself on the sofa.

"Oh, no. I wouldn't dare suggest haste. I expect you will want a fine public affair."

Prudence could have sworn he *had* said it, though, however teasingly meant. "'Tis a curious discussion, considering you haven't yet asked me." The boys burst into laughter.

"Begone, scalawags!" cried MacNeal. Peter and Roland fled.

The next day, when the lovers were once more alone, MacNeal took Prudence's hand and started to speak, but then leapt up and commenced pacing the room. She covered her mouth to stifle a smile. He spun on her and asked, "Does my discomfiture amuse you?"

"I beg your pardon, dear sir. After all we have been through, your sudden reticence surprises me. Come here and say what you planned to say: one week's courtship, you believe, is five days too many."

MacNeal's eyes went wide. "Good God! My thoughts, word for word! You astonish me." He sat beside her, took her hand, and drew it to his chest. Prudence's head filled with whispers, a half-heard conversation with no particular context. She had noticed the phenomenon before, but always assumed she was guessing his mind.

Prudence, what is this—

In a flash, their two minds became one. She knew exactly

what he meant to say, and she felt the anticipation of it welling up in his throat. "—strange connection between us?" she completed in a half-whisper.

A ripple of amazement passed through her head. A pathway, if one could call it that, had somehow sprung open between them. Prudence pushed back, trying to extract herself from his conscious and those secret recesses she had no desire to inhabit. Sticky and sweet as a half-melted toffee, the connection refused to sever.

"Unhand me, William," she murmured.

MacNeal did not let her go. Instead, his voice echoed, *I feel like I am caught in your soul.*

Prudence pulled her hand free. A vibration ran through her, like a door shutting far away. They looked at each other, questions tangling the air. "That's better!" she said brightly, though her nerves thrummed like the discordant strings of a harp. *Will I never be able to shed this unwanted Inheritance?*

MacNeal's face had gone ashen. "Better? What just happened to us, and how did you know how to stop it?"

"I didn't! I—I guessed."

"Ah, such evasion! I am completely unhinged, Prudence, whilst you're merely pensive!" He moved to take her shoulders again, then thought better of it.

His reluctance to touch her brought tears to her eyes. Prudence was desperate to steer the conversation back to the start, back to the question he had come here to ask. She thought soothing thoughts and ran a hand down his arm. A shudder went through him.

Glancing at the clock, she said, "Let us speak of that business some other time. William, you have five minutes before Aunt Amelia returns to reveal what's on your conscience."

"You already seem to know what I had planned to say."

She bent to purr in his ear, "Anyone could predict it, but I'd rather hear it directly from your lips." MacNeal closed a hand on her elbow, and she felt a charge grow between them as his courage returned. With effort, she found she could block out the words rising to his tongue.

"In that case," he said, touching his forehead to hers, "perhaps you'll forgive me for putting it bluntly: what is the use of prolonging our courtship? Prudence, say you'll marry me at once and let me possess you . . . completely!"

His lips brushed the lobe of her ear, and the sensuousness of his voice made his meaning quite clear. Swooning from emotion and the effort of staying out of his head, Prudence whispered, "Nothing, sir, would make me happier."

She reckoned they were safe now that MacNeal had no more secrets to divulge, but as their mouths came together in celebration, Prudence forgot her newfound ability to stand guard. Betrothal awakened the anticipation of further intimacy, and such thoughts supplanted their previous ones. She discerned the nature of this trouble but was powerless to stop it. MacNeal's private imaginings involved flesh and flying sheets and hot breath. She pictured herself arcing her body below his, and gasped as a bolt of fire raced through her.

"*Carissima!*" he breathed, tasting the tender part of her throat.

Longing became need. Need gave way to surrender. In a whirlwind of gradually cresting delight, flesh opened up and bones melted away. With a sigh, she slid sideways and the whole room went hazy.

"Breathe, silly!" At his gentle shaking, Prudence half opened her eyes. "Breathe, or else I'll have to call for the salts."

"I *am* breathing!" she groaned. MacNeal's concerned face came into focus. "Sorry," she rasped. "I reckon my laces are too tight."

"So you say. That was the kiss to end all kisses. I have no idea how it's possible for me to know such things about you."

Prudence inhaled sharply. "What sort of things?"

"Ohhhh . . . the sort of things, shall we say, that only a husband should know."

Prudence grew pink. Flashes of their shared thoughts continued to burst across her mind. She knew exactly what he meant—she had seen every inch of him, had run her hands across the broad planes of his muscles, yet never actually did so. The memory was at once embarrassing and highly arousing.

Bright spots rose on his cheeks. "Hmm. You and I must have a very long talk."

Footsteps sounded in the front hall. He sat bolt upright just as Aunt Amelia sailed in. She paused, noting his proximity to Prudence and the girl's helpless posture.

"I beg your pardon?" she asked tautly.

MacNeal jumped to his feet. "Your niece, madam, has agreed to be my bride."

"Ah!" approved Aunt Amelia. "Now *that* kind of announcement pleases an old woman!" She advanced to the sideboard and poured them all a strong drink, which Prudence and MacNeal accepted with a good deal more alacrity than was strictly necessary.

25 February 1820

Everyone agreed the wedding should take place as soon as possible. Mr. MacNeal wrote to the vicar of St. Lawrence in

Edingham-Greene, asking that the banns be read the first three Sundays in March, with the wedding scheduled for the following Friday. Aunt Amelia informed Lord Middlemere, whilst Prudence sent Josephine her personal account.

As was often the case, one of Josephine's letters crossed in the post. In it, she grumbled about the slow evolution of her portrait. Sittings consumed so much time that she couldn't properly care for the house, let alone Maria, who'd lately been feeling under the weather.

> *That I, of all people, should be obsessed with thoughts of domesticity astonishes even me! Oh, Prudence, I almost don't recognize this new Josephine.*

"I do, and she's a wonderful, more selfless Josephine," replied Prudence.

During her hours of posing, Josephine had reflected on the Winter Ball and drawn an interesting conclusion:

> *I think we have overlooked the most significant result of that night. Yes, you gained acceptance into Society and yes, you reunited with your true love, but do you realize you also defeated Lady Revelle? She gained neither your power nor your loyalty, and her scheme to part you from MacNeal failed. What more reason could she find to torment you?*

Prudence looked up, smiling. All true: in one month she would marry William MacNeal, and there was nothing Lady Revelle could do about that.

CHAPTER THIRTY-NINE

Edingham-Greene, Wiltshire
20 March 1820

Prudence, Aunt Amelia, and their two young companions arrived by coach on the Monday preceding the wedding. The girls greeted each other warmly. To Josephine's delight, she could discern no lasting traces of Prudence's winter illness.

"When does Mr. MacNeal arrive?"

"Thursday," replied Prudence, blushing happily at his name. "He's to stay the night at Mrs. March's. And your Lieutenant Quimby—will he be here, as well?"

Josephine shook her head. "He had to rush to Devonshire to sit vigil at his father's bedside. He's back at Cheltenham now, but he daren't ask for more leave."

Prudence squeezed the girl's hand. "Oh, no! I had so hoped to meet him!"

It was Josephine's turn to blush.

They went inside, full of information to exchange about trousseaus and plans for the upcoming wedding breakfast. After supper, Aunt Amelia and Prudence visited Middlemere's study to admire Josephine's portrait, which now hung beside her mother's.

"It's astonishing!" gasped Prudence, glancing first between

the real Josephine and her likeness, then between the two portraits themselves.

"Uncanny!" agreed Aunt Amelia. "I always thought she resembled Lady Joanna . . ."

The earl interjected, "And yet they are quite individual. I find myself less and less prone to confusing them these days." He looked sidelong at Lucinda March, who smiled with her eyes modestly downcast.

Aunt Amelia lifted an eyebrow but said not a word.

"But that's not all," Josephine told Prudence as they whispered together that night. "Two weeks ago, when Mr. Penney first unveiled the portrait, I was staring at Mother's, thinking it had perfectly captured the spirit of her legendary courage. Suddenly, Penney muttered in my ear, 'Those aspects of her character are also present in you. Perhaps you don't notice them when you look in the mirror, but I observed and recreated them with a special kind of paint.'

"'I beg your pardon?' said I, but no amount of persuasion could induce him to explain."

Prudence blinked. "Goodness, Josie, do you think . . . ?"

"Think what, dear?" asked Josephine archly. "That his paint is magical, perhaps?"

"Yes, of course, but the way that he answered you . . . Listen, remember when you guessed I had the ability to read other people's thoughts?" Josephine nodded. "You were right," admitted Prudence in a sorrowful voice. "Thankfully, it doesn't happen so often." She caught Josephine's narrow look. "Really, it has put me in some uncomfortable spots!"

"So you don't perceive everything that's currently in our minds?"

"No, that would be an unbearable cacophony, I should think."

"Which is why, when I asked you to tell me what I was thinking that day, you lost your temper."

"That's not the *only* reason . . . oh, poor Josephine, I was so unhappy back then! But no, I can't simply stare at you and divine whatever phrase you choose to be thinking. Anyway, there seem to be rules, and I've spent the past several weeks working it out."

"That's fantastic!"

"No, it's terrible! Do you have any idea what the average man thinks about?" Prudence shuddered and turned bright red.

"Prudence Fairfeather, you shame me!" They giggled together for a minute or two, after which Josephine lay back to ponder the significance of this revelation. "But if you are no longer handling the Talismans, what do you suppose this can mean?"

"I swear I am not. I left them under my bed back in London." Prudence heaved a sigh. "Whatever it means, the situation is untenable. I do not *seek* these powers—they are simply *happening* to me. But I've lost interest in magic, Josephine. I just want to be married and live a peaceful life."

"Then what will you do?"

A determined look crossed Prudence's face. "Next week, when the excitement of the wedding has passed, I shall build a great bonfire and, once and for all, I'll burn my Talismans. In me, at least, magic will vanish forever."

It occurred to Josephine that she ought to emulate Prudence by getting rid of those pistols hidden down the hall in her bureau. The smile left her face as an unsettling twinge pricked down her spine. All those times she had urged Prudence to do exactly that, all those months she'd wished the Talismans to stop affecting their lives. Now the prospect of living forever without them sent a pang of melancholy right through her gut.

"You won't miss it?" she asked. "You won't mind turning from the keepsakes, from their past and potential, leaving so many questions unanswered?"

"Miss it?" exclaimed Prudence. "I have learned enough to make me proud of my heritage, but if the price of happiness is never to learn another thing about the Inheritance, then gladly will I pay. Oh, Josephine, I feel so free already! My family's burden has lifted from my heart. Our parents and their secrets can finally rest in peace."

As much as she agreed in spirit with this, Josephine wondered how easy it would be at the actual moment of severance. After all, the Talismans had chosen *them*, not the other way around.

24 March 1820

Friday morning dawned clear and bright. A procession of carriages streamed from Greenbank into Edingham-Greene, disgorging passengers at the stately front door of St. Lawrence.

Just ahead of the bridal carriage, a barouche pulled up carrying the rest of the Westons. Josephine disembarked and stood aside to wait for Prudence and Middlemere. In the courtyard between parsonage and sanctuary, under the spread of a tulip tree bursting with buds, she spied William MacNeal receiving last-minute condolences from his friends Perkins and Tate. He glanced in her direction and threw her a wink. She looked away shyly. Something about his smile always caused her blood to thread faster.

"Robert Quimby. Robert Quimby," she muttered, thinking determinedly of a much dearer face.

When the groom and his party ducked in through a side door, Josephine nodded to the footman to hand down the bride and her father. Prudence ascended the porch, a vision in yards of pearlescent white silk. Her eyes were wide and blue and slightly watery from emotion, her cheeks flushed prettily from the unaccustomed attention.

Josephine reached up to adjust the combs keeping the bridal veil in place. "I wish you happy," she whispered.

Prudence grasped her hands. "Thanks to you, my dearest, most wonderful friend, I am immeasurably so."

The music within St. Lawrence swelled to signal the start of the service. Josephine and Prudence's eyes met, and they burst out laughing. After all that had happened, it hardly seemed possible they had reached this auspicious day. Lord Middlemere, looking proud and at ease, stepped forward to take the bride's arm. Josephine went before them and led the way into the church.

She wept copiously and unashamedly during the whole of the mass. Aunt Amelia elbowed her twice, but Josephine didn't care. A wedding was perhaps the most romantic moment of one's life. As Mr. Mitchell launched into a long, droning homily, a dreamy smile supplanted the flow of tears on her face.

My dress shall have three *rows of satin ribbon at the hem. And Robert—dear Robert!—will he wear the uniform, I wonder? His eyes will never leave my face, and when we kiss, it'll feel like the world is sliding away* . . .

Though she had no intention of making an immediate trip down the aisle, Josephine found it vastly entertaining to picture herself at the altar with Quimby. So intent was she on this epic creation, she barely registered the creaking of the ancient oak church door or the band of bright sunlight that briefly fell on Prudence and MacNeal. The usual shadows resumed once the door thumped to a close, exactly as the minister intoned, "—let no man put asunder."

Josephine sighed, dabbing her eyes with a handkerchief, and wondered why several congregants' heads had begun to crane toward the rear of the church.

"You may kiss the bride," said the vicar.

The couple sealed their vows somewhat self-consciously, after which everyone clapped and the vicar presented them as "Mr. and Mrs. William MacNeal." Hand in hand they turned to face the assemblage.

"Huzza!" shouted Josephine, provoking another jab from Amelia.

At this moment, the blood drained from Prudence's face and her eyes widened to dark saucers. Anxious to pinpoint the source of her distress, Josephine wheeled to face the back of the church. Behind her ranged dozens of family and friends, most of them taller than she. She hopped up and down, catching glimpses of two persons alone at the door.

"Who *are* they?" she growled, shoving past her father. She gained the aisle and aimed a glare toward the intruders. Though she had never laid eyes on either, she would have known them anywhere. A woman and a girl, standing shoulder-to-shoulder. "Christ!" she hissed, forgetting where she was, and wishing with all her heart she had a sword buckled to her side.

She stared and they stared, though their eyes focused on Prudence. The younger woman stood tall in traveling clothes of a warm chocolate color, her hands in a muff, her high cheekbones and sharp nose unmistakable. The other woman was resplendent in a snowy, ermine-trimmed redingote, her platinum hair piled high in an old-fashioned coif.

The girl's expression, though guarded, reflected genuine compassion. The woman's glittering gaze projected pure venom. Now a pulse of something unseen brushed past Josephine's shoulder, like a bolt of energy that contained whispered words. Languid, purposeful, the woman lifted her right hand, ostensibly to brush a stray hair from her brow. A large diamond ring stood out in bright contrast to her black calfskin gloves. The gesture took but a moment before her hand dropped.

"Make way! Make way! What's this about?" Aunt Amelia pushed past Middlemere and poked her chin over Josephine's shoulder. "*You?*" she breathed with perplexed recognition.

The organ burst into life, signaling the recessional. MacNeal took Prudence's hand and pulled her along. Josephine and Amelia backed out of the way. As the couple paused to acknowledge Lord Middlemere, Josephine seized Prudence's sleeve and hissed, "Is that *her*?"

Prudence had no time to answer, however, for MacNeal resumed his advance toward the door. When Josephine tried to follow, her skirt snagged on a protruding nail. She yanked viciously until the fabric tore loose, but having gained her freedom she found the aisle blocked with dozens of well-wishers. Now she could see nothing, nor could she move.

She spun on her heel and bolted for the side door, barreling into poor Reverend Mr. Mitchell. Mumbling an apology, she tore through the courtyard and rounded the front of the church. Prudence and MacNeal were already boarding their carriage. The celebrants gathered round, throwing flowers and rice. Josephine looked everywhere but could see no sign of the two unwelcome women. Then she spied a post-chaise disappearing down the lane.

"Drat!" she spluttered, stamping a foot.

A voice behind her said, "And why the high dudgeon?"

Josephine clenched fists and turned to face Edward. "Did you see them? Oh, the nerve! They came to spoil Prudence's wedding!"

"I saw two strange women, but I cannot say they did more than cause a mild stir. Are they friends of hers from London?"

"In a manner of speaking." Shaking herself free of this distraction, she said, "Summon the carriage, will you Eddie? We must reach Greenbank before the others arrive. Maybe then," she added when he strode off to comply, "I'll find a chance to question Prudence."

This wasn't so simple. The moment the Westons pulled up at home, the staff confronted Josephine with a hundred questions. She hurried down the rear hall, catching a glimpse of the newlyweds embracing in Middlemere's study, but she failed to divine whether MacNeal was comforting Prudence or they were simply enjoying a moment alone.

"You're upset," said Aunt Amelia, intercepting her in the kitchen and giving Josephine one of her patented hard looks.

Josephine stood with hands akimbo. "Those strangers— how vulgar! I can't imagine what possessed them to interrupt us like that!"

"Vulgar indeed. 'Twas a puzzling combination of persons, as well." Amelia peered at Josephine, as if expecting a particular response.

"Heavens, I have no idea why the two of them came." Josephine flagged a servant passing by with a tureen. "Not *that* ladle, Susan!" By the time she had finished admonishing the maid, Aunt Amelia had glided off to welcome the guests.

The wedding breakfast convened in Greenbank's ballroom.

There were speeches and toasts, and the couple was on several occasions ordered to kiss. Even Lord Middlemere and Mrs. March seemed to enjoy the romance; Josephine glimpsed them holding hands under the table, and for the moment forgot her various troubles.

At noon, the MacNeals made ready to leave. They were bound for Wharton that night and London the day after; their honeymoon trip to Europe would begin in late April. By now Josephine, who had still failed to get Prudence alone, was desperate to have a word with her friend. While the bride comforted a weeping Maria, she cornered MacNeal.

"Watch her closely," she said, clutching his arm. "You know what I mean. I am not convinced the Underwood conspiracy has run itself out."

MacNeal stooped to kiss both her cheeks. "My dear intrepid friend, you may depend on me. Hired men will accompany us home. Afterward, someone will always keep an eye on your cousin."

"Thank you, sir!" whispered Josephine, eyes shining with relief.

MacNeal embraced her, then moved off to bid adieu to Lord Middlemere, and at last Josephine had Prudence's undivided attention. Faced once again with the separation that a year ago had seemed so unbearable, she realized she could manage this new phase of their friendship. Even so, the girls clung to each other.

"Darling, that scene in the church," Josephine hissed. "Won't you tell me what happened?"

Prudence returned a bland smile. "I can't imagine what you mean."

"Those women—obviously Helen Morris and Lady Revelle.

Come, Prudence! I'm terrified for you. Did she cast another spell?"

Prudence shook her head slowly. "No, I don't think so."

"But I'm certain she did something. She threatened you, didn't she?"

Prudence's blue eyes slid sideways. "Enough, Josie. It's all water under the bridge."

"It *was* a threat! I knew it! I won't stand for it, I tell you. I'll—"

"Josephine," Prudence said firmly, "please do not get yourself worked up today. I have nothing to fear now with William by my side."

"That's true. He is so attentive, yet I worry your special day was spoilt—"

Prudence silenced her with a kiss. "Hush! Today you have given me a marvelous fete. It heartens me to see what a lady you've become. Write me as always—stint nothing in your dealings with a certain handsome gentleman—and in six months' time William and I shall set up house in London. Then you must come for a long visit, and we'll brook no kind of argument from Papa!"

MacNeal drifted by, touching his wife on the arm. The time for their departure had come. Josephine and Prudence embraced once more and spoke endearments through tears, then the newlyweds boarded an open barouche, decorated finely with flowers and streamers. They drove off to a chorus of cheers, passing beneath the budding sentinels of Greenbank's front lane. Silhouetted by sunlight shafting down through the trees, the lovers' heads met for a kiss. Josephine, atremble with mingled dread and delight, took Maria's hand and gave it a squeeze.

ACKNOWLEDGMENTS

To Deb for planting the seed and Rebecca for teaching me how to nurture it. To all those I subjected to the earliest incarnations (sorry). To those who did not believe in me, which only made me try harder. To my infinitely wise and patient editor, Lisa Stone-Hardt, who breathed life into my work. To Amanda Justice for reading this over and over with critical yet caring eyes. To Elaina Portugal for putting up with my ego. To Wise Ink Creative Publishing for all their help in making this dream a reality. To Mom and Dad, who have unfailingly believed in me. And to my three children, who grew up with their mother's face attached to a computer, I'm sorry. But I know you're glad I didn't helicopter you. Thank you all.

CC Aune's ramblings have led her through 49 states—nine of which she has called home—plus a fair number of countries. She has been a journalist and a contributor for the companion book to PBS's 2000 series *In Search of Our Ancestors*. Currently, she directs the blog *One Year of Letters*, which explores the internal landscape of writers. *The Ill-Kept Oath* is her debut novel.